# AS *Rich* AS A ROGUE

# JADE LEE

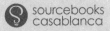

sourcebooks
casablanca

Published by Sourcebooks Casablanca, an imprint of Sourcebooks, Inc.
P.O. Box 4410, Naperville, Illinois 60567-4410
(630) 961-3900
Fax: (630) 961-2168
www.sourcebooks.com

Printed and bound in Canada.
MBP 10 9 8 7 6 5 4 3 2 1

# One

MARI POWEL'S ONLY WARNING THAT DISASTER HAD come to Hyde Park was when the parakeet said a new word. Normally the thing said slightly rude words like "clodhopper" or "bawdy basket." But this time, clear as the spring sky, the creature said, "winner, winner!"

Mari immediately used the excuse to set the heavy cage down. She'd been carrying the blasted thing throughout Hyde Park while Lady Illston showed it off. Lord Illston had brought it back from India a month ago, and it was a *ton* favorite. So popular, in fact, that Lady Illston allowed a different eligible young lady to carry the cage across Hyde Park during the fashionable hour. Today was Mari's turn, but she seriously doubted her shoulders were up to the task.

"My goodness," Mari said as she surreptitiously shook out her arms. "I believe that's a new word. Did you hear it?"

Lady Illston adjusted her parasol to peer owlishly at her. "A new word? Are you sure?"

"Quite sure." Mari looked hopefully at the two

gentlemen who had just joined them. Both were young and handsome but sadly dim. "Did you hear it?"

"I was listening only to your beauteous voice," crooned one. She'd mentally labeled him Dim #12. She'd already exchanged pleasantries with Dims number one through eleven.

"I wasn't speaking," she responded, wondering if she dared smile indulgently at him, as one might a slightly stupid younger brother. "He said 'winner, winner.'"

"By Jove, are you sure?" asked Dim #13.

"Yes, I'm—"

"That must mean he's here," Dim #13 interrupted. He popped off his hat and spun around, scanning the park with narrowed eyes.

"Who's here?"

"Winner, winner, of course," answered Dim #12, joining his friend in searching the crowd. "By Jove, there he is!" He immediately waved his arm quite forcibly. "Over here! Over here! There's a parrot for you!"

Actually, the bird was a parakeet, she thought idly as she tried to see what had gotten them so excited. Mari wasn't tall enough, and neither was Lady Illston, so the women were relegated to an awkward patience as the Dims continued their vulgar display. They did everything but jump up and down, and Mari suspected their restraint was simply an awareness that jumping would likely splatter mud on their boots.

"There's no need…" Mari began, but then the men finally parted enough for her to see the object of their adoration. "Winner," she whispered, dread lodging in her throat. Of course it was *him*. The one man who always won, making her the woman who lost.

As fast as she was able, she picked up the birdcage, trying desperately not to groan. Then she smiled as brightly as she could and tugged on Lady Illston's arm.

"Do you know, I believe your dear friend Lady Tennesley is over there. Let's go see."

"What? No, I want to meet—"

"Oh, she's waving. I believe she might have some delightful gossip to share."

Even the lure of gossip wasn't enough to distract Lady Illston. "Really, Miss Powel, it's quite ill-bred to tug on someone's sleeve."

Well, of course it was, but the lady hadn't objected to the gentlemen's behavior, had she? And she certainly didn't know that Mari was desperately trying to avoid the social disaster that was a few feet away and closing fast. "Winner! Winner!" cried the parakeet.

Then it happened. A deep voice she remembered in her nightmares spoke in that jovial tone of his. "Hullo, Greenie, how are you today?"

"Winner! Winner!"

"Of course you are. Such a magnificent bird."

Then Lady Illston tugged on Mari's sleeve. "Quick. Give him a treat. We must reward proper behavior."

Trapped. The man had spoken to them and was even now bowing his greeting.

*Stay calm*, she told herself, but it was no good. She could feel six years of bitter resentment rising in her gorge, despite her best efforts to swallow it down. Then her arms gave out, and she dropped Greenie's heavy cage back on the ground. Next she decided to hide her face as she fished around in her reticule for a treat. If she didn't look at the man, maybe she could keep a civil tongue.

"Miss Powel, I do believe you're looking more lovely than possible."

Worse and worse. He wanted to converse with her. She resolved to remain excruciatingly polite and tried to think of something innocuous to say. "That's a logical incongruity, you know. I cannot be more lovely than possible. It is obviously possible if I am it."

"Well, my goodness," Lady Illston gasped, and no wonder. Despite her best intentions, Mari was being rude. Fortunately, the jackanapes was laughing with good humor.

"Always so clever. What a delight to see you again." Then he extended his hand for hers, and she must, of course, give it to him. And with half the *ton* in the park right then, whatever she did now would be whispered to everyone within the half hour.

She could do this. She could be polite and not say exactly what she thought. She extended the tips of her fingers for him to kiss, then dropped into a stiff curtsy.

"Lord Whitly," she ground out. "I thought you were in India." Or hell, which was where she wished he'd stay.

"Just returned. One cannot remain forever in a foreign land. Eventually a man's thoughts must return to his native country and settling down."

That did it. Her gaze jumped to his on instinct. A man could not make a clearer statement that he was on the prowl for a wife, and she'd been on the hunt for a husband ever since he'd destroyed her chances over five years ago. And now he stood in front of her and declared his eligibility?

Lady Illston lost no time in leaping upon his

statement. "Oh, my lord, what a coincidence! I'm having a ball in a few weeks. Plenty of lovely young ladies there. All of them delightful."

"Capital," he said as he turned his beaming smile on Lady Illston.

"Winner! Winner!" agreed the parakeet.

Then he looked at her. The sun was full on his face, highlighting the ruggedness of his square jaw and large frame. His light brown hair had turned more gold in India, and its soft curls made him a dashing figure. Broad shoulders, big hands, and muscles everywhere, exquisitely revealed by perfectly tailored attire. He was everything handsome, rich, and eligible. A maiden's dream, and he was smiling at her.

"And you, Miss Powel? Will you be at the ball?"

"Not if you're there."

She clapped a hand to her mouth, horrified that she'd spoken her true thoughts aloud. She hadn't done that in five years. Five long years of watching her tongue, never stepping an inch out of place, of simpering, smiling, and carrying fans, not to mention shawls and birds—all of it gone in a second. She'd said the words that leaped to mind, and everyone about her gasped.

Everyone, that is, except Lord Whitly who arched his brows in every semblance of shock. "Miss Powel, have I offended you in some way?"

If she didn't still have her hand on her mouth, she would have gaped at him. Did he know nothing? She looked about her at the growing crowd. It wasn't just Lady Illston and the Dim pair. They now had four other parties joining them. And still her dratted tongue kept wagging. "Five, nay, six years ago, my lord, you did indeed offend me. Most grievously."

"Six years?" Dim #12 sputtered.

"But that's ancient history," agreed Dim #13.

"You labeled me the Wayward Welsh, though I didn't deserve the name. And what you did to my sister was worse."

He frowned. "Your sister? Oh, the Wild Welsh. I'd heard she'd married. Most happily."

Yes, Josephine had married and was deliriously happy, but that was only after five years of agony, fighting the epithet this man had given her. "Nevertheless, that doesn't mitigate your crime."

"Crime!" Lady Illston gasped, and she was echoed by the Dims plus the Misses Montgomery and their escorts. Meanwhile, Lord Whitly was defusing the situation with deep chuckles.

"I beg to differ with you there, Miss Powel. All's well that ends well, and all that."

"Winner! Winner!" the parakeet squawked.

"But it has not ended well," she said, wishing she could make him understand the hell she'd been living in. No man would marry a wayward woman. So she'd spent the last six years suppressing every instinct, every breath of life for fear of reviving that label.

"Naturally, I beg pardon for any unwitting insult."

"Unwitting!"

"But I cannot think that a casual word from me five or six years ago has caused the damage of which you speak. Truly, Miss Powel, can we not cry pax?"

Six years of guarding her every word, and still no suitors. He'd done that to her, and now he wanted to dismiss it as nothing. "My lord, some things cannot be mended with an apology. Look about you. Do you see how even now you wrong me? They think I am a shrew, and you the clever man."

"Surely not."

"Surely they do. You gave me a reputation six years ago. One that has dogged my every breath and prevented me from marrying. And now, just when I was set to escape, you return to dredge it all up again."

"But I didn't," he said, his voice betraying a hint of annoyance. "You did. I merely asked if you were attending a ball."

"Your very presence brings it up again, and well you know it." Except he didn't seem to know it. He seemed completely confused by her animosity, which made her hate him even more. To have such power to casually destroy her life, and he wasn't even aware of what he'd done.

Meanwhile, he was staring at her, his expression tight, his mouth curled down. "Surely you see that you give me too much credit."

"On the contrary, my lord, look about you. You have them hanging on your every word."

"*Our* every word, I believe."

Well, that was certainly true. Which left them at a stalemate. She would not forgive him, and he was left standing accused but unapologetic. Then he echoed her thoughts, which was disturbing indeed. She did not like to think they had anything in common.

"It appears we are at an impasse."

One glance around told her that he had the bulk of

the sympathy. It would be up to her to appear gracious or attach "shrew" to her "wayward" epithet.

"My lord—" she began, but that was when Dim #12 interrupted her.

"Why not settle it in the usual way?"

"What usual way?" Lord Whitly asked, and again, he was exactly echoing her own thoughts.

"A wager!" cried Dim #13. "Whoever gets the forfeit receives the apology."

"Oh yes," agreed Lady Illston. "That sounds like a great deal of fun."

"I will not wager on—" Mari began.

"I don't believe that ladies wager on such things," Lord Whitly said.

"Pish posh!" interrupted Lady Illston. "Ladies wager all the time. And the forfeit shall happen at my ball. Whoever wins shall have the apology from the other." She twirled her parasol in excitement. "But whatever shall be the contest?"

"Winner! Winner!" Greenie screeched again.

"Hush!" Mari said to the poor bird. "You really must learn another word."

Lord Whitly clapped his hands together. "An excellent suggestion. I accept."

To which the Dim pair heartily agreed with a back slap and "Jolly good" repeated multiple times.

"What?" Mari said, startled into looking right into her enemy's green eyes. "What do you mean, you accept?"

Lord Whitly smiled down at her as if she were a lackwit child. "Whoever teaches Greenie a new word first wins the wager."

"What? But I wasn't suggesting anything. I merely—"

"Doesn't matter," Lady Illston said with obvious glee. And why not? She and her bird had just become the center of a contest that would keep her in the forefront of the *ton* entertainment for the entire Season. "An excellent suggestion, my lord. Excellent indeed."

"You are suggesting," Mari said slowly, "that whoever teaches Greenie a new word first gets a public apology from the other?"

"Yes, yes," said Lady Illston. "It's a perfect idea."

It was a ridiculous idea, but the thought of him on bended knee before her, begging her forgiveness, was something she'd imagined for six years. It was her nightly ritual. She looked at the bird and thought things through. She'd spent a great deal of time with Greenie lately. It was a necessary evil in order to get this dratted walk through Hyde Park. Which meant she had much more rapport with the creature than Lord Whitly could possibly have.

"But what word am I to teach him?" she wondered aloud.

"Can't tell," said Dim #12. "Otherwise everyone else would take sides and be forever speaking it to the bird."

"Very true," agreed Dim #13, "but we must have a judge. Someone who knows the words."

"And equal time to teach Greenie," inserted Lady Illston. "I shall be the judge of that, as they must come to my house."

Lord Whitly's charm began to ooze from every pore as he bowed to Lady Illston. "You will make the most honorable judge, my lady. I feel secure in your hands."

The lady pinkened to an alarming degree as she tittered beneath her fan. Which meant he'd already gotten her in his pocket.

"But the words," Mari pressed. "They must be simple. I shall whisper them to you, Lady Illston, and you cannot tell anyone, or you shall end the whole contest."

Mari thought herself very clever for that part, because truthfully, Lady Illston could not keep a secret any more than she could keep her parasol still. Within a day, all of Society would know the words, and that would be the end of this charade.

"Well, come on then," Lady Illston urged.

Mari leaned over and whispered, "Happy day."

Lady Illston seemed to approve. "Very proper," she said with a nod. "Now, Lord Whitly, it must be two words. Come, come, what do you select?"

"This is a difficult decision, but I believe I must say what comes first to mind. Lady Illston, forgive the impertinence please." Then he leaned over and slowly brushed the hair away from her ear.

The woman giggled as he made a show of whispering in her ear. And when he was done, she gasped, and her eyes were round with shock. "Oh my, Lord Whitly. Oh my, indeed!"

"Not a word, or the game's up. You can do that, can you not, Lady Illston?"

"Oh my, yes. Oh my, of course."

Good Lord, he'd reduced the woman to a babbling idiot. Just what had he said? Lady Illston's color was up, and her eyes were bright. "Just a moment," Mari said. "If I am to be the center of gossip again, I should like the forfeit to be worth it."

"An apology isn't enough?" Lord Whitly asked.

What Mari wanted was a great deal more specific than words. She lifted her chin and said her fantasy in detail. After all, she'd been dreaming it for six years now.

"I want you on one knee, my lord, with flowers in your hand and the apology on your lips. And you will not get up from that position until you make me believe you are sincere."

"Oh, brilliant!" cried Dim #7. The man had joined the group during that last pronouncement. "He'll be there for a week."

Yes, he would, and that would be her revenge.

She looked at Lord Whitly and knew a moment's triumph. After all, no man would open himself up to such a forfeit. He'd be humiliated and possibly physically damaged. But instead of crying off, he bowed his head.

"I accept. But I shall add to your forfeit then as well."

"Am I to be on bended knee?"

"Certainly not. You will allow me a kiss."

She shook her head. "I cannot!" she cried.

"Oh, but you can," returned Lady Illston. "I am the judge, and I declare that a kiss will be proper. No one shall think the worse of you for it."

Of all the idiotic things to say. "You cannot promise that, Lady Illston."

"I can," she said. Then she looked to the crowd. "Come, come, don't you agree? This kiss will be perfectly proper. Lady Castlereigh? Lady Jersey?"

No. No, it couldn't be. This wager couldn't already have garnered the attention of two of the exalted patronesses of Almack's. And yet, while she stared, the press of bodies separated to reveal those two ladies plus a third. Lady Cowper, also a patroness of Almack's. If the three of them agreed, then everyone else must perforce follow.

"My ladies," Mari began, "this is not at all proper. I cannot—"

"And yet it seems it is already done," interrupted Lady Jersey. "Acquaint me of the particulars, if you will."

More than one person leaped into the discussion. The details of the offense and the wager itself were recounted a dozen times. If Lord Whitly had meant to capture the attention of all of Society, he had managed it neatly.

When the recounting was done, the three patronesses looked to one another, and then Lady Castlereigh gave the verdict. "We wish to see this apology," she said in ringing tones. "Therefore we declare it proper."

In the general roar of approval, the parakeet declared the future.

"Winner, winner!" it cried.

"Not him," Mari said loudly as she picked up the bird. "In the future, Greenie, that shall be my name."

And in this way, she began her war.

# Two

It was another two hours before Mari made her way back to her family's home near Grosvenor Square. Her father never spoke the name of their street. He had the money for the best lodgings in London, but not the pedigree for a true Grosvenor location. So they resided near to it, and she found herself trudging the last steps up to their doorway while her maid chattered behind her.

"Me cousin trained his rooster to crow when he whistled a particular tune. They would go to the pub and there'd be Jeb whistling and the cock crowing an' people buying pints 'cause they never heard anything like that afore. And then I heard tell of a man who trained a rat…"

If only the woman had advice on exactly *how* to train a beast. Then, thankfully, they were at her door, which the butler threw open with rigid pomposity. The man's name was Harvey Horace, and she'd mentally dubbed him Horrid Horace because he seemed to be disdainful of everything and everyone. That, of course, was exactly why her father had hired him, so Mari knew to keep her tongue. At least his presence abruptly silenced her maid, which she counted as a benefit.

"Good afternoon, Horace," she said as she stripped off her hat and gloves. Her arms felt like soggy linen, they were so heavy from lugging around that parakeet cage. Worse, the rest of the encounter in the park had given her a screaming headache.

"I'm going to take a rest, Horace. Please let me know when Papa returns." She would have to tell him that his daughter had become the center of gossip again, and she was not relishing the conversation. He was desperate to fit into the elite, for all the money and power it would bring to his business ventures. But he couldn't do that if his daughter was constantly getting into scrapes.

Meanwhile, Horace sniffed twice before speaking. "Lady Eleanor and Mr. Niles Camden await you at your earliest convenience."

She froze, her foot halfway suspended and definitely aimed toward her bedroom. "They're here?" she asked needlessly.

"In the front parlor." He spoke with such hauteur that she felt stupid she hadn't deduced her guests' location.

"Oh. Very well. Have you sent in tea already?"

"Naturally." The word was so disdainful, it was obvious she'd insulted him by asking.

She bit her lip. "I'll go in." She took a moment to smooth her hair. "Do ask Mama to join us when she returns."

She hurried forward as fast as she could manage without running, took a breath to steady herself, and was just starting her exhale when Horace threw open the door and announced her. Mr. Camden was on his feet quickly enough. Lady Eleanor rose as she always did: with grace and style.

"I'm so sorry you had to wait," she said, slipping into her best manners. "I trust Horace has seen to your comfort?"

"Most definitely," Mr. Camden answered. "Excellent man." He beamed at the butler before executing his bow to her.

"We've been quite comfortable," was Lady Eleanor's response as the two women held hands and smiled at each other. Eleanor was a true lady, the daughter of a duke, and as perfect a woman as Mari could ever aspire to be. And yet, part of her longed for the wild starts of her sister, the overly enthusiastic embraces, the way Josephine used to grab her hands and twirl her around. When was the last time someone actually touched her, skin to skin?

All those thoughts flashed through her mind in a moment of longing. But they were tucked neatly away by the time she sat down, her hands folded demurely in her lap. "Such a delight to see you this afternoon," she said, praying it would be true.

"You're looking lovely today," Mr. Camden said, "if a bit windswept. The spring wind is terribly chafing. I do hope your bonnet didn't suffer a mishap."

By which he meant she was flushed and untidy. Fortunately, she was saved from making an apology by Lady Eleanor.

"We heard about the wager."

"Already?" The word was out before Mari could stop it. It had only just happened.

"Of course," Mr. Camden snapped. "Not even lightning runs faster than gossip."

Something not literally true, obviously, but she was feeling too guilty to quibble. "The Ladies Jersey and Castlereigh, and even Lady Cowper, have declared the wager to be proper."

"Proper!" Mr. Camden said as he shoved to his feet. "I heard about it from Mama, who heard it from her maid. Apparently the servants are all aghast about it."

An hour and a half from Hyde Park to the servants. That must be some sort of record.

"I tried to stop it," she said. "I truly did."

"But it got away from you," Lady Eleanor said sympathetically. "These things take on a life of their own."

Mr. Camden's voice was disapproving. "But these things don't happen on their own. Something started it."

"Lord Whitly started it," Mari said grumpily, though inside she knew that wasn't precisely correct. He'd started it nearly six years ago. Today's event, however, was created by her own unruly tongue. "Surely it won't be anything more than a two-day wonder." It was a false hope, and everyone knew it.

"It will be the wonder of the Season," Mr. Camden said. "Betting on a bird. I thought you had more sense."

"So did I, truth be told," she said wearily.

At which point, Mr. Camden returned to his seat. His expression was doleful, his attitude one of great sadness. "I thought we were coming to an understanding, you and I. I had hoped to make our connection stronger in due course."

"Yes," she said, doing her best to keep her tone modestly sweet. "That was my hope as well."

"But this kind of behavior makes a man wonder if he will be the butt of gossip for the rest of his life."

Mari felt her hands clench, and since she couldn't very well grab her skirts and make telltale wrinkles, she untangled her fingers and allowed her hands to fall to her sides, where she clutched the seat of her chair. The hard wood cut painfully into her palms, but that was all to the better. And as she took a deep breath to control herself, she repeated the mantra she'd begun six years ago. *All Whitly's fault. All Whitly's fault.*

Which is when Lady Eleanor came to her rescue. Thank God, because Mari wasn't sure what the proper response was to a situation like this. Did she collapse into vapors? Start crying like an imbecile? Or simply sit there and allow everyone to chastise her? She could live through it if only she knew what the proper reaction was supposed to be. Trust Lady Eleanor to show her what one was to do.

"Well, Mr. Camden, I certainly see that you are in a difficult position."

"Too right—"

"But it's not irredeemable. *Any* attention can be turned to the good. It just takes a skillful hand."

By which she meant hers. And frankly, Mari was grateful for any assistance. "You know how to turn it to advantage then?" she asked Lady Eleanor.

"Of course. But that is not something to discuss in mixed company." Lady Eleanor rose to her feet, forcing Mr. Camden to stand as well. "Pray give it some time, Mr. Camden. You'd be surprised what a little notoriety can do for a woman."

Mari feared that he would argue the point. It was

clear he wanted to. But eventually his intelligence won out. He exhaled in resignation and then nodded.

"People say the Exchange is difficult to understand, and yet it follows understandable rules. I find Society much more confusing."

"As do we all, Mr. Camden," Lady Eleanor said. Then she waited with her hands folded and a polite smile fastened to her face as he took his leave.

Mari waited until the front door closed behind him before turning to Lady Eleanor with a grateful smile. "Thank you. I don't know what to say at times like these. He's furious, and rightly so."

Eleanor settled back onto her seat, her skirt perfectly smooth, her expression serene. "That is what your father paid me to do. I am here to smooth the way for you this Season—"

"I know, but—"

"Tut. Don't interrupt, because we have a great deal to discuss, you and I."

Mari nodded. "Your plan to turn this to my favor." She waited, her breath held. Lady Eleanor was a precise woman who would not begin until the perfect moment. But after two minutes of waiting, Mari ran out of patience.

"Lady Eleanor—"

"My plan is simply to listen. To you."

Mari stilled. Listen to her? No one ever listened to her, and it was rather annoying. The novelty of the experience had her at a loss. "Well?" prompted Lady Eleanor. "Tell me everything."

"Oh. Of course. Well, I was carrying that stupid bird, when he said—"

"Not that! I already know all about that."

Mari huffed out a breath. "It only just happened."

"Nevertheless." Eleanor scooted forward on her seat. "I want to know—exactly—what Lord Whitly said to you six years ago."

∽

Peter George Norwood, Lord Whitly, couldn't stop grinning, despite the afternoon's rather bizarre encounter with Miss Powel. Her bad temper was a minor blight on the marvelous joy of being back in England. And not just England, but a gaming hell, surrounded by genial fellows and eating solid English fare. Or more accurately, drinking the brandy. He took his time with his drink, rolling it around on his tongue, allowing the aroma to sink into his nostrils while the liquid bathed his teeth.

God, how he'd missed it. Too bad the dinner fare wasn't nearly as delightful. Sadly, the food seemed more bland than he remembered. Or he'd simply gotten used to Indian spices burning his palate. Either way, he was enjoying his drink.

"Blast it, Whitly, surely you can give us a hint as to what you're going to teach the bird," said one of his companions, a man who needed money and was going about getting it in all the wrong ways.

"He can't do it. Wouldn't be sporting," countered the youngest of his dinner guests, a youth who simply needed time to grow before embarking on a career.

"I'm not going to help him with the stupid bird," argued the first. "I'm going to wager on whether he'll manage it. Some things are harder for a bird to say than others."

The youth huffed out a breath. "That's not sporting either! We've all got bets down. Damned book at White's has three pages of them."

Four other voices broke in, all with an opinion as to what was sporting and what was not. Peter hid his smile behind his drink. Only in England did they have such conversations, and he loved every heated word. Gentleman's honor, a sporting wager, even the good-natured way they discussed cheating—it all amounted to jolly fun without fear of bloodshed.

Child's play, and he adored it.

It was, in fact, a large reason why he'd come home. The other, of course, was the aged, gloomy fellow sitting across from him, listening to the debate. It was all dark, brooding looks from his father, the Earl of Sommerfield, whose preference was for serious political debate and directing affairs of state. He'd foregone his usual brandy and cigars to meet with his son.

The earl had sent a summons an hour before dinner. Peter considered it the height of ill manners to cancel a dinner engagement already arranged, so he'd invited his father here, fully expecting a refusal. He was stunned speechless when the earl had stomped into the dining room of this barely reputable gaming hell.

"Welcome back to England's crowning jewel, my lord," said an elegant voice at his elbow.

Peter turned to see the face of a man he'd never met. The gentleman was dressed well enough, with expensive fabrics and a clean shirt, plus he wore a warm smile on his rather common face.

"I assume you mean London, not this particular hell," Peter returned. "It's pleasant enough, but not quite a jewel." Peter smiled because he thought it rude not to return an expression in equal measure.

"Of course, of course." The large man bowed. "Mr. Bernard Drew, my lord, at your service."

Ah, the new owner of this particular establishment. Rumor had it that he was the brother of the Duchess of Bucklynde. "Whenever you wish to play, I shall be happy to extend you a line of credit—"

"Off with you," interrupted the earl. "My son needs no credit, and certainly not from the likes of you. Thieves and sharps, every one of you." Then he glared around at Peter's companions until one by one, they grew uncomfortable.

Peter sighed. His father knew how to sour a room faster than anyone he'd ever known. Best try to make amends now, so Peter gestured to Mr. Drew. "Get my friends some more of this excellent drink," he said, ignoring his father's huff of disdain. Then he turned to his companions. "Pick a table. I will join you soon."

The younger set disappeared with alacrity. Only one lingered. His oldest friend, Ash, cocked an eyebrow behind the earl's back. Peter merely shrugged, then reluctantly gestured his friend away. The confrontation with his father was unavoidable, so he might as well get it over with. Besides, he'd figured out in his adolescence how to survive it. He thought about ladies' titties until the whole mess was over. And Miss Powel had nice ripe ones, likely with pert tips of a lovely color. Would they be pink or more dusky brown? He could drown out his father for hours, contemplating the possibilities.

"I cannot understand what you find amusing in those numbskulls."

"Good humor," he answered blithely. "But we are alone now. What is it that you wished to say?"

"Alone!" the earl spat. "In this place?"

"We are as private as we would have been at White's. More so, since it is quieter there. Things more easily overheard. Or I could attend you Thursday noon. I believe I offered that in my note."

"Thursday! As if I don't know that trick. Come Thursday, you would delay until Sunday."

That had not been his intention, but he couldn't deny there'd been a time when he'd used that trick often. "Well, we are here now, Father. What did you wish to say?" Miss Powel's titties would be full, round peaches and smell sweet. He couldn't wait to feel them puckering in his hands.

"Very well, I shall be brief."

Thank God.

"I need to know if you intend to see to your responsibilities."

A dark pink tip with a large rose circle around it. "Er…yes, of course I do. Uh…do you mean the finding of a wife?"

"Do you mistake me for your mother? The women are her concern. If you die without issue, your brother is perfectly capable of taking the reins when you fail."

Yes, his brother was more than willing to take up the reins. Though they'd have to find the miscreant first. At the moment, Lucius was campaigning somewhere…er…somewhere else. "Just where is Lucius at the moment?"

His father waved the question away. "Not here."

Obviously. Peter made a mental note to ask his mother. Disgraceful that he'd lost track, but then the military never kept the family well informed.

"If you're not here to demand I take a wife—"

"Hardly."

"Then what responsibilities do you wish me to pursue?"

"The estate! Bloody hell, it's like talking to a noddy. The title needs more funds. We're desperately lacking in improvements, and the canal isn't working as it ought. All that costs money, and if it's to be your land someday, you ought to see to its maintenance."

"But it's not mine now, Father. And I've already sent you all the money I could. That was, if you recall, the reason I went to India in the first place." It wasn't the only reason, but his father didn't need to know that.

"Don't mistake me for one of your lackwit friends. You've come back from India a nabob. It's all anyone can talk about. You and that dratted Welsh girl and her silly bird."

"You cannot believe what they say."

His father straightened up to his full height, which was impressive enough, though he was still sitting down. "Of course I can! You've fine clothes on your back, an emerald on your finger, and prime horseflesh that made the trip with you."

That was, in fact, about all he'd come back from India with, but no one knew that. And he meant to keep it that way for a good long time. "I mean to breed her, Father."

"Exactly. And you can't do that without money."

Peter leaned back in his chair, forced reluctantly to study his father as he might a maharaja. "I see you're in fine clothes, have excellent horseflesh, and wear a ruby on your finger. I'd say the only difference between us is the color of the stone."

"Which is why you need to shore up the estate—"

Peter snapped his fingers as if just remembering something. "There is one other difference." He leaned forward on the table, doing his best to appear intimidating without outright threatening his father. "You are the Earl of Sommerfield. You hold the title and the responsibility."

"We need the cash, Son. We need it desperately."

"Why?"

His father's face turned red. If they were alone, it would be the prelude to a tirade. But they were in public, and so Peter was able to stop it.

"I have the right to ask. If you want me to shore up the accounts, then I need to know why."

"Repairs on the estate," his father bit out. Peter could tell it was hard for the man to say that much without a great deal more vitriol.

"Where has the income gone?"

His father's face darkened another shade. "Expenses."

Peter waited to see if there would be more. Six years ago, he would not have had the patience. But he'd spent the last six years as the East India Company's taxman and had learned a great deal about patience. And about getting answers out of powerful men.

So he waited.

In the end, his father proved smarter than that simple ploy. He banged his hand down on the table and pushed to his feet. "If you want answers, then go read the accounts yourself. In Lincolnshire." Then he leaned forward. "But be sure to leave notice at your bank first to allow the debts to be paid from your account."

Clearly his father assumed that he would balk at the real work of sorting out the estate accounts. Before India, he probably would have. But now he leaned back and allowed a nostalgic smile to soften his face. "I should like to see the fens again." Odd how something so mundane could become so important after only a few years away.

"The money, boy."

He didn't bother responding. He didn't even look at his father, but pretended to gaze off into the distant past. In truth, he did have some lovely memories of the fens around his home. Fishing, fowling, and wenching. He kept at his pretend reminiscences for as long as it took for his father to lose patience with him.

Not long, as it happened, and in the end, the man muttered something foul before stomping away. Peter watched his retreating back, hating that the good drink felt sour in his stomach. His father was slipping to have allowed such a curse. Always before, it had been Peter who'd left cursing and stomping at the end of one of their battles. It was rather momentous that tonight his father had departed with less than total composure.

Peter didn't know what to think about that. Did he worry that his father had lost stature or glory in his own nebulous win?

He didn't know, and so he tucked the thought away. Then he made his way to a baize table and an amiable card game among his friends. And if his mind ever wandered back to his father or the estate and its accounts, he distracted himself in the usual way: Miss Powel did indeed have a fine set of titties.

# Three

"WHAT HAPPENED IN INDIA? I'LL WAGER IT WAS a woman."

Peter jolted. "What?" He peered through the dark at his best friend, Ash. They were walking to their rooms after a night of cards and good brandy. Peter had been ruminating on how hard it was to stay awake until dawn and wondering if he'd reacquire the knack now that he was back in England as a man of leisure. Fortunately for him, Ash appeared to be equally unused to cards through the night, so when the man had yawned, Peter had used that excuse to end the festivities. They were now ambling down the street in companionable silence. At least they were until Ash's sudden question. And even though he knew exactly what his friend was talking about, he decided to play stupid.

"I have no idea what you're talking about," he said.

"You've changed," his friend returned. "Significantly, I'd wager. That had to have happened in India. Probably a scheming Indian beauty."

"Don't be daft. It's been six years. Of course I've changed." He huffed. "I've got gray hairs."

"Horrible," Ash said, and he wasn't being sarcastic. He also wasn't leaving the topic alone. "You must have run afoul of someone in India."

Scores of someones, and only half of them were women. "It had nothing to do with the women," he said. "At least not any more than men."

"Seduced, were you?"

"Yes, thank God. Only thing that made the place bearable."

"Huh." Ash kicked at a stone, sending it skittering down the street. "I miss scheming, seducing, soiled women." Then he gave a happy sigh. "Thank God I'm back in London where I can be accosted on a daily basis."

"Shall I put the word out? That you're in the market for—"

Ash waved him to silence. "Too expensive, and in more than just money." Then he returned to probing into Peter's wounds. "I saw the earl leaving in a rage. What did you say to him?"

Peter smiled, though the pull of his lips felt tight. "I asked him to explain his spending."

Ash chuckled. "That's rich, coming from you."

True enough. Ash knew better than most exactly how many times Peter had been called to account by his father. The last had been the day before he'd left for India.

"Were you asking about Lady Charmante? She's known to be expensive."

"Who the devil is that?"

"Your father's latest paramour. I thought you knew."

The last thing he wanted to think about was his father's newest mistress. "I've only been back a few days."

"Huh." Ash sighed, as if in longing, but a moment later, he was back to asking questions. "So what did the earl say? Before he stormed out."

"You've got a lot of questions."

"I've stored them up."

Peter chuckled, then answered, "He said if I cared so much, I should go read the ledgers."

"Of course he did. So what are you going to do now?"

Peter paused to curse. He'd stepped in a pile of dog shit. That's what came from thinking about his father. "I'm going to read the ledgers. What did you think was next?"

"Truly?" The man looked genuinely surprised. "Jolly good."

"You didn't think I'd do it? I've always been decent with ciphering. I ought to be able to sort out the basics." More than the basics. His superior in the East India Company had taught him everything about proper and improper accounting. Maharajas were known for sitting on a pot of emeralds while claiming starvation. They weren't lying. Their people were starving, and their lands often struggled, but the maharajas themselves were living to excess in everything.

"Of course you could do it, I just…" Ash shrugged. "Well, as I said, you've changed."

"I looked at the ledgers when I was younger, too. Just had to do it without my father's knowledge."

"I know, but—"

"He says he needs money. My money to shore up the estate."

Ash's lips pursed. "Do you have it?"

Not even close. He had enough for a comfortable living in a village somewhere, but not to shore up Sommerfield. "I want to know why he doesn't."

"Ah. Well, if you need a hand, I've done nothing but look at account books these last years."

Peter smiled, but he could see the lines of strain around his friend's eyes and mouth. He'd noted it earlier when they were at cards. He'd thought it was about the man's wretched luck at the table tonight, but now it appeared there was more.

"I thought your lands were improving. That's what you said in your last letter."

"They were. Looked like we were coming around. I'd even begun to hope for the best." The man laced his words with mournful accents. As if he should have known that disaster lurked around the corner.

"You? Hopeful?" Peter teased, but underneath his light tone was worry. The one thing his friend needed most of all was something to believe in. Six years ago it had been the power of his own body and mind to effect his change in fortune. Apparently that hadn't worked, because once again Ash was rudderless.

"I'll never believe again, I assure you. We had a bad crop. That was hard enough, but a damned disease hit us in the fall."

During harvest. Bad time for people to be ill. "Dead?"

"Many. Mostly the old and very young."

"That's hard."

He nodded. "My hands are still cramped from bringing in the crop. If it were a bumper year, I'd be permanently stooped from the labor." Then he stopped long enough to arch his back and stretch his shoulders.

"Thank God I'm back here, where a man doesn't have to hunch unless it's over a willing woman."

Peter chuckled as they continued their slow amble. He nodded to a few men and smiled at a few tarts who came their way. He smiled, but declined their offers. Their titties simply didn't compare to the ones he'd been dreaming about since his afternoon in Hyde Park. And while his mind was pleasantly fogged, a quiet realization slipped in. Ash hadn't been to a Season in years. Claimed it was too expensive, but he was here now. That hadn't struck Peter as unusual until just this moment.

"You're looking for an heiress."

His friend nodded. "Got an eye to Miss Powel." Then his step hitched before he resumed at a slower pace. "I take it you object."

Peter frowned. "I didn't say anything."

"You growled at me."

Had he? "I...I was clearing my throat," he lied.

Ash sighed, the sound coming from deep inside. "So it's true then. You've come home to marry."

No sense in denying it. "I have."

"And you want Miss Powel."

"I haven't decided." Another lie, and Ash knew it.

"What phrase are you going to teach that bird?"

He didn't have to say a thing. For all that they'd been apart for six years, Ash knew him best of all. It took the man all of ten seconds to realize the truth, and then suddenly Ash gripped his arm and jerked him to a stop, speaking in a low tone.

"Damnation, man, you've only been back a few days. You haven't even had a look around, and you certainly can't have selected a bride."

"You want her," Peter pointed out. "Isn't that good enough?"

"No, it bloody well isn't. Why her? And when? When could you possibly have decided on this course?"

Six years ago, to be exact, but he didn't tell his friend that. He didn't need to, because Ash started cursing, loud and fluently. So well, in fact, that a few gentlemen stopped to listen and even clapped when he was done.

"You've gotten better at that," Peter said.

"I've had practice."

"I can do it in a dozen languages now."

Ash rolled his eyes. "You make those words up."

"Used to. Don't now." And perhaps that was the heart of how he'd changed. He was now everything he'd pretended to be before. Ash was the choleric one, his moods swinging between delight and despair. Peter was the affable fool, or so people said. They both knew the truth was far more complicated than that. And in the end, they began walking again, the silence returning to a comfortable place.

"So what happened in India? What were you doing while I was digging ditches and learning how to shear sheep?"

"The usual. Horse races, card games, pistol matches. Oh, and I learned how to throw knives."

"Whatever for?"

To save his life. And it had on more than one occasion. "It was fun to learn."

"Keep your secrets if you must, but it's not healthy, you know. Causes an ague."

"To keep secrets?"

"Absolutely. Had a cousin who would never say boo to anyone. Always doing things nobody understood. Then one day, dead from an ague. That's what comes from keeping everything held off behind a blank smile and an empty stare. All those thoughts twist around themselves until you die."

Peter laughed, but when his best friend in the world gave him a hard stare, he relented. He said what he'd told no one, and he used the simplest terms he could find. "I was a taxman, Ash. I got money out of wealthy, powerful men who didn't want to pay. It was difficult work, often violent, and all done with a smile." He grunted. "Turns out I was perfect for the work."

"Violent? But you're a terrible shot."

"I'm an acceptable shot." Better than acceptable now. "And an excellent fighter. Especially with knives."

Ash drew up in horror. "You beat the money out of them? I don't believe it. You got weepy when that kitten died."

"*You* bawled. I was simply trying to show you a moderate example."

"Bollocks. Tell me the truth, did you really beat them?"

Peter tried to laugh, but the sound came out strained. "I got the money any way I could, Ash. I found out what they needed most, got it, and then bargained for what I wanted."

Ash's eyes narrowed. "You've always been uncommonly good at that."

Peter shrugged. If he had an unusual talent, it was the ability to see exactly what a person needed most. It was an internal knowing. A stupid parlor trick he'd played with as a boy, but in India, the talent had been refined to a sharp blade, and if he could use that knowledge to force someone to live up to their responsibilities...well, then he did it without regret or guilt.

"What happened?" Ash pressed again. "Exactly."

Peter looked back at his friend. "The same thing that happened to you, exactly. We survived the best way we could."

Ash accepted that in his usual manner. He frowned and glared. A dark expression that had lost its effectiveness on Peter by the time they were nine. Eventually, Ash released a huff of annoyance, and they resumed walking. Turned out it was the best choice the man could have made, because a few minutes later, Peter added one more thing.

"I came home to end all that, you know. No more violence. No more nonsense. Just good brandy, hearty beef stew, and an English rose in my bed."

"She's Welsh."

"Near enough."

"And she really doesn't like you." Ash chuckled then. A slow roll of sound that worried Peter more than all the man's glowers and frowns.

"What's so funny?"

"You really don't know, do you?"

"Know what?"

"Just how powerfully that woman despises you."

He hadn't the foggiest. "Whatever did I do?"

His friend's grin grew wider. "I don't think I'm going to suspend my pursuit of the wealthy Miss Powel."

"Just a minute—"

"But I'm not going to court her either."

This time Peter knew it when he growled. Bloody hell, when had he started making that noise? "Just what do you intend, then?" His voice was hard and low.

"I'm going to stand her friend. As you blunder your way about her heart, I will stand by and offer her a safe shoulder to cry on."

"I sincerely doubt she'd cry. More like beat me about the ears with her reticule."

Ash snorted. "Perhaps six years ago, but you've been gone a while, and the situation has changed."

Yes, he'd noticed that. The vibrant, powerful woman he remembered now wore boring dresses and severe hair. "Who has been advising her? It appears they're trying to destroy everything good about her looks."

His friend frowned. "That was all the talk a fort-night ago. It's Lady Eleanor."

Peter turned forcefully toward his friend. "Eleanor's never been vicious, and she's always had excellent taste. Why would she dress Miss Powel like a sack of wet oatmeal?"

"That's overstating the case, don't you think?"

Peter arched a brow.

Eventually his friend shrugged. "Oatmeal is perhaps close to the mark, but she's nothing like that."

"I know she's not!" Peter huffed. "I want to know what happened that she's acting as if she has no more flash than weak potage."

His friend opened his mouth to speak, but his words stopped, and his face took on a quizzical look. "Eleanor has just started to sponsor her, but I think she has always appeared as you see her now. There was no discussion of a change in appearance."

Peter shook his head. "I don't like it."

"I don't imagine she cares what you think," the man answered, which only served to irritate Peter. He knew she had no regard for his thoughts. She'd already made that abundantly clear. But why was she dressing herself to such disadvantage?

"Something must have happened," he deduced. "Something damaging made her want to hide herself away. And don't try to tell me it was that insult she thinks I gave her. That's a distraction from the real problem." The very idea of someone hurting her made him want to growl again.

"Excellent." Ash clapped him on the shoulder. "Then we'll see whom the lady wants. I'd thought there'd be no contest between your wealth and my lack thereof. Our titles are relatively equal, thank Heaven, but I see now that it won't be about money. Lord knows she's got plenty of it."

"What will it be about?"

"That's simple. Who's the better man?"

⁂

Mari smiled at Lady Eleanor, pleased to have a willing ear to share her tale of grievance. "It all began at Lady Farbridge's ball six years ago. It was my first Season, and my sister Josephine and I were so excited to go. You know how it is with young girls. Everything is so special. It was only my third ball, and I was still dazzled. Jo was hardly any better, though she'd been out longer than I."

"I missed that entire Season," Eleanor mused. "I was traveling with my father, and we couldn't be back in time."

Mari nodded. "I suppose it was a Season like every other, so you didn't miss much. But I was young and had never done anything so thrilling." Funny how, in all her private reliving, she'd never thought of how little she'd understood about anything. Everything had seemed so important. The number of people at the balls, the ladies in their gowns, the dandies in their lace, and the Corinthians in their shiny boots. She'd been devastated to be suddenly cast out from it.

"Well?" Eleanor prompted. "What happened?"

"I was wearing a gown I adored. Pale lavender with tiny seed pearls along the bodice and in my hair. Understated but elegant."

"I quite approve."

Of course she would. Eleanor's style had always been refined.

"My sister, of course, had to have color. She wore a modest gown but of a bold russet color. Almost orange."

"I've never met your sister. Did it suit her coloring?"

"Close enough, though the ruffles were not her style at all."

The two women shuddered.

"We began to talk as one does before the dancing. Our cards weren't full by any means."

"You are Welsh," Eleanor hedged.

"And new money. I know. To my mind, it was perfect. Everything perfect."

Eleanor leaned forward. "Get to the important part."

"I wanted some punch. It was dreadfully hot in the

room. Sally and I—she's Mrs. Clarkin now—headed for the bowl, but it was such a crush that we were constantly stopping. And that's when I heard it. Lord Whitly was speaking to Mr. Fitzhugh."

Eleanor's face pinched. "He's a bounder, that Fitzhugh. Fortune hunter is the kindest thing I can say about him."

Mari looked down at her hands. "Yes, and a terrible gossip, which of course made everything worse."

"What were they saying?"

"I stopped, you see, because I heard them say my name. Mr. Fitzhugh was asking advice. He intended to have a go—his words—at my sister or me and wanted to know who was the better catch."

Eleanor sighed. "Both of you were far too good for him."

"Yes, but I didn't know that. Whitly's answer destroyed me." She took a deep breath. "He asked whyever would Fitzhugh want either one of us? The elder was wild and the younger wayward."

Eleanor's eyes widened, and her lips formed a perfect O of surprise. "So that is how you came by your names."

"Yes," she said bitterly. "From that moment on, everything we did, from the most innocent flirtation to the cut and color of our gowns was scrutinized and used as proof of our inappropriateness."

"Oh dear. I hadn't realized that was Lord Whitly's doing."

"Jo tried to be restrained, but it isn't in her nature. She's very high-spirited. She soon learned that no matter how dull she appeared, no matter what she did, the name followed her. She laughed too loudly; she gestured too broadly. Heavens, she was even criticized for the way she sipped her tea."

"But she's happily married now, yes?"

"Yes, thank Heaven, but it was only after five Seasons." Horrible, difficult Seasons. And then all the time in between listening to her father bemoan their lack of accomplishment. As if any of it was their fault.

"And you?" Eleanor prompted. "How has it been for you?"

Mari sighed. "You know how it's been. Miserable. Do you know why my gowns are a single color? I can never wear two colors or even a pattern."

"You can't be serious."

"I am. I wore a lovely yellow gown with a dark blue shawl once and was called flighty and clearly wayward."

Eleanor pursed her lips. "That's ridiculous."

"I know, and yet the label persists. If I sing anything but the slowest dirge, it's proof that my upbringing has been too lenient."

"Heavens, is that why you never sing?"

Mari nodded. "Or dance much. Or do anything but wait hand and foot on the dowagers. I have been the model of propriety—I daily want to scream—all because one night Lord Whitly called me wayward. The blighter!"

"Well, to be fair, I doubt Whitly knew you would be plagued by that moniker."

Mari clenched her hands in her lap. "I don't care. He was speaking to a notorious gossip and knew his words would be repeated."

Eleanor patted the couch near her hand. "I think

you overestimate how much a gentleman thinks about anything."

Mari huffed out a breath. "That's all the more damning. One careless word to Fitzhugh, and I have spent six years wearing dull dresses and serving tepid lemonade to dowagers."

Eleanor waited a moment, clearly thinking about her story. In the end, she pulled her hands back into her lap and gave Mari a wan smile. "You have been the soul of propriety, and that is why I agreed to help you."

That and the generous sum of money from Mari's father. Mari didn't know the exact details of the arrangement, but she knew that Lady Eleanor had begun aiding a few very select ladies in their match-making efforts. This year was her turn.

So everything was established for a perfect Season. After six years of complete dullness, no one called her *wayward* anymore. She'd worn a patterned gown two nights ago with no ill effects. It had been yellow with tiny white dots. Hardly visible, which was why she'd allowed it, plus a very daring lace trim. And she'd gotten away with it! Then out of the blue, Whitly returned and confronted her in Hyde Park. Suddenly, she was a topic of conversation again. The label would more than resurface; it would gain new life, and she would be back to beige again. And sitting along the wall at every event, without a single suitor.

"Oh, I shall kill him!" she fumed as she set aside her tea. She couldn't drink it anyway. She was sick to death of it, when she truly, desperately wished for a stiff drink of claret. Or better yet, brandy. And that was another thing she hadn't had for six years, all thanks to Lord Whitly.

"Don't fret," Eleanor soothed. "This isn't nearly as disastrous as you might think. It's a harmless diversion."

"Other ladies can have harmless diversions. Thanks to Lord Whitly, the Wayward Welsh can't do any of it without being spurned."

"Well, yes, that is a concern. Mr. Camden did seem rather put out by the wager."

Her best matrimonial possibility already running because of Lord Whitly. "It's not fair! I haven't done anything wrong. Why is it so hard for me to find a husband?" The need to be married grew stronger every day, like an itch she could not scratch. She wanted to plant roots, to have a home of her own with children and responsibilities. Unmarried women were not allowed such things, and she hated it.

Lady Eleanor sighed, lifted her tea, and sipped it with perfect serenity. Or pretended to, because when she set the cup down, the liquid hadn't lowered. Then the lady looked long and hard at Mari. And she kept looking, so Mari ended up smoothing down her hair. Had some of the strands gone *wayward* again?

The woman must have understood her thoughts, because Eleanor smiled and picked up her tea again. "No, no, don't go doubting your looks. You are in fine fettle, best I've seen from you in a while."

"I am incensed."

"Yes, and it gives a lovely color to your cheeks."

Mari sighed. "I shall just have to win that wager."

"Well, of course, I'm sure that's important too, but I was thinking of Mr. Camden. Are you sure he's who you want? As a husband, I mean. He is rather, um, steadfast in his niceties."

By which she meant he was a bore prone to priggishness.

"He's smart and wealthy enough that I don't fear he's a fortune hunter."

"That's true," Eleanor allowed.

"We can converse, he and I."

"Truly? About what?"

"Mostly about his investments and the state of the country. Political things." Though primarily, he talked while she asked questions. He loved it when she asked questions so he could answer them with all the pomp of an Oxford don.

"I hadn't realized he was political," Eleanor mused.

"He isn't really, but I think he'd like to be. He's taking a chance with a Wayward Wife, so to speak."

Eleanor's eyes narrowed imperceptibly. "Yes, I can see that would be awkward for a political man."

"He told me exactly that. He hoped my wayward ways were behind me. And when I explained—quite vehemently, I might add—that it was all Lord Whitly's fault, he was quite kind."

"Really?" Eleanor didn't sound as though she believed it.

"He can be very sympathetic. He understands how Society works and admires my restraint all these years."

Eleanor's expression brightened. "I certainly admire it. I thought it was your natural inclination."

"It is, a little." A very little. "And anyway, it doesn't matter. I've done it. Mr. Camden admired it, and now Whitly's ruined it."

Eleanor didn't speak, just sat there smoothing an invisible ripple in her skirt and thinking. Mari could only pray she came up with something brilliant that would end the rumors altogether and make Whitly pay for his perfidy.

Then finally the woman spoke, her voice tempered, as was her wont. "So you have your heart set on Mr. Camden?"

"My heart? Good God, no. He simply fits my requirements."

Eleanor's eyebrows rose. "Requirements?"

"I was afraid my father never showed them to you. He's uncomfortable with what he calls a woman's mercenary side, though truthfully, I'm only doing what he taught me."

"I am all agog. What did he teach you?"

"To outline clearly one's desires, and then act to achieve them. I shall show you. I keep it with me and look at it every day." She fished the well-worn paper out of her reticule. "It's my requirements for a husband, and as you can see, Mr. Camden fits all of them."

The lady looked at the page, her expression blank. Eleanor was the very definition of feminine serenity, and it wasn't until this very moment that Mari realized how completely irritating that was. She had no clue what the woman was thinking. Which meant Mari soon started babbling.

"The first is obvious. No fortune hunters. With my dowry, they've been thick about me, and I cannot stand a one of them."

"Of course not," Eleanor said with a sniff.

"The second is relatively clear, too. He has to be

a man of acceptable moral character. Note the word 'acceptable.' I'm not looking for a cleric. I'm not so naive as to think a man can't enjoy gambling, drinking, or anything else in moderation."

Lady Eleanor arched a brow. "Are you aware of some of the vices you are allowing?"

Mari frowned. "Well, Mother has told me that most men of influence have a mistress. It's practically a requirement."

Her companion nodded slowly. "I think I understand. You want a man of moderate temperament."

"Exactly. No showy displays, no shocking vices." And a man who had made his fortune gambling or racing, as Lord Whitly claimed, was out of the question. "The third requirement is harder to define. You see, I don't need any money. My dowry alone could keep a modest man comfortable for the rest of our lives, but I wish for more. I want a man who will be important in London Society. I want to help him become important."

"So you want a title."

"No," Mari said with a smile. This was where she thought herself very forward thinking indeed. "I know Papa is mad for a title, but so many peers are ninnies. They want my dowry so they can continue to gamble and wench. I want a man who wants something beyond his next meal."

"So that is why you haven't wed so far." Lady Eleanor set the list down, her expression vaguely troubled. "And that is why you look to Mr. Camden."

"He has a bright financial future."

Eleanor nodded. "I see your problem, then. You

are looking for the rarest creature of all: a man of influence who travels through the *ton* and who has no obvious vices. My dear, that is no one but a clergyman, and yet you state clearly in the next item, no clergy. If I may ask, why do you object so strongly to the religious?"

"Because their wives have to be even more circumspect than I've been. If I thought these last six years have been a trial, imagine constantly having to be the epitome of moral rectitude. It would be maddening."

Eleanor gifted Mari with one of her rare true smiles. "We are of the same mind, you and I. And now that I know you will be content without a title, then I see no impediment in getting you to the altar by Season's end."

Well, that was a relief.

"Except, of course, for the obvious one."

Mari nodded. "Lord Whitly."

"I was going to say any temptation to willfulness on your part. I see now that your natural inclination is not nearly as restrained as I'd been led to believe."

"It is only because Lord Whitly has interfered."

"Well, that is as may be, but you must restrain yourself. One impetuous wager can be survived. Especially as Lady Castlereigh and the others have approved it. But any more such nonsense, and even I will not be able to redeem you."

Mari took a deep breath. So her path was clear. She was to be circumspect in all things no matter how much Lord Whitly provoked her.

"You may count on me." She refolded her list. It might be a list about a man's requirements, but in truth, it was all about her. About the woman she would have to be to attract a man like that. She returned it to her reticule, next to her folded list of possible husbands. Many of the top tier were crossed off as unattainable or unsuitable. Mr. Camden was the highest available to her now, and he was number twenty-seven.

Meanwhile, Lady Eleanor clasped her hands together and started to rise. "Do you intend to go to Lady Barnes's ball tonight, Mrs. Winter's musicale, or the theater?"

"The theater tonight, and Lady Carlyle's ball tomorrow."

"Very well. I shall see you tomorrow then, as I'm to the musicale."

Mari scrambled to follow. "But…but what are we to do about Lord Whitly?"

"Ignore him. You have the approval of myself and the patronesses of Almack's. If you cannot turn that to your advantage, then you are not as clever as I thought."

Mari stared at her a moment, then blurted out her thoughts. "But you are here to help me." In fact, Papa had *paid* her to help.

"And I am. I am giving you my approval. The rest is up to you." Then she gave her a beatific smile. "Don't fret so much. I think your gowns are perfectly sound."

Then she departed. Horace must have been listening, because he opened the parlor door with perfect timing. Mari stood silently, watching as Eleanor donned her outer wraps and walked away.

Mari never said a word. She most certainly didn't scream or rail that the woman had been paid to give better advice. That she'd been less than useless in offering sympathy. And most of all, that Mari absolutely, positively did not want to wear *perfectly sound gowns*!

Which meant there was only one thing left to do. One simple and perfect choice. She was going to teach that dratted bird to say "happy day," and then she was going to stand over Lord Whitly and gloat. Yes, she was going to savor every second that man was on his knee before her, and she wouldn't let him up until Easter!

# Four

"HAPPY DAY, YOU DRATTED BIRD."

Peter and Lady Illston's butler paused outside the back parlor door. It wasn't good form to laugh while in the company of someone else's butler. Indeed, it wasn't good form for the butler to be chuckling under his breath either, but the two men exchanged amused glances and then—good man—the butler bowed and withdrew.

That left Peter free to open the door quietly to the parlor in which Miss Powel was trying to tempt the parakeet with a piece of apple.

"Come on, Greenie, I have a bit of apple for you. Happy day. Happy day. Happy day."

The bird tried to reach for the apple, but she pulled it away, thereby demonstrating that she knew nothing at all about training birds. Specific treats should be tied to the phrase. Therefore, the creature ought to be stuffed on apple right now as she kept repeating "Happy day."

He began to think he would likely win this wager. Which made it unfortunate that he had little interest in their wager one way or the other. He'd come here for an entirely different purpose.

Still, that didn't stop him from appreciating how her body twitched with her frustration. She was an animated woman with a nice bum, neatly outlined as she leaned over the table and tried to entice the creature. Given that he was built on a large scale, he liked a woman with curves.

Mari was a woman of middling height, perfect complexion, and bright amber eyes. Her breasts were lush, her hips tempting, and her lips were on the proper side of sinfully dark. But mostly, she was alive in his mind in a way that no other woman ever approached. And right now, she was dropping into a nearby chair, clearly at odds with the world.

"You're an awful bird, and I hate this game," she grumbled.

He was too amused by her to realize his mistake until it was too late. With Miss Powel in a chair, the bird could see him. And right on cue, the creature greeted him.

"Winner, winner!"

Peter grinned at the bird and crossed into the room. "Good morning, Greenie." A simplistic, stupid name for such an intelligent bird. "Miss Powel."

He tried not to notice how she'd leapt from her chair, her bosom jiggling and her color deepening to a delightful rose.

"Lord Whitly!" Shock and horror on her face. "What are you doing here?"

"I believe your hour is up, Miss Powel." He gestured with one hand to the mantel clock. With the other, he fed the creature a bit of carrot, which was greedily consumed. "Good bird."

"Oh," she said as she obviously took in the time. "Nevertheless, you should have announced yourself."

"I'm sorry if I startled you," he said, but she suddenly gasped and clenched her fists.

"And now you know my phrase!"

He leaned against the table, wondering why she chose to wear such an insipid shade of pink. It was so dull, even the matching ribbon looked bored.

"I knew it before," he said, "so there's no harm done there."

"You couldn't possibly."

He nodded as he looked at her hair. She'd done it up into a tight bun that pulled her skin flat across her forehead. Bloody painful to look at. He wondered why she didn't have a headache.

Meanwhile, he answered her unspoken question. "You didn't shade your mouth when you whispered it to Lady Illston. I could read it off your lips."

She gaped at him, her hand going to her mouth. Pity to cover up one of her best features. "That's not possible," she said.

"I assure you, it is." And when she simply shook her head, he allowed himself to revel in one of his fondest memories from his childhood. "I had a playmate as a boy. His father worked at the stable, and we often ran off together to explore. Then one year, he took a fever. An ugly disease, but he survived. Except he was deaf from then on."

"Winner, winner!" the bird cried.

"Greedy thing," he said as he passed the creature more carrot.

"He could read language off a person's lips? How extraordinary."

"He was much better at it than I, for obvious reasons, but we learned it together. And I kept up the knack because…" He shrugged. "I suppose I don't like it when people keep secrets from me."

"But that's cheating!"

He tilted his head. She couldn't possibly think that. And yet looking at her flashing eyes, he realized she was truly that innocent. To think that cheating was comprised of reading someone's lips. Replacing the bird was cheating. Preventing the woman from spending time with the creature was cheating. Knowing the woman's phrase was just simple skill.

But rather than explain that, he decided to pursue his primary goal. The one where she tumbled headlong into love with him. And that, of course, began with simple flattery.

"It is not cheating. And I cannot help it if I find your lips particularly fascinating."

She blinked at him, and her cheeks flamed like fire. Obviously she wasn't used to compliments, because she immediately began stammering.

"You—I—" Her hands went from her mouth to her blazing cheeks, and she glared at him.

"Don't cover up. Your looks are stunning when you blush," he added.

"I never blush!" she said, her tone full of accusation.

He grinned. He liked watching her when she was

flustered. "Then occasionally, you have a particularly florid complexion."

Her hands dropped to her sides, and she visibly got control of herself. "You are an odious man."

And right there was what he'd come to discover. She obviously still held him in contempt, but for the life of him, he couldn't see why.

He shifted his weight so he was sitting more fully on the table. It wasn't a proper way to be in front of a lady, but he was trying to encourage her to feel less proper around him. They were alone. It was a lucky stroke that Lady Illston's butler was amenable to bribery.

But far from being more casual in his presence, she tightened even more. Her hands twitched, and her brows narrowed. Clearly, she didn't like his air of insouciance, so he relaxed even more. It was the imp in him, he was sure, but he did like vexing her.

"I have a wager with one of my oldest friends," he began.

"I'm sure you do—"

"It's about you."

She blew out an annoyed breath. "I'm sure it is."

Well, there was a wealth of meaning in that, but she didn't elaborate, so he leaned back and studied her slowly as he spoke. He wanted to memorize every nuance of her reaction.

"He believes you hold me in such contempt that if I were to propose to you right now, you would throw my words right back in my face. Worse, you would crow to every one of your intimates the insult I had done you by offering to make you my countess."

She lifted her chin, and her eyes flashed fire. He hadn't thought amber eyes could make him think of searing heat, but her expression downright burned.

"Do you mock me, sir?"

"Not in the least." He leaned forward. "My position is that you would be appropriately flattered and would weigh my offer with the consideration it deserves."

"Well," she said with a laugh, "I would certainly do that." By which she meant she would discard his proposal as if it were bad meat.

He shook his head at the insult. He was due to inherit an earldom. Surely she understood that. "I cannot credit that a woman of good sense would toss aside a future earl so cavalierly."

"Good sense? Is that how you would describe me?"

"Well, of course—"

"I thought it was *wayward*."

He sighed. "You cannot possibly still be angry about that."

She jolted forward a step, and he had to scramble off the table to maintain the slightest semblance of decency. Meanwhile, her fists landed on the table on either side of him. It was a startling, masculine gesture, one that made him want her even more. Especially as it put her face right close to his.

"Of course I am still furious! How can you be so thickheaded? Do you know what my last six years have been like? Everyone thinks me wild."

"Wild? I thought that was your sister."

She hit him. She flat-out punched him across the jaw. He saw it coming. He'd have had to be blind to miss it, but she did connect with his chin, though it glanced painlessly away. Then she stepped back and shook out her hand, muttering under her breath.

"Fisticuffs! That is what he brings me to. Damn, that hurts."

He looked at the way she jerked in front of him. Like lightning dancing, spastic and beautiful all at once.

"Well, obviously you have no brothers to teach you how to do that properly."

"I do most certainly have a brother!" she snapped.

"Younger, then, and remiss in your instruction."

"He… I… I have no need to learn how to hit a man." She took a deep breath, shot him a glare that practically sizzled across his skin, and straightened up to her full middling height. "Your friend has won his wager with you. I would indeed throw your proposal back in your arrogant face."

"Because I named you wayward to a scoundrel who meant to dupe you? So he would stay away?"

"Yes! What? No!" She crossed her arms below her bosom, plumping them nicely. If she weren't still pacing back and forth, he might have thought it a practiced move. Now he suspected she was merely keeping herself from trying to punch him again.

"Fitzhugh is a jackanapes, through and through," he said. "I was doing you a kindness by steering him away from you."

"By saddling me with a label that was repeated over and over for the last six Seasons?"

He shrugged. "You were already labeled Welsh. Wayward or wild could hardly make it any worse."

She gaped at him. Her mouth popped open, her

eyes shone bright with unshed tears, and she seemed to vibrate with suppressed emotion.

"That's not true!"

He studied her body. Indeed, it was something he was prone to do quite often in his memory. But in this case, instead of focusing on her more feminine wiles, he looked at her tight shoulders and the way she bit her lip, a little more on the right side than the left. In truth, she looked a little lost.

"It is true," he said as gently as he could. "*Welsh* is little better than a gel from the Colonies. Surely you know that."

"No," she said, shaking her head. "No, it's because you said that horrid thing."

He didn't contradict her. In general, he found arguing to be a great waste of time. So he simply waited while she fought with her thoughts. Eventually, she would realize he was right, but it might take her a while. But then that imp inside him pushed him to tease her. "And besides, it's true, isn't it? I mean, everyone is a little bit—"

"You, sir," she interrupted, "are a boor!"

He'd been called much worse, but still the words stung. "And you, my dear, are…" Innocent. Spirited. Beautiful. "Wayward."

"Oh!" She reacted as a woman this time. Open palm as she went to slap him. Again, he saw the move coming and easily caught her arm. But instead of releasing her or allowing her to draw back, he jerked her close to him. He pulled her tight, so her breasts lifted and lowered against his chest. Her ruby lips were parted and so close, and her amber eyes were right before him, as mesmerizing as any cobra in India.

"Shall I tell you what I remember of that night?"

"No—"

He spoke right over her. "I remember asking you to dance and being pleased when you agreed. Then step by step, whenever we were close, you began to eviscerate me."

She nearly choked on her gasp of outrage. "I did no such thing."

"You whispered things into my ear, so soft I had to bend to hear them. I thought they would be sweet confessions or delicate words."

"You had just damned both me and my sister. I heard it clearly. And then, I watched Fitzhugh repeat it to everyone at the ball."

He barely heard her. He was too caught up in the memory of her words from that night, of the tight horror in his chest, and the dull agony of knowing he had to complete the dance or lose composure in front of the whole *ton*. "You called me a useless fribble, wasting my life and my money away. You named me cruel and lazy. But more than that, you said I was the worst kind of Englishman, because I did nothing of any value." With his free hand, he lifted her chin until they stood eye to eye. "You called me useless that night, Miss Powel. You destroyed me."

He hadn't meant to reveal that to her. In truth, he hadn't even thought those words in such a way before this very moment. But the strength with which he gripped her, the anger that seethed in his blood, and the resentment that blistered his tongue as he spoke, all pointed at how hideous that moment had been for him.

Broken furniture was useless. A drunken servant was useless. He was a peer of the realm, or would be when he inherited. By definition, he was not useless.

And yet in the short time of a single dance, she'd laid his soul bare and named it useless. It was only his pride that had made him finish the dance before he gave her a dismissive bow then fled. He'd gone as fast as he could to the nearest brothel, where he'd gotten himself blind drunk then robbed by the strumpets. And when that hadn't worked to blot out her words, he'd run all the way to India.

And that had been the making of him.

That too was why he loved her. Because she had said exactly what he'd needed to hear in exactly the way to force him out of his lethargy. If she hadn't flayed him alive, he'd likely still be sunk deep in drink and cunny. And all anyone would ever say of him was...

"Useless," he repeated in a hissing whisper. "You named me useless."

"Clearly I was wrong," she said. "You were powerful enough to make me suffer for six years."

"And you were vicious enough to send me to India, where, I assure you, I had much worse done to me than a little name-calling."

She blinked, and her mouth pursed into a sweet O. She smelled of apples and musk, and without even looking, he knew her nipples were tight. She was aroused, and he was painfully hard. Clearly one of them was insane. He for desiring her when she'd been so terrible to him. Or she for hating him and yet allowing herself to remain panting in his arms.

"I am not wayward," she said, her chin hardened with stubbornness.

"I am not useless."

She swallowed. She looked at his lips, and he let his gaze drop to her breasts. Plump and pointed. He tightened his grip on her. She didn't even try to escape.

Instead, she met him eye to eye. Her head was canted back, exposing the arch of her neck. His gaze was burning downward at her, and he wanted nothing more than to free himself from his clothing and let her see what she did to him.

"Are you sure?" he pressed.

"What?"

"Sure you would refuse my offer?" Then he leaned down slowly toward her. Their breaths mingled, hers sweet with apple. Did she know he'd chewed mint before seeing her? Could she smell it like he scented her?

He touched his lips to hers. Her breath caught on a gasp, but he did no more. Just held there, his lips slanted across hers where she'd parted to allow him entry. A touch. No more.

And then he bit her. A tiny nip along her bottom lip. She shuddered in reaction. He might have thought she was repulsed if he didn't feel her body surge forward. She checked it as soon as it happened, but he felt it nonetheless.

"You destroyed me, Miss Powel, and I am better for it."

Then he pulled away. Slowly, because he still worried

he'd throw her onto the table and take her, propriety or no. She did nothing but stare at him. Her cheeks were red, her lips even more so, but she said nothing. And when he'd eased two steps back, he straightened his coat. It did nothing to hide his erection to a discerning gaze, but her eyes never left his face. Did she even know to look? Or feel for it? Did she understand what she did to him?

Then with a slow, dazed look, she pressed her fingers to her lips. She held them there, her eyes fluttering. Good God, he realized, he knew exactly what she needed. She needed to be touched, to be caressed, to be worshiped in a very physical way. If he had it right, she was starving for it.

He almost did it. He could give her all the worship she desired, but it would be a fool's game. She was not ready to accept him yet, and he would not go where he wasn't wanted. Even if it was exactly what she most needed.

"I am leaving for a few days," he said, his voice tight. "I suggest you use that time to your advantage."

Her eyes blinked and focused on him, but she still said nothing. She gave him nothing but her amber eyes and parted lips.

"With Greenie," he explained. "But talk to a trainer first."

She frowned. "A trainer?"

"Horse trainer. Dog trainer. Falconer. Anyone. You're a miserable hand at it, and I consider it gentlemanly to allow you at least a few days to figure out the basics."

"The basics?"

"Yes," he said. "It isn't fun to play with someone so miserably outmatched."

Then he had a choice. It was either flatten her on the table and take what they both wanted from her body or escape before he lost all credibility with himself and her. It was a near thing. He wanted her that badly. But eventually, he forced himself to leave. Or more accurately, he fled all the way to Lincolnshire, because that's what she did to him. Made him insane with want even as she cut him to the quick. It's what she'd done six years ago, but he refused to allow it to happen again.

He wasn't a boy anymore, and when he returned, it would be to fight toe-to-toe with her. And by God, next time he would win, simply because this was the very last time he was leaving before all was settled between them.

# *Five*

MARI STOOD BESIDE THE SILENT BIRD AND TRIED TO manage in a world gone insane. But first she had to stop her lips from tingling. Her body was recalling in vivid sensual memory the exact way he had touched her. The press of his lips, the heat of his breath, and the startling nip with his teeth. He had kissed her, and she ached with the need for him to do it again.

No, no, no. She couldn't desire Lord Whitly. He was the man who had destroyed her.

But what if she was wrong?

It wasn't possible, but what if...

For years, all she'd heard was Wayward Welsh. It had never occurred to her that *Welsh* was the problem.

She could fight the impression of wayward. Indeed she had been, but there was nothing she could do about Welsh. In truth, she was rather proud of her heritage and had never sought to hide it. Was she truly barred from the best husbands in the land simply because of where she'd been born?

It wasn't possible.

And yet maybe it was.

And maybe she'd been a complete idiot.

She slumped backward against her chair, not even remembering when she'd sat down. And when the bird chirped at her, she blindly fed it some apple.

"Happy day," she murmured, though those words would now forever mark the day she'd deciphered how much of a fool she'd been. "Sodding day," the bird squawked.

She jerked, and another apple bit slid out of her fingers. The bird pounced on it, gobbling it down in three quick bites.

"Sodding day," it cried again.

"No, no, I did not teach you that."

Mari glared at the thing, but it just cocked its head and waited.

"Sodding day," it chirped.

"Bloody bird," she shot back. Then she grabbed her reticule and departed. There was only one woman of her acquaintance who would know the truth of the matter. One woman who would tell her if the problem was wayward or Welsh. One woman—Lady Eleanor—who when finally confronted, answered in two short sentences.

"Of course the problem's Welsh. I thought you knew."

No, she hadn't. But now that she did, she planned to make a few significant changes to her wardrobe, her attitude, to her whole public persona. If she didn't have to fight the idea she was wayward—

"But it shouldn't make any difference," said Lady Eleanor, interrupting Mari's excited plans.

Mari jolted. "Of course it does. It means I've been fighting the wrong label."

"But you still want to marry an influential man. And that means you have to remain circumspect. You need to be an asset to the powerful, not a detriment."

Oh. Of course.

It took Mari a moment to get over how crushed she felt. Once again, she'd thought to escape her self-imposed prison, but it was not to be. She had to stay the course.

"Thank you, Lady Eleanor. I can see that my thoughts ran away with me."

"You really should stay away from Lord Whitly. He seems to have a deleterious effect on your wits."

Mari nodded as she blocked the memory of his kiss from her brain. "I completely agree," she forced herself to say. "In the future, I shall avoid all contact with him." Even if it was a kiss. Even if it was a lot of wonderful kisses.

Lady Eleanor beamed. "I knew you were a bright girl."

❧

"You're looking eminently respectable this evening."

Mari was feeling rather old today as she stood languishing at the come-out ball of yet another debutante. Six Seasons was too long for any maiden, and she very much feared that Wayward Welsh was going to give way any moment to Ape Leader. But she had to keep a positive outlook despite her fears. So she turned to Ashley Tucker, Lord Rimbury, and gave her new friend her brightest smile, even though he obviously disagreed with the sameness of her attire.

"Thank you," she said sweetly. "I'm rewarding myself for a week of completely proper behavior."

He arched a brow at her bland yellow gown. "That's a reward?"

"It has white dots."

"Really?" He squinted at her gown. "Damned if I see them."

"They're very tiny dots."

"I'd look closer, but I believe at least two of the dowagers would beat me about the ears with their canes."

"Yes, they probably would." As usual, she was standing near enough to the older ladies so she could be called to their side at a moment's notice. It was the only way she kept herself from dancing too much.

Meanwhile, she was pleased with the distraction that Lord Rimbury afforded her from feeling too old. "I've had a very productive day. This morning I spoke with a dog trainer, and I have high hopes for teaching Greenie my phrase."

His smile turned lugubrious, which on him was a very droll look. "Then I congratulate you on your progress, if not your choice of celebration."

She laughed merrily—but not too loudly—and then turned her attention to the gathering. "I think the dancing will begin soon," she said. The musicians had pulled out their instruments.

"I would beg for a dance, but I know you prefer to talk."

Not true. She preferred to dance, but as she was being circumspect, he was one of the few gentlemen with whom she had equal delight in conversation. Therefore, if she had to sit out, then at least she could do it with someone who was entertaining.

"I have reserved your usual spot at the dance just

before supper," she told him, showing him where she had scrawled his name on her card.

"Then I shall be delighted to escort you early to the buffet tables. I hear Mr. Hario sets an excellent table."

She nodded, knowing this was likely Lord Rimbury's only meal today. It was the other reason she reserved the dance before supper for him. This way she could be sure he had plenty to eat well before the food ran out. Her father had named Lord Rimbury "another damned impoverished nob," but she rather liked his gloomy sense of humor. He adored giving dire predictions about everyone and everything, and that never failed to make her laugh. And sure enough, a moment later, he was gesturing at a dandy across the room.

"I wager that Baron Pattinson rips the lace off his cuff within the hour."

"Don't be silly," Mari countered. "The baron is a fop of the first order. He wouldn't be casual with that lace any more than I would suddenly toss away my favorite fan."

"Ah, but the baron is trying to attract a new mistress."

Lord Rimbury also had the best gossip, usually tidbits that rarely reached an unwed lady's ears. "What, here? This is a coming-out ball."

"I never said the man was smart. Only that as men, we cock up the thing we love most. It's in our nature. And for Baron Pattinson, that means…ah…there it is. Spilled wine on his sleeve."

Sure enough, the baron was now red-faced with fury at the Corinthian who had been careless with his wine. Unless it was done on purpose.

And as if reading her mind, Lord Rimbury answered her unspoken question. "Deliberate. Definitely."

"But—"

"Those two have despised each other since the baron married the beauty and the Corinthian got the prune-faced one." His voice dropped to a depressed register. "It's on account of the baron being worth five times as much, even though he is ridiculous. You ladies are a terrible curse to us men, you know."

"Well, it's because you always…" She hesitated, wondering if she could actually say it. But the interest in his eyes made her lift her chin. "Because you always cock up when it's most important."

"Wisely said, Miss Powel."

"You said it first."

"I know." He gave her a mournful face, which made her laugh all the more. After a week of such exchanges, she might have been completely smitten except for one thing. For all his joking, she detected an undercurrent of bitterness. He truly did believe that men always cocked it up and that a woman was always the cause.

A week of this was only mildly irritating. A lifetime of it would be tedious in the extreme. So she enjoyed his company, tried to shine in her patterned gown, and waited for a better choice of husband.

"Peter Norwood, Lord Whitly."

She looked to the top of the stairs at the announcement. His was the one name she would always react to, for good or ill. And there he was at the top of the stairs, looking larger than life. He was outfitted in a jacket that fitted his wide shoulders to perfection.

A snowy-white cravat flashed a large emerald in the center. Narrow waist, long legs, and an arrogant lift to his chin completed the picture of aristocratic perfection. The sight of him made her breath catch. She also found herself pressing her fingers to her lips as she remembered their delicious kiss.

"Don't look so impressed," murmured Lord Rimbury. "He'll find a way to cock it up."

"There's nothing to cock up," she said primly as she whipped her hand from her mouth. It was all she could manage. Apparently her gaze wouldn't leave Lord Whitly as he descended the stairs and greeted their hosts. For such a large man, he moved so fluidly. "He was still wrong in what he said to me, but I may not be as angry as I was before."

She finally managed to tear her gaze away from Lord Whitly to look at Rimbury. "You said you've known him for years?"

"Since we were boys."

"And you've remained friends?"

"For the most part."

"Then there was no woman to destroy your friendship? No harpy who tore you apart?"

She hadn't thought it possible. Suddenly, Lord Rimbury's face drew in tight, and his eyes looked deeply sad. Always he was dramatic in his expression, but never with this quiet dread. "Not yet," he said softly. "But the evening is still young."

She meant to ask him to explain, but at that moment the musicians began their first dance. Mr. Hario escorted his daughter Isabelle onto the floor. The girl was dressed in white with deep blue ribbons for accents. It was a perfect come-out gown for a young lady who couldn't stop grinning. This was her night, and Mari smiled to see the delight in the child's face.

"Are there dots on this dress, or did you spill something on it?" a rich voice said. Lord Whitly, of course. His tone was matter-of-fact, almost dismissive, but he had one of those voices that rumbled excitingly on the ear no matter what he said.

"Dots," she snapped. "It's a pattern." She hadn't meant to sound quite so shrewish.

"It looks like you spilled milk on it. The dots aren't even regular."

"That's part of the *pattern*."

"I think it looks bloody ridiculous. Why wear a pattern that doesn't look like a real pattern, especially since almost no one can see it?"

"Because it's not wayward, you oaf!" Less than one minute in his company, and she was on the verge of screaming. Fortunately for her, Lord Rimbury was standing in earshot and suddenly burst out laughing. And when both she and Lord Whitly looked at him, he shrugged.

"I told you," he said, still chuckling. "We can't help it."

"Ash," Lord Whitly grumbled, "what are you going on about?"

"Peter," Lord Rimbury returned in exactly the same tone, "whatever possessed you to come to a ball in such a state?"

Lord Whitly looked down at himself. "Is this not the right fashion?" Then he smoothed down his hair. "Have I got it wrong?"

"You look most elegant," Lord Rimbury said with a grin.

"It's your behavior that is lacking, my lord," Mari clarified.

At which point the man frowned at her, then his cheeks pinkened. She wouldn't have believed it if she hadn't seen it. He appeared embarrassed, perhaps even ashamed.

"I beg your pardon," he said, and she could detect no lie in his words. Then he stepped back and executed a handsome bow. "Miss Powel, a pleasure to see you this evening."

She dropped into a curtsy. "Lord Whitly, I see you have returned to London."

"Yes." Then he stood there, staring at her as the conversation lagged. Finally she decided it was incumbent upon her to speak.

"Was your trip successful? You didn't tell me where you were going."

"Successful?" He reached back, likely to rub a hand over the back of his neck, but was stopped by his clothing. He ended up upsetting his hair instead. "I suppose in a way."

"Where did you go? You never said."

"To the family estate in Lincolnshire." His expression softened. "It's beautiful this time of year. Actually it's beautiful every time of year. I've missed it."

"India did not compare?"

"To the green fields of Kesteven? Not in the least."

The set was forming up, and her partner came to her side, bowing perfectly before her, his expression fashionably bored. He acted the proper gentleman, and she found him much less interesting than Lord Whitly. Still, she must keep to the proprieties.

"If you'll excuse me. I believe Mr. Midean has come to claim his dance."

"Of course." But then he held out his hand to her arm, stopping her. "But if I may, is there a dance left for me?" He quickly caught her arm and stroked over her glove until he grabbed the dance card attached to her wrist.

"Perhaps it would be better if—" she began, but he was already scrawling his name boldly across two lines. He returned her card to her, releasing her arm much more slowly. His fingers seemed to linger on her glove, and the heat burned through the fabric as if it were parchment. Her lips began to tingle in memory, and she was so distracted by the dual sensations that she didn't at first realize what he had done. But then she forced herself to look away from his eyes and down at the card. "You've claimed two waltzes," she said.

He nodded, his gaze almost distracted. "I cannot understand why they weren't claimed, but never fear. You shall have a partner now."

Meaning him, obviously, the dolt. As if she couldn't get a partner without his beneficence. "That's because I don't dance the waltz," she said firmly.

That brought his gaze back hard to her. "You don't dance it? Whyever not? It's all the rage in India."

"I've never received permission."

That wasn't exactly true. She'd never *asked* for permission. Even though every other debutante eventually got the nod for the scandalous dance, she'd never taken the risk, fearing it would appear too wayward.

"That's nonsense," he said. "You're not a green girl. Just dance it."

She didn't dare, and she was about to say so, but she'd run out of time. The first notes of the next dance had started, and Mr. Midean was clearly irritated. That would never do. He was a rising star in the legal arena, and she considered him an excellent potential husband. Number 31 on her list, in fact. Her father wanted a title, but she was more interested in intelligence and potential influence, which Mr. Midean had in abundance. So she pushed Lord Whitly from her thoughts—or she made a valiant attempt at it—and turned her smile onto Mr. Midean.

An hour later, she was still thinking of Lord Whitly instead of her dance partners. She'd seen him talk with Lord Rimbury, then steadily make the rounds of the room. He greeted many people, danced with a few young misses, especially the wallflowers, which she thought was sweet, and then sort of meandered about the room.

If he'd settled with one knot of gentlemen or another, she would have known better what to think of him. If he'd stood with the bankers, well then he was a man of finance. If he'd stayed to chat with the politicals, then she could classify him with them. It was clear from his dress that he was neither dandy nor Corinthian, though he was greeted by both sets.

In truth, he seemed to be wandering in search of something or exploring to some mysterious purpose. But what? She hadn't the slightest clue, except he spent an inordinate amount of time catching her looking at him. Annoying man. What was he doing watching her so closely? And why was she looking back all the time?

She refocused on her partner, finished the set, and then instead of wandering to where Lady Eleanor was holding court—which happened to be near where Lord Whitly stood talking with an aging solicitor—she went to her more typical place near the dowagers. They greeted her like a Greek chorus, all happily in accord. But that lasted only as long as it took for them to smile.

"Goodness, my dear, we all thought you'd forgotten about us."

"Of course not—"

"Lady Mary here thinks Mrs. Wotton has suffered a brain fever that hurt her sense of color. Look at that gown. It's purple!"

Mari glanced across the room at the gown in question. It was a beautiful color in her estimation, and worn by a married woman with two nearly grown girls. Eminently proper, but apparently the dowagers didn't agree. She was about to express that she admired the gown, but Lady Mary spoke first. "Mari dear, will you pick up my shawl? It seems to have fallen, and Lily will step on it before long."

"Of course—"

"I wouldn't step on it if it wasn't always underfoot." An aged hand clutched at her elbow. "Would you mind getting us something to drink? I don't know about these footmen. Not a one has come 'round to bring us refreshments. Most disgraceful."

Then they were back to being a Greek chorus, all nodding as they disparaged the staff at various parties dating back two score years.

She left them to it, heading to the tepid punch. She would have to make several trips for all of them, but she was used to it by now. She was just considering whether she could manage a fourth full glass without spilling when they were all plucked from her arms by a set of large hands.

"What—"

"Why the devil are you acting as a servant?" Lord Whitly's expression was fierce, and his hair had gone even more askew than before.

"I was getting drinks for the dowagers. They—"

"I'm well aware of what you're doing, but it's not your job."

She huffed out a breath. "Of course it's not my job, but they're thirsty, and no one—"

He snapped his fingers beneath one footman's nose. "You will get a tray and serve every one of those ladies punch. And claret. And anything else they want. Do you understand?"

"But...but, sir..." The hapless man gestured to the punch bowl. Apparently his job was to pour lemonade.

"What is your name, young man?"

"Thompson."

"Well, Thompson, I expect you are capable of figuring out how to have the lemonade bowl manned *and* get the ladies their drinks, are you not?"

"Er, yes, sir."

"My lord," Mari corrected.

"What?" The man turned widened eyes to her. Truly he was rather young, and she felt bad for putting him on the spot like this.

"This is Lord Whitly, young Thompson. And I shall

stand here and explain the situation to anyone who asks. So do what you must to get the ladies served."

"Yes, my lady."

She smiled at the boy, and he blushed all the way up through his ears. But then paled when Lord Whitly practically growled at him.

"She isn't waiting long, Thompson. Go."

"Oh! Yes, sir. Er, my lord. Um…"

Lord Whitly bared his teeth and made shooing motions. The footman scampered away.

"And that," said Mari, "is why I gave up trying to get the servants to carry the drinks. You've not only frightened that poor boy—"

"If that frightens him, God help him if he ever sees battle."

She snorted, a most inelegant sound that she immediately regretted. "He's a footman. He's not likely to see battle. And now you've probably upset things below stairs. It's a delicate balance down there."

"Bollocks. They weren't doing their job."

She sighed. "Have you been gone so long from London Society that you have forgotten everything? Or did you never pay any attention to it in the first place?"

"You think you will be the topic of conversation tomorrow for this?"

"I do."

He frowned at her. "Very well, shall we make a wager on it?"

"I am attempting to be circumspect."

"This is a perfectly proper wager. If not a single word of gossip ensues from this dastardly lemonade bowl incident, then you shall walk with me in Hyde

Park during the fashionable hour. I regret that we cannot go driving, as I have not yet purchased any type of conveyance."

"That shall not be a problem, my lord, as you have no chance of winning."

He arched a brow. "Very well, and your forfeit shall be…?" He lifted his chin as he appeared to think about it.

"Another apology for doubting me?"

He waved that aside, then snapped his fingers. "You'll go riding with me instead. Do you have a horse?"

She did, though she was not a very accomplished rider, and rusty to boot. Horsemanship was one of those wild activities denied to someone who wanted to prove she wasn't wayward.

"I haven't been riding in a very, very long time."

"Then you should enjoy it."

Assuming she didn't fall on her face in the mud. "You must swear not to laugh. My horse is very sensitive to laughter."

"Your horse?"

She shrugged. "Her feelings are easily hurt."

"I shall endeavor to be deadly serious all morning." He gave her a teasing look. "I will meet you at nine of the clock tomorrow."

Just then young Thompson scurried back to the lemonade bowl, so Lord Whitly extended his arm to her. It would have been rude not to take it, so she set her fingers on his sleeve and tried not to marvel how, even through the layers of clothing, she could still feel his muscles flex.

Over six Seasons, she'd held the arms of scores of

men. Dandies, Corinthians, impoverished lords, and a few nabobs. None of them had made her aware of his muscles or size beside her. Neither had they made her feel comfortable. Always she was an accompaniment to the gentleman's presence. She was the woman on his arm, the lady who added to his consequence.

She felt none of those things beside Lord Whitly. She simply felt at ease. She wasn't intimidated by his size. In truth, he made her feel rather womanly beside his broad shoulders and powerful stride. His arm was there to support her if she should stumble. He didn't seem to need her to compliment him. Indeed, she tried by mentioning that his coat fit him very well and he looked quite fine in it.

He gave her a glance and a shrug, almost belatedly remembering to say, "Thank you."

She chuckled, because truly, she'd never met a gentleman of the *ton* who had such little vanity. It put her quite in charity with him. So they ambled happily to the dowagers, who simpered and flirted with him, greatly honored that he'd condescended to pay them any mind.

He charmed them smoothly, though she could tell only part of his attention was on them. He was distracted, for all that the elderly women were flushed with pleasure. She wanted to ask what he was thinking. She wanted to push to a deeper intimacy with him, and yet that was the most ridiculous thought ever. Friendship could not be sought in the middle of a London Season. And intimate friendships were impossible.

There was no time during a ball to discuss anything of substance, no space for more than a nod and a smile.

There were dozens of people she saw every Season and knew nothing more about them but the cut of their clothes and their attitude on the weather. And yet here she was desperately trying to think of a way to ask what was he thinking? What disturbed him so deeply that he'd pulled at his hair and forgotten to greet her properly? And why was he still at her side, discussing knee pains with the dowagers when he should be attending to whatever had him so distracted?

Then the musicians started tuning again. The break was over, the next set beginning to form. No time to ask. No silence in which to push for understanding.

"Oh, listen," said one of the dowagers. "They're starting again. You young people go dance. That's what we're here for, you know, to watch you enjoy yourselves."

"Oh, and look, Miss Powel, here is that handsome Lord Byland come to claim you. I'm afraid you'll have to give her up, Lord Whitly."

"I'm afraid I must," Whitly said, and he almost sounded regretful. "Fortunately, I will reclaim her hand soon enough. She has consented to waltz with me."

"Waltz?" gasped the nearest dowager.

"Miss Powel, really?" cried the next. "You're going to waltz?"

"Oh, my dear, I don't think that's quite proper," added a third.

On the objections went. Enough that it became quite uncomfortable, until Lord Whitly raised his hand for silence. Strangely enough, it worked, and each member of the dowager chorus quieted.

"I cannot believe my ears," he said solemnly. "How could you think the waltz is anything but proper? Is it possible that you've never tried this dance yourselves? Can it be said that you condemn something without having tried it?" She had no idea how he could know that, but it was true. As far as she was aware, none of them had ever tried the waltz.

The dowagers gasped. And then quick bursts of answers exploded all around.

"Well, we'd never!"

"Not at our age!"

"Such a thing to ask!"

He waved away their objections with a casual sweep of his large hand. "Then I shall make it my purpose to get each of you a partner for the waltz. You can't very well object to something unless you've tried it."

"What?"

"Oh goodness, no!"

"Who would want to dance with us? No, no, that's for young people."

Mari glanced to Lord Whitly. His eyes danced even as his lips curled.

"You like the challenge," she abruptly said, surprised enough to speak her thoughts aloud.

His gaze jumped to hers. "What?"

"Everything's a wager to you. Will the footman leap to your tune? Will there be a scandal as a result? Can you get the ladies to dance?"

He straightened. "Yes, no, and of course." She snorted, and he arched his brow. "Do you doubt my ability?"

"Of course I do! You can't get all of them to dance, and certainly not the waltz."

His grin widened. "And if I manage it? Before the evening is done?"

Mari didn't know how to answer. She was acutely aware of Lord Byland standing, cooling his heels, and yet she couldn't force herself to move away from Lord Whitly. Not with him turning that arch look straight at her.

"If you manage it, my lord, I shall…I shall tell you a secret. About me."

His eyes widened. "What ho, that's an exciting forfeit."

"And if you fail—which you surely will—then you shall tell me one about you."

He chuckled, the sound rich and deep. "And if I have no secrets?"

"That's a bounder, if ever there was one."

He nodded. "True enough. Very well, I accept." Then he turned a gimlet eye on each of the dowagers. "And I expect you ladies to help me win my forfeit."

"No," Mari returned archly. "I have spent the last six Seasons in attendance on these venerable ladies. I assure you, they will help me."

Then there was no more time. The first notes of the new set began, and Mari had to rush with Lord Byland to find their places.

But what about the waltz? she wondered. And what secret was she about to learn from Lord Whitly? Because she knew the dowagers. They had been damning the waltz since its first appearance in the London ballrooms. Even so charming a man as Lord Whitly would fail in getting them on their feet for so scandalous a dance.

Right?

# Six

"LADY STOTT, I IMPLORE YOU," PETER SAID IN THE most charming voice he could manage. "Surely you would enjoy a dance. I'll go as slow and gentle as you like. You must know, I could carry you if you stumble. Never fear that you will fall."

"It's not fear, my boy," the elderly woman said, her eyes sparkling and her cheeks flushed. "I will not do such a scandalous thing in public. I will not." She punctuated the statement with a thump of her cane.

"But, my lady," Peter pressed, "all the other women have consented to join." They damn well ought to have. He'd pressured, cajoled, and outright bribed gentlemen to get their elderly relatives onto the dance floor. It had been a devil of a difficult thing to accomplish, but he had managed it. All except for Lady Stott. She'd outright refused her own grandson, and now Peter was at his wits' end trying to win her over.

Meanwhile, a sweet chuckle sounded to his right. It was warm and seemed to reverberate down his spine. Miss Mari Powel, of course, coming to his side for her very first waltz.

"I brought you more lemonade, Lady Stott," she said as she extended the drink.

"Thank you, my dear. Now go on. They've started the waltz."

"I don't think so," Miss Powel said firmly. "I've decided to sit down with you for this dance."

"What?" Peter said, frustration making his voice curt. "You can't possibly mean to deny yourself—"

"As all of Lady Stott's friends have deserted her…" Miss Powel gestured to where the dance floor appeared a slow whirl of septuagenarians. "It's only fair that I remain with her. After all, she's doing this to help me win my wager."

No, the woman was doing it because this was the most attention she'd been paid in a decade. Lady Stott needed a good spanking for putting her own needs ahead of Miss Powel's, but he couldn't say that. Instead, he turned to his intended waltz companion.

"Miss Powel, I insist," Peter huffed. "You have promised me this dance. You cannot deny me the pleasure of your company." Or the chance to touch her again. Through the fabric of their gloves, of course, but he would take what he could get. And if he managed to brush her anywhere more intimate, then it would be a victory indeed. But he couldn't do that if he couldn't get her on the dance floor. "It wouldn't be sporting," he said with what he hoped was a cajoling smile.

"I've never quite understood men's definition of 'sporting,'" she said, rather gleefully he thought. And full of mischief. "Besides, you may have my company right here. We can converse however you like."

Well, that was an opening she was going to regret, but he knew better than to grin. Instead, he turned to the dowager. "Do you know that Miss Powel has promised to tell me a secret if I get you to dance?"

"I'm not deaf. You said it right here." Then she tapped Miss Powel's leg with her cane. "But as she has no secret to share, I'm afraid we will have to content ourselves with hearing about yours."

Not bloody likely. Whatever he shared, it would not be with an aging dowager with a taste for gossip. "Every lady has a secret," he said, deciding to try flattery. "I'd wager you have plenty, and you are definitely a lady of the first order."

The woman chuckled, her pale cheeks flushing. But then a moment later she was waving her hand in dismissal. "Women's secrets are boring. They're always about who said something cutting to someone else." She leaned over toward Miss Powel and spoke in a loud undertone. "Men's secrets, on the other hand, are so much more interesting. Especially a man who made his fortune collecting money from those Indians."

Never, ever. But he was playing the dandy right now, so he put a hand to his chest in pretend shock. "Miss Powel, surely you wouldn't share whatever secret I confess."

"Only with me," put in Lady Stott.

"With no one," corrected Miss Powel, her expression prim as she turned to the lady. "You would not respect me if I were a gossip."

"Tut, tut. Gossip is the only thing that makes you interesting, my dear."

Miss Powel shook her head. "That's other people

gossiping about me. I will not swell their ranks by joining them."

Peter smiled, at last seeing his opening. His whole goal had been to get the woman to dance, but now he saw a larger possibility. "Lady Stott, did you truly mean that gossip was the most interesting thing about Miss Powel? Surely not."

"Well, of course she has many commendable attributes."

"Thank you—" said Miss Powel.

"But you are correct, my lord. Gossip about her is our primary pastime."

It took a moment for Miss Powel to understand the statement, and Peter took pains not to interrupt. "What? Surely you don't mean that."

"Of course I do," said Lady Stott, clearly unrepentant. "Not in a nasty way, of course, but because we adore you. What else would we have to discuss if not who had wronged you, what you should do about it, and how you fared today? Plus, we've spent many evenings trying to guess what phrase you intend to teach Greenie." The lady turned to shoot Peter a glare that was equal parts threat and glee. "After tonight's demonstration, my lord, you are likely to be discussed in great detail."

"Not in a nasty way, I hope."

Lady Stott lifted her chin and sniffed. "That remains to be seen."

Meanwhile, Miss Powel seemed to be completely nonplussed. And no wonder. She had just realized that her staunchest allies were the ones who perpetuated the very gossip she apparently abhorred.

"B-but you cannot mean you discuss me often. I'm completely unremarkable!"

Lady Stott thumped her cane on the floor. "We discuss that as well."

While Miss Powel stared, Peter had a chance to appreciate her shocked expression. He could tell her mind was churning away, but at what, he had no clue. He rocked back on his heels and enjoyed the shifting rose of her skin, the dark red of her mouth, and the way her bosom lifted and lowered in agitation. The sight would fill his fantasies for some time to come, he was sure. Especially if he imagined other places for her mouth. Or that she would be arched above him—

"The dance is over, my lord," Lady Stott said. "You have lost your wager."

He brought himself forcibly back to the present. One quick glance around showed him that indeed, all the dowagers were tottering flushed and happy back to their seats. Unless…oh dear. Flushed was certainly true, but not a one appeared happy.

He had thought by forcing the dowagers to dance he could show Miss Powel that defying convention was simply a matter of deft handling. That even the staunchest detractors could be brought around.

Apparently, he'd vastly overrated his ability to persuade elderly ladies of anything. Every one of them was complaining as she tottered to her seat.

"Damned difficult thing to do on these old bones."

"Charlotte, mind your tongue!"

"My grandson can't manage to step to the rhythm for all that he smiles and tries to charm everyone. Can't keep his feet going where they ought."

"Horrible dance, twirling a woman around like that. Made me quite dizzy."

Peter desperately tried to salvage the situation. If the women kept up their complaints, he'd never have the chance to dance in close quarters with Miss Powel. "Surely, ladies, it wasn't that bad," he ventured. "Now you can see—"

"We have tried your dance, my lord," snapped a woman he'd never met before. "And we declare it to be scandalous."

He looked to the dance partners, all gentlemen he'd somehow badgered to do their parts. They didn't meet his eyes. To a man, they were all bowing as fast as possible before beating a hasty retreat. But he was quicker than one fellow. A man he'd gone to school with who had condescended to dance with his aunt for the ghastly sum of three guineas.

"What happened, man?" he asked in as low an undertone as he could manage.

"Exactly what I told you would happen. They danced. I believe Aunt Agatha even had a lovely time, though my arms will never be the same. Woman has a grip like a strangling snake. But if there's one thing these ladies like more than the attention, it's the pleasure of ruining everyone else's fun."

"That's harsh," Peter said, but one look about him proved the point. The ladies each looked mighty pleased with herself even as she condemned the activity.

"Oh, go on with you!" snapped the man's aunt. "Call my carriage. I feel quite ill."

A chorus of agreement sounded from all around.

And that was it for the dowagers. They all started gathering their things. Soon there wouldn't be a one left.

"Not so fast," he said, his voice taking on as much of a commanding air as he dared. It worked. They all stopped and looked at him. "I am dreadfully sorry that you disliked the dance, but I am afraid I cannot be swayed by your opinion. I adore the waltz, as I'm sure Miss Powel will too."

"Harrumph!"

"Cheeky boy!"

"Ridiculous dance!"

"And now," he continued, doing his best not to let panic enter his expression. "Lady Stott, if you would please take my hand? I shall have the orchestra play a special waltz just for you and me."

Lady Stott had been busy gathering her shawl, but at his words, she lifted her chin and pursed her mouth. Then while everyone in the ballroom listened, she turned to Miss Powel.

"My dear, you have won your wager. I am going home." Then she winked at him. Him! "Best make it a good secret, my boy. Otherwise this whole display will have been for naught."

"It was meant for me to learn her secrets," he grumbled.

"Then next time, do not place a wager against a clever woman." And with that, she stomped her cane down with a thump before walking regally away.

One by one, the other dowagers made their exits as well, each giving him a sniff of disdain. He looked to Miss Powel, his expression bemused. He had no idea how he had suddenly become an object of such fun for them. And not just them, but one glance around the ballroom showed that everyone, from the guests through the servants, were watching the exodus and turning sympathetic gazes on him.

"Huh," he finally said. "That certainly was not what I expected."

Miss Powel laughed. It came out at first like a snort, and she rapidly covered her mouth. But a second later, she could not restrain herself. A peal of delight burst from her lips—high and musical—and she was soon joined rather awkwardly by others. Quiet titters, a couple of "By Jove's," and Miss Powel giggling hard enough that she had to press a hand to her side in apparent pain.

Then she looked at him, amber eyes tearing, her perfect mouth drawn back enough to show white teeth, and such merriment of body and soul that he had to laugh with her. How could he not? She was a delight to look at as she gasped for breath. And besides, he deserved it.

So he laughed, and as he burst into amusement, so too did the rest of the ballroom, until everyone declared this the best ball of the Season. Which meant that when he'd regained his breath and she hers, he held out his hand to her.

She looked at him, her brows pinching a little above her nose. "What?"

He pitched his voice loud enough for the musicians to hear. "I believe we missed our waltz, Miss Powel."

She straightened and looked at her card. "Don't be silly. It's a cotillion next."

He turned and looked at the musicians. "A waltz, if you please," he commanded.

The conductor nodded and lifted his arms. A moment later, the first notes of a waltz began. And while she was still staring at the musicians, he stepped forward and took her hand, pulling her upward from where she'd been leaning against a chair. A quick tug, and suddenly she was in his arms.

"You are a complete hand, aren't you?"

"I am trying to lose gracefully. You have won our wager."

"Really? And yet somehow I feel as if you have gotten exactly what you wanted."

He waggled his eyebrows at her. "Then perhaps I am an equally clever gentleman."

She smiled at him, her expression the warmest he had ever received from her. "It occurs to me that you have also won our other wager."

"Oh?"

"Yes," she said ruefully. "No one is likely to discuss our display by the lemonade now."

He'd been so focused on getting the dowagers to dance, he had forgotten all about the lemonade. Goodness, he was on quite a winning streak with her. Too bad the main prize was still well out of reach.

"My lord?" she asked as she settled into position in his arms.

"What?"

"You looked quite serious there for a moment."

"I'm always serious," he said, his voice grave, "when I have a beautiful woman in my arms."

Then he swept her into her very first waltz.

# Seven

MARI MEANT TO RESIST HIM. AFTER ALL, HE'D NEVER actually asked if he could dance with her. He'd simply scrawled his name on her card and then proceeded to create this whole charade around it. And yet she never quite formed the words.

Instead, she felt his fingers as they intertwined with hers. He had large hands, but as her own fingers were rather long, they seemed to match quite well. Then she felt his other hand slide around her waist. His touch sent shivers down her spine in a delightful way. Never had she felt such awareness of a man in front of her, of his legs so near, of his face as he looked so intently down at her.

She ought to chastise him for taking liberties, but she let him draw her closer. His arm moved higher on her waist to wrap more around her back, which allowed his forearm to press ever so lightly into her shoulder. She felt surrounded by him, but not oppressively so. Then he began to move.

She didn't have to think about matching his steps. The rhythm of the music was steady, and his body was perfectly in tune with it. He guided her easily with just the slightest pressure. It felt as if they were one body. She breathed his air, he held her everywhere, and together they flew.

Heaven.

She could have danced like that for hours. She wanted to, but something this magical couldn't last long. Their steps slowed and eventually stopped. She stood still in his arms, her head dizzy from the dance and her body flushed with excitement. Champagne giddiness, she thought. As if there were bubbles of laughter in her blood and brain. Lord, if he weren't holding her, she might just float away.

"You dance wonderfully, Miss Powel," he said, his voice thick.

"I don't think I've ever enjoyed anything more," she said. No, no! She wasn't supposed to be in his thrall like this. She wasn't supposed to sound so breathy or feel tingles all over her body. It was not how a proper lady felt.

She could hear the titters around them. And if she looked, she knew she would see spiteful women whispering behind their fans. She knew what they were saying. Hadn't she been hearing it for the last six years?

Wayward Welsh.

"You have ruined me again, my lord," she said, startled to realize that there was only defeat in her voice. She wasn't even angry with him. It was what the man did.

She dropped her arms, and he let her go, raising his arm to escort her back to her place near the now-empty seats for the dowagers.

"I think I shall go home," she said mournfully. She hadn't the stomach to face the spiteful tabbies over supper. Not when she was so busy damning herself for her behavior.

How could she let him sweep her good sense away? It wasn't just the dance, though that was reason enough. But add in the entire wager with the dowagers and the way he'd ordered the orchestra to play a waltz just for them, and she felt mortification all the way down through her toes. It was an ill-bred spectacle, and she had allowed it.

"You cannot leave," inserted Lord Rimbury as he sauntered up to her side. "That'll make them talk all the more." He looked at Lord Whitly. "You should be the one to depart."

Whitly frowned. "Why would I allow gossip to dictate to me one way or the other?"

Did he understand nothing? "You're a wealthy man who will one day inherit an earldom," she said. "Of course you wouldn't allow gossip to deter you."

"Exactly." He folded his arms across his chest, a self-satisfied smirk on his face.

"But you aren't the only one being affected by your actions," added Lord Rimbury.

Lord Whitly opened his mouth to respond, but no sound came out. His brows lowered in a dark glower, and his gaze hopped between his friend and Mari. And then he looked at the people around them, all whispering to one another. "It is only talk. Why do you let it hurt you?"

Because she was an unmarried woman in search of a husband. Because she wanted to be one of them some day. Not a bitter ape leader, but a woman accepted and powerful in her own sphere of influence. Because she dreamed of leaving her father's Welsh name and taking on an English one with a family of her own.

But she knew saying all that would not only be useless; it would reveal too much of what she held tight to her secret heart. So instead, she said what came easiest: to blame him for his inadequacy instead of looking at her own.

"You will never understand women if you do not consider that your actions have consequences not for you, but for anyone in a weaker position."

He shook his head. "I have not hurt you, Miss Powel. Whispers behind fans are of no consequence. When I cause someone to poison your food or shoot you from the shadows, then you may harp at me. But this..." He gestured disdainfully to the people around them. "This is trivialities trussed up to be important."

She gestured with her hands, a quick flick of her wrists to deflect his words. She wished they could, in truth, but she made sure her disgust of him showed plainly. "Why do you come into Society if you have no comprehension of it?"

He sighed, his expression frustrated. "Why indeed?"

She glared at him, wondering if he meant to answer his own question. But instead of speaking, he looked at her as if she could possibly fathom his motives.

Meanwhile, Lord Rimbury released a low whistle. "It's dreadfully hot in here. Should I get us something to drink?"

A brandy, she thought, but she didn't say it. Instead,

she smiled at the man who was becoming a friend. "I should love some lemonade."

"Excellent," he answered, but before he left, Lord Whitly held out his hand.

"No, I'll get it. I'm afraid you're right. I should not have come here until my mind was settled."

"Ah," returned Lord Rimbury. "So it was bad at home, then?"

Oh dear. She'd been cutting up at him, when something dreadful had happened. And yet the man simply shrugged. "You know how tedious it is to look at endless pages of numbers. I fear my mind has run to madness after a week of it."

"You were looking at your family accounts," she deduced. It wasn't proper for her to speak of it, but she hated pretending to be a birdbrain. She often assisted her father with his ledgers when he wished to be especially private about it. And of course, any woman who wanted to hold a prestigious title would need to understand household money.

But rather than explain, he flashed a condescending smile. "Never fear. The title is still well heeled, and my own prosperity is not to be questioned."

She wasn't questioning it. She'd been trying to be sympathetic. "Well, thank God for that," she snapped. "Heaven knows you'd never survive penniless and without expectations." Then she gaped at her own audacity. "Good God, you've made me shrewish." How had he managed to take her so quickly from the joy of that lovely dance to this moment, when she couldn't speak a civil word?

She watched as his jaw clenched, the muscles in his

throat working hard, but no sound came out. In the end, he executed a quick bow. "Lemonade then. I shall return slowly."

She curtsied to him before watching him head for the drinks. "I don't know what it is," she said to Lord Rimbury. "That man brings out the worst in me."

"I think he brings out the honesty in you."

She shook her head. "I wouldn't call what I just said honest. I expect he'd do fine dropped anywhere in the middle of anything. He is a winner, after all." And by extension, that made everyone else—including her— the loser.

"I don't think he sees it as a game. Perhaps that is the problem."

"What? Life?"

"Society, Miss Powel. You and I both see it as a game to be played and danced according to set rules. But I'm afraid Lord Whitly sees something vastly different here."

"But what could he possibly see?"

Rimbury shook his head. "For that answer, I'm afraid you'll have to ask him."

She would. In fact, the moment he returned with the drinks, she would find a way to understand this man who persisted in making all of her careful resolutions shatter into nothing. She turned, scanning the place where he'd last been, but didn't see him. Instead, she spied a footman heading their way. He was carrying a tray with two glasses of lemonade.

"Where'd he go?" she murmured.

Then she saw him. No one else could have that broad a back or so casually perfect brown locks. That was he at the top of the stairs as he left the ballroom, departing just when she'd screwed up the fortitude to ask him a serious question.

❧

Mari did not enjoy waking early in London during the Season. In summer, she was always up and about while the sun was just topping the rise. The fresh air called to her, and she had plans in the summer. She helped her sister with her garden and in her stillroom, and her young twin cousins were always courting disaster somewhere. Not to mention that the village was an endless source of need, and she'd found purpose in helping at the school or at a task with the vicar's wife. But mostly she felt alive in the country in the way of a tree finally setting down roots.

Except, of course, they weren't her roots. They were her parents' roots, and all the work she did helped their standing grow in their village and on their land. None of it was her own. And none of it would bear fruit for herself or her children.

She desperately needed her own family, and to that end she husband-hunted. She endured long hours at balls and musicales. She slept late to preserve her looks, and maintained very strict diet and cosmetic regimens for optimum appearance of health and beauty.

Therefore, it was unusual and with grave reluctance that she struggled out of bed the next morning. It was a testament to how desperately she wished to speak with Lord Whitly that she managed to rouse herself at all. Plus, it was the only time to speak with him before her session with Greenie and afternoon calls. So she dragged herself out of bed, and dressed in a riding habit that was many Seasons out of date and scratchy to boot. Then she chose the most docile horse they owned and headed to Rotten Row with a groom trotting behind her. She approached the Row slowly, her composure already starting to desert her. The avid riders were out in full force today, and the thunder of horses' hooves pounded in her head. She saw perhaps a dozen gentlemen and nearly as many women. They rode like the wind and laughed with gleeful delight. Their horses were beautiful and their tack designed for show.

What had she been thinking? There was no possible way she could show to advantage among these people. She hadn't ridden in years and was already becoming sore.

She was just turning around to tell her groom they were heading back, when she saw him: Lord Whitly flying toward them on a moderate-size horse. Pounding down the stretch toward her, his creature was fast.

She stopped to stare, as did many others, especially the women. And when he finally drew up, his cheeks were red, his eyes dancing, and he turned to Lord Rimbury, who thundered in behind him.

"Good Lord, she's amazing," Lord Rimbury said as he pulled his stallion to a trot. "Odd-looking to be sure, but damned fast."

The mare wasn't odd-looking, at least not for a horse from India. It had a gorgeous reddish color coat, though not so even as to be fully prized. The inward-turning ear tips were no doubt what appeared odd-looking to Lord Rimbury, but Mari knew it was the whorls underneath the creature's eyes that were the most damning of its features.

Meanwhile, Lord Whitly grinned and smoothed down his horse's mane. "She's a beauty," he said before leaning forward to speak to his mare. His words were in Hindi, but clear enough to Mari, who had spent several years in that foreign country while her father made his fortune. "You're my best lady," he said. "And you'll get fine oats tonight."

"A beauty to be sure," she said in that same language. "And I'll wager you got her for a song with those whorls."

He turned to her, his eyes widening in surprise. "Miss Powell! I didn't know you spoke Hindi."

"I don't as a rule," she said in English. "It's been a very long time." Then she looked about her and flushed. She hadn't even realized she'd come close enough to converse with the man, and yet suddenly she was beside him. A moment later, he aligned his mare with hers and they began walking together.

"You obviously remember enough," he said in English. "And you're right, the eye whorls dropped the price significantly."

"What?" asked Lord Rimbury as he joined her on the other side. "What do you mean?"

Mari gestured to the hair pattern along the horse's nose. "A whorl on the nose is unlucky, but on the neck is very good. Better still would be a whorl on the fetlocks, which means victory."

"The devil, you say," Lord Rimbury exclaimed.

"You know your Marwari horses," Lord Whitly commented.

No, she didn't. But since gentlemen enjoyed horses, she'd read up on the Indian breeds when she'd begun husband-hunting. It gave her a relevant topic of conversation and a way to cast her time in India in a beneficial light. Not every man thought a childhood spent outside of England a good thing in a woman.

"I had a groom in India who liked to share tales," she said.

"Truly?" he asked. "I didn't think grooms chattered to the young ladies of the house."

"I pestered him until he talked to me," she said, a little unnerved that he listened so closely to what she said. It startled her enough to reveal the full truth. "And I read more about them when I learned that gentlemen often love anything to do with horses."

"Of course," he said, his tone neutral.

Meanwhile, on her other side, Lord Rimbury pulled out his pocket watch and muffled a curse. "I'm done for," he said, his tone morose. "Have to get cleaned up before meeting with the banker about a pasture property."

She turned to smile at him. "Are you acquiring, my lord?"

His expression lengthened, and she realized belatedly that he was more likely selling than buying. But before she could stammer out an apology, his mournful look turned dramatic.

"Would you love me better if I were, Miss Powel?"

She shook her head and answered honestly. "No, my lord, I would not. I find my affections have nary a whit to do with land."

He tipped his hat to her. "Which makes me appreciate you all the more." Then after a quick nod to Lord Whitly, he wheeled his stallion away. He took his time doing it though, letting it prance about and draw some attention before he settled it with a fond pat on its neck. And then he had the creature walk crisply away.

"Oh," she said softly. "He's thinking of selling his horse too, isn't he? How very sad."

"How did you know that?" Lord Whitly asked, his tone frankly surprised.

She shrugged. "As far as I can tell, he doesn't make a show of himself. But since he did just then…"

"You deduced it was to show his horse, not himself."

She shrugged. "I had hoped his finances were in better frame."

"The title's on solid footing," Lord Whitly said, his eyes canting away. "But he's feeling the pinch right now. It's only temporary, and he's doing the right things to keep the ship afloat, so to speak."

"By hunting for an heiress?"

His gaze leapt to hers. "You know?"

She sighed. "Of course I know. It's the only reason titled gentlemen attend to me."

"You underestimate your allure."

She nodded and looked away. He'd spoken a routine compliment, and so she took it as meaning nothing. And yet he pursued the topic. "You're clever, beautiful, and well-dowered. I cannot understand why you haven't been dragged to the altar by one such as him."

"An impoverished gentleman?"

"A man with the good sense to see what you're worth beyond your father's money." He cast her a sidelong look. "Is it your father or yourself who has been shutting the matrimonial door on so many of your suitors?"

She startled at his words, a little flustered by his plain speaking. "I…um, both, I suppose. My father will not countenance a fortune hunter." Neither would she. It was, after all, the first thing she'd written in her list.

"And well he shouldn't." His gaze narrowed. "But could you overrule him? If your heart led you to a man, would you be able to persuade him to allow it?"

She stiffened. "I am eight and twenty, well into my majority, and able to marry as I please."

He nodded as if he had suspected as much. "So it is your heart that has to be caught."

"No, my lord. A child has a heart. A woman in Society needs a clever mind."

"And yours has not been seduced." He said that as if it were perfectly normal to speak of seducing a woman directly to her face.

"My mind is ever my own."

He nodded as if he were thinking something important about what she'd just said. In the silence that followed, she decided to demand her forfeit.

"I was startled to see you leave last night, my lord," she said as they turned their horses around on the path. Truly, riding in London was distressingly restrictive. There was no room to wander, and all the while, other, more skillful riders were constantly galloping past. "I had not thought you so unsporting as to try to avoid paying your forfeit."

He reacted as she expected, with a jolt and a dark frown. "Avoid paying? Never!"

"But you did leave rather precipitously."

"Yes, I did," he acknowledged as he rubbed at his chin. She twisted enough to stare directly at him. Thankfully, it eased some of the strain on her spine from sitting sidesaddle. "Why did you leave so quickly?"

"I learned that my father was in the cardroom. I had not thought he would be at a come-out ball, but apparently someone prevailed upon him, and so he was there."

"So you left?" Certainly she knew that fathers and sons could have strained relationships, but she had not thought theirs was so difficult.

He gave her an awkward shrug. "I trust that you will not bandy this about. It's not so much that we cannot stand one another. Well, it is, but no more than the usual father and son."

"That cannot be true."

He looked at her and then nodded slowly. "I simply wish to control the manner in which I communicate with my father. In a cardroom at a come-out ball was not the best location."

"Especially since you had just made a spectacle with the dowagers? And by waltzing with a Welsh chit?" She counted herself heroic for not adding the word "wayward."

He frowned a moment then shrugged. "He will no doubt call me to account for that."

"I wish to call you to account for that." And when he gave her a quizzical look, she amended her statement. "I wish to call in your forfeit. You are to tell me a secret."

He turned their horses down another lane. "I believe I just did."

Had he? Oh yes, that his relationship with his father was seriously strained. "But that is not the secret I want."

He flashed her a delighted grin. "I don't believe that was part of the forfeit. You do not get to choose which of my confidences I reveal."

She pulled back as if shocked. "Surely you wish to give a good account of yourself, my lord. A paltry forfeit does not reflect well upon you. Not upon the winner, winner." She said those last two words as Greenie might, high and with a parakeet's chirp.

"You count my strained paternal relationship as paltry information?"

"I do, my lord." She leaned forward. "I wish to know something a great deal more important than that."

"At the moment, I cannot imagine what that could be. I'm afraid my mind is greatly consumed by—"

"Why are you in Society if you have such a great disregard for it?" She spoke impetuously, trampling over his words in her rush to get the question out. He had such power to distract her that she feared losing track of it altogether if she did not say it quickly.

But once spoken, she began to regret her question. It was what she had wanted to know almost from the very beginning. Why was he here? Why did he accost her in Hyde Park that first day? Why did he seek her out at last night's ball?

But the more the questions crowded in her mind, the more his expression made her doubt her own sanity. Or his. Because far from quietly considering her request, he stared at her in stunned surprise.

# The Seattle Public Library
University Branch
Visit us on the Web: www.spl.org

## Checked Out Items 7/16/2018 15:02
### XXXXXXXXX8733

| Item Title | Due Date |
| --- | --- |
| 0010087842802 As rich as a rogue | 8/6/2018 |

# of Items: 1

**Balance Due: $1.00**

Renewals: 206-386-4190
TeleCirc: 206-386-9015 / 24 hours a day
Online: myaccount.spl.org

Pay your fines/fees online at pay.spl.org

In the end, she had to prompt him to speak. "My lord?"

"Truly, Miss Powel, I cannot guess whether I am especially bad at this or if you are being willfully obtuse."

"If I am obtuse, my lord, I assure you it is not willful."

"Then perhaps I have lost all ability to function in English Society."

He didn't seem particularly pleased with that statement, and well he shouldn't. She tried to form something conciliatory to say, but at that moment a pair of Dims went galloping past while hooting in a nearly drunken manner. Her horse shied, her seating slipped, and it was all she could do to stay atop her mare. It was fortunate that Lord Whitly was large enough—and quick enough—to reach forward and grab hold of her bridle, otherwise she might have gone for her own wild run on an uncontrolled horse.

It took a moment to quiet her mount and another few after that for her heart to settle to a slower tempo. And all the while, he stood there, his body flexed as he held her horse, and his attention riveted to her.

"Are you steady, Miss Powel?" he finally asked.

"Y-yes," she said somewhat breathlessly. "I'm afraid I am out of practice."

"It was not your fault. Those young bucks should be whipped." His gaze scanned her quickly. "You are sure you're not harmed?"

"I didn't fall, my lord. I was merely startled."

"Yes."

Silence.

And then he spoke, his words loud and clear. "Miss

Powel, I left for India with one purpose in mind. Certainly, I wanted money and a certain degree of notoriety, but uppermost in my thoughts was one thing: I wished for your regard."

He paused, his gaze skittering away, and no wonder. To say such a thing to a woman was awkward indeed. She couldn't fathom why he was saying it to her.

"Sir, if this is some sort of tease, then it is in very poor taste."

"Of course it's not a tease," he snapped, his brows drawing down. This time he looked her full in the face, but his expression was less than cordial. "You named me useless, and I realized you were right."

"B-but... I..." She snapped her mouth shut. She had no ability to make sense of his words. Six years she had lived thinking him her nemesis. The one man who destroyed her out of casual disregard. To hear that he had left the country because of her was like saying the moon had decided to take a stroll down the street simply because she'd wished it. He was too large and powerful a creature to be swayed at all by her opinion.

He straightened in his seat, gently releasing her mount, who had calmed much more quickly than its rider. "I returned to England for the fulfillment of that one desire."

"Er...what?"

"Miss Powel, I returned to seek your regard. And, naturally, your hand in marriage."

Which was when, with absolutely no one riding nearby, she did in fact tumble off her horse.

# Eight

PETER WOULD NEVER HAVE BELIEVED IT IF HE HADN'T seen it with his own eyes. It appeared to him that after hearing his proposal of marriage, Miss Powel was so repulsed as to jerk backward away from him. Her eyes were wide with shock, and her mouth gaped into a dark red O of horror.

Shock, when he'd thought himself clear in his intention for more than a week now.

Horror, when he was the heir to an earldom.

And so she jerked away from him, which at that moment meant sideways on her saddle. Then another gasp—and this time he was too slow to react—before she desperately pulled on the reins. Too hard, too fast, which made her horse shy badly, and down she went with a squeak of alarm and a tumble of skirts.

He leaped off his mare, steadied both horses, because the last thing anyone wanted was for her mount to step on something breakable—like her body—and then, when her groom got there, he tossed the reins to the young man before rushing to her side. A quick look told him she was unharmed, though some injuries might not show for a while. Her face was red with embarrassment, but she seemed to move easily enough as she flounced her skirt back into order. Not before he'd seen two nicely trim ankles leading to very shapely calves, but he was trying to be a gentlemen and not make things worse.

Meanwhile, he didn't have to look up to know that she was already a subject of fun among the dashing gents and ladies. He spared a moment to glare at the nearest group, giving them a silent warning to look away and be quiet. He didn't know if it would work, but he tried. And thankfully, they at least moved back.

Which left him staring helplessly at Miss Powel and wondering what exactly he could say to make the situation better. He couldn't think of any social inanities, so he settled on what he did know: basic medicine.

"Is your chest tight? Is there pain or numbness? Does your head hurt?"

She glared down at her feet. "I landed on my—" She cut off her words. "On the softest part of me."

Hardly, since as far as he could tell, she fell on her bum and not her breasts. But that was not an appropriate thought, so he did his best not to look at those lush mounds so near him.

"Nothing is hurt except my pride." She tucked her feet under her, and he held out his hand to help her up. He thought for a hideous moment that she would disdain even that, but she grabbed it quickly enough. Then he pulled her easily to her feet.

"Let's walk this way, shall we?" He gestured to an empty pathway.

"So long as it's away from here, I shall be delighted."

He watched her gaze travel over their onlookers. He saw her mouth pinch tight and her cheeks color, but she didn't say more.

"Don't worry. People fall off their horses all the time."

She slanted him a defeated expression. "Why yes, I'm sure it happens hourly. Someone somewhere in the world falls off a horse every hour. Today was just my turn." She began moving away slowly. "I just chose to do it in front of the horse-mad set." Then she looked to her left and winced.

"What is it?" he asked. "Pain?"

"No, no. I just saw Mr. Randall. Or rather, he saw me."

"And he offended you?"

She snorted, but the sound came out more as a mournful laugh. "No. I shall simply have to cross him off my list of potential husbands."

He frowned. "Mr. Percy Randall? The horse-mad puppy with delusions of oratory genius?"

She turned to him. "You know him." It wasn't a question.

"We all know him. His attempts to match his father's eloquence have been the subject of laughter since he was in school." He cut off his words there, but that didn't silence his thoughts. The woman was considering Percy Randall, a braying ass if ever there was one, but she fell off her horse rather than accept him?

"I thought I could help him," she said almost too softly to hear.

At which point, his temper snapped. They'd walked

far enough to be relatively private, so he drew to a stop and touched her arm. He wanted to grab it and haul her around, but he did not.

"I will have an explanation, Miss Powel, or I will drag you to the nearest doctor, for you are obviously concussed."

She gaped at him. "Concussed? Because I didn't accept your proposal?"

"Because you fell off your horse rather than accept it. And yet you'd willfully consider an idiot like Percy Randall!"

She dropped her hands onto her hips and faced him squarely. "Percy Randall has a temperate nature—"

"Unless you damage his horses."

"He will be in the House of Commons soon."

"Speaking nonsense about horse-trading laws."

"And his father is a brilliant, influential man."

"What the bloody difference does that make?"

She huffed out a breath. "I could help him. Host political salons. Aid his work against slavery. Any number of things."

"Then you should marry the father."

She threw up her hands. "He already has a wife."

"I don't," he snapped. "I don't have a wife, I will inherit an earldom, and my conversation is about more than horseflesh spoken in a stutter."

She pressed her lips together in a mulish pout, but a second later she was off defending that ass again. "He doesn't stutter often. Just when he's at a loss for words."

"Which happens whenever he speaks about anything but his damned horses."

She huffed out a breath and turned to look behind them, presumably at Percy, but Peter had had enough of this ridiculous conversation. It was merely a way to avoid speaking of his proposal. So rather than let it continue, he caught her chin between his thumb and forefinger and drew her face around to his.

"Percy hasn't proposed, Miss Powel. I did. And I will have an answer."

She stared at him, then she abruptly jerked her chin back. "First of all, you didn't propose. You informed me of your intention. There wasn't a question anywhere in there."

Of course there was. Except when he thought back, perhaps he hadn't exactly phrased it as a question. "Well, if you need—"

"Good Lord, no!" she cried. "Truly, I begin to think you're the one concussed. Lord Whitly, whatever possessed you to think that you and I would suit? We cannot be five minutes in one another's company without sniping at each other. Can you imagine a year of that, much less a lifetime?"

Bloody hell, but she was being difficult. "We would rub along just fine if you would cease seeing me as the enemy."

"And what evidence do you have of that?"

He stared at her. Her eyes were bright in the sunlight, and her cheeks were flushed. She had one eyebrow arched and a tilt to her chin. She was challenging him with every fiber of her being. The problem was she was challenging him with *words*, and he was not a man who used words well. "I just know," he ground out. It was something he'd tried to explain a dozen or more times and had always failed. He couldn't even understand it himself. There were times in his life when he just knew what other people needed in their life: money, attention, discipline. He knew his father would never be pleased with him, simply because Peter had a mind of his own. And he'd known when she'd cut up at him that first time at the ball that every word she uttered was *true*. He was a useless man floundering on a path that led nowhere.

And so he had changed.

He knew when he returned and saw her with that bloody parakeet that he would find her beautiful until the day she died. Her skin could wrinkle, her hair could turn gray, and she could gain four stone in weight, but he would still lust after her. He didn't know why, he just knew he would.

And sometime in the last six years, he'd known that he would marry her. That he *had* to marry her because she was the woman for him. But how did he tell her that? He couldn't, and frankly, he'd never thought he would need to.

"I've got a title, wealth to spare, and a temperate nature."

"I'm well aware," she said, her voice not hard so much as frustrated. "Though you can never be classed with so simple a word as 'temperate.'"

He didn't know if that was a compliment or not. Knowing her, probably not. "Do you wish for a political career? I have considered it, and certainly I will one day serve in the House of Lords."

"But it is not your passion."

"It isn't Mr. Randall's either!" And damn it, they were back to that braggart, which was the last thing he wanted. Behind him, his mare was growing restive. He needed to keep her walking and eventually stable her. With a grimace of frustration, he gestured to Miss Powel.

"Shall we walk some more?"

She stifled a word. It was most likely a curse, which had him smiling. He liked that he could make her swear, though he wanted to hear the word rather than have her swallow it down.

They fell into step beside one another, the air thick with unresolved questions. But he had no way to answer them and only more problems. "I never imagined that I would have to fight so hard for the woman of my choice."

"Because you are a wealthy lord?"

"Yes."

She sighed and kicked idly at a stone. "If you wish to pursue this, you need only speak to my father. He will put me on bread and water and lock me in a dungeon until I accept your proposal."

His eyes narrowed. "Your father would do that?"

"Probably," she said with a laugh. Her expression was easy despite what she was suggesting.

"So your father is a harsh man," he pressed. This was something he needed to know.

"What? Papa? Well, no more than the usual, I suppose. He's considered merciless in business."

"How merciless?" In his experience, a man's business practices could be very ugly indeed. "I need particulars, Miss Powel."

She faced him squarely. "Then you should talk to my father."

He took a deep breath. "Very well," he said. "I will."

It took her a moment to process those words and then another breath before she grabbed his arm in alarm. "Oh no. I misspoke. My father is the gentlest man in the world, and you should definitely not speak to him."

Now they were getting somewhere. "Afraid of bread and water, are you?"

"Yes! Well, no, not literally. Good God, why are we speaking of my father? You are correct, he is the one who wants the title and would do a great deal to see me wed to you. But after the vows are exchanged, you would not be shackled to him. It would be me in your bed. Day in and day out with a wife who spends most of her time wanting to throttle you."

He heard her words, but most of them were lost under the fantasy of her in his bed. Of her beneath him night after night and well into the morning, when he could wake her with sweet kisses and bold thrusts.

"My lord?" she pressed when he had been silent too long.

He forcibly drew himself out of his reverie. "So what is it that you want in a man, if it isn't a title or money?"

She glanced at him but quickly looked away. "Shall I name for you the countless well-heeled peers who would be a nightmare as a husband? There are exactly fifty-three."

"Are those the eligible gentlemen?"

She shuddered. "Goodness, no. The unmarried or

widower titles number thirty-seven. Beyond that, there are over a dozen in my acceptable column, and exactly none who wish to court me, a wayward Welsh cit."

"Lord Rimbury is courting you."

"Well-heeled, my lord."

"I am courting you."

"You are in my nightmare category."

He turned to her. "Why?"

"And here we are full circle. I have explained to you that we do not suit. We fight constantly. You make me want to do violence. Every single one of my good intentions fly to the boughs the moment you enter a room. You make me insane, my lord, and—"

He did not allow her to say more. He knew her words were meant to dissuade him, but he heard what she didn't say. He heard that she lost her careful plans when he was around. That she was mad for him. And if they were wed, she would be this creature who challenged him at every turn to speak better, to think more clearly, and to act in every way better than the lummox he had been. That he often still was.

So he kissed her.

He jerked her into his arms and put his mouth on hers. He wrapped her tight against his chest, knew the glorious feel of her breasts flush against his torso, and when her mouth opened on a gasp of surprise, he thrust his tongue inside.

He would have stopped if she'd fought him. At least he believed he would have. Either way, it didn't matter. His mouth slanted across hers, his tongue boldly thrust between her lips, and though she started out stiff in shock, a moment later she turned sweet.

Her tongue began to thrust and parry with his. Her arms, which had been caught spread open, now went slowly up to his shoulders. And her hips, that perfect cradle of womanhood, pressed pillow-soft against his thickness.

He groaned as he felt her body mold against his. His mouth pressed harder; his tongue danced faster. She matched him. He knew she would. And then one of her hands that had been clutching his shoulders slid up over his neck and into his hair. And when he would have eased back, when he would have softened his possession of her, she gripped his head and pulled him to the angle she wanted.

Their mouths were sealed together, and her tongue pushed at his. She might even be biting down just a bit, just enough to add spice as her leg rose against his thigh.

Hot. Hungry.

Lust slammed through him, and his hands dropped to her hips. While she pulled at his head and shoulders, he hauled her against his groin and thrust against her belly. Throbbing delight rolled through his organ. His buttocks tightened again and again. Her leg pressed against his thigh. And their tongues dueled in a fever of need.

It went on forever and only for a blink of an eye. For a glorious time, he lost himself completely in her. The heat of her body, the scent of her musk, and her erotic whimper of need inflamed his blood.

It was the most glorious kiss, beyond even his fantasies. Except that they were in public. And someone was tugging on his arm. Something was pushing her away, and that someone was a man. Then he felt it: a sharp whip across his backside. A crop hitting hard and painfully on his flesh.

He pushed Mari behind him as he rounded on the danger. His left hand became a fist while his right drew his knife with a reassuring hiss. He was well into his throwing position, a split second from releasing his blade with deadly accuracy, when his mind came back to him.

The interloper was not a man at all. He was a boy. Miss Powel's young groom, not out of his teens, and he had been protecting his mistress, as all good servants did. The boy's face blanched, but he did not give ground.

"My lord, there are people coming," he said in a high-pitched undertone. It didn't work. The words came out more as a squeak, but it only underscored that this child was not a threat. Neither were the pair of well-dressed gentlemen walking their horses a bare hundred yards away.

Except, of course, they were. They were members of the *ton*, turning to look at him now with sharp eyes and curling lips. And him, standing there with his fist raised and his blade out. So he threw the dagger.

It flashed in the sunlight as it tumbled through the air. And then it landed—*thunk*—in the trunk of a tree a few feet beyond their horses' noses.

"I say!" one of the gentlemen gasped. The other said nothing as he was settling his mount.

"And that, Miss Powel," Peter said loudly, "is how one throws a dagger."

He looked back at her, his breath held for fear

that she would be mussed beyond recognition. Her eyes were gratifyingly dazed, but they cleared quickly enough. Her riding habit was no more out of sorts than expected, given that she'd tumbled into the dirt some minutes ago. And her hair…well, that too could be explained by her fall, though he longed to pull the remaining pins from her curls and toss her hat to the wind.

"G-goodness," she said, her voice wobbling but growing rapidly stronger. "That's quite impressive."

He held her gaze, silently asked her if she was well. She dipped her chin slightly, a barely perceptible acknowledgment.

Then he turned to the tree and his blade, pretending to be startled when he saw the horses and their riders. "What ho," he called. "You came out of nowhere."

"You should be careful where you throw that thing. You could have impaled one of us."

"Stuck us like a pig," the other whined. "And then what would we do?"

"Squeal like one, most like," he muttered under his breath.

Beside him, he heard a muffled snort and was startled enough to turn. It was Miss Powel, her lips pressed tightly together but still twitching at the corners. Was she laughing? He wanted to pull her hand away and see her release her joy wholeheartedly, but they were still in public. So he jogged to his knife, pulling it out of the tree with a quick flick of his wrist. Then he sheathed the blade and gave an insouciant shrug to the gents.

"Sorry, what," he said in his most jolly idiot tone.

"I'll be more careful next time." Then he waved and returned to her side. Except when he reached for her, she shrank back.

That hurt. After that kiss, to have her pull away was a visceral wound that bit sharply into his belly. Enough that he had to take a moment to be sure his tone remained neutral.

"If you are ready, we should mount up again and ride to your home," he said. Then he held out his hand to her. She was not in enough riding form to mount without help, and he would not allow her damned groomsman the privilege.

She looked at him for a long moment. Her eyes were dark and her expression unreadable. Was she angry? Resigned? Inflamed? He was all of those things, and a thousand more, all jumbled together with a still-throbbing lust.

"Miss Powel?" he pressed, his jaw clenching against the tide of his churning emotions.

"Yes. Um, of course. Th-thank you."

She took his hand. Small, delicate bones engulfed by his palm. He wrapped his fingers around hers and lent her his strength as she mounted. He would give almost anything for them to be holding each other with bare hands instead of their gloved ones. Especially since hers were shaking, and he wanted to soothe her with a caress. A slow draw of his fingers down her flanks, and then, in time, between her thighs. He sighed. She was like a flame that danced and flickered before his eyes, but tortured his body to the point where he thought he'd burn alive.

"Good thinking about the knife," she whispered.

She seated smoothly, then pulled back her fingers to tuck them neatly around the reins and into her lap. A breath later, and all that glorious fluttering of her eyes disappeared. No more trembling. No more light. Just a steadily calming expression and the suffocating descent of propriety.

"You were born to be a countess," he murmured.

Her gaze sharpened on his face. "What?"

"Cool and proper," he said. "I have never been more pleased and disgusted at the same time." His own heart was still beating hot and insistent. His mind kept flashing lascivious fantasies that he tried to banish but failed. And worst of all, his legs felt shakier than a newborn colt's. He was in a miserable state, and she sat atop her horse like a queen.

He waited a moment, but she had no words for him. Just as well, as his mind was still churning along wholly inappropriate paths. So he went to his horse and mounted up, wincing as he settled astride. Damnation, this was going to hurt.

Then they rode sedately, thank God, to her home. It was as he'd expected for her residence. Ostentatious but not exclusive. A place for the wealthy without title. And as he dismounted to escort her up the walk, a butler opened the massive door and stood there with a curled lip like a disdainful statue. He had to speak now before they were within earshot of that man. He had no patience with supercilious butlers.

"I believe I have answered your question, have I not?"

He felt her startle and then saw her brows narrow in confusion. "My lord?"

He waited a moment. He was learning that with her, timing was critical. So he paused until he had her full attention.

"*That* is why I believe we will suit." He leaned forward and whispered the last. "Most erotically suit."

He completed his lean forward with a bow before he kissed her hand. Then he retreated as fast as he could manage while she stood gaping after him.

# Nine

THE BLIGHTER. THE BLOODY, ARROGANT, PRESUMPTUOUS *man*. To think that one kiss, one long, overpowering, amazing kiss could make her rethink her entire life's plan simply because it was… Well, it was a bloody good kiss.

Lord, she was still tingling. Thank heaven Nicols had been there as her groom. If he hadn't interfered when he did, who knows what might have happened in the park where anybody—most especially Dim #2 and Fop #14—could have seen. And gossiped.

Certainly she'd been kissed before. Any number of unscrupulous gentlemen had tried to lure her into a compromising position just to force their marriage. But she knew better than to wander into dark corners with impoverished men.

That didn't mean she hadn't allowed a kiss or three. One sweet press on the lips from the very nicest Dim, and two sloppy, repulsive kisses from potential husbands. She'd rapidly crossed them off her possible list, because a lifetime of that had made her want to retch. And then of course that earlier nip from Lord

Whitly, which hadn't truly been a kiss. More of a tiny bite. There had been no…well, none of what had just happened between them. So it didn't deserve the label "kiss."

Except now she knew what a real kiss was like. One drugging press of his lips, and she'd all but stripped naked for him. She was beginning to think she *was* concussed. There was no other explanation for her behavior.

Horrible Horace cleared his throat from his place in the doorway, and Mari belatedly realized she'd been standing in the walkway, gawking like a love-struck mooncalf.

Well, no more. Once again—perhaps for the thousandth time—she resolved not to let Lord Whitly discompose her again. She was so determined, in fact, that she intended immediately to write down strata-gems to avoid succumbing to his dubious charms. She would carry the list in her reticule and look at it often. Right after she taught Greenie his phrase and made sure to win that wager.

She breezed inside and was halfway to the stairs when Horace upset her plans, and he did it with a single name.

"Mr. Camden," he intoned behind her.

She froze, waiting for him to pronounce the rest of her doom.

"He awaits your pleasure in the parlor."

Of course he did. Just when her mind was filled with Lord Whitly, her best husband candidate decided to make an early call. She looked at the mantel clock. "It's rather early for callers." It wasn't even eleven.

"He claimed he had an appointment with you. Your mother is entertaining him at the moment. Tea has already been served."

An appointment? As if she were a banker? Gentlemen called on ladies; they did not have appointments. But she didn't say that out loud. It was just one of the things she would have to teach Mr. Camden if they wed. She took a breath, smoothed her skirts, and went to the parlor. Horace knew his job and was there before her, announcing her with echoing accents that were hardly necessary in the intimate room.

Mari walked in, a smooth greeting on her face. Mr. Camden rose to his feet, his wispy blond hair floating about his ears as he tugged the crease out of his pants. Her mother turned as well, her face warm with welcome. Then both of their eyes widened in shock.

"My dear," her mother gasped. "Whatever happened?"

Good God, they couldn't possibly *see* what she'd done with Lord Whitly. Were her lips still swollen? Her breasts still heavy? Could other people truly discern—

"Your riding habit is covered with dirt," her mother continued. "And your hat is… Well, I never liked that hat anyway. You should throw it out."

Mari looked down, relief flooding her with a dizzying flush of heat. Of course. It wasn't the kiss they could see but the results of her fall.

"I'm afraid it's been a long time since I've been riding," she confessed. "I should have realized I needed to change before attending you."

Then she turned and cast a dark glare at Horace. He was hired to be a pompous, proper butler, but not at the expense of the house. She had been unable to dismiss him as long as he kept to that line, reserving his obnoxious behavior for riffraff and not them. But now he had crossed the line, allowing her to appear in such a state. Finally, she would be able to speak to her father about dismissing the man.

She watched his skin pale, and he swallowed nervously. One dragon down, she thought with satisfaction. But now she had to salvage this situation as her mother gestured her forward.

"But you ride beautifully, my dear. Was it the horse?"

"I ride adequately," she said as she leaned down to kiss her mother's cheek. "But not for a very long time. The bruisers at Rotten Row startled me, and I'm afraid I fell into the muck."

"Oh, that is a terrible time to ride," said Mr. Camden in dark tones. "Especially if one is out of practice. No way to appear anything but at a disadvantage."

Which had been her thoughts exactly. "I'm afraid I could have used your advice earlier, Mr. Camden. As it was, I had to endure an inglorious tumble."

Her mother clasped Mari's hand. "You're not hurt, are you?"

"Only my pride." Then she looked at Mr. Camden. "If you will forgive me, I'll dash upstairs and become more presentable. Then I shall attend to you properly."

Mr. Camden executed a smooth bow. "I would like that most especially, Miss Powel. I have something interesting to discuss with you." He glanced outside. "It's a fine morning. Perhaps we could take a stroll down Bond Street."

In the morning? That was the time gentlemen shopped. Women were rarely seen there until after one. But it wouldn't do to correct him. She simply nodded and flashed a warm smile. "Fifteen minutes, no more. I promise."

"I will wait as long as needed," he said graciously. Or it would have been gracious if he hadn't then proceeded to consult his pocket watch. Really, did he intend to time her? Perhaps. Which meant she had better change quickly.

With a quick look of apology to her mother for abandoning her, Mari took herself off. Fortunately, her maid was up in the room, and together they stripped her out of the habit, wiped off the mud that had smudged her chin, and then brushed out the terrible mess that was her hair. Good Lord, had she really appeared in public like this?

"Tie it back, as severe as you can manage," she instructed her maid. Mr. Camden preferred her neat as a pin. Plus ten minutes with him would do more than any number of stratagems for keeping her wayward nature in check. He had a dampening effect on all of her less proper thoughts.

"Do you think he'll propose?" asked her maid Ginny.

"I don't know. Maybe."

"An' if he does…?" she asked.

"I…" She swallowed. He was on her list. The one set on her dressing table in full view every moment she was in London, and often in her reticule for when she needed to consult it. It was labeled "Acceptable husband candidates." Mr. Camden was number 27. Certainly not high on her list, but to be fair, sixteen of the higher names hadn't ever even danced with her. She'd never spoken a single word to twelve of them.

So considering that, Mr. Camden was very high up on the possibility list.

"But do you want to marry him?" pressed Ginny.

She wanted a home. She wanted to begin her life as a wife and a mother. And she wanted a productive function in Society. For that, she needed a husband of influence. But she couldn't quite bring herself to say the word *yes*. Not after throwing herself into Lord Whitly's kiss.

Lord, she wanted more of those kisses too. She wanted to be held in that man's arms and touched in his bed. She wanted everything her sister had whispered about. She just hadn't expected that her first experience of wonderful kissing would be with Lord Whitly.

"I shall give him every consideration," she finally managed. Then they were out of time. The clock chimed the quarter hour, and she stood up so quickly that Ginny accidentally dug a pin deep into her scalp.

"Bloody he—" She bit off her curse. None of that. Even she knew that ladies did not curse.

"I'm so sorry, miss!" Ginny said, but Mari waved it away.

"It was my fault entirely. Now do I look neat and tidy?"

"As a pin."

"Then I believe I am ready to hear whatever it is Mr. Camden wishes to say. And I shall undoubtedly say yes," she abruptly decided. It would be a yes. It had to be a yes, because potential husbands number one through twenty-six had barely given her a second glance.

Five minutes later, she and her suitor were walking

at a fast pace down the street. It wasn't so fast as to be rushing, but it was certainly faster than a pair ought to walk on a casual stroll.

But then Mr. Camden was of a more hurried nature. It was a telltale symptom of the rising rich that Lady Eleanor had often deplored. Gentlemen who had things to do and places to be were most assuredly not aristocrats bred to enjoy the leisurely pace of their class. Therefore, if Miss Powel wished to catch a peer in her matrimonial net, she had never, ever to give the appearance of being rushed.

Sadly, at this particular moment, Mr. Camden set the pace, and Mari was forced to maintain it or be left behind. She chose to maintain in the hopes that the man would slow the moment he began to speak. But she did try to hint to him as she tilted her face up to the sun.

"It's a beautiful day, don't you think? I adore a slow stroll on a sunny day, don't you?"

"Careful," he warned. "Don't want your skin turning brown."

Right. His mother was quite fond of her skin-bleaching creams and had even sent a pot to Mari as a kind gesture. Or a hint. It was hard to tell which. Nevertheless, Mari looked down from the blue sky and waited with every appearance of calm for Mr. Camden to get to the point. It took him another two hurried blocks before he finally managed it.

"I have had some very exciting news, Miss Powel. Very exciting indeed."

"I am breathless with anticipation."

"I had a frank discussion with Lord Rossgrove. Do

you know of him? He's been very active in my circle, intimate with the men who watch the Exchange. And he's extremely influential in the Anti-Corn Law League. Quite a forward thinker." The man spoke in rapid tones, his excitement obvious as the words went on. "He's got a sharp mind, you know. Is well monied and has a genial attitude toward the common man too. My spirits are lifted whenever I have the great fortune to be in his presence."

"My goodness, Mr. Camden. You sound quite enamored." She was teasing him for his flowery language. She was sure he never spoke of her with such warmth, but he did not seem to understand her meaning.

"Oh, I am, Miss Powel. I am most enamored. Especially as he condescended to ask me to dine with him for nuncheon."

Now the man slowed down, his eyes crinkling at the corners as he grinned at her. Clearly she was supposed to understand what that meant, but she had no true idea. Except, of course, that gentlemen never met for nuncheon. That was a time reserved for workers.

"Do tell me what happened," she finally pressed as he was nearly hopping back and forth in excitement.

"Lord Rossgrove has a nephew. Young, wild lad, dashing with the ladies and all that. Bit of a buck about town."

"Mr. Oscar Morgan, yes, I know of him." Then she remembered what had happened. The young man had been racing his curricle in a wild manner from…well, somewhere to somewhere else. It was hard to keep track with the youngest bloods. But he had an accident in Piccadilly Circle, broke a spoke, and crashed. One of the horses had to be put down. But even worse, Mr. Morgan had banged his head and took days to regain consciousness. Days with the family praying by his bedside. "Oh dear. Do you mean *that* Mr. Morgan?"

"Yes!" Mr. Camden answered, somewhat gleefully.

"I'm afraid I don't understand."

"You don't? Of course not. Ladies don't follow this sort of thing, but the boy was to stand for the House of Commons, sponsored by his uncle."

"Oh," she whispered, finally putting the pieces together. "You think Lord Rossgrove wants you to stand for the seat instead?"

Mr. Camden grinned. "He has said so already. When we met."

"But that is marvelous! It is exactly what you wanted, is it not?"

"Well, of course it is, but I never expected that it would come so soon. I'm a bit young, you know, to have garnered such attention from so significant a man. He shows great condescension to take an interest in me. Great fullness of spirit and an extraordinarily keen eye."

She wasn't quite sure what he meant by the fullness of spirit or extraordinarily keen eye, but she knew better than to argue. This was an incredible opportunity for Mr. Camden and exactly why he was on her list in the first place. He had a significant future ahead of him, and she could be the woman at his side, helping him do good work in the nation.

"I'm so pleased for you, Mr. Camden. What is your next step?"

"As to that, Lord Rossgrove had a few reservations.

It is natural in a man with such true insight that he would have some requirements. A need to be sure that I would measure up."

"Requirements?"

"Before he could fully support my campaign, he would like certain proofs, so to speak, of my suitability. Trifles, really, that I am all too eager to demonstrate."

"I see," Mari said slowly. "What are they?"

"Well, first and foremost, he believes, quite rightly, that a man can be considered mature—something most dreadfully important in any man who wishes to lead—only if he has, to wit, a wife."

It took Mari a moment to sort through the man's verbiage. He did not normally talk in such a round-about manner, but when he was most excited, the worst of this tendency showed through. And as his sentences were very complicated, Mari could deduce that he was most excited. So excited that she nearly missed the importance of his statement as he stood before her, blinking his dark brown eyes.

"Mr. Camden?" She frowned as she pushed through his words. "Lord Rossgrove would like you to wed before he supports you to his nephew's seat?"

"Yes, yes, that is it exactly." He swallowed. "And, you see, in a man so attuned to the subtle rules of Society, he had some few suggestions as to whom that lady might be."

Oh dear. That she understood very easily. "And…" She hesitated. Did she push the point? Demand to know her situation, or play the shrinking violet? Two weeks ago, she would have chosen modesty. But having spent the last week being battered about by Lord Whitly, she was sick to death of being diffident. So she lifted her chin. "Was I on Lord Rossgrove's list?"

He swallowed. "Sadly, no, Miss Powel."

"Then I'm sorry, Mr. Camden, I cannot see Lord Rossgrove in a kindly light."

"Of course not, of course not." Then he bit his lip. "I told him of your many fine qualities and my deep respect for your person. He did of course refer to what he called your wayward Welsh ways, but I assured him that you have grown past such nonsense and are now a most respected and quiet woman."

"I do try, Mr. Camden."

"Yes, yes, and so I told him. Though he had heard about the wager, you see, with the parrot. That made it more difficult to convince him."

Of course it did, and here was yet another difficulty she laid at Lord Whitly's feet. "But did you convince him?"

He flashed her a slow smile, one filled with canny understanding. "I am pleased to tell you that he was impressed by my determination. He could see that my affections were firmly engaged."

They were? "I am gratified to hear that, Mr. Camden."

"And so, Miss Powel, he would like to meet you."

She stared at him, her mind whirling. "Meet me?"

"Yes," he said. His eyes grew serious as his excitement drained away. He reached forward and took her hand, drawing it tight to his heart. "I should like very much to marry you, Miss Powel. I believe you and I suit extraordinarily well."

"I—" she began, but he did not allow her to continue.

"We have a shared vision, you see. I believe you would make an excellent wife and mother to my aspirations. But none of that can come to fruition, none of our hopes can appear unless you pass muster with Lord Rossgrove."

"I see," she said, her voice quiet. "And if I do not?"

"Then I will have no choice but to end our association. Please understand, I have a great personal liking for you, but without Lord Rossgrove's support, my aspirations might as well be wishes on a falling star."

"But surely he's not your only option."

"He is the one here now. And if you cannot manage his approval, then you are not the helpmeet I need."

She exhaled slowly. He was right.

"I mean no disrespect, Miss Powel."

"I know," she said softly. "Is there a time and place for this inspection?"

He didn't even wince at the word she used. "He has invited you to call on him for tea tomorrow."

"Me?" she said. "Won't you be there?"

"No. Indeed, he was quite specific upon that point. You may bring your maid and no other."

She nodded. She had wanted to begin establishing herself as an asset to a husband with aspirations. Apparently God had seen fit to test her even before she wore an engagement ring. "I won't disappoint you," she said firmly.

"Good, good," he said as he resumed walking. "And if I might be so bold, pray do not wear pink."

She jolted. "What? Whyever not?"

He gave her a pitying look. "Because the color is flippant."

She took a moment to allow the idea to sink in. Or perhaps what she needed to understand was the way Mr. Camden was staring at her, as if the character of a color was common sense. "What does he think of jonquil?" she ventured, not expecting an answer. She was simply trying to make a joke as a way to diffuse her nerves.

"Jonquil would be most unwise, Miss Powel. Most unwise indeed."

# Ten

It's generally considered crass to speak to a woman's father while still hard from kissing his daughter. Unfortunately, given the amount of lust Miss Powel inspired, Peter would be unlikely to find a time when he was not achingly ready to plant himself between her thighs. Which meant there was no point in delaying his discussion with her father. If only he could find the damned man.

Mr. Powel did not frequent the usual gathering places of gentlemen. He'd certainly been seen at White's, Brooks's, Watier's, and Boodle's, but usually as a guest and without any predictability. There was a coffeehouse near the docks that he sometimes enjoyed, and every gentleman wandered through a gaming hell or three at some point. But in general, no one could predict when or where the man would appear, except to say that he had an office on Cowper's Row.

An office like a solicitor or a banker, very bourgeois. So it was that Peter tromped up the steps into Mr. Powel's London office and found himself struck dumb.

He had been in many offices in his life. The head-master's office at school burned dark in his memory, as did his father's ponderous edifice of dark wood and condescending tomes. But he'd also found happiness in his messy corner of the office he'd shared with a half dozen other East India employees. He'd cooled his heels by enormous, ornate desks in India, and once sat scribbling for two days next to an elephants' watering hole. But this place—this vast space of Mr. Powel's office—was as near to heaven as Peter had ever imagined.

Mr. Powel's place of business took up an entire floor of the modest building. Whereas most offices had doors and walls, this space had none of those things. It was an imposing place of desks, all covered in paper. Three secretaries sat shoved into the farthest corner. Fortunately it was near a window, so the hunched men at least had light. But the rest of the floor was filled with tables covered in sketches, notes, and a treasure trove of maps.

And in the center of it, like a maestro conducting his orchestra, stood Mr. Powel. Or rather, he walked, muttered, and inspected, moving from one spot to another, pulling out a map, making notes in corre-spondence, and occasionally tugging at his hair.

"Is it teatime already?" Mr. Powel said as he set down a well-worn diary. He pulled out his pocket watch absently, but then abruptly glared at it. "No. No, it's not." Then he looked up, his amber eyes widening in surprise. "And you are not the tea girl."

"No, I am not." Peter sketched a quick bow. "Peter George Norwood, Lord Whitly, at your service."

"I know who you are. You're Sommerfield's heir, and the gentleman who waltzes, trains parakeets, and tosses my daughter off her horse."

Peter felt his lips twitch in a smile. "I definitely waltz, am middling at best with birds, and sadly, I was simply too slow to catch her. I did nothing to knock her off her seat."

"Then what caused it? She's not a gel who simply falls off her horse."

Very true, but Peter had no wish to talk so quickly of marriage. Not when Mari's heart was so unreadable. What Peter came here to discover was the character of her father, which at the moment appeared more unpredictable than his wealthy cit image would suggest.

"I'm afraid you'll have to ask her that. She wouldn't explain it to me either." Then he wandered to the closest corner, clearly devoted to waterways. He saw maps of canals, seas, and oceans, with sharp lines as used by sailors to navigate. Lolling lopsided in the middle of the table sat a model of some sort of sailing vessel such as a boy might fashion, but there were three others that looked meticulous in construction in a neat row behind. He waved a genial hand at the top map and decided to start with flattery. "This looks very impressive. I probably couldn't understand half of it. Have you plans for something exciting?"

The man frowned, clearly not easily swayed by flattery. "I always have plans. Ideas at a minimum. Only a dolt has nothing in his head." He tilted his head, his eyes narrowing. "You were in India. What do you know of the caravan routes?"

"Inside or out of India?"

"Out."

"Very little, I'm afraid." Peter picked up the farthest model boat. "I traveled extensively inside the country, but only took the usual sailing route out."

Mr. Powel joined him at the table, his thumb holding a page in another diary. It showed a rough sketch of Turkey, bisected with a jagged red line. Presumably the route the diarist took through that country.

"You were a taxman, as I recall," Mr. Powel said. "Pulling rubies out of the maharajas."

Emeralds more often, but he wasn't about to argue. Neither was he going to elaborate.

Meanwhile, Mr. Powel leaned against the table, his expression turning pensive. "I worked shipping during my time in India," he said bluntly. "Messy business, cutthroats everywhere, but I learned the value of transport." He rubbed absently at a smudge on his hand. "Can't make a profit if you can't get the goods to market."

Peter nodded, then wandered to the next corner. The left wall was covered by the roads of England, drawn in a precise hand, while the right was dedicated to the Continent. Both were covered with smudge marks, as if traced repeatedly with a dirty finger. "So that's what this is? New routes to get Indian goods to market?" If Powel succeeded, that would be a treasure beyond price, but the risks were enormous. He peered around the table. There were stacks of books that looked to be more journals and travel records.

"It's one of my notions," Mr. Powel hedged.

A serious one, obviously. Peter started to wander to the next table, his eye catching on a map of the

English canal system. "You seem to have a great many excellent notions, at least according to my father."

Mr. Powel didn't answer. His gaze was alternating between Peter and a larger map of Turkey, this one not nearly as specific as the one in the diary.

"He says you have the Midas touch."

"Your father exaggerates," muttered Mr. Powel, his attention centered on rooting through another set of papers beneath the map of Turkey.

Peter paused, watching the man intently, wondering how best to approach this unusual man. "Don't stare. It's rude," Mr. Powel admonished, all without lifting his gaze from his papers.

"You sound just like your daughter."

"She's an uncommonly intelligent woman." Then he looked up. "Both my daughters are, though I never would have guessed it of Josephine at first. Mari at least thinks before she acts. Good quality in a woman."

"In any person, I imagine."

Mr. Powel finally turned to stare directly at Peter. "Is that why you want to marry her? Because she's levelheaded?"

Peter didn't answer. Thanks to his father's love of discipline, he was uncomfortable discussing anything precious to him. And India had honed that reticence into lock-jawed silence.

Meanwhile, Mr. Powel continued, his gaze unnervingly direct. "You don't need her dowry, not if you're smart with what you've brought back from India."

"You seem to know a great deal about me, Mr. Powel, when I know so little about you."

"Pah," the man said with a wave. "We know a

great deal about each other, I'd wager. Still doesn't tell me why you're here."

Peter idly picked up a sketch of a new kind of carriage. Intriguing design, obviously meant for stability, not speed. "I'd think it was obvious. You've made a great deal of money for my father. I'd like to invest some of my blunt."

Mr. Powel's expression tightened in confusion. "If that's what your father considers a great deal, then your title isn't as well-heeled as I thought."

"He said thousands of pounds." £3,621 to be exact, according to the ledger. And that was only the newest ledger entry.

Mr. Powel smiled a broad grin that showed crooked teeth but made his face light with humor. "It's humbug, son. He's invested with me once, and the profits are growing slowly."

"Just the once?"

"Still growing."

Peter nodded. "Interesting. He said it was in a shipment of spices from India." That's what the ledger recorded. Spice sales. Seventeen entries.

"Spices, bah," Mr. Powel said as he dropped the diary. "Too touchy, and the English palate isn't as accepting as everyone pretends. Silk is the better investment if you can keep the vermin out of the stores."

Peter agreed, but he was more interested in the three thousand pounds his father had recorded. "But my father said it was spice."

Mr. Powel dismissed him with a wave of his hand. "Your father can say what he wants to whomever he wants. Earls usually do."

"I'd like to know more."

Mr. Powel turned his back. "Then talk to your father."

"I'd like to invest."

The man didn't even pause as he pulled his chair over and settled down in front of his maps of Turkey. "I'm sorry. I have nothing available right now. Talk to me in a few months."

"Even if I have tens of thousands of pounds?"

"Even so."

Peter crossed his arms. Flattery hadn't worked. Appealing to the man's greed got him nowhere. Time to start looking for a vice.

"Perhaps I'm approaching this the wrong way," he tried. "I'm newly returned to London, have some extra blunt you don't seem to want. Is there a gaming hell you'd recommend?"

"No."

"Haarkata Lane was a wonder, was it not?"

The mention of India's most infamous street of whorehouses got nothing but a sigh.

Not the usual vices, then. "I miss Indian food. You're right about the English palate being used to dull fare, but it seems mine has expanded in six years away. Any recommendations?"

The man set down his map and turned to look at him. "Everyone seems to think that you're a jolly good bloke. That's what they say, you know. Jolly good bloke. And yet I find you remarkably irritating."

Whereas Peter was finding himself remarkably entertained. He'd forgotten how much fun it could be to ferret out a difficult man's character. Most people would have revealed more by now.

"Some people take longer to notice my good qualities."

The man snorted in answer, and Peter counted that as a good sign. He was laughing—after a fashion—rather than tossing Peter out on his ear. Meanwhile, Peter decided to offer one last temptation before abandoning the vices altogether. He pulled out a special box and set it on the table between them.

"What's that?"

"Something I'm willing to share in the name of getting to know my future father-in-law."

Now Mr. Powel did set down his map to look Peter fully in the eye. "That's a confident statement, given how often I've heard Mari curse your name."

"She is also taking a while to see my good qualities."

Again the snort, this time a bit louder. "She has good sense."

Peter only shrugged, which gave Mr. Powel time to lean forward, setting his elbows on his knees. "I won't force her to marry you, title or no. I'll stop her if she's hell-bent on a bounder, and if I don't like you, I'll cut off her dowry too."

Peter shook his head. "You won't do that. You dote on your girls, and you'll make sure she's provided for." It was a guess, but a good one as the man folded his arms.

"She'll have what she needs in ways that will prevent any jackanapes husband from touching her money." He lifted his chin, an angry glint in his eyes. "It can be done, you know. I can set her up without letting you have a ha'penny."

"I have no doubt." He pulled out a stool and dropped

onto it, setting his ankle on his knee. It wasn't an easily defensible position. He'd never do something so awkward in India. But this was England, and he seriously doubted any of the secretaries in the corner would skewer him with a knife. So he took the casual pose and hoped he looked confident rather than arrogant.

Apparently it was a good choice, because Mr. Powel released another snort, this one soft and appreciative. "All right, Lord Whitly." He reached for the box. "Let's get to know one another."

He popped open the lid to see a box of the finest hashish in England. It might even have been the only hashish in England, but Peter wasn't going to keep it hidden. A tool was only good if one used it, and he considered hashish one of the best in his arsenal.

Mr. Powel's eyebrows shot up in surprise, and then he lifted the box closer. He pinched the substance, feeling the consistency and quality of the product like a true connoisseur.

"I've had better," he mused.

"But not in years, I'll wager."

Mr. Powel flashed a rueful grin. "Not since India. Do you have more?"

Peter shook his head. "This is the last of it, though I could probably get more."

"So could I, but I don't."

Peter could guess the reason, but he waited for the man to elaborate.

"I've seen people destroyed by this."

"Hashish? Or opium?"

"Both, though opium's done the most damage."

That was Peter's belief as well.

Mr. Powel set the box back on the table, but he didn't shut the lid. "Do you eat it or smoke it?"

Peter had done both, but he pulled out a pipe. "Only if you wish, sir. I have no interest in seeing you destroyed."

The man chuckled. A fine improvement from the earlier snorts. "So you mean to loosen my tongue this way."

"I've never heard of you drinking to excess. You barely gamble, and the tarts have never met you. By all accounts, you are an upstanding family man." He didn't add the sneering word "businessman" that so often accompanied that description. "But every man has a vice. I'd like to see how deeply yours runs."

"Not that deeply. Even when the hashish was plentiful, I tried it only a few times." He arched his brow. "What about you?"

"There's a knack to pretending to smoke. You can't completely prevent its effects, but it does keep a man sharper than the others."

Mr. Powel nodded. "Smoked a lot, did you?"

"The maharajas did. I pretended." His expression tightened. He didn't mean it to, but sometimes old memories fought to come out no matter how he schooled his expression. "It saved my life on many occasions."

"Now there's a tale I should like to hear."

Peter shook his head. "Not today." Then he decided to try honesty. "It doesn't haunt me as it does some men, but I don't want to look behind me. I am attending to the future. And your daughter."

The man waited a moment to see if Peter would

bow to the pressure caused by an expectant silence. He didn't. So in the end, Mr. Powel stood up, snapping the box closed with a quick flick of his wrist.

"Very well, my lord, I believe I should like to introduce you to a chef trained in all the best Indian dishes."

Peter matched the man's movements, pushing to his feet. "The best dishes?"

"Tamed considerably for the weakened English palate."

"Not too considerably, I hope."

The man grinned. "He'll burn your tongue if you want."

That was something to get Peter's attention. Meanwhile, Mr. Powel was laying it on thick, tempting him with every Indian delight he'd thought he'd never miss.

"He's just finished a new batch of bangla as well. Took him years to perfect the brew."

"Bangla" was a single word to describe a multitude of alcoholic drinks, some vile, some delightful. "I'm intrigued," he said truthfully.

"Then we'll see about your hashish and your tens of thousands of pounds."

So the man did have a streak of greed. Well, that was true of the best businessmen, and Peter would not fault him for it.

"There's only one condition," the man continued, throwing words out as if they were no more important than a comment on the weather.

"Yes?" Peter asked, doing his best to appear equally casual.

"I need to know your vice as well." Then his eyes

became piercingly direct. "You're moderate with your money, haven't been to the whores or spent much time in the gaming hells. Your superiors speak in glowing terms, and the maharajas curse you as a white demon who eats their young."

Repulsive. "I have never eaten anyone's young. I got what was due to the company and England. No more, no less."

"I know. That makes you remarkable. But where in all that is your vice?"

"That's easy, sir. I have a potentially unhealthy obsession with your daughter."

The words hung in the space between them, filling the air while Mr. Powel studied him and he returned the regard. It felt like the mutual call of "en garde!" before a fencing match.

"Very well," Mr. Powel finally said. "The stakes are high, then. Impress me, and I'll not stop my daughter from marrying you, should she wish it. But what shall I get in return?"

"Tens of thousands of pounds for investment."

Mr. Powel shook his head. "I will not sell her to anyone."

Good. Peter hadn't meant it that way anyway. "A titled son-in-law, then."

"Pah. You titles are always tripping about here and there. I turned one away just yesterday."

It was likely a lie. Peter knew Mr. Powel did indeed have a lust for the peerage. But maybe not for just his daughter. "You have a son, do you not?" He already knew the answer.

"He's on his grand tour."

"And there is something you want from me. For your son." It wasn't a question, and Mr. Powel didn't treat it as one. Instead, he grinned and turned to his row of secretaries.

"Mr. Harper, please draw up the usual marriage contract for Lord Whitly. We'll see what he thinks of it."

It would be a disaster, no doubt. Fortunately, he knew a man with an excellent head for contracts, who actually enjoyed the things. Meanwhile, he decided to taunt his adversary, who likely enjoyed a good negotiation as much as Peter did.

"Impressed so easily? Is your daughter mine, then?"

Mr. Powel's answer was a laugh. Not just a simple chuckle, but a belly laugh that grew until the man was wiping tears from his eyes. Peter might have been insulted, except there was such good humor in the sound that he was hard-pressed not to join in.

But in the end, the man sobered enough to speak. "Keep your hashish, my lord. I think I shall be vastly entertained without it."

"I am very willing to share," he responded.

"You should throw it in the fire. You'll need all your wits to fence with me, and I am nothing compared to what Mari will put you through."

Peter pretended to consider that. He pursed his lips and furrowed his brow. In the end, he took the box and walked over to the row of secretaries, setting it down in front of Mr. Harper. "My gift to you," he said. "To smoke or eat, as you will. I suggest trying it with this afternoon's tea."

"At home," growled Mr. Powel. "And do not report for work until your head has cleared."

Peter shrugged as if to say, as you wish. But then he winked at the row of wide-eyed young men. "There's enough to share with your friends." And not so much that it would harm them even if they smoked the entire box. "Just think kindly of me when we have occasion to cross paths."

Then he took the time to greet each man, memorizing their names and mannerisms. A great deal could be learned from young secretaries who had reason to be grateful.

Mr. Powel watched the entire proceeding with an amused air. He likely understood what Peter was doing and apparently approved, since he didn't stop it. Or perhaps he trusted to the good sense of his men.

Then it was on to the next steps in this negotiation: a genial meal, some spicy bangla, and whatever hints he could learn about Mari.

# *Eleven*

MARI GLOWERED AT THE BRIGHT SUNSHINE AS SHE clomped her way up the steps to her home. From now on, she would remember never, ever to rise early, because it completely disordered her day. It was barely past teatime, and she already felt like a wet rag hung out to dry. The bruises from this morning's fall ached liked the devil, she had a headache from a terrible session with Greenie, made worse from sitting fruitlessly at Lady Eleanor's salon. She'd wanted to get a single private moment to ask the woman about Lord Rossgrove, but had been unable to manage the feat. And now the blasted sun chose to shine bright and hot right in her eyes. All she wanted to do was be on her bed and cover her eyes with a lemon cloth, but…what the devil was that noise? Was her father singing? In the middle of the day?

Horace pulled open the door for her, his expression so pained as to immediately brighten her mood. Then she heard another masculine voice join her father's. It was deeper and richer, and was surprisingly sweet to hear. And she knew just whose it was, especially since the words were spoken in Hindi.

"Lord Whitly?" she asked Horace, her expression turning as sour as the butler's. Then it hit her. Lord Whitly was talking to her father. About their marriage. It had to be, and she wasn't ready for that. Not if Whitly got her father to pressure her before she brought Mr. Camden up to scratch.

"Yes, Miss Powel," Horace answered. "In the dining room for a late luncheon."

"Oh, oh no."

Luncheon? It was past tea. Didn't matter. They were here, and from the sounds of it, they were having too good a time with each other. As if to underline the thought, her father abruptly burst out laughing. It was a big sound that boomed through the house and usually made her smile. This time, it made her grind her teeth in frustration.

And then, the other realization hit her. "Cook finished the newest batch of bangla this morning, didn't he?"

"Precisely," Horace intoned. She looked to their disapproving butler and immediately resolved to make sure the understaff got half the current batch. Why should she be the only one with upset plans? Watching Horace trying to control a too-jolly crew would make the day marginally better. Meanwhile, she decided to grab for her nearest ally.

"Please ask Mama—"

"Your mother is currently making calls."

Of course she was. If the men weren't right now discussing her future, Mari would be out the door as well. "Very well," she said as she stripped out of her hat and gloves. "I shall…" Her voice trailed away. Her father had stopped crooning and left the tune to Lord Whitly. Lord, he had an exceptional voice.

It was slow and filled with tenderness. She didn't know enough Hindi to understand the words, but Lord Whitly's voice infused it with pain. Slow, melancholic longing that called to her in a way she couldn't understand. Mesmerized, she walked to the dining room but did not enter. She stood in the doorway, her eyes filling with tears for no reason at all.

She blinked them away. She was not a watering pot and knew how to get her emotions under control. So she focused on the way Lord Whitly lounged in his seat, stretching his legs out before him as his head dropped against the back of the chair. His hand was on his chest, and his eyes had slid closed. Clearly inebriated, and yet his song continued.

Her father saw her. His cheeks were flushed, and his eyes were bright, but he didn't do more than acknowledge her with a nod. He too was caught up in the ballad, if that indeed was the term for so beautiful a tune.

Then it was done. Lord Whitly exhaled the last note on a sigh and opened his eyes. He wasn't looking at her, but at her father, and when he spoke, his words were gravelly with emotion.

"There. Now you have it."

Her father planted his chin on his hand. "What?"

"The best thing I brought back from India. That song."

"Ah. And did you learn it from a beautiful woman?"

Lord Whitly smiled, the expression nostalgic. "I did."

Mari found her mood souring, and she pushed off the doorjamb. Good God, had she really been lolling against the doorway like a lazy chambermaid? She moved into the room, making sure her steps were crisp and her words even more so.

"I see chef has finished his latest batch of bangla." She scanned the table to see the remains of a half dozen of her father's favorite Indian dishes. "And you've had quite a feast as well."

There was the rapid scramble of feet as the two men rushed to stand. Meanwhile, her father grinned at her.

"Best Indian chef in all of London," he said.

"The only one, Papa."

Lord Whitly bowed his greeting. "This was the finest meal I've had since coming home, and I extend my highest compliments to your chef."

"He's a good man and a good cook," her father said with a warm smile.

"He's an average cook, but an excellent brewmeister," Mari returned. Then she took a deep breath and forced herself to smile, as if she wasn't worried to death that her father had just engaged her to this man. "I didn't expect to see you here, Lord Whitly. Did you and father discuss anything significant?"

Her father waved his hand in too wide an arc. "It's all significant. We have more in our heads than fripperies and balls."

This was a standard complaint among her father and the ladies of the household. Their usual response would be to tease him about his less-than-fashionable attire. For a man who desperately wanted to rise in the ranks of the social elite, her father was woefully bad at dressing himself.

But instead of the usual comment, her gaze caught and held with Lord Whitly. He was looking at her with an intensity she found rather thrilling. He hadn't moved from his formal stance, but his eyes were trained so tightly on her face that she couldn't look away. And she couldn't deny the flutter of delight she took at his attention. Then he ruined it completely.

"Your hair makes me wince. Doesn't it hurt?"

She touched her pins, noting that many of her curls had escaped, so she quickly attempted to settle them back into place.

"No, no," he said. "You're going to give yourself a migraine." Then before she could stop him, he pulled out several of her pins.

"Oh!" she cried, trying to stop him. But he was quicker than any man—especially an inebriated one—ought to be. A moment later, every lock on her head was released to fly about her face in abandon. And as quick as that, her head felt better. The ease on her scalp made her eyes flutter closed for a moment in relief as her hair tumbled down her back.

"Stop that!" she said as she tried to brush them back into order. It didn't work. Not without the pins he was dropping so casually onto the table. "Give those back to me."

Lord Whitly shook his head while her father dropped back down into his chair. "He's right, you know. You look much prettier with everything…" He waved vaguely about his ears. "Loose."

Had her father just suggested she become a loose

woman? If the man wasn't in his cups, she'd admonish him, but he was smiling fondly at her, and she couldn't bring herself to naysay him.

Lord Whitly's mood, however, was something else entirely. She turned to him with a stern glare. "When I need advice on my toilette, I shall be sure to ask someone else."

He huffed out a breath. "What happened, Miss Powel? Why would you do this to yourself? A beige dress? The entire thing makes me sad."

She felt her mouth gape open. What was the polite response to so outrageous a statement? I did it because this was the only way to get married? Except, of course, she wasn't married. I did it because the gossips delighted in hurting me whenever I wore something interesting? Very true, but he wouldn't understand the way women sniped at each other.

Before she could frame a response, he rubbed a hand over his face. "Damn, I've become maudlin." He glared at the bangla. "That's a good drink, but stronger than I thought."

Obviously. What sane gentleman picked the pins out of a woman's hair? "What are you doing here, Lord Whitly?"

Her father's head snapped up. "You said she was expecting you!"

Lord Whitly grimaced. "She ought to be. I can't help it if she forgot."

Mari dropped her hands onto her hips. "I have not forgotten anything."

Her father groaned. "He said you were to go walking in Hyde Park today. Because you lost some wager about lemonade. Really, Mari, I thought you knew that ladies don't make wagers."

She opened her mouth to give a blistering retort—drunken father or not—when she realized he was right. She had wagered and lost. A walk in Hyde Park had been the forfeit. She couldn't remember one thing with her hair all fly-away and Lord Whitly standing so close.

Meanwhile, the blighter in question grinned at her father. "See? Can't help it if she forgets."

"Did you really forget?" her father pressed. "You? The one with the perfect schedule in her head?" He looked at Lord Whitly. "Amazing mind, my gel. Remembers everything."

She blew out a breath. "It's been a difficult day. I rose too early."

"And fell off your horse," her father said. "Your mother told me."

Mari had no response to that, so she turned to Lord Whitly and tried to be gracious. "I can see that you're not quite yourself right now, so perhaps we should delay our walk." Maybe until after she brought Mr. Camden up to scratch.

"I am perfectly well, thank you," he said with a smooth bow punctuated with a flourish that had gone out of style two hundred years earlier. "I merely await your convenience to amble." Then he cast her a mischievous look. "Perhaps you wish to change your gown?"

"You won't like anything else I own either," she muttered. Then she tried to think things through logically. She wished to learn what Lord Whitly and her father had discussed. She wanted to know more about his secrets too, and any number of things that had kept her wondering through the night and had prompted her to rise too early this morning. And the best time to get him to talk was when he was soft from drink.

In short, now was a better time than most for her to go strolling with him. She just had to keep her temper long enough to gain the answers she sought.

"Very well, Lord Whitly, it would be my pleasure to walk with you this afternoon."

"Excellent!" Then he offered her his arm. She took it gingerly, setting just her fingertips on his sleeve, but then he settled his other hand atop hers. Large and all encompassing. Just a forearm. Nothing so exciting about that. Except she was excited by it. She did marvel at his easy strength and the hard bulge to his upper arm. He was a powerfully built man. And he was looking at her as if he wanted to eat her.

She ought to be frightened. She told herself to be on her guard. Instead, she flushed and looked away, both embarrassed by his attention and flattered by it. They started to walk out of the room, but before they could leave, her father called out.

"You really think stability in the carriage is the wrong choice?"

Lord Whitly turned back, Mari with him. "I think that carriages in India overturn from trying to outrun bandits on bad roads. If you want to transport your silk from the interior up through Turkey, you need to design a carriage with a protected seat for a sharpshooter."

"Have to find a reliable sharpshooter first. At least half of them are in league with the bandits."

"Plenty of men coming out of the military, some

of them with great skills. My brother would know of a few."

Her father arched a brow. "But would he recommend me to them?"

Lord Whitly smiled. "He would if I asked."

"Hmmm. I'll think on it." Then he plopped his chin on his fist and stared darkly into his empty cup of bangla.

Lord Whitly waited a moment, obviously unsure what that meant. Mari couldn't blame him. Her father's moods were unpredictable at the best of times. So she squeezed his arm, trying not to get a surreptitious thrill at the motion.

"He'll be like that for an hour or more. It's what he loves to do best after a good bout of bangla."

"Talk about carriage designs?"

"Stare into space and mutter about ideas. He tends to overflow with them when in his cups." She gestured with her free hand as one of his secretaries slipped into the room and sat down, pen and paper at hand. "Mr. Harper is here to record whatever comes out."

"So his ideas are good?"

She shrugged. "Only one or two in a hundred. But it doesn't matter. He has so many."

"One or two good ideas could set a man up for life."

She nodded and was strangely pleased that he understood her father. She'd heard the whispers about him. Her father was an odd-duck bourgeois. A town cit who had delusions of being better than he was. Only his family and a few of his investors knew the true genius of the man. And now, perhaps, Lord Whitly saw it as well.

"So is that what you two talked about?" she pressed as they headed for the front door. "Carriages in India?"

"Some." They parted at the door to accept hats and gloves from Horace. "He is sending around a marriage contract for me to peruse."

Her step hitched, and her heart beat painfully in her throat. "Oh?" she said, scrambling to keep her voice from a high-pitched squeak of alarm.

"I shouldn't be too concerned. It's the initial gambit. The terms will be outrageous, and if I accept them without argument, your father will likely ban me from the house."

If she was alarmed before, now she was tending toward horror. "What?"

"It's the game of negotiation. Surely you've seen it before. A suitor appears avidly at your side, and then abruptly disappears."

Well, of course she had. Scores of times. "Because they didn't accept the terms of the negotiation?" How humiliating to have her future dickered over like a meat pie at market.

"Or they were insulted. I believe it's one way your father tests the gentlemen who come for your hand. If they don't understand how to barter, then they won't manage your dowry well. And that, I gather, would be a capital crime."

She didn't know how to answer. She'd never thought deeply about the subtleties of the marriage contract. She had been more interested in thinking about the man than the money.

Meanwhile, he held his arm out to her again,

winking as he spoke. "Never fear. I know this particular game very well."

"And do my wishes matter to either one of you?"

He gave her a fond pat on her hand. "Of course they do. A great deal." His expression shifted into devilry. "But that has nothing to do with the marriage contract. In that, I think your father and I shall take a great deal of joy in growling at each other like distempered dogs." They stepped onto the walkway and began a pleasant pace toward Hyde Park. "We have that in common, you know," he added. "Your father and I."

"Acting like dogs?"

He chuckled. "A love of negotiation. I never realized how much fun it was until India, when my entire livelihood depended on well-struck bargains."

She shook her head. "I dislike it intensely. I rely on knowing what an item is worth and then paying that much and no more."

"Which works extremely well for a pair of shoes or a horse, but not so well with a wife." He lifted her hand and pressed a kiss to the back. "If we had to measure your worth, I would be beggared paying for you."

A pretty compliment indeed, made all the more striking because he said it with little inflection. It was a statement, not flattery, and she turned mute from the heat his words generated in her belly. Warm, liquid yearning that might even be called desire. Which pushed her into an irrational state of panic. Desire, after all, was much too wayward for her.

So she rushed her words, everything spoken

without forethought. "What do you know of Lord Rossgrove? Have you ever met him? He would not be in your set, though naturally your father would know him. They're both political. And the men of money often speak together. But I'm not sure if you know anything of him, because you've been in India for a long while."

She bit her lip, cutting off her abrupt flow of words. He arched a brow, his expression bemused. "Is Lord Rossgrove the tolerant uncle of Oscar Morgan, disinterested father to Stephen, with a prune-faced wife and a love of sugar plums?"

She blinked. In one question, he'd told her more than she'd learned in an afternoon of searching. "I-I believe so," she stammered.

"Then I am somewhat familiar with him. Why do you ask?"

"I mean to impress him tomorrow, and I wish to know how."

His head jerked slightly as he stared at her. "That's a fool's gambit if ever there was one."

"Why?"

"Because he only cares about power, and as lovely as you are, you have none. You cannot gain entrance to his sanctum unless you have something he wants. And since you don't, you are doomed to fail."

"But he has asked to speak with me. Indeed, he has commanded it."

That got his attention. His brows drew down, and his hand tightened over hers.

"I have surprised you," she said with a childish kind of satisfaction.

He nodded slightly, as if to acknowledge the statement. It was a small thing, clearly done without conscious thought, because his mind was likely working out the reasons for her summons. But she noted it in the way one might note a spectacularly colored coat or a beautiful song. Clearly, he felt no problem with admitting she'd beaten him in this small way. She'd surprised him. But whereas she took satisfaction in winning, he couldn't care less. She couldn't imagine Mr. Camden admitting so tiny a thing. Nor her father. She had to trick them into listening to her. For a "winner, winner," he was decidedly casual about losing.

And while she was still absorbing the magnitude of that, he inquired about her abrupt confession. "Do you know why Lord Rossgrove would summon you?"

"I have an idea, yes."

He waited in silence when she didn't provide the answer. He didn't begin to reason it out with guesses or silly comments. He simply ambled with his quiet attention fixed on her. It was unnerving. And in that awkward moment, she found the truth tumbling out once again.

"I believe he wishes to put Mr. Camden up for a seat in the House of Commons."

"The one that was meant for his nephew?"

Mari nodded. The man was in London barely a day, and back in the country for less than two weeks, but he knew gossip from a month earlier.

He tilted his head. "Do you have a relationship with Mr. Camden that would bring Lord Rossgrove's attention to you?"

She nodded slowly. "I believe I do."

"So you are engaged?" There was a dangerous edge to his voice that made her shiver. Not in fear. Everything about him was pleasant in this casual stroll on a lovely afternoon. But there was a note to his voice that made her breath catch and her nipples tighten.

Good Lord, that couldn't be true, but the sensations were undeniable. How humiliating. Even her nipples were wayward.

"Miss Powel?" he prompted while she was busy being embarrassed by her breasts.

"Oh, um, no. Not as yet. I believe Mr. Camden is waiting for Lord Rossgrove's approval before he speaks to me."

"What man seeks another's approval before choosing a wife?"

"What man barters for his bride like a cantankerous dog?"

His lips twitched in response, and again he dipped his chin toward her. "I shall not debate my choice of bride," he said, his voice low. "The bargaining is merely for fun."

"Your sense of fun is distinctly lost on me."

"Is it?" he challenged. "Truly?"

She bit her lip and shrugged. He touched her arm, stopping her forward movement as he looked hard at her face.

"Never say you cannot laugh with me. I remember the sound from six years ago. It has haunted my dreams, Miss Powel. It has lived in my heart ever since that day."

"I laughed?" She couldn't remember it. "Out loud and at a ball?"

"It was a bold sound, filled with joy with a musical lift at the end." Then he did it. He laughed in his deep baritone, lifting the final notes at the last moment. It was so odd a sound that other strollers stopped to stare. And then he frowned. "No, that's not it," he muttered. Then he did it again. Loud and full, in a higher register before doing a strange trill at the end.

She laughed. She couldn't help it. He sounded so bizarre that the giggles burst from her. And then— belatedly realizing what she had done—she clapped her hand over her mouth just before the lift at the end.

"Yes!" he cried. "That's it exactly." He pulled her hand away from her mouth. "But don't cover it up. It's the most wonderful sound ever."

"You have had entirely too much bangla," she said, her voice stern.

"Not me," he said, his expression sobering. "I begin to think you have not had enough." Then he sighed, and they began walking again. "I cannot understand why you have locked yourself away. You dress dull, you cover your mouth and never laugh, and you think of marrying a man who must get Rossgrove's approval. Has England gone mad, or is it just you Welsh?"

"Is it mad to think of my future? Is it mad to act in a way that will not incite gossip?"

He grumbled under his breath. They had come to the edge of Hyde Park, where the *ton* was out enjoying the lovely afternoon. The drive was clogged with carriages, and the pathways were awash in the color of ladies' gowns and bonnets. "Tell me you can look on that and not laugh."

She looked where he gestured, but saw nothing untoward. It was merely the fashionable throng parading about the grass. "I see nothing to be amused—"

"The lady wearing the stuffed swan in her bonnet."

"Oh, Baroness Burke's hat. Well, her husband accidentally shot the swan, and since she'd just paid a great deal of money to get it set up on their pond, she thought she ought to have some use out of it."

"So she stuffed it and mounted it on her head?" He cast her a look, obviously waiting for her sense of humor to surface.

"Well, yes, I suppose that is rather silly. But no more so than Lord Norman over there, dressing all in white with blue feathers. Do you know, he trails the things behind him like breadcrumbs. Says it helps people remember where he's been."

Lord Whitly chuckled. "It must give the chambermaids fits trying to clean up after him."

"Oh no," she answered. "It's his tailor who curses his name. They quickly ran out of birds with blue feathers and have gone to dying the things. For the first week there were feathers everywhere, but now he's only got a few pieces that aren't denuded. See?" She gestured to where the baron was strutting, huge blue-dyed peacock feathers bobbing up from the back of his coat. "He's very protective of them now." As they watched, a young woman reached out to touch the things, and the baron jerked away. Though they couldn't hear what was spoken, it was clear that the lady was receiving a severe dressing-down.

"And you don't find that funny at all?"

Of course she did. But she hadn't allowed herself

to laugh at it in years. Six years, to be exact. "Young, unmarried ladies aren't supposed to laugh at their elders."

"But how can you not?" he returned. This time he pointed to a clog of carriages. Three moving one way, a fourth and two riders heading the other. And all six were caught trying to turn a corner from opposite directions. The resulting jam-up was punctuated with "By Jove!" sniffs from one overdressed dandy, and "Ridiculous imbecile!" returned by three others.

She chuckled. How could she not when the lone tiger in the dandy's curricle dropped his chin on his fist and rolled his eyes. Lord Whitly snorted.

"Dandies should not drive curricles."

"Not unless his tiger is a bit older than ten and can control his expression."

"What? Oh Lord, yes, that is funny. I was thinking that the entire mess happened because the dandy was adjusting the fall of the lace over his belly."

She smiled. "Is that what happened?"

"It is."

They sidestepped the increasing chaos. Meanwhile, off to the right was a crowd of fashionable people surrounding Lady Illston's newest victim. Miss Rose May was the poor maiden carrying Greenie's massive cage.

"Do you wish to greet them?" he asked, pointing to the grouping.

"God no," she answered. She'd had more than enough of Greenie lately. They turned to the right, nodding to a separate clutch of people. She noted, naturally, that everyone was decidedly more friendly to him than to her. But no one outright snubbed her, which was a relief. Still, she couldn't help but tally the steadily shrinking number of women who treated her with warmth.

"What has you sighing so quietly, Miss Powel?" he asked after they had passed through the worst of the congestion.

"Was I sighing?"

"Or your bonnet has sprung a leak."

She chuckled, and then abruptly quieted. How had this come about? She was on Lord Whitly's arm and laughing. Or at least smiling. "Miss Green will accidentally forget to invite me to her ball."

"Who?"

"The girl dressed all in green, my lord. The one who—"

"Kept tittering like a mouse?"

"Er, yes. But I was going to say the girl with the large bonnet to de-emphasize the size of her nose."

"Is that why I nearly poked out my eye on that huge bonnet? Because she thinks her nose is large?"

"To be fair, it is rather large."

"It… Oh, yes. I suppose it is. But a bonnet doesn't hide that."

"It did from you. You were too busy avoiding blindness."

He nodded. "Very well, I'll grant you that. But why would you sigh over missing a silly girl's ball?"

"Because her mother is a grand hostess and a woman I respect. She could be a great help to me in the *ton*, and by extension, I could then be a great help to my husband."

He took a moment to digest that. She was surprised again that he seemed to truly consider her words.

She'd expected him to toss her comments aside as female machinations, which was what her father called her thinking. But instead he nodded.

"I can get you invited to the ball, if that is what you wish."

"How? By indicating that you wish to attend? I expect that your invitation is already resting on the front table of your residence."

"No doubt, but I shall only attend if you do."

"Which will make her even more of an enemy. Do not snub one woman in favor of another."

He groaned. "But I *do* favor another."

"And if you make it a choice between myself and her, then I shall lose. She is in the more powerful position, with her mother a grand hostess. If you make an ultimatum such as that, then you will declare me her enemy."

"But she already is, if she will not invite you to her ball."

"And if you draw no attention to it, then it will settle out after she finds her husband and establishes her position."

He looked at her and nodded slowly. "And you care because you are looking ahead. To what her mother can do for your husband."

"That is how this game is played." And now they came to the crux of what she wanted to know. "I would consider you, my lord. I would think of you as a possible husband, except you see none of this. You care for none of this. You will be an earl one day, and you have no ambition."

His eyes narrowed, and for a moment, she saw

something cross his expression that made her gasp. It was dark and powerful. Like glimpsing the heart of a thunderstorm. But then it was gone, though his words came out in a low, clipped tone. "You know nothing of my ambition."

She ought to take the warning of that spilt-second expression, but she'd always loved thunderstorms, and so she challenged him, trying to see if she could provoke him to explain. "Then tell me. You wish to be my husband? Then tell me not only what you want to do, but what I will do as your wife." She tightened her grip. "Do you not understand? Do you not see what I need?"

"Work," he said, clearly shocked. "You want to work."

"And you want to play."

"No." He turned to her. "What I want is something a great deal more significant."

She waited. It was a clash of wills between them right there in the middle of Hyde Park during the fashionable hour. They faced each other, brows drawn together, eyes flashing. She did not soften, and neither did he. If anything, he grew stronger, bolder, and his words came out like the crack of lightning, even though they were spoken low enough not to be overheard.

"I will show you." He spoke it like a challenge, and she was startled to find herself rising to the bait. "Tomorrow night, can you escape your chaperones?"

Without the least bit of effort. She might be an unmarried virgin, but her parents trusted to her good sense. Which would be severely lacking if she went out at night alone with this man. "What do you mean to do?"

He smiled. "Trust me."

And God help her, she did.

"Midnight," she said. "Meet me at Lady Stokes's masquerade."

# Twelve

THE NEXT MORNING WAS RUSHED, EVEN MORE SO
because she'd spent the night wondering what Lord
Whitly could possibly want to show her. Not to mention a few highly inappropriate dreams that left her
restless and achy in places best not mentioned. Worse,
they weren't technically dreams, since she'd been
awake when those imaginings had wandered into her
thoughts and refused to leave.

She felt as though she'd barely closed her eyes
when her maid woke her with the message that Mr.
Camden was waiting for her downstairs. He'd arrived
two hours early for her meeting with Lord Rossgrove,
insisting she be escorted. He also insisted that he was
being helpful when he inspected her gown, her hair,
even her shoes before he pronounced them acceptable.
Well, almost acceptable, as she'd chosen a softer, less
headache-creating hairstyle. He wanted her to change
it to her usual severe style, but she refused, saying that
she could not be clever with Lord Rossgrove while
suffering from a migraine.

Naturally, Mr. Camden was nervous at her word

"clever," but she refused to be swayed. Lord Whitly had somehow induced her to become bolder with her statements, and she was loathe to give that up, even for an meeting as important as this. She was a clever girl, and Lord Rossgrove needed to understand that if they were to work together in support of Mr. Camden's career.

So they left an hour before the appointed time, her maid serving as a bored chaperone. All three rode in her father's carriage because it was more richly appointed than anything Mr. Camden could afford. And then, after all the pomp and anxiety, Lord Rossgrove kept them waiting in his front hallway. They weren't even shown into a parlor but left sitting on a bench.

It was a calculated move, she was sure, meant to show that they were petitioners for favor. Mr. Camden kept murmuring how gracious the man was to see them in his home. Obviously, he didn't understand the tactic, and frankly, his ignorance was becoming an irritant. Worse, no matter how much she reassured him that he had no need to hover, Mr. Camden would not leave.

Thankfully, after half an hour cooling their heels, Mr. Camden managed to restrain his anxiety long enough to sit down. In gratitude, Mari patted his hand and smiled.

"Never fear. I know what I am about," she said softly, hoping it wasn't a lie. She had been thinking hard about how to handle this interview. Lord Whitly's comment that she had no power rankled. If the only thing Lord Rossgrove respected was power, she would pull on the trappings of it like a cloak. A smart man would not be fooled by such things. A petty man would resent her for it. Either way, she was determined to figure out exactly what kind of man Lord Rossgrove was, and for that, she had to out-pompous the butler and out-power Lord Rossgrove.

It would be a challenge indeed, but she relished the chance to try.

"Lord Rossgrove condescends to admit you into the library. Mind you do not touch, eat, or drink any-thing. You may sit if he offers it, but you must stand if he does not. And do not under any circumstances approach him closer than ten feet. That is the width of the desk plus the chairs. Do you understand? If he allows you to sit, you will claim the one farthest away. And you will show appropriate gratitude if that happy event should occur."

It was that last comment that was the tipping point. She arched her brow and gestured to her hat and gloves, which rested neatly on the table appointed for such things.

"And you are not to touch my hat or gloves, sir, unless I specifically bid you to. If you should detect so much as a smudge on the silk, then you are allowed to clean it quickly with a brush—no bleach, for that would mark you as a fool—and I expect you to under-stand that I show you great favor in permitting such a thing. Normally only my most trusted maid would be given such a task."

Mr. Camden gasped in horror, but Mari did not waver. To her distinct pleasure, the man stiffened in rigid outrage before bowing to show grudging respect.

It was gone a moment later when he walked her with achingly slow steps to the library. He quietly opened the door, announced her, then silently withdrew. She didn't hesitate but proceeded to the chair closest to Lord Rossgrove's desk, where she waited, her brow arched, for him to stand, the way any gentleman would in the presence of a lady.

He didn't stand. In fact, he remained hunched over a ledger, which he perused with the intensity of a miser over a stack of coins. It was pretense, she was sure. He was merely waiting to see if she would sit, thereby accepting his rudeness to her as if she were a servant.

She did not.

In the end, he looked up, pretended to be surprised, and pushed to his feet.

"Miss Powel, please do sit down."

"Thank you, my lord." She made sure her voice was hoarse, and she cleared her throat delicately as she sat.

Lord Rossgrove frowned. "Are you well, Miss Powel?"

"Merely a dry throat, my lord. London can be so dusty." By saying this, she pointed out that his butler had not served her tea, and he heard the underlying criticism clearly.

"Didn't Fletcher serve you? Bother the man." Lord Rossgrove grabbed a bell and rang it in a loud clang. The butler appeared before the sound stopped echoing.

"My lord?"

"Bring Miss Powel some tea," he said. "And be quick about it."

Fletcher, poor man, forgot himself so much as to

drop his mouth open in shock. But he recovered and quickly withdrew.

Excellent. It appeared that the trappings of power were working for her. So she settled into a relaxed position and smiled blandly at Lord Rossgrove, doing her best to imitate Lady Eleanor in body, speech, and attitude. At the moment, Eleanor would wait for the gentleman to take control of the conversation, and then she might or might not deign to respond.

Meanwhile, Lord Rossgrove mirrored her relaxed position and extended it, going so far as to let his head loll against the wing of his enormous desk chair. He was a tall gentleman with graying hair and large teeth, but his dress and attitude were restrained. Odd that so severe a man would have so wild a nephew, but young men didn't always follow the examples of their elders.

"I can see why Mr. Camden favors you," he said finally, his voice slow and his lips pinched tight.

Mari had no idea how to respond to that, so she said nothing, merely arching her brow and tilting her head slightly as if she were listening intently to him or perhaps a bird twittering outside. It was a favorite pose of Lady Eleanor's. It worked beautifully, because Lord Rossgrove stumbled back into speech.

"You're above average pretty, know how to keep your tongue, and it appears you've surprised my butler. That's rare indeed."

Again she made no response, but it didn't work as well this time. His expression tightened, and his next words came out like the snap of a whip.

"Most ladies would be thankful for the compliment."

Power, she reminded herself. Pretend to the

Queen's own power. Or at least Lady Eleanor's. "Compliment?" she said sweetly. "My apologies. It sounded more like a list of attributes, such as I might note the color of your furnishings or the large numbers in your ledger."

He looked down as if surprised to see the tallies open before him. Then he smoothly closed the book. If he'd snapped it shut, she would have thought—possibly—it had been a mistake to leave them where she might see them. But the way he moved was too calculated a gesture. Which meant he had intended her to be impressed by the figures there.

She wasn't. After all, her father had equally grand numbers in his account book. So she smiled blandly at him and waited for tea. And again, he was the one who spoke.

"It was gauche of me to allow you to see that, but now that you have, let me be blunt. I am a wealthy man of great influence." He preened a bit at that, and she knew that Lord Whitly had pegged him exactly. He gloried in his power and the wealth that brought him more power. "I believe I should like to exert myself on Mr. Camden's behalf."

"I'm sure he will be most grateful."

"He ought to be." Then the man smiled at her, though the expression never touched his eyes. "How grateful are you?"

She arched a brow. She was becoming quite good at Lady Eleanor's expressions. "Why would I be grateful for consideration shown to Mr. Camden? There is no connection between us, no reason that his fortunes will affect mine one way or another."

Lord Rossgrove was surprised by that. "There is no understanding between you two?"

"No, my lord."

"Then why are you here?" Now the man began to show his true colors. He was irritated with her, but no more than she was with him.

"I am here," she said tartly, "because you invited me, and I was curious. Plus, I believe your political interests and Mr. Camden's are aligned. He seemed to wish this meeting, and because I bear him good will, I agreed to call upon you this day." Then she unfolded her hands and waved vaguely in his direction. "Was there some reason you wished to speak with me?"

He opened his mouth to respond, but at that moment, there was a quiet knock at the door. Fletcher, she assumed, with the tea tray.

Lord Rossgrove grimaced then grabbed his bell, ringing it with a loud clang. How obnoxious. He could simply have said enter, but he had to ring that thing as if it he were calling in sheep to their pen.

The door opened, and Fletcher stepped ponderously inside with a tray. He moved slowly to the table and set the thing down with the stiff airs of an octogenarian.

"Oh, be done with it, man," snapped Lord Rossgrove, clearly out of temper.

Fletcher straightened in shock. It took him a moment to recover—slightly longer this time than before—but then bowed and departed with alacrity. Meanwhile, Mari began to see the appeal of obnoxious butlers. One had a great deal of fun discomfiting them.

She waited until the doors shut before reaching for the tea service. "Shall I pour?"

She was assuming the role of hostess, much as Lady
Eleanor had done at Mari's home. Lord Rossgrove
nodded, his eyes narrowed as he clearly revised his
opinion of her. For the better, she hoped.

"Cream, my lord?"

"Sugar only," he answered. "One spoonful."

She served him, then herself. And she allowed only
the tiniest portion to wet her lips. After all, she wasn't
thirsty. The tea had been a statement, not a need. So
they sipped, looking at each other over the rims of the
delicate cups. Then Lord Rossgrove spoke, his words
casual as he caught her completely by surprise.

"Tell me of Lord Whitly. What do you make of him?"

"What?" Damnation, why would the mention of
his name seize up her belly and set her heart to a frenzy
inside her chest?

"Lord Whitly. He's shown you marked attention,
waltzing and the like. You have some silly wager
going about a bird. And I understand he threw you
off your horse."

Gossip. Was her every action to be forever bandied
about? "Lord Whitly is…" She couldn't bring herself
to say *friend*. "Someone I've known for many years.
He's recently returned from India and—"

"Presumably is a suitor for your hand. Will you
choose him over Camden? He's got the title and
the blunt that Camden lacks." He leaned forward,
pressing his advantage while she was still ridiculously
aflutter. "What do you see in Mr. Camden that is
missing in Whitly?"

A purpose. A direction. A damned goal that she
could support. But she couldn't say those things. Her

choice in husband was none of his business, so she resorted to Eleanor's tactic. She pushed to her feet, forcing him to scramble to his.

"Thank you for inviting me, Lord Rossgrove. This has certainly been an enlightening visit. I hope you—"

"I won't do it," Rossgrove interrupted.

"What?"

"I won't put my money behind Camden without you."

"Whyever not?"

"Because you're the making of him. Can't imagine what's taking the fool so long to tie your fortune to him."

Well, that answer was clear. Because she hadn't allowed herself to be bold and powerful before. She'd spent all her time quietly nudging when she should have been shoving. Or demanding. How lowering to realize that her nemesis was right. Without Whitly's advice, she'd have been a quiet mouse of a woman without power or notice from anyone.

Well, if she was to own her new power, she had best learn to use it. So she lifted her chin.

"How disappointing," she drawled. "I had thought you smarter than that, Lord Rossgrove."

His brows snapped together. "What?"

"Mr. Camden is whip-smart and loyal. Two things you desperately need. Your political ambitions align, and he'll never betray you. If he has a failing, it's that he won't see your faults until it's too late for you both."

Rossgrove arched a brow. "Presumably something that won't be a problem if you are at his side."

She nodded slowly. "Very true. But you would be a fool to let him slip away, with or without me."

He snorted, dismissing everything she said with the brutish sound. "I expect to hear of your engagement within the week." His eyes narrowed. "Bring him up to scratch, Miss Powel."

As if she hadn't been trying! But she was insulted by the order, and so her tongue got the better of her. "Or what, my lord? You will put your insensate nephew in the seat? Perhaps you favor a farmer, who will be ignored by everyone and make you a laughingstock? You have no power to command me, Lord Rossgrove."

It was the wrong thing to say. Never dismiss the power of a man who hoards it like gold. She knew that, but her tongue had gone beyond her, and so he slapped her in the most civilized way he knew how.

"I can see your wayward temper has gotten the better of you. It must be your Welsh blood that makes you unsuitable. No wonder you haven't gotten married yet."

The words were deliberate, the dismissal infuriating. How could he know the exact words to cut her to the quick? It was all she could do to keep from bursting into tears. Not one minute before, he'd been praising her as the making of Mr. Camden. Then she allowed her temper loose, and he dismissed her as a Wayward Welsh. Worse, he was waving her away as he sat down to his ledger with those grand numbers in neat little columns. Then he finished it with a final cold statement.

"Tell Mr. Camden that I shall be looking elsewhere for a candidate."

Bloody hell. She'd mucked it up completely, and now Mr. Camden would bear the brunt of her ill temper. This appointment would have been the making of him, and she'd destroyed his every chance. But far from spurring her to apology, she tossed aside everything and let her anger boil over. "I shall tell him that a fool and his money are soon parted. Your greatest wealth is your family and friends, and yet your nephew is wild, your son won't remain in the same vicinity as you, and your cronies are fast disappearing. You are waning, Lord Rossgrove, and since your friends and family are gone, your gold will soon disappear as well." She shook her head. "You have failed this interview, my lord. I wish you well, but I doubt it will come to pass." And with that, she opened the door herself and sailed out straight past the shocked Fletcher.

Mr. Camden had been sitting at the bench, worrying his hat into a frayed state. He jumped to his feet when he saw her, and his eyes widened. "Miss Powel?" he asked, his voice a high squeak.

She bit her lip and shook her head. She'd harmed him. She'd destroyed his chances with Lord Rossgrove, and she didn't know what she could say to fix that. In the end, she just squeezed his hand.

"I'm sorry," she whispered. "I tried very hard. I really did, but…"

She watched Mr. Camden's face pale. His skin blanched white, and his eyes shone bright. But only for a moment, then the look was gone. He grabbed their things from the side table and wordlessly held open the door.

"You might be able to fix things," she offered softly. Then honesty forced her to say the truth. "I don't know how, though. Not with me as your bride."

He shook his head. "Never mind that now. There are other patrons, other seats in Commons. Come let us walk in this fine weather. Your maid can take the carriage home."

He was being nice to her when she'd just destroyed his future. "You are very kind, Mr. Camden."

"Not at all, Miss Powel. Not at all." He took her hand, placed it on his arm, and they began walking away. They were barely down the first step when Fletcher closed the door with a ponderous thud. Mari tried not to mind. She was busy looking at a lovely white cloud in the sky as pointed out by Mr. Camden. He said it looked like a bird.

She tried to see it. She truly did. She told him emphatically that it was a magnificent cloud bird, but in truth, she felt too miserable to see anything but a dark, hulking cloud.

# Thirteen

"WINNER! WINNER!"

"Shut up, you bloody bird," Peter groused. But then when the creature tilted its head and appeared confused, Peter relented and fed him a bit of carrot.

"Winner, winner," Greenie confirmed, and Peter sighed.

It had never occurred to him that he'd fail to win his choice of bride. Naturally, when he was in India, he had worried that Miss Powel would marry someone else, but at the time he had more pressing concerns. But now that he was home and she unwed, he had never expected that she would be reluctant. Worse, that she would still think so little of him.

What is your plan?

Bloody hell, just because a man didn't bellow his thoughts far and wide didn't mean he wasn't thinking of them. Or working toward that end. In truth, *she* was critical to his plan, and she was proving to be quite difficult.

Besides, he got the distinct feeling she was simply putting up obstacles out of obstinacy. Which meant that no matter what he said to her, she would find some objection. He knew the root of the problem. She had been told from the cradle that the only way a woman could succeed was to be caged in, restrained, and hampered. She was so used to others putting obstacles in her way, she didn't realize it had become a habit for herself as well.

That, of course, was the real reason she'd remained unwed. Between her father's vigilance and her own misunderstanding of what she really needed, she was left setting boulders all around herself. Few men would brave such a thing. But then few men knew exactly what fire lay behind all those barriers. He had kissed her. He knew.

But he was getting damned tired of boulders.

Which led to his current question and the source of his ill temper with Greenie. Was Miss Powel worth the effort he was investing in wooing her? Ash was right that he hadn't looked around at the current crop of bride-hopefuls. Surely any number of them would be an eager substitute for Miss Powel.

Except he didn't want anyone else. They all seemed pale to him. Less vibrant, less interesting, less everything than Miss Powel. Which was ridiculous, he knew, and yet he couldn't shake the feeling.

Logic told him to start looking for someone else. Emotion told him to stay the course, because Miss Powel would eventually realize that there was more to life than endless rules and restrictions.

"Winner, winner!"

He sighed and fed Greenie another bit of carrot. As a winner, he knew that when one direction was blocked, he had to move around the obstacle, adjust his thinking, or even change his target to something else. He was a man of reason, damn it, and he would not be swayed by emotion. As important as Miss Powel was to his ultimate goal, she wasn't indispensable. Another woman could grace his bed, wear his title, and give him children he'd love.

Which meant he would give her up, he decided, and his heart sank to his gut and soured his mood.

"Happy sodding day!" the bird squawked, and immediately, Peter's attention sharpened.

How perfect that the moment he decided to give up Miss Powel, fate brought her to him. She was behind him right now, presumably come for her time to train the bird. Well then, perhaps he should win her favor in some small way.

"No, no, Greenie," he said. "Happy day. You're supposed to say 'happy day.'"

He heard her soft exhale. "Do not think me so easily gulled, my lord," she said. "You have not been teaching that bird my phrase. You did it just because you knew I was at the door."

He smiled. He knew she was smart. That was one of the reasons he liked her so well. "True," he commented, "but I thought to help you get your hour with Greenie started."

Then he turned around, and immediately his expression darkened. She was standing beside Lady Illston's butler, and everything about her screamed repressed. Her hair was pulled back until her eyebrows neared her hairline, and her dress was the most boring beige he'd ever seen. That was bad enough, but when he looked at her amber eyes, expecting that sparkle of animation he'd come to love, he saw red rims and a flatness that had him cursing under his breath.

"What happened?" he asked, his voice low and threatening.

She pulled up short, and her gaze flicked to his. "My lord?"

He glanced at the butler and made a tiny gesture with his chin. The man bowed himself out, closing the door behind him, which required Miss Powel to step farther into the room. Peter went to her side immediately, reaching for her hands, which he lifted into his. She barely resisted him, and he grew even more alarmed.

"I insist, Miss Powel. Something dreadful has occurred, and I must know what it is."

She shook her head, and a telltale sheen of tears glossed her eyes. "It is not something to concern yourself with. I've just done something terribly stupid, and someone else has paid the price. I feel quite angry with myself and…" She shrugged. "Well, there is nothing to be done but to learn from my mistake and beg pardon." She looked away. "And to wish I would learn once and for all."

He drew her deeper into the room and pulled out a chair for her. She sat down across from Greenie, who greeted her in the usual way.

"Happy sodding day."

Miss Powel cast a dark look at the bird then held up a bit of apple. "Happy day," she said with emphasis. If ever a phrase did not fit the tone, that was the one. Nevertheless, she fed the bird some apple while Peter studied her listless expression.

"What happened?" he said softly. "I will not stop pestering you until I know all."

She did not look at him, but spent her time staring at Greenie. Peter saw the classic lines of her profile, the uplift of her nose at the very tip, and the oblong shape to her ear. Her skin was porcelain clear, but the freckles intrigued him more. The slightest dots, mostly along her nose. And a mole just short of her hairline, exposed only because her locks were drawn back so harshly.

"Miss Powel…" he began, then he touched her cheek. He knew she longed for someone to caress her. "Mari, please tell me."

She swallowed, and when he feared she'd pull away, she pressed her forehead against his stroke. A moment, nothing more. That was progress, but also a sign of how deeply distressed she was.

"Do you know why I have hated you for six years?" she asked, her voice low.

"Because you thought I was responsible for your lack of suitors?"

"Because you accurately named the flaw in my character." She looked to him, and the amber in her eyes was very clear. Bright brown ignited by emotions. "I am wayward. I long to laugh out loud, to dance wildly, and I say things, my lord. Oh, you have no idea the things I want to say that I hold back. And sometimes, no matter how hard I try, I say them anyway."

"What did you say?" He could tell she did not want to admit her words to him; she was that deeply ashamed. But again he touched her cheek, using what she most needed to encourage the confidence. "You cannot think I will condemn you."

She snorted, then pressed a hand to her mouth. "Of course you will. I condemn myself."

He gently drew her hand away from her face and lifted it to his lips. "I swear to stand your friend."

She looked into his eyes, and he held his breath. Everything between them hung poised in the balance. If she could not talk to him when they were in private, when she was so clearly distressed, then there would be no honesty between them ever. So he held her gaze and prayed that she could find it in herself to trust him.

"I was unspeakably rude to Lord Rossgrove," she said. The words were quiet but reverberated with dismay. "He was to stand patron to Mr. Camden, and I thought to be bold and powerful." She looked up at him. "You told me that. He values power, so I…"

"You *are* powerful, Mari. Just not in a way he respects."

"I called him a fool who would soon be parted from his money. I told him his children couldn't stand him and his friends had abandoned him. I told him he was waning, and now he will not help Mr. Camden." Her eyes swam with tears. "I could bear it if it were just me who suffered. Heaven knows I have done stupid things in my life, but this was Mr. Camden's future. He had a chance at that seat, and he would be diligent in his efforts in the House of Commons. He is a good man, and I have ruined everything for him merely because I could not hold my tongue."

The tears were trembling at the edge of her lashes. He'd watched them form and hold there. Even in this, she could not allow herself to break free. So he knelt before her and brushed his thumb across them, smearing the wetness across her cheeks.

"Lord Rossgrove is an ass."

She snorted softly, and he counted that a victory. "I cannot tell every ass exactly what they are. Not if I want them to help me."

But it wasn't help for herself that she'd been looking for. She'd been trying to help that annoying sapskull Camden. He couldn't fault her heart, even if he damned her choice of men.

Meanwhile, he tried to stroke his fingers into her hair, but the pins had pulled everything hard to her head. With a muttered curse, he started tugging them out. He couldn't stand it when she tied herself down like this.

"What are you doing?" she gasped.

"You have restrained everything to punish yourself, and I will not abide it. Rossgrove is an ass who deserved every word you said. Probably more."

She gave him a wan smile. "Much more, but we needed him."

"There are other patrons."

"No—"

"Hush." He pressed his fingers to her lips. "Listen to me."

She quieted, and he took the opportunity to release all of her pins and fluff out her hair. She let her head drop back, her mouth parted on a sigh of delight, so he took the time to knead her scalp. He rubbed her in his own clumsy way and then felt his groin tighten painfully when she released a low moan.

"You have such large, wonderful hands," she

murmured. Then she abruptly straightened up. "Good God, there I go again."

He pulled her hands down and held them still with one hand. He wasn't going to let her cover her words. "I enjoy your thoughts immensely. I dislike it when you wear ugly colors and pull your hair back like that. And I hate that you tie back the best part of yourself."

"My hair?"

"Your everything." He held her hands in her lap, but that didn't stop her from shaking her head.

"I speak without restraint, and Mr. Camden loses his patron."

"Lord Rossgrove would be a nightmare of a patron."

"I said something stupid in India as a child and cost my father a great deal of money."

"Your father should not have let a child know important things."

"He didn't. I snooped." She bit her lip, and he felt a surge of lust at those even white teeth on the dark pink of her lips.

His eyes widened. "Do you know all your father's secret places, then? Where he hides his important things?"

She nodded, clearly pleased with herself. "I even know where the secret ledger is, the one with the most important numbers written in his own sloppy hand."

He frowned. "You have been in his offices that much?"

She grinned. "He doesn't keep it there. It's not even in the library at home, but in his bedroom underneath the chair he sits in when he reads. He pulls it out at night when he can't sleep."

He released a slow whistle of admiration. "Clever girl."

"Bored girl." She sighed. "Wayward girl."

"Shall I tell you a secret?" he whispered. "Being wayward is not a flaw. Some might even say it was attractive. Mesmerizing." The last word came out on a sigh.

They were eye to eye now, with him drawing closer by the second. She didn't pull back. Indeed, she didn't do anything but look into his eyes and part her lips. It wasn't an invitation. The woman was too innocent to know what she looked like with her hair tumbled about her shoulders and her eyes liquid with emotion. But he took it as one anyway.

He cupped her face in his hands, and he tilted her to just the right angle. Then he pressed his mouth to hers, needing to taste the sweetness there.

She sighed against his lips, her breath tart with lemon. That was a surprise. It was likely from a drink she'd had recently, and he told himself he was simply exploring how deep the new taste went. He pushed his tongue between her teeth, thrusting just enough but no more. She met him there, and they played, tongue to tongue.

It was a quiet kiss. A sweet one that did not ask too much of an innocent girl. But then he lost himself to her. He felt the roar of hunger build in his blood, and his thrusts into her mouth became bolder. His hands were cupping her head, holding her to him as he plundered between her teeth.

She released a sound somewhere between a mew and a groan. Was it desire? He couldn't tell, not with his heart pounding in his ears and her hands clutching him.

She was holding onto him, he realized. Gripping his shoulders and pulling herself closer. Yes, that was permission. So he let his hands shift. He abandoned her hair to cup her shoulders, to slide down her arms, and then he molded her breast between his fingers.

She gasped against him, pulling back with her eyes wide. She didn't need to speak. He knew the sight of a startled virgin. But he also saw hunger in her eyes and a need that echoed his own.

"There is pleasure in being wayward," he rasped. "I can show you."

She shook her head. "I shouldn't."

Not quite a denial.

"I won't take your virginity. No one else will know."

He saw the struggle in her eyes. Passion against prudence. He dropped his forehead to hers.

"What I show you can be done alone too," he said. "Something to pleasure yourself when no one else is looking." He tilted her chin up. "Do you know about this thing? Has your mother never told you?"

She shook her head. "But my sister..." She bit her lips.

The Wild One. "Does she know?"

"She said it's wonderful."

"But she didn't tell you how?"

"No."

"Shall I show you?"

She glanced to the closed doorway, and he answered her unspoken question.

"Lady Illston is away on calls. We are entirely private here."

"But the servants—"

"Will stay away. I promise."

She shook her head. "You cannot know that."

"I do know that."

"How?"

He shifted his hand, letting his thumb roll over her breast where the nipple would be beneath corset and shift. It was a small thing, done light enough that she might not even feel it. Except he watched her lips part on a gasp and knew that she was as excited as he. And while she was distracted, he made his confession.

"I bribed the butler to keep away. He will be sure of the rest of the staff."

Her eyes widened. "You what? When?"

"Weeks ago. And every time I think you might be here with me."

She shook her head, clearly surprised by his foresight. "But why, when…" Her voice trailed away. It took him a moment to understand what she hadn't said. To realize that what he valued most was the very thing she decried.

"I'm fascinated by wayward," he said honestly.

Then he pulled her to her feet. She was pliable in his arms, loose-limbed despite her hesitancy. He tugged her close, letting himself feel the fullness of her breasts against his chest, the sweet scent of her hair, and the heat of her breath against his neck.

"Do you trust me?" he asked. "I swear I will not cause you any harm. No one will know."

"I will know," she answered.

"That is the best part."

He felt her smile against his neck, and again, he took that as consent. He was pushing the bounds of propriety, but he knew to the depths of his soul how desperately she needed the touch of another person. Someone who cared for her. Someone who could show her that wildness didn't have to cost anything.

He gently urged her to lean back against the table. It was high enough that it would brace her perfectly, if she allowed it. Then with a quiet prayer that she remain, he moved quickly to the door and twisted the key in the lock, just to be sure they would not be interrupted. Then he returned to her.

"You are a beautiful woman," he said as he stroked across her cheeks and admired the sweet openness of her face. "It destroys me to know you hate the best part of yourself."

Her lips tilted up. "The part that forgets to guard her tongue? Who insults wealthy, powerful men?"

He smiled. "Exactly so." He kissed her again. Slow and sweet, letting her get used to the taste of him while he reveled in the sweetness of her. And soon she was gripping his shoulders, pulling herself toward him.

He broke the kiss. His breath was short, but hers was stuttering, lifting her breasts in tiny jerks as she struggled to restrain the feelings coursing through her.

"Let yourself feel everything," he said. Then he took her hands and guided them to the table. He wrapped her fingers around the edge and squeezed slightly, so she knew to hold on. "Don't do anything but feel."

Then he began to rain tiny kisses all over her. Her cheeks, her neck, the curve of her shoulder. He felt her shudder beneath his lips, and when she moaned softly, he fought to keep himself from taking her in the most primal way.

It took a moment for him to control himself. Long enough for her to focus on him, a question in her eyes. He held her gaze and answered.

"I will stop if you want. Just say the word." He began to stroke her legs. Hard muscles, long flanks, trim calves as he gently stroked her skirt up. "Do you know how your body can feel? Or have you been so busy fighting yourself that you never even allowed yourself to ask?"

She bit her lip, telling him her answer. She had spent six years—probably many more—fighting her nature. He nuzzled his head down to her neck, grazing her flesh with his teeth before biting softly. Just a pinch before soothing it with his tongue.

"Jo told me of such things," she murmured. "But I didn't understand it."

"And you want to know."

"Yes."

He wondered if this was part of her drive to get married, even to someone as far beneath her as Mr. Camden. Did she hope finally to express her passions in her marriage bed? Oh, he prayed so.

And while his balls tightened high and hard, he slipped his fingers beneath her skirt. How many times had he imagined just this event? The sweet length of her legs, her parted lips, the tight buds of her nipples barely noticeable beneath her gown.

"Close your eyes," he urged. Her lids flickered closed, and he leaned forward to kiss her as a reward, though whether it was for her or him he didn't know. And as he moved, his hands naturally slid up her legs.

She was wearing stockings. Practical cotton, and at

the top, a ribbon tied tight enough it cut into her leg. Smooth fabric, hot woman quivering as he touched her, and then he tugged the ribbon tie undone.

"This is very wicked," she murmured.

Her eyes were open again. And below her waist, her legs were tightening. So he stopped his progress, gently caressing. He flashed a dark grin. "I mean to show you that wayward can be very good. Did you want me to stop?" She had to agree, or it would not work. "Mari," he said gently, "tell me what you feel."

She licked her lips, the pink dart of her tongue making his cock surge, but he held himself still. "I feel hot," she said. "I cannot catch my breath."

He waited, knowing there was more but needing her to find the words.

"My...chest is full and..." She swallowed. "And tight."

"Your breasts, you mean." His gaze went to the full, lush mounds.

"Y-yes."

"And here," he said, squeezing her thigh slightly. "What do you feel here?"

She opened her mouth to answer, but then shook her head.

"Are you wet?" he coaxed.

She nodded.

"That is very good. Do you know how the act is done?"

Again she nodded. "But you said—"

"I won't take your virginity, Mari. I swore that to you."

"Yes," she said, as if reassuring herself.

"But there is a pleasure that can be had without that." Again he squeezed, daring to creep his hands higher. A bit more. An inch. Then he held still. "Say you want this, Mari. You have to tell me that you—"

"Yes. Please…" She swallowed. "Please show me."

He wanted to crow aloud in pure masculine pride, but he held it in check. He would not startle her. And while he waited, her thighs relaxed, and he slid up the last inch. He felt her curls against the tip of his fingers. She jolted when he connected, but then quickly stilled. Her buttocks were tight, lifting her high, but not away from him. Not if he kept still and waited for her.

A moment.

A bit.

She eased back down, and this time her legs were spread a little farther. Enough for him to crook a finger and slide between her petals. She gasped, and her eyelids fluttered.

"How does that feel?"

"So…so…" She opened her eyes, and there was humor lighting the amber depths. "Wild."

He grinned in response. Then he held her gaze, locking his eyes with hers as his fingers began to play. Strokes, pushes, swirls. He learned the curve and the wetness of her. The plump center and the welcoming depths. And while her eyes became dazed and her mouth opened on a slight gasp, he reminded himself that he could not take her. It was immoral. He would lose her forever. Then those words fell away.

Nothing held his attention as she did. Her moan as he pushed against her clit. Her gasp as he penetrated her with two fingers. Or her cry as he began to speed up his pace. Tighter. Harder. He pushed against her bud while her skin flushed and her eyes grew wide. She thrust against him as he pushed a third finger inside her. And when he drew his thumb up, long and slow against her nub, she keened with hunger.

He knew when she was close. Her breath became nothing but a hitch, and she arched up to his hand while her legs spread wide for his plunder. Then her belly went rigid, and he knew he had no more time.

Abruptly, he straightened while still keeping her aroused. With his free hand he pulled her sideways then caught her, so she fell into the crook of his arm while his mouth slammed down on hers. Her arms had flown up in surprise, gripping his shoulders while he pushed hard against her nub. Quick circles, faster. Tighter. Harder.

Detonation.

Her body went wild, and he caught her scream in his mouth.

Amazing.

He kept her riding that excitement as long as he could. He held her while she bucked in his arms, and then waited until she eased before stroking her again. He let her feel the bliss forever while he kept her cries of delight to himself. And he thanked God in Heaven that she had gifted him with her first experience. God, how beautiful she was. And how perfect he wanted this to be for her.

But it could not last forever. In time, she jerked her hips away from him. Too much, he realized. And so he slowly took his hand from between her thighs.

When she released a tremulous laugh into his mouth, he knew it was safe to rise up from her lips. He still lingered, nipping along the edges of her mouth, pressing tiny kisses along her cheek, and then simply holding her, his lips pressed to her temple.

He could spend an age like this and be content. She was languid in his arms. His body clamored to possess her, but he would not disturb her lingering pleasure.

With that thought in mind, he looked up at the mantel clock. Hell, Mari's hour with Greenie was almost up. Which meant the butler would be returning soon. The man was honor bound to prevent her from staying beyond the allotted time.

Peter had to get her presentable soon. He looked back down to her face, seeing the light catch her amber eyes, making them warm with sun even as she blinked herself back to awareness.

"You should allow yourself to be wayward more often, Mari," he said.

She smiled and spoke in teasing accents. "I have not given you leave to use my Christian name, Lord Whitly."

"I am taking that leave." He pressed a kiss to the tip of her nose. "But only in private."

"I suppose I am wayward enough to allow it." Then she stirred. Their embrace was done, and so he helped her to stand, though she still leaned heavily against the table. Her legs were weak, but she put strength into them quickly. Too quickly, in his mind. He would rather lift her into his arms and carry her to bed.

Instead, he took a wicked pleasure in watching her fingers fumble as she retied her stocking. He couldn't stop himself from caressing the length of her thigh, though she blushed furiously at his boldness and quickly dropped her skirt back down. Much too soon her dress was back in order. He flatly refused to allow her to return to her severe hairstyle, so he secreted half her pins in his pocket. He mourned even the few locks she pressed in place with the remaining pins. Then he looked at the mantel clock and knew he had to leave.

"I will slip out without the butler noticing. You remain with Greenie until the butler comes to retrieve you."

"How can you go without someone seeing?"

"I can do it," he said. There were any number of ways to slip through a household unseen. Then he touched her cheek. "Pull at your hair while you are trying to train Greenie. That will explain your lack of pins."

"I need those back, you know," she said. "I'll be a ragged mess in the first wind."

"I would buy all the pins in England if I could keep your hair tumbling about your ears."

"That would make for a very untidy England."

He looked at her then as she smoothed down more unruly curls. She had such fire inside her, if only she would let it out. The lure of tempting her to wild abandon had hooked deep into his soul, and he knew he would continue to poke at her until he had seduced her completely.

With or without marriage, he would have her. It was a sobering thought to a man who believed himself a moral creature. Then that knowledge brought something deeper and darker to his mind.

If he could not stop himself, if nothing would prevent him from exposing her every wayward desire, then he had to tell her all. About himself. If she were exposed, then he would need to be as well. Not just the pieces he'd meant to show her tonight. Not the half measures meant to placate her, but *everything*.

That was hard. That was a terrifying thing, but he would do it if it meant winning her to his side.

"Tomorrow night," he rasped before he could change his mind. "I cannot manage it tonight, but tomorrow. I will find you at the ball. Bring a dark cloak if you have one."

Her eyes widened, and she nodded. No hesitation, no regret, just a solemn trust that he would keep her safe. Which was all the more damning, because he knew he was the rake here. His every intention was to seduce her to his side.

# Fourteen

MARI WATCHED PETER SLIP OUT OF THE ROOM. SHE hadn't been given leave to use his Christian name, but in her thoughts he would forever be Peter.

Peter the handsome.

Peter the strong.

Peter the man who showed her why every woman worked so feverishly to get married.

It was for that feeling. For that explosion of pleasure. For that amazing experience of joy that sang through her heart and mind long after he'd left.

"Greenie," she whispered, "I didn't know. Heavens, why didn't I know?"

"Happy sodding day!" the bird chirped, and Mari was so happy she didn't even remonstrate with the creature. But she didn't feed the bird either.

"Happy day," she said firmly as she held up the bit of apple. "Oh, Greenie, it is such a happy day." Then she fed it to him.

She remained in that state of bliss for a minute more. Maybe as many as two, but before long, doubts began to creep in. Had it truly felt as wonderful as she remembered?

Her belly still quivered when she thought of it. Her breasts were heavy, and the memory of his face as he whispered that she was safe—well, that set her to wetting her lips and wondering when she could be wayward with him again.

"Happy day," she said as she fed Greenie a bit of apple. "Happy day."

Then her gaze happened to land on her reticule. Inside it was her neat list of requirements in a husband. She certainly had an item to add now, didn't she? Though God only knew how she'd phrase it.

Waywardness in bed?

Waywardness in the afternoon?

Waywardness often.

She giggled and fed Greenie another bit of apple without remembering to speak the phrase. It was some moments later when she thought of something else. Something that horrified her down to her toes.

What if waywardness wasn't always this much fun? What if it only occurred with certain gentlemen?

How horrible to be trapped for the rest of your life doing that with a man who didn't make it wonderful. She now knew how amazing it could be, but what if Mr. Camden, for example, made it dull? She might be an unmarried virgin, but she'd overheard enough to know that men weren't always good in bed.

She shuddered in horror. Worse, the more she thought of it, the more frightened she became. Mr. Camden didn't like her being wayward. He'd remonstrated with her on that very thing any number of times. What if he made this thing as restricted and sedate as he liked everything else?

But that made no sense. The very nature of what they'd done was to be unrestrained. She couldn't imagine doing it while still being tied into a corset and with her hair gripped into a fist-like bun. That would be horrible.

She had to know. She couldn't possibly marry a man who didn't enjoy this.

The mantel clock chimed the hour, but instead of looking at it, her gaze went to the table and the place where her fingers had gripped the wood. Her face heated, and her legs shifted with a secret thrill. What a difference a single hour had made. Now she had a whole new requirement in a husband, and nothing would satisfy her but to know if Mr. Camden could make her feel like that as well. She didn't even know if the gentleman still wished to marry her, but she could not have an answer for him until she'd learned the truth of this.

So it was that when Lady Illston's butler knocked quietly on the door, she was already reaching for her reticule. A moment later, she'd collected her maid and climbed into her carriage. How easy it was to be wicked, she realized. Here she had just had the most scandalous experience imaginable as an unwed woman, and yet she had adhered to the proprieties. Or at least the appearance of them. And better yet, with her maid in the carriage with her, she had someone here to help her adjust her hair to a less flyaway style.

The trip through London was tedious as always, but it was necessary. Indeed, the urgency to answer her question was building to the point that she feared she would do something extremely improper. But she couldn't seem to stop herself. So when the carriage stopped in front of Mr. Camden's office building, she went in with her head held high.

It wasn't proper for her to be here. Ladies, especially unwed ones, didn't enter such places of business, even with a maid in tow. She did it anyway and barely even blinked at the shocked expressions of the men toiling in wretched darkness at their desks. At least her father's place of business let the secretaries sit by windows.

"Wait here," she instructed her maid. Then she turned to the nearest secretary and spoke with an imperious accent. "Please show me to Mr. Camden's office."

"Er, um, is Mr. Camden expecting you?"

She didn't want to be mean to the man, but a certain level of boldness was required. "If he were expecting me, he would be waiting out here."

"Oh. Of course." To which the man glanced awkwardly at his fellow workers, as if to say *what should I do?* Mari didn't allow them to answer.

"Direct me to his office now."

Her tone was enough to make him leap out from behind his desk with a "Yes, miss." A few moments later, he led her to an unimposing door in a row of unimposing doors. How disappointing for Mr. Camden, she thought.

"I'll announce myself," she said before her escort could knock. "Good day, sir."

He flushed at being so clearly dismissed. Meanwhile, she turned her back on him, rapped loudly on the door, and turned the knob.

She sailed through the room as if she had a right to enter like this, only to be stopped short at the cluttered disaster that was this tiny space. Books, papers, and ink bottles choked every surface. Or at least what she could see from the fitful light that made it through the very dirty window. And in the middle of it all, behind a small desk, sat Mr. Camden, hunched in obvious misery, one hand wrapped around a bottle of gin.

"I said no one—" His words cut off as his red-rimmed eyes caught sight of her. "Miss Powel?"

"Oh goodness." She glanced behind her. Yes, the secretary was still standing there, his mouth even more gaping than before. "I believe you have work to occupy yourself?" she said tartly.

The man flushed a dark red. She shut the door on him. Then she turned to face Mr. Camden, who was scrambling to his feet, knocking over a stack of papers as he did so.

"Bloody hell," he cursed, then cursed again as he tripped over another stack. He righted himself quickly enough, though his expression was particularly florid, before giving her a critical frown. "Ladies do not visit a gentleman's place of business."

"Gentlemen do not become gin-soaked in their offices in the middle of the afternoon," she responded.

He pushed out his lower lip and managed to look like a particularly stubborn boy. "What a man does is his own affair."

She was about to say something churlish in response, but she held her tongue. Obviously the man was a great deal more upset by Lord Rossgrove's defection than he'd let on before. In one light, it might seem almost chivalrous that he'd pretended not to care that she'd mucked up his chances. Now, of course, she saw that he was deeply affected and it was all her fault.

Given that, she was predisposed to forgive him an afternoon's inebriation. So she felt very warm toward Mr. Camden as she stepped carefully over a pile of books and took hold of his hands.

"I am terribly sorry about earlier today. I came to… to find out how you fared."

He opened his mouth to answer, but an especially noxious burp came out instead. He flushed crimson then covered his lips. "I beg your pardon," he muttered behind his hand.

"It's all right. I do that sometimes as well," she offered.

He reached beside him and grabbed a jug of water hidden behind a tall bookcase. He quickly poured himself a drink then swallowed the liquid in loud, steady gulps. Mari waited patiently, wondering how she could turn the conversation to where she wanted. Also, she wondered where exactly she could sit among the stacks of books. Meanwhile, Mr. Camden finished his glass, set it down with a click, and then turned to her with a compressed smile.

"That should do it," he said overly loud. "I'm fit to be seen." He straightened his waistcoat then gave her a cheerful smile. "Now, what can I do for you, Miss Powel?"

How to answer that? She reached for his hands again. She wanted him to caress her like Peter had so she could compare the two experiences. She wanted a kiss, but it would be too bold to ask for that. So instead, she smiled at him and stayed with her first lie.

"I came to see how you fared."

"I've been laid low, as you see." He gestured wanly toward the bottle of gin. "Even tea taken with my mum failed to cheer me up."

"Oh dear." She knew that tea with his mother was one of his most cherished rituals. "Was she horribly disappointed?"

"She was. She took to her smelling salts three times, I'm afraid. Seeing her set so low was what brought me back here and…" Again he gestured to the bottle. Or he might have been reaching for it and checked the motion. It was hard to tell.

"My. Three times," she echoed feebly. "But do you forgive me?" she asked. "After all, I've heard it said that Lord Rossgrove is…well, somewhat of an ass."

His eyes widened, and he drew back. "You must not say such things! Not of so great a man!"

"Oh," she said, dismay pooling in her belly. This was not going at all as she'd planned. "But surely if he doesn't see how perfect you are for his plans, if he doesn't recognize—"

"All is not lost yet." He grabbed her hand and patted it overly hard. "Never fear, he may still come around. Women say such silly things sometimes. Surely he understands not to listen. He'll realize that soon enough. I shall write him a letter tomorrow. Something that apologizes for you. Love is such an unpredictable thing, you know. Sometimes a man cannot control whom he marries."

There was her opening. There was the question she longed to answer, and she voiced it without checking her words. "So is that it, Mr. Camden?" she asked. "Do you…do you love me?"

He looked at her, his eyes widening to the point where she could see every reddened vein, even in this dim light. "Well, Miss Powel, um, I mean... I'm not one who speaks well on these things."

She blew out a breath, feeling her head start to ache. "Just a yes or no, if you please. It would make things so much clearer."

"Oh. Oh yes, I see." He paused and looked at her, obviously waiting.

She returned his stare, her own eyebrows rising in anticipation. "Mr. Camden?"

"Yes."

Her insides tightened, but not in a pleasant way. "Yes?"

He blinked. "Yes?"

Was he echoing her question or answering it? "Mr. Camden!" she cried. "I don't understand your meaning."

And then it happened, nearly as she'd hoped. He leaped forward and took her head between his hands. He wasn't as large as Lord Whitly, and his aim was off, so one of his fingers landed painfully in her ear. But the intent was the same, and that was what she focused on. Better yet, his mouth was headed toward hers, and she obediently closed her eyes in anticipation. After all, the view of the man's pointed nose was not all that appealing.

Then their mouths met.

His was wet and tasted of acid. She pulled back in shock, even though she had been the one to create the situation. But as she gasped, his tongue invaded her mouth.

Oh. Oh my. She hadn't remembered this being so

very wet before. And his tongue was forceful, nearly gagging her.

She tried to enjoy it. She really did. She did not want to think that she could only enjoy waywardness with Lord Whitly. But...oh, this was getting very slobbery.

She coughed and wrenched backward, breaking the seal of their mouths. She tried to step back, but there was little room, and he was holding her tightly, kissing a wet trail along her cheek. In her mind, she just kept thinking *No, no, no. This is not how it is supposed to go!* But he obviously couldn't hear her, and his hands now slid down her back to grip her bottom.

That was wrong, she decided, as panic began to tighten her throat. She was shoving at him now, pushing against his chest and trying to squirm away. He must have misunderstood, because he gasped out a fevered, "Miss Powel!"

Which was when she lost her temper. Thankfully, she had a brother who had taught her a few things. She was in her strong half boots, and while Mr. Camden was busy trying to angle his face back to hers, she lifted her foot and slammed it down hard onto his.

He leapt back with a howl, only to trip over a stack of books and tumble to the ground. The sound was deafening, but no louder than the rapid pound of fury in her ears.

She knew she was being irrational. She had instigated this particular encounter, but it was supposed to be pleasurable. It was not meant to leave her face slimy and a feeling of nausea in her gut.

Mr. Camden was righting himself while she busily

fished out a handkerchief from her reticule and wiped her face. Meanwhile, a sudden pounding on the door had her cursing under her breath.

"Mr. Camden! Is everything all right?" called the secretary.

She looked to Mr. Camden, who was red-faced as he pushed himself to his feet. "I'm fine," he snapped. "Just tripped over the books, is all."

"But—"

He stomped over to the doorway and wrenched it open. As Mari was still patting her hair back into place, she found this to be particularly alarming. Hopefully the young man didn't see anything. Although one look at his wide eyes had her cursing anew. Just how discomposed did she look? Was *wayward* now emblazoned across her forehead? Or perhaps it was written in her wild hair.

"Go back to work," Mr. Camden snarled in a darker voice than she'd ever heard before. Apparently it was a shock to the young man as well, who jumped as if poked. Then he nodded and scrambled away without so much as a peep.

"He will talk to his friends," she said miserably. Bad enough to be the subject of gossip among the *ton*, but it upset her to know that now she would be an object of fun among Mr. Camden's subordinates. Whatever had possessed her to think this was a good idea?

Meanwhile, Mr. Camden turned back to her, his expression tight. What he had to be angry about, she didn't know. This was all his fault. What man turned kissing into an attack by an ill-bred mastiff?

"Your hair is untidy," he said as he straightened his waistcoat.

"You made it so," she shot back as she tried to smooth the strands down. She couldn't without a brush, but she did her best.

"No," he countered, "it was messy when you first arrived. I noticed it right away."

Of course he did. "I don't like pinning it so tight. It gives me a headache."

"And I don't like wearing shirt points that stab my neck, but there are some things we do because it is appropriate."

"You're not wearing high shirt points," she said. "And that is nothing like spending the day with something trying to pull your scalp off your head."

He dropped his hands onto his hips, his expression severe. "You are discomposed, Miss Powel."

That was the final straw. The nerve of any man talking to her like a stern father when he was both a disgusting kisser and in no way affianced to her. And after weeks of careful cultivation on her part!

"And you, Mr. Camden, need not call on me ever again." Then, just to prove the point, she pulled her list of gentlemen out of her purse, flattened it on the only clear space of his desk, and with great flourish, crossed his name out.

Number 27 no more.

Then with a huff, she spun on her heel and stomped out.

# *Fifteen*

PETER GOT THE MESSAGE WHILE HE WAS STILL DRESSING for Lord and Lady Vinson's ball. He'd spent the day trying to ferret out the differences between his father's ledgers and Mr. Powel's statement that there had been only one middling payout from their joint investment. All it had gotten him was a headache. Now he was looking forward to an unencumbered evening with Mari. He was both anxious and excited to tell her the things he needed to share. And it turned out that both those emotions led to a state of arousal that was highly embarrassing in the presence of one's newly hired valet. But then his father's footman rushed into the room, and he had to redirect his thoughts.

"Mrs. Evans sent me, yer lordship," the man huffed.

Mrs. Evans was his father's cook and Peter's best ally in that household. "Really?" he said, lifting his chin so his new valet could finish off the cravat. "Whatever for?"

"Said she remembered that name you'd asked for. Her cousin's cousin's nephew, she said." The footman's expression spoke volumes about the illogic of running through London just to relay such a benign message. What it really meant was that something odd was going on at his father's household.

"Did she say more?"

"No, milord. Just that her memory being what it was, it be best if you came right away. I tried to get her to write it down, but—"

"Don't question her, man. Mrs. Evans has her own way of doing things, and neither you nor I can change that."

The footman didn't have an answer. Didn't matter. Peter let his valet finish off the cravat, and then he pulled on his coat. He'd look damned stupid riding a horse in all this finery, but a hackney would take too long. Mrs. Evans had said to come right away.

So he flipped the footman a coin as thanks and then left. He made it to his father's back door in a frustratingly slow twenty minutes. When he slipped in the kitchen door, he could see she was ready for him. The entire kitchen area was empty except for Mrs. Evans, who was just pulling a kettle off the stove and bringing it to three teacups already laid out on a tray.

"Mrs. Evans," he said warmly. Some of his happiest childhood memories were of the two of them sharing a bit of tea and a sweet. "I got your message."

"Got here faster than I expected, but your boots have suffered."

Peter looked down and sighed. He'd been quite pleased by the shine on his Hessians, but now they were mud-splattered, and somewhere he'd picked up a scuff. "Where is everyone?"

"I sent them on errands or let them dally as they want. Figured it would be best to speak to you alone."

"It's serious, then?"

She didn't answer. Instead, she picked up the tray and smiled at a third person who'd just walked in the room. "Mrs. Osborn, just in time."

The housekeeper? He barely knew her, but obviously the two women wanted a private word with him. "Good evening, Mrs. Osborn," he said with a generous dip of his head.

"Lord Whitly," she returned with a curtsy. "I thought we'd be cozier in my sitting room."

"Excellent idea," returned Mrs. Evans, as if this hadn't been planned. Then she led the way, with Mrs. Osborn holding open the door. A minute later, everyone was seated on rickety little chairs around a tiny table that was too small for the tea tray, but they made do.

"Well, this is lovely," he said by way of opening.

"It's not fancy enough for you, I'm sure," said the housekeeper. "But we enjoy a comfortable chat every now and then."

"Indeed we do," agreed Mrs. Evans.

Peter opened his mouth to comment, but the ladies went on as if he weren't there. "Why, just yesterday we were talking, weren't we? About how I found little Betsy crying her eyes out."

"Terrible thing. Seems she must have tripped in the back parlor. Was bruised something awful."

Then both women looked directly at him. Was it his turn to talk now? "Something awful?" he echoed dumbly.

"Yes. The back parlor is where your father likes to read his paper. He does it when the maids come to dust, you know. Says he likes looking at something pretty."

Oh hell. He knew his father enjoyed a little pinch and tickle with a lively maid every now and then, but he'd always done it with willing servants. It sounded as if his father had gotten more aggressive. "Just how badly was Betsy hurt?"

"Oh, not bad at all," Mrs. Osborn reassured him. "Just a bump and a scare, but she won't go in to dust again. Not with the earl there."

"No," he agreed. "No, she shouldn't. Have you mentioned this to my mother?"

"Lawks no," said Mrs. Osborn with a laugh, though the humor didn't reach her eyes. "What with her being in the country this Season, we're more like a bachelor household these days."

A bachelor household. Which meant his father was getting wilder with his mother away. Hell. "Tell me about the footmen employed here. Good men?"

"Yes, milord," both women said together.

That was something.

Then Mrs. Osborn set down her teacup with a small sigh. "But we've only the two, and they're young. Not very large, neither."

And his father was a large, imposing man. "I'll send around two more." He eyed the women. "You'll see that they're incorporated into the household?" He'd make sure they knew their job was to protect the women staff from his father. Bloody hell, this was awful.

"That would be easy as pie," Mrs. Evans said with a relieved smile.

"Is there more I should know?" he asked, his mind already slipping to Mari. He had a courtship to continue.

"Just that we had an odd visitor not more than an hour ago," Mrs. Evans said.

"Oh yes," continued Mrs. Osborn. "The boy. Comes by now and again. Can't be more than ten, dirty, and always has a message for his lordship."

"A message for my father?" He couldn't imagine the earl allowing a filthy child into his household, much less his presence.

"Yes, my lord," said Mrs. Evans, picking up the tale. "Lives near the docks, as far as I can tell. Always starving, and his eyes are going hard, if you know what I mean. But not completely. Not yet. I make sure to have some food for him, poor thing, and I've earned a bit of his trust from that."

The housekeeper poured herself some more tea. "Comes in, speaks to his lordship, and then leaves. Unless we can distract him with a bite to eat."

"Is it always the same boy?" Peter asked.

"Oh no," said Mrs. Evans.

"But he's the right boy," said Mrs. Osborn. "The right one to speak to, if you had some tarts for him. Best to catch him before he sees the earl."

"And some good stew. That boy likes my stew."

"Everyone likes your stew," said Peter, though his mind was on this child. "Do you know where he goes?"

The ladies shook their heads but then began giving him details, as if they'd just remembered them. Either way, the facts spilled out.

"His name is Tie because he's good with knots—"

"But I think it's really Tyler. And he wasn't always living like this, mind you."

"No, milord. He talked about a mum that smelled

of cherry tarts, but she was killed." Her voice changed, her accent becoming thicker, more like a dockside worker's. "She was kilt. That's how he said it."

"Terrible thing to see a boy so calm like that. She was kilt, and then he went to live with the others."

Peter frowned, his apprehension growing by the second. "What others?"

"The other boys," said Mrs. Evans, but it was the housekeeper whose gaze grew hard and her tone angry.

"And a leader. Boy calls him Silas. Don't know anything more than that."

"I do," came a male voice from outside the door.

All three of them started, but Mrs. Osborn rapidly grimaced. "Come on in, Robin. Got ears like a cat, that one."

Mrs. Evans sniffed. "Especially when he presses them against doors."

The door opened, and a young footman appeared. His eyes were a wide green, and his ears were large in his long face, but what Peter noticed most was his sheepish grin. "I know where to find Silas, milord," he said, ducking his head. "Tavern near the docks. Named the Striking Eel."

"And how do you know that?"

The footman didn't answer, but Mrs. Evans huffed out a breath. "You followed him, didn't ye? That other time. With the bigger boy."

Robin lifted his chin. "I didn't like what he said to Daisy."

A maid of all work, and apparently the boy was sweet on her. Well, he'd take what information he could. "And he's there most nights?"

"Don't know. He was that night."

"Very well," he said, pushing to his feet. "Thank you all for a very educational tea, but I've got an appointment—"

"But it's happening soon," interrupted Mrs. Evans. Peter froze. "What is?"

"Whatever they're planning!" she huffed out in an irritated voice, and Peter had the distinct impression that she would have thumped him on the forehead if he were within reach. "I'm not a woman who gossips, my lord. I been with this house since I was younger than Daisy, and it ain't right what's been going on. This is a fine family, and I won't have the maids being hurt or thieves at my table."

He slowly sat back down. "Thieves, Mrs. Evans?"

"He's grouchy as a bear until one of them boys comes around." By which Peter guessed she meant his father.

"And then he's nervous afterward, but there's a look in his eyes," added Mrs. Osborne.

"That's when he goes for the maids," added Robin. "Like he's excited and can't keep it inside."

"And then there's money to pay for new livery," said Mrs. Osborne quietly.

"And for good beef," said Mrs. Evans.

"And his tailor," added Robin.

Peter was silent. Bloody hell, he didn't want to think it of his father, but part of him wasn't surprised. The earl had certain standards, and he wasn't about to let things slip just because of a bad crop or three.

"Tonight?" he asked quietly. "You're sure—"

"Whatever's to be done has to be done quickly," pressed Mrs. Evans. The other two nodded gravely.

There was no questioning the seriousness of their expressions or the risk they were taking to tell him what they suspected. As the eldest son, it was up to him to make sure his father wasn't doing something stupid with the maids or…anything else.

This was England, for God's sake. Corruption shouldn't run rampant here. Certainly not in his own family. He sighed and grabbed a piece of paper from Mrs. Osborne's desk and hastily scrawled a note for Mari. Then he handed it to Robin.

"You will give this to Miss Mari Powel and no other." He fished out his invitation from his pocket and gave it to the footman as well. Then he looked to all three. "I owe you a great debt. You have my gratitude."

Mrs. Evans pulled out a wrapped piece of linen. "Give this to the boy. That'll calm him. Maybe get him to talk."

Cherry tarts. He'd know the smell anywhere. "If these can't, then nothing will," he said.

Mrs. Evans colored prettily. "And there's another for you to eat while you change clothes."

He looked down, belatedly realizing what he was wearing. He couldn't possibly go dockside looking like this. Not unless he wanted to get coshed on the head. Fortunately, he had exactly the right type of clothing to wear, but it would delay him even longer before heading to the Striking Eel.

"Best you go slowly there," Robin said. "Or wait for me."

Peter frowned. "How familiar are you with this tavern?"

Robin shook his head. "I'm not. But I grew up

near the docks, milord. I know a few things. That's a rough place."

Peter thought about it but decided not to risk the footman. "Just get that message to Miss Powel. I'll be careful." And armed.

Robin bowed quickly and left. Peter departed barely a minute behind him, his thoughts grim. He'd been anticipating a night of seduction, and now he'd be skulking about as if he were still in India. At least he could take comfort in the fact that Mari was safely away from the danger he'd be facing tonight.

∽

Mari's smile was becoming strained. She very much feared it looked more like a grimace of irritation rather than the welcoming smile of an unwed maiden. Even Lord Rimbury noticed, though he declined to comment beyond asking if she had the headache. But her huff of disgust after the supper buffet pushed him to a more direct question.

"Did he finally arrive?" he asked as he peered around the milling throng of guests.

No. "Whomever do you mean?" she asked, her tone sweet. Or at least trying to be sweet.

He cast her an arch look. "You've alternated between clenching your teeth at your dance partners and glaring at the doorway. It must be Peter. You only get that furious tick in your eye when he's nearby."

"But he's not nearby," she said tartly as she once again glared at the door.

"Which vexes you to no end," he said as he lifted her gloved hand to his arm. "Tell me why." It wasn't so much a command as a charming wheedle. Everything was so confusing right then, with her being wayward, and Mr. Camden being so awful. She wanted to talk to someone. She wanted to experiment. She wanted out of her damned boring gowns. This one was a smoky blue that could have been interesting if it had the tiniest bit of decoration.

But the gentleman she wanted to discuss, experiment, and undress with wasn't here. And she was hard put not to scream in frustration. Which wasn't Lord Rimbury's fault, so she smiled and started to make up some excuse. Except for all that he played the fop, the man was much too perceptive. "I'm afraid—"

"My lord, Miss Powel," came a pompous tone from their right.

They turned to find two footmen standing awkwardly beside them. The one with the pompous tone wore the livery of the household. The other wore the colors of the Earl of Sommerfield. She and Lord Rimbury exchanged a concerned look. "Is something amiss?" Lord Rimbury said.

"No, my lord," the pompous one said.

"I have a message," said the other. "For Miss Powel. His lordship said to hand it to her and only her."

That was surprising. And attracting notice. "Very well. You may give it to me."

The young man did, and she quickly ripped open the missive. It was written on coarse paper in a bold hand.

*I am unavoidably detained. I pray you will forgive me. I hope I may be allowed to call on you tomorrow.*

*—W*

She frowned as she looked up at the footman. "Is Lord Whitly well?" It wasn't appropriate to question the man, not in the middle of a ballroom, for all that most everyone was still at the supper buffet, but she couldn't stop herself. She had to know if he was all right.

"Yes, miss. He's just otherwise occupied."

Well, that didn't answer anything at all. She glanced at Lord Rimbury, who was frowning at the missive. And then he was abruptly overcome by a massive yawn.

"Oh dear Lord," he grumbled when it was done. "How gauche of me." Then he gave her a deep bow. "I fear I have been enjoying the Society rounds too much these days. London does that to me," he said with a gleeful twinkle. "I do love this city, but I think I shall take my leave."

"Of course," she said, not believing him for a second. Especially as the two footmen had withdrawn, and Lord Rimbury was sauntering after them with every appearance of casual speed.

Something was up, and Lord Rimbury was going to figure it out. Well, what was sauce for the goose was sauce for the gander. She'd already sent her mother home, claiming she'd be escorted back by one of her friends. That meant this was the perfect time to escape, before the other guests came out of the buffet room.

So while Lord Rimbury and the footmen exited, she ducked out the side door and rushed around to the front. Fortunately, it was a warm night, and she didn't need a cloak. A moment later she saw them climb into a waiting hackney. Now was her chance. Thank God her wild sister had taught her a few things.

She rushed forward as fast as her slippered feet could carry her. She wove between the trees, then dashed between two sitting carriages. And just as the hackney hit the shadows, she leaped onto the boot and let it carry her away too.

# *Sixteen*

MARI WAS CHILLED ALL THE WAY THROUGH BY THE time they reached their destination. It was a dockside pub in a dangerous part of London, and she felt fear slide through her bones. She'd never been alone like this. And though her sister had gone on adventure after adventure, Mari was usually more prudent.

But it was too late now. She was here, and for the first time ever, she was grateful for the dark blue of her gown. The quality couldn't be disguised, but the color hid her from view, especially since she'd stripped off her white gloves. She was still trying to decide what to do when the hackney doors opened. Lord Rimbury's voice came through clear as day.

"Peter's in there? Whatever for?"

"Keep your voice down," said the footman as he stepped out. "He's looking for a boy named Tie, who knows something about what the earl's doing."

"What *is* the earl doing?" Lord Rimbury asked as he disembarked. "Never mind. If you knew, we wouldn't be standing out here. Lord, it stinks." Mari couldn't help but agree. Uncoiling her frozen limbs, she jumped off the carriage while Lord Rimbury paid the driver. But then she was standing there in silk slippers and a dark blue gown, with bare arms and feeling rather stupid. Just what had she hoped to accomplish by coming along? She slipped into an alleyway, keeping her eyes and ears open for an opportunity, but all she heard was more bickering between Lord Rimbury and the footman.

"Come on. Let's go see what we can do," Rimbury said as he headed for the tavern. The footman grabbed his arm.

"You can't go in there dressed like that! We'll get knifed for sure."

Lord Rimbury looked down at himself. "As rough as that?"

"Aye," the footman responded with a thick dock accent. "I grew up nearby. I can fit in, but not in these clothes. And you'll—"

"I'll wait outside. In the shadows. You go get us clothes."

The footman was understandably confused. "But I thought we'd wait outside. Safely—"

"I'm not leaving my best friend to die unprotected. We can't go in dressed as we are, so go get us the right clothes." Then he headed to the exact same alley darkness where Mari was crouched listening. *Oh no!* Then she heard it. A babe's fretful cry. The sound came from a broken window a story up in the building that crowded the tavern. Luck was with her. She found a way inside the building quickly, then up the stairs as she skirted a gin sot sprawled in the hallway. The babe was truly upset now, and she focused on that as a woman's crooning voice tried to hush the child. A moment later she was at the door, listening hard. No man's voice.

She knocked on the door. "Please," she said through the door. "I don't mean any harm. I need help." She swallowed and pitched her voice lower. "I can pay."

She suspected that last part was what had the woman opening the door, her eyes narrowed with distrust. Goodness, she looked tired. Once she would have been a beautiful woman, but it was late at night, and she had a fretful baby squirming in her arms. Her blue eyes had heavy bags under them; her blond hair was dirty. "Wot?"

Mari smiled in her most coaxing way. "Please, it's just me. May I come in?"

The woman nodded and stepped back, only to have her eyes widen in surprise when she took in Mari's elegant clothes.

"Wot you doing out 'ere?"

"It's a long story," she said gently. "But I need to be dressed differently if I'm to leave safely."

"It'll take more'n different clothes."

Probably true, but she'd start with her dress. "I will trade you," she said. "My dress and shoes for yours. And a cloak."

It was a good bargain for the woman. She'd be able to sell the dress alone for enough food for a month. And a quick look around at the terrible condition of her flat made Mari want to give her more.

"How do you survive?" she asked quietly. "Do you have a husband? A way to get money?"

The woman nodded. "He's a sailor, but he ain't been 'ome for a while. I work down there when I can." She gestured with her chin toward the tavern. "But Rudy don't like the babe coming with me."

"No, I don't expect he would," Mari said. "Do you have anyone to help you?"

"Me mum comes 'round, but she's got troubles of her own."

Of course.

"And she's not quite as respectable as me." The woman lifted her chin. "I was married right and proper in a church. You ain't got no cause to be thinking less of me."

"I don't," Mari said hurriedly. "Not at all." But she couldn't help thinking that if this was respectable, then what of the life of ill repute? Was it better? Or infinitely worse? Meanwhile, she began to unbutton her gown. "So will you do it? Do you have clothes to trade?"

The woman nodded slowly, still wary. "Over there."

Since the woman was still holding the babe, it was left to Mari to sort through the pile. There was a cloak hanging on a peg that would serve her fine. The dresses, however, were dropped on the floor in a cluttered pile.

"What's your name?" she asked as she crouched down to find the most suitable of the bunch.

"Ellie."

"Hello, Ellie. I'm Mari." She set down her gloves then pulled out a dress that looked like the only possibility. Ellie was rail thin, and Mari would never fit into anything the woman normally wore. But there was a fuller gown there, probably worn during Ellie's pregnancy.

"May I have this?" she asked. "I'll give you my gloves and my dress." Then she saw rough shoes that would likely work. "I'd like those as well, and I'll leave you my slippers."

Ellie nodded, but her eyes were still wary. "Wot brought you 'ere?"

A dozen lies hopped to her lips, but there was no need for them. Instead, she decided to prod for information. "I'm looking for a boy named Tie. I'm told he runs in that tavern down there."

Abruptly, Ellie sidled backward. "'E's one of Silas's boys. You don't want to mess with 'im."

"Who is Silas?"

Ellie frowned at her. "'E's not a good man."

Mari took a moment to think, then she slowly pulled off her ear bobs. They were simple dark sapphires, tiny enough to match with her sedate image. She held them out to Ellie.

"Tell me everything you know."

～

Peter set down his drink and tried not to throw it against the wall in frustration. The ale here was lousy, the stench hideous, and worst of all, there was no point to being here. He understood the benefits of lying in wait, in listening to the grumbles of folk who had information he wanted. He knew he had to wait here for Silas or Tie or someone who knew something that would help him figure out what his father was up to. But so far, he hadn't learned anything but that the barmaid would tup him for a penny, a half dozen cargos were being unloaded, and no one was paid enough.

The idea that he had given up a night spent with Mari to fester in this shithole was enough to make his mood very, very foul.

He stared at his drink, wondering if he could stomach another draught. Three new sailors came in, bursting with pay that they longed to spend, and the pair of thieves by the fire hunched closer together, no doubt planning the best way to rob the boys before they spent it all on drink.

Then a voluptuous barmaid, with assets spilling out of her gown, slipped into the seat across the table from him. He sighed, unwilling to engage in enough conversation to send her away, when her scent teased his mind. Not a true scent, not in this morass of ale and piss, but a clean smell that might have had lemon in it, but certainly did not reek of the usual tavern wench. Which was why he lifted his gaze enough to see her face.

Mari.

Bloody hell.

Questions crowded into his mind. How had she found him? Why was she dressed as a common tart, in clothes too bloody tight? And how the hell did he stop her from causing a riot when the three sailors took note of her assets?

"Come over here," he growled at her.

She blinked at him. "What?"

"Come over here," he snapped. Then he shoved back his chair enough to give her room and patted his lap.

She drew back, clearly shocked down to her toes. "I will not!"

"If you're dressed as a tart, then you'll act the part. Unless you'd rather spend your time with them?" He jerked his chin at the meanest-looking huddle of men, all of whom had hard eyes that recognized she wasn't typical in this place.

"I'm not dressed as a—"

"Mari, goddamn it, you're going to get us both killed." It wasn't a lie. He'd seen worse in India. He caught her wrist, then firmly, steadily, inexorably pulled her out of her seat and over to his side of the table.

She stumbled around and settled just where he wanted her. In his lap with her arm on his shoulders and his hands settled possessively around her waist. And then, just to see how brazen she was, he let one hand slide down her thigh. A couple flicks of his wrist at her skirt, and his fingers were underneath, stroking the silk of her stockings.

She gasped in surprise, but he was busy nuzzling beneath her hair. Sweet lemon scent, clean and fresh. God, he wanted to sink into her perfection, but he couldn't. Not here, not now. But soon, he promised himself. Very soon.

He became bolder with his fingers, and she slapped her hand over his, flattening his palm against her thigh. "You are exposing my leg to everyone here," she growled.

"Then swing your legs around across my lap. They'll be hidden underneath the table." Plus, it would give him better access to her body.

"Bad enough that I'm dressed as a barmaid—"

"A tart," he corrected. "Barmaids don't come close to splitting the seams of their dresses."

She looked down at where she was near to bursting past the worn threads. "I tied my corset as tightly as possible. I can barely breathe."

"Then I'll have to get you out of it as soon as possible," he said as he helped her adjust her legs over his. She accidentally nudged his thick cock, and he hissed with pain and arousal. Damn, if they were attacked while he was in this state, he would be hard-pressed to protect either one of them.

"You will not!" she said primly.

"I will," he promised as he pulled her tight enough that he could glare over her shoulder. And then she jiggled across his lap. She was simply finding her position as she tried to tug her skirt over her legs, but the movement knocked against his cock again.

"Sit still," he growled. "Or move more gently."

"What?"

"Good God, I thought you were raised in the country. Surely you can understand that a man needs gentle handling."

"I was raised in India," she retorted. Then at his arch look, she flushed. "I'm sorry," she said more quietly. "Have I hurt you?"

He pulled her in tight enough that she could feel his erection pressed hot and throbbing against her thigh. And the dark thrill that went through his body at the pressure had his hands sliding to where they should not be. Not yet at least.

"I'm made of hardy stuff," he said as he nuzzled again into her shoulder. He brushed aside her luscious mane of hair so he could watch the room even as he nipped at her neck. And then, when she was shivering in his arms—and the room had returned to its normal business—he lifted his mouth to her ear.

"Why are you here?"

"I came to help you."

Of course she did. "And how exactly does dressing as a tart—"

"A barmaid."

He huffed rather than argue. "You cannot help. You need to go home."

"I know all about Silas, and Ellie will let me know when Tie shows up. Oh, and Lord Rimbury and a footman are hiding outside, just in case." She drew back and beamed a smug smile at him.

"You…what?"

"Did you think you were the only one who could skulk about in taverns?"

The very idea that she'd been here…that she'd been *skulking*, left him cold with horror. "Tell me everything," he said in a low voice tinged with true anger and nearly overwhelming terror. "Now."

She rolled her eyes, then settled against his shoulder. He wrapped his arms around her, his actions more protective than sexual. And yet he couldn't deny the need that pulsed inside him.

"It wasn't difficult," she said, obviously pleased with herself. "I jumped on the back of Lord Rimbury's hackney. Then I found a woman and traded my clothes for hers, and my earbobs for information."

He rubbed his hand through her hair—her glorious tumble of auburn locks—and felt her earlobe. It was naked, and he tugged on it just to hear her murmur a throaty purr. "But why?" he said, genuinely confused. The magnitude of what she'd done was just filtering into his awareness.

She exhaled loudly. "You promised to explain things to me. You promised to do it tonight. I cannot help it if you made it blasted difficult to find you."

"But, Mari—"

She pressed her finger to his lips. "Have I helped you? Have I gotten the information you need?"

"You haven't told it to me yet!"

She blinked. "Oh. Right. Silas runs a thieving ring of boys. They steal cargo somehow. They've got at least one wealthy protector—some say more—and Tie is the youngest of his crew."

"Somehow?"

She shrugged, and in that too-tight gown, her breasts were a distracting sight. "Ellie didn't know. Though Silas comes here more nights than not, which implies that his home is nearby. And it's not just him, though he's in charge. He has three lieutenants, though I don't think it's right to call boys raised to steal by a military rank. Insults the real lieutenants, don't you think?"

Peter dropped his forehead against her temple, shaking his head slightly. "I quite agree," he said rather than reveal how flabbergasted he was by her knowledge. "Three lieutenants?" he prompted.

"Boys he's raised. Big ones. They go everywhere with him as a kind of guard."

Peter absorbed this information, making quick plans. All he need do now was to wait for Silas to show and tail him. Thanks to Mari, he had a much clearer picture of the situation. If he stood watch, eventually he would find out who the wealthy protector was. And maybe he'd even grab little Tie and figure out exactly what his father's role was in all this.

All thanks to Mari. "You're a wonder," he breathed against her skin.

"That's what I keep telling myself, but no one else seems to notice."

"I notice," he said. He noticed a lot of things about her. Like the way she let him hold her legs and caress the soft swell of her thighs. Like the way her breasts were pressed against him, and she'd even allowed herself to run her hands through his hair. This was more than a proper woman playing a part. This was Mari, who was desperate to escape the harsh rules of proper behavior. And he was just the man to help her do it.

"Kiss me," he said as he maneuvered her face toward him. "Kiss me like a tart who is about to be paid very, very well."

Instead of doing as he asked, she arched a brow. "A tart would give you nothing without coin."

"Whatever you want, Mari. Just kiss me." There was raw hunger in his voice, a need that burned through his blood and hardened his cock. A desire that he focused on her, and he watched with satisfaction as her eyes widened and her nostrils flared. Then she slowly, hesitantly, leaned forward. Her lips touched his. Her mouth parted, and her tongue darted out. Her arms tightened around him, and she pressed her breasts against his chest.

*Yes.*

He took her mouth. He slanted his across hers and thrust his tongue inside. He might have done a great deal more. He might have flipped the tavern owner a coin and taken her right upstairs to bed. He was that desperate to be inside her. But just then the door slammed open, and a rough voice called out.

"Drinks fer me mates. Drinks fer ever'body, thanks to me new nob friend!"

He didn't want to look up. He didn't want to let anything distract him from the wonder that was Mari. But this was odd enough that he couldn't ignore it. Because anything odd in surroundings such as this was dangerous.

So he broke away, and then he hissed out a curse. There, held roughly by a man who could only be Silas, was his best friend, looking much the worse for wear.

"Oh dear," murmured Mari. "They've caught Lord Rimbury."

# *Seventeen*

MARI IMMEDIATELY SCANNED LORD RIMBURY'S FACE
and body for damage. He was roughed up, certainly.
His jaw had a swelling bruise, and his cravat would
never be the same. But he seemed to be standing well
enough, though his eyes burned with fury.

The other men had fared worse. Bruises abounded,
many were missing teeth, and one was limping. But
it was hard to tell whether Lord Rimbury had done it
or that was their natural state. Either way, they held
Peter's friend firmly by his cravat—using it as a kind
of noose—and randomly shook him just to be mean.

It quite made her blood boil.

She started to go to his defense, but Peter's arms
tightened about her. "Not yet," he said in a low tone.

She disliked waiting, but knew he had the right of
it. They probably needed a plan, but she hadn't the
least idea what.

"At least they haven't seen the footman."

He glanced her way. "Robin?"

She shrugged and leaned in tight to whisper into
his ear. "I never got his name. He brought me your

note at the ball and then left to find different clothes for Lord Rimbury and himself." She shifted on his lap, and his hands tightened, holding her still. "I could step out and find him."

"No." The word was curt and cold for all that he nuzzled against her neck. "It's too dangerous. I want you right by my side."

"So I can protect you?" she teased, even though this was no laughing matter. And yet a part of her couldn't help but soar. Finally, she was having an adventure that would live up to her wayward name.

He growled his answer. Then a moment later, he said, "I'm going to try and buy him. Easiest way to avoid a fight."

There were so many questions but she didn't have time to ask. Suddenly, Peter growled loudly at her. "He's not that pretty. You sure you want 'im?"

It took her a moment to adjust, but she knew her cue. "I am."

He gave her a loud smack on the lips, then he turned to the leader. "Me laidy wants to play with yer lordling over there. How much fer a night with the bloke?"

Lord Rimbury's eyes widened in shock. "I am not—"

"Shut up!" Silas said, cuffing him roughly. Mari bolted upright, even though Peter kept a firm hand on her arm.

"Hey! I want him kept pretty." She made no attempt to disguise her voice beyond a rough accent. It didn't stop Lord Rimbury from recognizing her, and his eyes widened with horror.

"Bloody hell," he breathed.

Silas wasn't letting him go, though. "He's my toy, and I ain't sharing."

Peter stood, slouching a bit as he cuffed an arm around her shoulders. "Aw, come now. Ye've stolen his purse, humiliated him in front of ever'body. Why not make a few extra coins on him while you can?"

Silas ground his teeth together, apparently considering his options. Clearly he wasn't a fast thinker. Meanwhile, Peter tossed a coin at the barmaid.

"A round of drinks on me."

The knot of men around Lord Rimbury cheered, then Peter stepped in front of her. "Come on," he coaxed. "Let a bloke entertain his laidy."

"A guinea," Silas said, his eyes narrowing.

It worked! They were going to get out of here without so much as an ugly look from anyone but Lord Rimbury. Except Peter laughed, his tone almost spiteful.

"Don't be daft. He ain't worth it, and I ain't got it. Two shilling an' no more."

"Two shilling?" Silas scoffed. "For a night with a lord?"

"Two shilling, and I make sure 'e don't set the constable on ye tomorrow."

The waitress was handing out tankards of ale as fast as she could. Mari could see the mark of fear in her eyes, and she hoped that as soon as the men got to drinking, they'd think less about Lord Rimbury. They certainly couldn't hold him as tightly with their hands wrapped around their drinks.

Meanwhile, Peter was pressing his point. "Didn't think about the constable, did ye? That there is Lord Rimbury, he is. Right bugger of an idiot, but no one said the nobs had any sense."

Silas's eyes narrowed as he looked him over. "And 'ow would you know that?"

"'Cause we were set to meet 'im here. Didn't think the bugger'd come dressed like a fool."

Lord Rimbury straightened up in mock insult. "I came attired as a gentleman ought."

Peter snorted. "There you go. Now let us be on our way, all nice an' quiet, or there'll be the devil to pay come morning."

That was enough for Silas's henchmen, especially with the ale on the table now. They dropped like rocks into their seats and tucked into their ale with nary a peep. Not so for Silas, who apparently disliked being reasonable.

"I got a lord in me pocket, and not just a lackwit boy, neither. The constable cain't do nothing t' me."

Lord Rimbury looked shocked. "I'm older than I look! And I could have you—"

"Shut up!" growled both Silas and Peter at the same moment. Apparently that was enough to make Ash silence his tongue.

"And 'oo is this great nob o' yours?" Silas scoffed. "Some wealthy toff with more money than brains?"

It looked for a moment like Peter was going to answer. Mari could tell he wanted to brag, but knew better. So in the end, he lifted his chin. "Four shillings."

"I'll pay the damn shillings," Lord Rimbury snapped as he jerked his cravat free.

"With wot?" Silas asked as he held up Lord Rimbury's purse. It was fine old leather, tooled with the family crest. "This 'ere's me own. Found it just today." And he showed his foul teeth as he grinned while he thumbed the fine stitching.

It was a mistake.

Lord Rimbury had been resigned up until that point. He'd been battered and outnumbered five to one. But right now, seeing that bastard fondle his family crest was apparently too much for him. He moved faster than Mari thought possible. He grabbed the leather with one hand while the other punched Silas hard in the face.

Everyone was caught flat-footed. Everyone, that is, except Peter.

He was on the lieutenants before they could do more than sputter into their ale. He dropped two with heavy blows to the head, another with a quick shove to his chair that sent him toppling, and the fourth stopped short when he saw Peter's knives.

When had he drawn those? Sharp steel that he held with perfect confidence.

Meanwhile, Lord Rimbury was locked with Silas in a furious battle. They were swinging at each other, the purse still gripped by both men. It was only now that Mari realized the tavern had emptied out except for the eight of them. Which meant that no one else was hurt, except the furniture, as the two beat at each other.

Which was when Mari saw her opportunity. Lord Rimbury twisted around, and suddenly she was presented with Silas's back.

She wasn't as tall as she'd like to be for this movement, but fortunately, she knew how to jump. So she did.

With a tankard of ale in each fist, she jumped high enough to slam both of them down on Silas's head.

*Whack!*

The crockery shattered. Ale splashed everywhere. But the big man didn't do more than stumble. Goodness, he had a thick head.

Fortunately, it was enough that his hand went slack, and Rimbury got his purse back. Then with his free hand, he delivered such a solid blow to the man's face that Silas went flying.

Which was when the other four attacked. They rushed Peter together. Mari was startled enough to scream. She'd been so busy watching Silas drop, that she didn't see much more than a flurry of movement.

And then she watched as Peter started fighting. But not with his knives. He used his fists as they wrapped around the knife hilts, punching, dodging, even kicking when needed. A few moments later, it was all done.

With a quick flick of his wrists, he sheathed his knives into holsters hidden inside pockets of his loose-fitting pants. Lord, she'd been sitting on his lap, and she hadn't even noticed them.

Meanwhile, he bent to Silas, quickly pulling the brute's face around. The man was out cold.

"Good work," he said as he began rifling the man's pockets.

"No need," Rimbury said as he wiped blood off his lip. "I got everything he took from me." He'd already returned his purse to his pocket.

"A moment," Peter growled as he drew out a tarnished silver flask. He stared at it a long moment, quietly rubbing his hand over the dented side. Then he grimly put it in his pocket.

"You're robbing him?" Rimbury gaped.

Mari had a similar thought. Whyever would he want such a battered thing, for all that it was silver? Peter didn't answer. Merely continued turning out the man's pockets. He found a purse, weighed it quickly in his hand before tossing it over his shoulder.

Mari spun. She hadn't even realized the tavern owner was standing there, his eyes glowering and his hands clenched into fists.

"For your trouble," Peter said. "With my apology."

"I can't take 'is money. He'll kill me," the tavern keeper said.

"Tell him I stole it."

The man chewed a moment, then nodded. Meanwhile, Rimbury was crouching down beside Peter, his hand going to the flask. Peter passed it over, likely because it freed up his other hand. Then the air was split by low cursing from Lord Rimbury.

Peter didn't respond, but his expression became more grim.

"What?" Mari pressed.

"I'll answer your questions," Peter said quietly as he ushered her out the door. "But let's get away from here first."

At last. They were thinking exactly the same thing at the same moment. It was almost enough to urge her into an impetuous kiss.

She didn't. Not with Lord Rimbury watching through his rapidly swelling eyes. But she did touch Peter's arm, intending to thank him. Before she could get out a word, she saw his face.

Fury.

Peter was flat-out furious with her. This wasn't going to be a comfortable conversation at all.

"Oh dear," she breathed.

"Just so," he agreed.

# Eighteen

ONE OF THE FIRST THINGS PETER LEARNED IN INDIA was how to prioritize emergencies. Wounds first. Crazy women second.

Now that they'd run six blocks away from the docks, nearly knocking over Robin where he hovered anxiously by the tavern, Peter was able to grab hold of his best friend and see just what kind of damage he'd suffered.

"I'm bloody fine," muttered Ash as he wiped at his lip. It was bleeding sluggishly, but in all other aspects he seemed normal. Better than normal, in fact, as he flashed Peter a grin. "I haven't had a good row in ages. God, I love London."

"You're soft in the head," Peter answered, though reassured by his friend's cheerful answer. "Are your ears ringing? You're limping a bit. Is that—"

"Bugger off." He glanced significantly over at Mari. "And exactly how did you come to be here, and dressed like that, no less?"

Peter didn't give her a chance to answer. Just the sound of her voice distorted his focus. "She jumped on the back of your hackney," he ground out, "then bartered for the clothes."

"Really?" Ash said, his eyebrows going up. "That's surprising."

It was bloody brilliant, especially since in ten minutes she'd learned more than he'd discovered in hours. But that didn't change the fact that she was a gently reared woman with no ability to defend herself. She'd wandered through the docks without protection and had joined into a brawl. And she'd been the one to deliver the key blow!

He didn't know whether to kiss her for being brave or throttle her for being reckless. So rather than give voice to the riot of emotions inside him, he kept a firm arm wrapped around her waist and focused on the others. But that didn't stop her from talking.

"I'm experimenting with waywardness," she said primly.

"Hmmm," returned Ash. "I'm not sure that was the kind of waywardness Peter meant to inspire."

Too right.

"Too bad," she returned hotly. "If I'm going to live up to my reputation, then I get to pick exactly how and—"

"We'll talk about that in a minute," interrupted Peter. Then, when she opened her mouth to argue, he turned to her so she could see the absolute fear in his eyes. "I'm still terrified by the sight of you clapping those mugs on Silas's head."

"It was brilliant," Ash said.

"He could have hurt you and…" Peter swallowed, cutting off his next words.

She looked at him, her eyes narrowing. "Finish your thought."

"And it would have destroyed me to see that. To be the *cause* of that."

"The cause?" she said, turning so he had to release her. He didn't. He gripped her even tighter. "I chose to come. I chose to help. If I was hurt, then that's my fault, not yours."

"Doesn't fadge," inserted Ash with a wobbly shake of his head. "Might have worked before he went to India, but not now. Peter pays attention. And he takes care of what he sees."

He watched her absorb those words, her eyes darting quickly between the two of them. Then she frowned. "Me?" she asked in a small voice.

God, what more did she need to get it through her thick head? "Yes, you." Then he dragged her tight against him and took her mouth with all the ferocity his churning emotions demanded. He was probably moving too fast. Up until now, he'd made sure every step of this dance was slow enough for a virgin to handle. But not now. He was feeling too raw from seeing her wade into a bar fight. Far from being startled, she responded as if she'd been desperate for just this very thing. She wrapped her arms around his shoulders, she pressed her body flush against his, and she nipped at his tongue before thrusting hers into his mouth.

"Pete! Damn it, you can't do that here!"

She fell back, though he kept her from stumbling. And the two of then looked at each other. Her eyes were wide, her lips were dark red, and her breasts were peaked and so damned intriguing that he couldn't get a thought through his head besides a dozen ways to taste them. "Oh hell," Ash grumbled. "Robin, can you find us a hackney? I've got an eye on them, though I'm not sure I can stop a woman who is bent on ruination."

Peter stiffened, ready to flatten his best friend for that, but Mari held him back.

"He's right," she said softly. "I've lost my head."

Peter shook his head. "No, you're finding yourself. Though why you chose a dockside tavern to do it in, I'll never know."

She sniffed. "You had to go all the way to India. I suppose I am ahead in this game."

Ash chuckled. "She's got you there."

Peter didn't answer, his mind too fuddled with thoughts of her to form a witty response. Fortunately, Robin was quick about his task. A hackney rolled up a moment later. Peter made sure both Ash and Mari were inside, then he stopped to speak with Robin, keeping his voice low.

"Just how well do you know the people around here?"

"I grew up not far—"

"Well enough to find out where Silas runs his boys? Where they meet and work from? What they're planning?"

Robin nodded. "And wait for Tie?"

"There's a waitress here who said she'd send word if Tie shows up."

Mari poked her head out. "Ellie. She lives right beside the tavern."

Robin nodded. "I can find out what you need."

"I'll take care of matters at the house. You know how to reach me?"

"Yes, my lord."

"Don't take any risks. And you come talk to me when you're done."

"Yes, my lord."

Peter took a moment to clap the young man on the shoulder. He was sturdier than he looked, and unlike Ash, he was dressed like a local. Spoke like one too. "No risks," he said as he pressed a coin into the boy's hand. "Be extra careful."

Robin nodded, then Peter climbed into the carriage and settled himself next to Mari. The footman disappeared like magic into the mists while Ash knocked on the wall to signal the coachman.

"Where are we headed?" Peter asked as he pulled Mari tight against his side. She didn't resist, which had him smiling in the darkness.

"I gave him directions to Miss Powel's residence."

"No!" she cried. "I still have questions, and you, sir"—she poked a sharp finger into Peter's ribs—"have promised me answers."

He grabbed her pointy finger and wrapped his hand around hers. Then he drew it to his lips for a gentle kiss. He did this because he needed to touch her, but also because he needed time to think. Unfortunately, she was not going to give it to him.

"I risked a great deal tonight—"

"I know," he growled.

"And I did it so we could have our conversation. I cannot marry a man who has no focus."

He dropped his head back against the squabs and

took a deep breath, but it was Ash who answered for him.

"You don't understand him at all, Miss Powel." His voice was soft, and he was the most serious he'd been since coming to London. "Didn't you hear what I said earlier? Peter sees things. He doesn't talk about them. Doesn't prance about. He just sees things and—"

"And I build things," he interrupted. "Solid foundation, first."

"—he takes care of what he wants."

Mari huffed out a breath, lifting her free hand in a gesture of frustration. "I don't know what any of that means."

"It means I want you, Mari. It means I want to marry you."

"And do what?"

Make love to her nonstop for weeks. Plant his children inside her. Grow old beside her. Look at her face, argue about nonsense, hold her tight when things got difficult, and then kiss her senseless whenever she wanted. All of those thoughts, plus a thousand more, flew through his head, but none of them made it out of his mouth. They got jammed somewhere in his throat. At least until Ash kicked him hard in the shin.

"Hey!" he cried.

"Jesus, Peter, the one thing you never figured out is that women need to be talked with. You've got to tell her everything. More than what you share with me."

He knew that. Damn it, he knew! "It's not so easy to put into words."

Ash sighed. It was a sad sound and painful to hear.

"Miss Powel—Mari—are you determined on this course?" Ash asked. "On him?"

She sniffed, pulling herself slightly away from Peter. "I'm determined to make him explain."

"Very well." Ash rapped on the hackney and called out a new destination. "That's my direction," he said by way of explanation to Mari. "I'll leave you to it, but whatever happens, Miss Powel, I beg you to remember something."

"What?"

"Peter is my dearest friend, but if it came to it, if I had to choose... Mari, I would choose you."

Peter felt the impact of those words hit her body. She jolted, but fortunately for him, she didn't lurch toward Ash, she shrank inside herself.

Then she released a mew of frustration. "Being wayward is so much more difficult than I thought."

Meanwhile, Ash pushed himself forward, grabbing her free hand. He would have taken both, but Peter refused to release her other one. "Surely you've noticed my attention."

"Of course I have. But..." She shifted awkwardly on the seat. "But you only want me for my dowry."

This time it was Ash who released a low, bitter chuckle, the sound grating and wrong from Peter's ever-cheerful friend. "If you think that, Miss Powel, then you are as blind as he is mute. Perhaps you deserve each other."

Mari had no response to that—just a silent cringe— and though Peter wanted to thump his friend hard for speaking so cruelly to her, he said nothing. Ash was right. If she truly thought he wanted just her dowry, then she was a fool. Or perhaps blinded by her father's assumptions. Either way, he could not damn his best friend for wanting her.

Even so, he had no intention of releasing her to follow him. Not yet. Not until he found the words to explain himself to her. Meanwhile, Mari was still struggling to respond.

"My lord…" she began, but there was nothing beyond that.

"Ashley," he said. "Just once, say my real name."

"Ashley, you honor me more than I can say."

"But you want him." It wasn't a question. And lest Peter feel the joy of that, she immediately crushed his happiness.

"Not exactly."

"Then what, Mari?" Peter growled out. "What do you want? Who do you want?" And if she said that damned Camden puppy, he was going to put his fist through the carriage wall.

"Do you not understand?" she said, irritation underlying her words. "This is too new to me. You men are encouraged to think of your own wants from the earliest cradle. What will you do today, Master Ashley? Where do you want to go, Master Peter? We women are told what we will do and how we are to think. We are not asked anything, ever."

"I have asked," said Peter.

"And so I jumped onto a hackney and clapped a villain with tankards of ale to meet with you. Do you not think I have been daring enough for one night?"

He did. She was. But, oh, how he longed for so much more from her.

Meanwhile, his best friend acted the gallant. "Of course, Miss Powel," Ash said as he lifted her hand and pressed a kiss to her knuckles. "Just think on what I have said."

"I will."

A moment later, the hackney stopped. They had arrived at Ash's lodgings, and when he pushed open the door, Peter got another flash of his friend's swollen face.

"Ash, are you sure you're all right? I can send for a doctor or—"

"Shut up, Peter." His words were harsh, but the smile was genuine. "Just take care of Miss Powel."

"You know I will."

And that was it. They shared a moment of understanding as only two childhood friends could. Then Ash gave a jaunty wave and sauntered away. Which left Peter alone at last with Mari. If only he knew exactly what he wanted to say to her. How to say it. In what way to say it. And...

She kissed him.

He'd been looking back from Ash to her and trying to find the words, but she apparently hadn't wanted any. And the moment her lips touched his, any ability to talk was obliterated.

# Nineteen

FROM NOW ON, KISSING WOULD BE MARI'S FIRST choice when she had no idea what else to do.

Too excited from a barroom brawl? Kiss Lord Whitly.

Too surprised by Lord Rimbury's sudden devotion? Say good-bye to the man and kiss Peter.

Too frustrated, too angry, too confused by everything that had happened this night? Kiss Peter until her thoughts stopped whirling and an entirely different maelstrom built inside her.

Perfect.

Especially with the way he was taking hold of her body, pulling her roughly against him while he devoured her mouth. Damn her skirts and this too-tight corset. She wanted to wrap herself around him and do things she'd never ever imagined before. Animal things. Wayward things. Except he was trying to hold her back. His arms were tight, but his mouth was suddenly absent. He pressed his forehead to hers while their breath heated the air between them.

"Mari," he gasped out. "What are you doing?"

She didn't answer at first. It was too bold—even

for her—to say what she wanted out loud. Besides, she couldn't catch her breath or clear her thoughts. Thankfully, the driver thumped on the top of the carriage.

"'Ey now! Where to?"

"Not home," she said quickly. "Not until you've explained."

"Do you know what you risk being private with me? Do you know what I want to do right now?" If she had any doubt, he grabbed her hand and pressed it against the hard, hot center between his thighs. It seemed to pulse under her hand, and she squeezed it as much out of curiosity as anything else. But when he groaned and shuddered against her hand, she knew she wanted to do more. A great deal more.

"Not home," she repeated firmly.

She heard him swallow then nod. "We are going to marry, you and I."

He was stating it firmly, and she saw no reason to argue with him. She wanted this time with him, and she would risk her reputation for it. A quiet part of her said she was risking a great deal more, but she ignored it. The voice was too small to defeat the hard beat of her heart against her ribs.

Peter called out a direction. She guessed it was to his rooms. She swallowed and touched his face. Only now did she realize that she sat on his lap and that her pins were scattered all over the floor. But it was his face she explored. The rough texture of his cheek, the hard cut of his jaw, and the full delight of his lips.

He pressed a kiss to her fingertips. Then he nipped at them. And then, he sucked her index finger into his

mouth. The feel of his wet tongue stroking her had
her belly quivering in delight. His arms were still tight
about her body, but whereas his left arm wrapped her
hips, the right was free to stroke across her thighs and
up her waist.

She ached for him to touch her breasts again. Her
nipples were tight enough to hurt, but her mind was
focused on the slide of his tongue over her finger.
The scrape of his teeth against her skin. And the way
her heart just kept beating, a thousand tiny throbs
throughout her body.

But then he turned away.

"I have to tell you about India, Mari," he rasped.
"You want me to explain. I have to... You have to
understand what happened there."

"Yes," she said as she dropped her head against
his shoulder. His neck was right there, and this close,
she could make out the pulse point beating almost as
rapidly as hers. She pressed her lips there. Then when
that was not enough, she licked the skin, tasting salt
and smelling bay rum.

He groaned and let his head drop against hers.
"This is too fast," he said. "You don't know what you
do to me."

"Is it the same thing I feel? The same..." How to
describe it? Wetness? Aching? Breathless desperation?
"Never before has anyone made me feel this way."

His hands tightened. A quick grip hard enough to
make her gasp. And then he loosened his hold. Just
enough to let her breathe. "Yes," he said, his voice
thick. "Yes, but more."

She didn't think it was possible.

"You're a virgin. You don't underst—"

She kissed him. She didn't want to hear anything about what she lacked as a woman. She knew he didn't mean to insult her when he said that. She *was* a virgin. But his words made her think of all the exotic women he'd been with. Beautiful courtesans who knew what to do. What was she compared to them? Nothing. So rather than face that, she kissed him and did everything she could to erase them from his mind.

She felt him resist. Was she not doing this right? But then a moment later, he surrendered to her. He leaned back, taking her with him until she was sprawled against his chest and straddling his hips. And there, he kissed her a thousand different ways. Slow and teasing, only to be startled by a hard, hot thrust of his tongue. Tiny nips accented by a slow suck on her lower lip.

And while she was lost in his kisses, his hands did a slow sweep of her back and bottom. He caressed her body then squeezed her bum. She lay fully atop him, pressed against that hot, hard length that so fascinated her. Especially when he began to thrust. Not demanding, not even big movements. Just a slow, rhythmic press into the softness of her belly. And how she yearned to explore that further.

"Oy now! Get out!"

The angry words were followed by a hard rap against the top of the carriage. And from the tone, the driver must have been doing it for a while.

Beneath her, Peter let out a soft curse. "This is too dangerous for you," he said.

"No one will know me. Not dressed like this."

It was true. With her hair wild and her clothing that of a dockside tavern worker, she looked as far from a pampered daughter of the elite as it was possible to be. She saw the struggle on his face as he fought with his gentlemanly code. It really was quite sweet of him.

"I'm not leaving," she said. "We might as well get me inside."

That decided him. It didn't hurt that the driver rapped on the carriage top again. "I'm coming down!" the man called.

"No!" Peter answered as he gently set her away from him. "We're getting out." Then he frowned at her. "I wish you had a cloak." He shrugged out of his coat and handed it over to her. "Put that over your head as if it were going to rain."

He waited while she did as he asked, putting the jacket over her head. Suddenly she was surrounded in his scent, spiced with the tease of bay rum. She breathed deeply and pulled the sleeves of his coat against her nose. And then there was no more time as Peter pushed open the door.

"Thank you for your trouble," he said as he gave the man several coins. Then he held out his hand for her.

She took it, feeling the expanse of his fingers wrap around hers. She gripped him, holding tight, while excitement popped in her blood, and together they moved quickly up the walkway to his bachelor rooms.

It was a simple home in a quiet boarding house, not something one would·expect of the future Earl of Sommerfield. He pulled out a key and quickly opened the front door. Then they tiptoed up the stairs and to the back. He opened his door and pulled her inside before quickly shutting it.

"The old gentleman who runs this house is a genial sort, not one to pry. But he's got ears like a dog."

She frowned. "Will he be angry that you've brought someone here?"

Peter's lips twisted into a self-mocking smile. "Not at all, but as you're the first female I've brought home, he'll certainly take note. And I'd rather not risk even that."

She smiled, inordinately pleased that she was the first to breach this inner sanctum of his life. She didn't intend to waste the opportunity. So while he lit a brace of candles, she walked deeper inside and tried to absorb everything she could.

Her first glance told her the place was a mess.

Her second glance told her the place was a mess of papers.

And once there was light, she saw it was an organized mess of research. In truth, looking around, she thought it was very much like her father's office, except in a smaller place and with vastly different interests.

"Agriculture," she said as she picked up one pamphlet. "Politics," she said as another sheaf of notes discussed the latest foreign policy debate.

"Tariffs," he corrected.

Same thing to her uneducated mind.

"Accounts," she said as she made it to another stack with an open ledger sitting on top of a listing pile of correspondence. There were other notes there as well. A hastily scrawled list of items with numbers beside it and dates going back two years. She picked it up, something burning hard in her mind, but she couldn't place it. There was something unusual about the words, but she didn't understand it. Canal. Sheep. Wheat. Not unusual words, but they meant something.

Beside the words and numbers were endless notations. Large numbers divided three ways, four ways, as much as seven ways, with differing permutations and additions. Most were scratched out.

"What are you doing here?" she asked as she held up the pages.

He had been busy cleaning up. Setting stacks of papers aside as he cleared space on a chair. But at her question, dismay rippled through his features.

"I'm looking for evidence of a crime."

Well, that was intriguing. She looked back at the paper, but he gently pulled it out of her hand and set it aside. "What crime?"

"Theft. Fraud. I'm not exactly sure. Maybe nothing."

She looked into his eyes. "You don't think that, though."

He rubbed his hand through his hair, the gesture distracted. "I'm looking, Mari. So far, I haven't found anything."

She pressed a palm to his chest, loving the way her hand was so small against his muscle. "But you feel it. You know something's wrong."

He gripped her fingers and pulled them up to his lips, his eyes drifting closed as he held her fingers there against his mouth. Nothing more, he just held her still.

"Peter?"

"I can only think of you right now. The rest is…" He shook his head. "Too much."

She smiled. That was what she wanted to hear.

Well, not really, she admonished herself. She'd come here to find out his secrets. But now that she was here, she was more interested in his touch, in his kiss, in all those wonderful wayward things he'd been showing her.

She stepped closer to him, she lifted her face toward his, and she gently pulled her hand—and his—aside, so nothing would stop them from kissing.

"If we start," he said, his voice thick, "I will not be able to stop. And then you will never know what I meant to tell you this night."

That wouldn't do. "So tell me," she said as she boldly pressed her body against his.

He swallowed, and even in the muted candlelight, she could see that his eyes burned over her face. He wanted her as fervently as she wanted him. It was a heady thing, this desire. And within a moment, she would give in to it. "I was beaten in India," he rasped. "Attacked, imprisoned, and nearly killed thirty-seven times. It was so common that it became almost routine."

She pulled back, blinking the haze from her eyes. She repeated his words in her mind, trying to sort out if she had heard him correctly. "You were jailed?" That wasn't what she meant to ask. It was merely the first word that reverberated in her thoughts.

"Often. But it is not like gaol here. It was simply a way of making me stay put for a time. Not for crimes." Then he shrugged. "Unless it was for a crime. But I usually didn't get caught."

She shied a step backward. He didn't stop her, but she knew he watched her—taut and anxious—to see how she would react to everything. He was being dramatic, she supposed. She recognized the ploy from her sister's antics. He was saying things as boldly as possible while watching to see if she'd run. It was a way of getting her truest—worst—reaction before moderating it with facts.

But she'd played that game too often with Josephine for her to fall for it now. So she settled neatly into the chair he had cleared, then folded her hands as a way to keep from reaching for him. She wanted to be clearheaded while they talked. Or at least less distracted.

"I think you need to start from the beginning, please."

He nodded. It took him a moment to clear another chair and settle across from her. And though she watched his eyes, she was very aware of his hands as they fidgeted at his sides. Of his shoulders starting out tall but slowly slumping as he leaned onto his elbows. And of the way his eyes seemed to look at something very far away.

"I left for India because you were right. I was wasting away doing nothing but arguing with my father. A man can only rebel against his pater for so long before he goes mad. And I was three-quarters gone by the time we danced and you told me exactly what a useless thing I had become."

"I shouldn't have spoken like that," she said, guilt a sharp spike in her chest.

His gaze cut up to her. "We started with plain speaking, Mari. Do not run from it now."

He was right. She had maneuvered and manipulated to get to this moment. She should not have interrupted. Then she abruptly reached forward and touched his hand where he gripped his knee. Gently, she spread her fingers and covered what she could of his hand. "I'm sorry. Please, I want to hear it all."

He nodded and started his tale.

# Twenty

PETER HAD NOT ALLOWED HIMSELF TO THINK ABOUT his experiences in India. It was over. He had returned to England. But the struggle to speak now told him more clearly than anything that the past was still large and ugly in his mind whether or not he told anyone.

"I wish I could say I went to India to become a man. Mostly, I left in search of change. I was sick to death of who I was and needed to become something else. Except the moment I landed in India, I fought every day to be as lazy and indolent as I'd ever been." He shrugged. "Fortunately, my immediate superior at the Company did not suffer fools gladly."

"What did you do for them?"

Her voice was quiet, and her hand a warm balm over his. The two grounded him as nothing else. Whenever his memories threatened to bury him in that wild and exotic land, she kept him firmly anchored in Mother England and all the blessings of home.

"I collected taxes. In many ways, the business there was an occupation of India by England. Decades ago, we invaded, supported our position with guns, and declared ourselves in charge. The maharajas bought peace by promising us taxes and then daring us to come and get them."

She shifted uncomfortably at his assessment, but when he looked at her, he saw she was simply thinking. "Papa has often said that India is a heathen place that needs our civilizing hand."

He arched a brow, challenging her to speak her true thoughts. She had spent many years of her childhood there, and he wanted to know her opinion.

"That is what he said, but I simply saw different people. Different ways of thinking and doing. Just…different."

"You were not allowed in the dangerous places." India was more than different. In places, it was savage.

"You were captured." He couldn't tell if that was a question or a statement.

"Not the first time." He flipped his hand over, needing to grip her fingers. He was trying to be honest, but when he looked back at the idiot he had been, he could see only arrogant stupidity.

"I enjoyed the ledger part of the work. Don't tell Ash. I've never admitted it to anyone, but the numbers line up in my head easily. Always have."

"That's not something to be ashamed of."

"Tell that to a young boy judged purely on his ability to swive everything in a skirt."

She smiled and squeezed his hand. "I promise not to tell a soul."

He returned the squeeze and allowed himself a

moment to focus on her breasts. Sweet, beautiful breasts that fitted so nicely in his hands and responded to the smallest caress. He would touch them soon. He would marry them and the beautiful woman who possessed them. And soon, all these memories would fade in favor of her pillowy softness.

"Peter?"

He forcibly reordered his thoughts. "I wanted to think that my task was a simple one. That because I was an impressively sized man and a future earl that the Indian leaders would bow to my authority. They did not."

"When you went to collect the taxes they owed?"

He nodded. "I thought the deviousness would be in the ledgers. That they would hide their wealth and not pay what was owed to England."

"They didn't hide it?"

"They did," he said with a bitter chuckle. "But that was the smallest of the problems." He looked up at her. "They simply refused to pay. And there I was, thinking my name and my title were all that was needed."

"Didn't you have men with you? Soldiers or someone to protect you?"

"Certainly. But even so, we were always few against many. And I was in the maharaja's palace, demanding he pay money to a conqueror."

Mari shook her head. "But it is a business. A shared trade to England. Why were you collecting money from them? I thought the money came to you first, and you paid them."

"Sometimes. Sometimes not." He was impressed

with her knowledge of basic business practices. Most women would not understand even that. "I was sent to collect money whenever money was owed. First, I was sent to teach me a lesson. I was an arrogant fool uninterested in learning what was needed. Later, I went because I was good at it."

"But how did you do it?"

"I studied the ledgers, figured out what was owed, and then asked for the money, and was refused." He flashed her a smile, not averse to playing to the drama of the situation.

She returned the smile, but her mind was clearly working hard on the problem. How to get money out of a maharaja who had no interest in paying? "Did you steal it?"

"Not the first time, though it became one of my best tactics later."

"That's how you got gaoled."

He nodded. "A few times." He glanced away, unable to express how dangerous prison was. Trapped like a rat in a hole, surviving only by the whim of the guards and the dubious attention of the maharaja. Many times he felt more animal than man.

He hadn't realized he was lost in his memories until he felt her hand on his face. A cool caress across his cheek. At first he flinched away from it. Sometimes the softest touch was the most dangerous. But then he saw who caressed him. He remembered where he was and dragged his attention back to the present.

"It was terrible, wasn't it?" she asked.

"Yes." He swallowed, needing to rush through the

explanation. No longer interested in the fun of telling the story. "Once I realized my mere presence and title were not enough, I fell back on what I understood. What I was good at."

He waited for her to catch up. For her to figure out his solution. It didn't take her long.

"You were a gentleman well skilled at…what gentlemen know."

"Which is?"

"Riding, gambling, and swiving."

He smiled at the way she said that last word. Her chin had lifted, as if she dared him to argue with her use of the word. He didn't, because he liked hearing scandalous words on her lips. "I was also good at wrestling. Hand to hand, like the Greeks."

She nodded. "You gambled for the money?"

"Yes. Cards, horse racing, and wrestling were my best choices, but I learned other skills."

"Knife throwing."

He wasn't likely to forget her surprised expression when he'd thrown his dagger in Hyde Park.

She dropped her hand onto his leg, still leaning forward as she studied him. "And that worked. Betting with the maharajas for the money they owed."

"For the most part, yes."

"But did you never lose?"

"I did. Often at first, but I got smarter at it. Better. And then there were my thieving skills."

"Are you a good thief?"

"Yes. Though there are some who are much, much better." He shrugged. "I employed a few to be part of my personal guard."

"Ah." She was impressed by his cleverness. She didn't understand that he'd had to be clever or die. "So you won the money. And did they pay?"

"Yes. That at least was something we English shared with the Indians. Publicly, they always pay their gambling debts."

"And privately?" Before he could answer, she had already guessed what had happened. "Did they rob you of it?"

"Often. Which is how I first learned to thieve. I was robbed and had to steal the money back."

"That's amazing."

He supposed it was. Given how incredibly unprepared he'd been, it was astonishing that he'd survived, much less thrived. But he'd learned quickly and fought desperately. "I did not do honorable things, Mari." In fact, his honor had been the first and easiest casualty of his life in India.

She tilted her head. "I suspect you were as fair and honest as possible in the situation."

He didn't quibble with her words, even though she was very wrong. "There are things I don't fully remember," he said, barely even realizing he spoke at all. "Times I lost all sense of honor."

Her fingers danced across his mouth, and he kissed them out of reflex. Like a man gripping his only lifeline in a stormy sea.

"You survived and came out stronger."

He shook his head. Did she not know how fragile he felt? A scent could drag him back into his memories. Fetid water, heavily spiced food, the manic laughter of a trapped man. It didn't happen often, but when it did, he was caught unprepared, and the experience always left him shattered.

"You have just returned," she said, her fingers continuing to stroke across his face. "Perhaps you merely need more time to remember who you were."

"I don't want to remember who I was, Mari. Don't you see? I came home with a purpose. Every moment in India made it all clearer."

Her caress didn't change, but he saw her eyes widen and her mouth curve with excitement. Here was what she'd been pressing him to explain but the idea was so precious to him he had difficulty voicing it. Thankfully, she knew how to be patient and wait for him, and in time he found the words.

"I saw such abuse in India. The wealthy destroyed the weak. The poor did anything to survive. Terrible things because it was that or die."

"It can be a terrible country."

"And so I came home, Mari. I came home to be damned sure that it does not happen here."

She pulled back, clearly shocked. "Evil maharajas here? Mobs of beggars in the street? Don't be ridiculous."

He looked at her, seeing her innocence and the blind faith she had in her heritage. He didn't blame her for it. Not so long ago, he had shared her opinion a thousandfold. But not now. Not anymore.

And it wasn't long before she was biting her lip in consternation. "Well, yes, I suppose I will allow that there are thieves and bandits in England."

"And beggars in the streets."

She nodded slowly. "Yes, though not like it was in India."

"Not in the same numbers or the same way, but the desperate poor exist everywhere."

She took a breath. "Yes."

"But you have been told to ignore them."

She nodded. "There are too many and I cannot help one without a thousand—"

"Mobbing the carriage or murdering you in the street for what little you have." He was merely reciting what he had believed and what the wealthy had been telling themselves for thousands of years. "It is not true, you know. You can help in small ways and it is a blessing."

She nodded. "So is that what you want to do? Help the poor?"

"Not in the way you mean."

He spread her fingers open as he traced the creases of her white palm. He noted with pleasure that she had calluses, so she was not completely a lady of leisure. In London, her time was occupied with husband hunting, but in the country, she probably did a great deal. "I saw the evil of men's hearts in India, and it wasn't just in the maharaja's. The English were greedy."

She winced but did not look away. "I am disheartened that we are not as civilized as we pretend."

"I want to build a home here. I want to make Sommerfield a place that leaves no room for barbarity. I want to serve the people I protect and be sure that their needs are met."

She tilted her head. "That is the responsibility of every lord over his land."

"And yet so many do so little."

Her eyes abruptly widened. "You mean to force them to live up to their responsibilities?"

He snorted. "I doubt any man has that power." He took a breath. "I mean to begin with Sommerfield. And when that is a utopia, I will look to my compatriots." He shrugged. "I hope my example and my voice in the House of Lords will help."

She rocked back in her seat. Her gaze darted across his features, but steadied as she looked at his eyes. She was a woman who needed only a few pieces of a plan for her to fit much of the puzzle together. So he waited, feeling exposed for admitting so simple a thing.

Yet it wasn't simple. Creating a utopia in the middle of England would be a constant battle against all the smaller vices. And that was nothing against the dread of sickness or natural disaster. Nothing brought out the barbarity in man faster than a few weeks of hunger and a few longer weeks of hopeless despair.

"I need to stand somewhere and have that place be strong and beautiful."

"Sommerfield and England." She smiled, and it chased the last of the shadows from his thoughts. "That's a beautiful ambition."

"Will you join me? As my wife?"

"Yes." A single word, whispered at first and then repeated louder. "Yes."

The most beautiful word in the English language.

He kissed her. First her hand that was still on his face. Then her wrist. But a moment later, she tumbled into his arms, her face pressed to his, her laughter filling his soul.

*Yes.*

Then she gasped against his neck, her breath hot but short with distress. He pulled back to look at her face, seeing her widened eyes while her hands clutched at his shoulders.

"Mari?"

"I'm sorry," she said, embarrassment pinkening her cheeks. "I must get out of this corset. It's too tight."

He grinned. Well, if it was a matter of her health, then of course he must oblige.

# Twenty-one

IT WAS AMAZING HOW EVERYTHING IN LIFE COULD align in an instant. Her wants, her husband, her entire future lay before her now—a glorious picture of a home and children, with happy workers in a peaceful country. And in the center of it all was this man working steadily to maintain the noble civilization that was every Englishman's birthright. She saw it as clearly as daylight, and it fit her like a dream come true.

In fact, the only thing that did not fit was this dress and her blasted corset. And while a certain degree of breathlessness added to the excitement of being wayward, this was too much. The last thing she wanted was to faint just when she'd finally gotten the answers she sought.

So she leaned back. This was a working woman's dress, and so the buttons were in front. She started to reach for them, but he blocked her hands and set them on his shoulders.

"Let me," he said.

She did, and the sight of his large fingers deftly releasing her buttons had her heart beating triply fast in her throat. He was undressing her. And she wanted him to.

The buttons went farther down, lost in the folds of the dress. Rather than search for them, he slipped his hands beneath the fabric and bracketed her waist with his two hands.

"Good God, that's whalebone. No wonder you can't breathe."

Of course it was whalebone. That's what a proper woman wore. And it apparently made it very easy for him to lift her up and set her on her feet before him. She wasn't a tiny woman, and so the thrill of him doing such a thing made her belly quiver with delight.

"Turn around," he said as he gently guided her.

Her dress pooled as she moved. Then she felt his fingers on her back, pulling at the ties that cut off her breath. And then…a miracle…they began to loosen.

She took a breath and then another. Air. Thank heaven. She was light-headed from the sudden freedom.

"Do you want it just loose or off?"

"Off." She wanted to be completely, totally, irrevocably free. And now that she was an engaged woman, she could cease the strict restraint of every aspect of her life. She could breathe in so many ways. And maybe even wear patterned clothing.

The ties fell apart, and she pushed the hated thing down before kicking it away.

She wore only her shift now, fine muslin that fell to her knees. And he was behind her, his hands on her hips, his fingers gripping her slightly as she filled her lungs with air and leaned back against him. He braced her on her sides, warmed her back and bottom, and pressed his mouth to the curve of her neck.

"You smell like English ale," he said.

She twisted slightly. "What?"

He tightened his hold so she couldn't pull away. "I like ale." Then she felt the scrape of his teeth across her skin and the wetness of his tongue. "But you taste sweeter." Another slow nip. "And spicier."

She wanted to say something clever. Some sort of worldly response to his seduction, but she had no words. Just the shivering delight of his body around hers. His lips at her neck and his hands gently sliding around her hips to her belly.

"What should I do?" she whispered.

"You will marry me."

It wasn't a question, but she answered it nonetheless. "Yes."

She felt him smile against her neck, and then he tugged her fully against him. She felt the sheer size of his body behind her, the strength in his thighs as he bracketed her, and the breadth of his shoulders as he pulled her arms up over her head.

"What are you doing?" she asked, her voice thick.

"Hold on to me."

There was nothing to hold, arched as she was like this. Her left fingers found his head and played in the thick curls of his hair. Her right hand touched nothing but air, but he balanced her back against him so she remained stretched out in the most decadent pose she could ever imagine. Especially as his hands were now free to roam over her body.

He skimmed over her belly, but quickly found her

breasts. His touch was light through the muslin as he stroked across her nipples. The feel was both rough and too light as the fabric scraped across her peak. "Take it off me," she whispered. She didn't know how she had the temerity to say such a thing.

He stilled for a moment. "You're sure?"

"Yes."

He lifted up her shift. He worked slowly, first gathering it up in his fists at her waist, then raising it all the way off while she shivered at her sudden nakedness. Her arms came down, and she meant to cover herself. There was bold, and then there was brazen. This was beyond both.

"Shhhh," he whispered against her temple. "You're beautiful. Let me look."

He gathered her arms and again pulled them high, draping them over his shoulders. She again found his curls—this time with her right hand—while he stroked the underside of her left arm where it stretched over their heads. Then he turned them both a bit.

"Look how beautiful you are."

She opened her eyes, startled to realize she'd shut them tight. But at his urging, she focused on a round mirror on the wall. It wasn't so large as to show her full body, but she saw enough. Skin pink and pale in the candlelight. Her body narrow as she arched, her breasts heavy. And there he was behind her. His eyes were nearly luminous as he looked at her. His hands were tan, his shirtsleeves a rough blue, and he held her as if she were porcelain.

"Take off your shirt," she said. She wanted to feel him as naked as she. His flesh, his heat. He smiled and pulled back to strip off his workman's shirt.

"Wait a moment," he said.

She watched in the mirror as he stripped off everything. Shirt, shoes, and stockings, then his pants. All until he stood naked and proud. His organ was large, even in the reflection, and she saw the dark reddish color of it amidst the golden of his hair and skin.

"Are you frightened?" he asked. "I'm large, but we will fit, I promise you."

"I should be."

"But you're not?"

No. She was intrigued. Excited. She looked into his eyes. "I'm delighted." Finally, she could begin her life unfettered.

He grinned in answer, but when she went to kiss him, he stopped her. "I have dreamed of this," he said. "Let me watch you before I lose control."

"Watch?" she asked, but then he turned her back to the mirror. He guided her arms again, stretching her out against him as he touched her. Skin on skin, calluses brushing across her in increasingly powerful caresses.

He stroked her breasts, then palmed her nipples. She gloried at the size of his hands and the way his eyes watched her flesh spilling through his fingers.

Then he took hold of her nipples and twisted them, pinching and pulling while she writhed against him.

He supported her as she arched into his hands. He nudged her head back, and she relaxed against his shoulder. And she moved up and down on the hot fire of his organ where it pressed thick and wet against her bottom.

"Lift your knee," he said.

She had no idea what he meant until he nudged his

thigh between her legs. She bent her left knee, and he immediately used his leg to pull her open as he braced his foot on a nearby stool.

She still wore her stockings, bright white against the dark hair of his leg. The mirror didn't show below her navel, but she could see his leg and hers intertwined when she looked down. And she could feel as his finger pressed down her belly before sliding to the wetness below.

She had felt this before. She knew this sensation. The fullness, the erotic rub. He spread her and speared her. Touching everywhere with thick, callused fingers.

Then the invasion deep inside her that wasn't enough. She ground against his hand, wanting more.

Her breath caught, and fire burned across her skin.

"Yes," he said against her ear. "Come for me."

She barely heard him, though she knew the tone of command. How silly to order such a thing, and yet she strained to obey. Faster and faster he rubbed her, tighter against her nub. Deeper inside her as she moved in ways outside of her control.

She had no idea how he kept her upright. Perhaps he held her. But her thoughts, her body, all of them spiraled to the movement of his hand, the heat of his breath, and his one single word.

"Now."

*Yes!*

Sweet detonation as she fractured apart in his arms. A flood of sensation too myriad to contain. *Yes!*

Then suddenly she was in his arms more literally. While her mind had been floating, the pulses continuing at a slowing pace, he had picked up her boneless form. He was carrying her to his bedroom, cradling her in his arms.

She blinked, too pleasured to do more than press a kiss to his neck.

She felt his hands tighten where he held her, then he gently set her on his bed. Her head was pillowed in the blanket. Her legs dangled off the side.

"Mari," he whispered.

She stroked the hard angle of his jaw as he leaned down above her.

"You will be my wife," he said.

"Yes."

"I cannot wait for our wedding night." This time his statement was almost a question. Almost, but not really.

"I know." She didn't truly know. Her mind was not yet her own. But as she spoke, he began to caress her breasts again. Brief strokes, almost reverent. Then she felt his lips there. Suckling on her nipple and bringing everything back into focus.

He couldn't wait for their wedding night. He meant to take her now. As a husband did a wife. As a man possessed a woman.

He spread her legs, easily stepping between her knees.

He would have her virginity, and she would be completely, irrevocably tied to him.

She felt him there, a large presence at the entrance to her womb, but he didn't push inside. His hands slid to her flanks, lifting her knees until she gripped him. Then he leaned forward, his expression stark, his eyes dark.

"Mari," he whispered. "Mari, say yes."

She touched his jaw, feeling the muscles twitch

there. She touched the sensuous curve of his mouth, and then she tightened her knees.

"Husband," she whispered. "Yes."

He thrust.

Pain flashed through her consciousness. Bright and sharp enough to make her cry out. He was so big. He was so very *there*.

He stopped when he was fully embedded. His mouth was tight, and she saw him swallow, but his eyes were on hers. He watched her face as she breathed shallowly and waited.

She softened.

She didn't know how it happened. Perhaps it was just the pain fading away. She was still stretched and too full, except not as much. Not bad.

Oh. Oh yes.

She began to like the feeling of fullness.

"Is there more?" she asked.

He flashed a grin. "Much more."

He eased back slowly. She felt his withdrawal and whimpered.

He leaned down and pressed a kiss to her nose. Then another to her cheek. Then her lips, teasing them with his tongue.

She teased back. Nipping. Kissing. Entwining tongues in a dance—

Thrust.

He pushed inside her again. Hard but not sharp this time.

Nice, especially as he ground his pelvis down against her.

Right there.

Very nice.

Then he raised up away from her mouth. Somehow her hands had gone to his shoulders, holding him to her, but she was not strong enough to keep him with her.

"Again," she said.

Thrust.

Very nice!

She gripped his hips, wanting to hold him to her. Wanting to increase the pressure. Just wanting. Then she smiled at him.

"Come for me," she said, barely knowing what it meant, but liking the echo of his words.

His eyes widened in surprise, and then he grinned. It was as if she had let loose his reins. Suddenly, he was thrusting into her harder than before. A wild tempo of impalement. Again and again.

His breath rasped in her ears as she held on. Her body thrummed with every impact, and she felt her body spiraling up with him. Another glorious splintering soon, but this time with him. He slammed one last time, and his body shuddered.

She felt him deep, saw his face as he surrendered to the release, and thought for a split second: This man gave everything. No half measures, no partial gifts, but everything. To a woman who made lists, measured every word, and never gave everything of anything to anyone. This was almost beyond comprehension.

Then he took her with him. Her body exploded. No half measures, no itemized list. Everything she was changed completely.

And she was amazed.

# Twenty-two

It was done. She was his, and the magnitude of that gift robbed him of speech.

He collapsed beside her on the bed, careful not to crush her. She was still languid with pleasure, and he was thankful he'd managed to control himself long enough for her to come again. It had been a near thing, but this time—and every time—should be perfect for her.

He reached out and gathered her to him. She snuggled close, settling her head on his shoulder, her breasts on his chest, and her hand in his. He pressed a kiss to her fingers, feeling the rightness in that. She belonged with him.

She slept.

He drowsed, but forced himself to stay awake. She had gifted him with her body; the least he could do was be sure to keep it safe. And that meant being careful that she returned home before her reputation was destroyed.

A half hour.

An hour.

He spent the time making plans for her dowry.

He would make Sommerfield into a paradise. And he would do it with her.

⤬

"Mari. Wake up, sweetheart. We need to get you home."

Mari hated waking. When she slept, she went deep and generally refused to get up until she was ready. But there was something special about rousing to the sound of Peter's voice. To the gentle way he squeezed her shoulder and nibbled at her lips.

She opened her eyes on a smile, and she stretched her arms around him. Up this close, she could see his eyes crinkle as he returned her smile, and she was reminded again how handsome he was. Then she ruined the moment with a jaw-cracking yawn. She slammed a hand to her mouth to cover it, but it was too late. He'd already seen it.

"Sorry," she said behind her hand.

He grinned and pulled it away from her mouth. "Don't ever hide from me. I want to see it all."

She shuddered in horror at the thought. "No man wants to see everything."

"I do." Then he pressed a kiss to the tip of her nose before pulling her upright. "But we cannot linger here. Not unless you want everyone to know what we have done tonight."

It was a testament to how far she'd fallen that part of her didn't care. They were to be married. What difference did it make if things were done quicker than completely proper? But it was a very small part. She'd been reared to be a lady, and no lady lingered in a man's bed before marriage. Unless...

"Surely we have time for—"

He kissed her. Swift and hard in all the best ways. But just as she was beginning to truly enjoy it, he set her apart from him.

"A lifetime with you will not be enough to satisfy me. So for now I will get you safely home."

She laughed, but then heard the rumble of a dray on the street. Surely it was too early for that.

He must have seen her confusion, because he answered her question before she could ask it.

"It is just after four."

Four? She gaped at him. "But the servants will be up soon."

His expression turned wry. "Just so."

She grimaced as she quickly donned shift and coarse stockings. The shoes were distasteful, since they pinched her feet, but it was nothing compared to the hatred she felt for her corset. But as the dress was too tight for her, it was wear it laced rib-crackingly tight or go naked in the street.

"You must help me," she said as she fitted the garment to her chest.

"I dislike that you must be disguised," he said as he quickly closed the buttons on his own attire.

"No more than I. Believe me, I will be the one gasping for air." She twisted so the ties were facing him. "Next time, I shall be sure to barter with a larger woman."

He gripped the ties but didn't pull. "There will be no next time. I will not put you in danger like that again."

"You didn't put me there in the first place," she countered. "I found you. Now pull. It's almost daylight." It was far from daylight, but she was beginning to fear discovery and was anxious to be demurely back at home.

He pulled the ties, but not hard enough. She could still take a breath. She cast him an arch look. "Is that all the power you have, my lord?"

He blinked then frowned down at the garment. "I don't know how you stand it."

"A woman does what she must to find a husband."

He hauled on the ribbons, but again, he was holding back. At this rate, she'd never be able to close the gown. Meanwhile, he grumbled into her ear, "You have already found a husband."

"Which means I will have to appear as a countess at your side. You will not want me looking fat."

"I would have you naked in my bed and never in one of these things again."

She chuckled, shaking her head at his silliness. He truly did mean what he said, but she knew there were requirements of a lord and his lady. He would see to the land and his people. She would have to see that they were respected in Society and acted in a proper fashion.

"Come now, my lord. It is bind me tight now, or take me home in a gown that gapes in the front for all to see."

That was enough to spur him to action. With a grunt, he set one hand to her waist while the other hauled back on the ties. She exhaled as she must, and within moments, she was restricted as any *not* wayward Welsh could possibly be.

"Excellent," she said. Quietly and with a shallow pant.

"Abhorrent. I like you better lush." Then he turned

her around, and his gaze dropped to her breasts. "Though I suppose there are some advantages," he murmured as he stroked a finger slowly across her breasts.

She felt her skin heat, and her breath caught. "Kiss me," she whispered.

She needn't have asked. He was already leaning in. So they kissed. Not deeply, but long. And when they separated, his gaze was intense.

"We will marry as soon as the banns are read."

She dropped her hands on her hips. "I cannot manage a wedding fit for an earl in three weeks' time."

"Between you and my mother, I am sure you can."

"But—"

"I have waited six years for you, Mari. I am impatient to begin our life together."

She'd been dreaming of the day she'd be mistress of a home since she was old enough to pick up a doll and order her brother's soldiers around. "Finish the contract with my father, and I will see what can be done about the wedding."

He agreed with a swift kiss. "Hurry now. If we linger much longer, I will have you back in my bed."

She smiled at that thought and pulled on the gown. It was tight, but she managed it, though there was nothing to be done about her hair. The pins were long gone. She tied it back, pulled on the heavy shoes, and pronounced herself ready. Two minutes later, they were in a hackney and headed to her home. It wasn't a long distance, but they spent every moment in each other's arms. She doubted she would ever tire of kissing him. Then the hackney stopped. She would have lingered, but he refused to allow it.

"How will you get in?"

"I have a key to the back. Everyone's asleep and won't stir for another hour." Half hour more like, but she didn't quibble.

"Have you done this before?"

"No, but my sister did. Sometimes she just needed to run free, even in London."

"Dangerous."

"I know. But she was quick and careful. Just like I will be."

He nodded, pressed a last kiss to her lips, then pushed open the door. "I will call on your father today."

"I will be waiting." Then she hopped out of the hackney and ran as quickly as was possible in the corset around to the kitchen entrance. She opened the door quietly, tiptoeing as she slipped inside. But a moment later, she realized her mistake.

The kitchen was well lit.

She turned slowly, dread rising from the pit of her stomach to choke off her breath. Then she turned around to see her parents, the cook, a young boy, and Horace, all staring at her.

"Sodding hell," cursed her father.

She couldn't help but agree. What was she supposed to do now? Her best choice, she decided, was to distract them, so she smiled at the dirty boy eating some honey bread. "Hullo there. You're a new face."

Her father slammed his hand down on the table, making everyone jump. "Where the devil have you been?"

"At Lord Vinson's ball," she said with a bright smile. "It, er, was a masquerade ball."

Her mother huffed out a breath. "It was not!"

"Well, it was for me. Afterward."

Her mother's eyes narrowed dangerously, and her voice dropped to a more menacing level. "You said you were staying with Georgette."

"Yes, well, I intended to." Lies upon lies. "But my help was needed elsewhere and…um…in disguise." This was not going well at all. However had her sister managed to sneak about? One wayward night, and Mari was floundering. She glanced significantly at Horace, then back at her father. "Must we discuss this right now?"

Her mother sniffed. She had the angriest sniff of any woman alive. "I rather think it's too late to try discretion now."

"Mother—" she began, but she hadn't a clue what she wanted to say. And then her brain finally caught up to the situation. At least as far as the people in the room, as she focused on the boy. "Wait a moment. Are you Tie?"

The boy's eyes were round, and his mouth was jammed full, but he still managed to nod at her.

"You're the reason I'm dressed like this. We've been searching all over dockside for you."

"Mercy me," murmured the cook.

"Dockside!" gasped her mother.

"*We?*" said her father with a growl.

Trust her father to narrow in on exactly the point she wished to avoid. He could be angry at her all he liked. Heaven knows she deserved it, given what she'd really done this night. But she did not want that fury turning on her future husband. That would not do at all.

"That doesn't matter," she said much too brightly as she focused on the child. "The point is that finally we've—that I've finally found you. Or you found me. Was it Ellie who told you?"

The boy nodded his head. He'd finished off his bread and was reaching for his cup of honey tea. But when she stepped toward the child, her father intercepted, his hand hard on her wrist.

"What have you been up to, Mari?" His voice was low and dark. Darker than she'd ever heard from her father.

"Papa, it's nothing."

His voice dropped to a low timbre, barely audible in the near-silent room. "Were you in my bedroom? Have you been looking at the ledger?"

She frowned. "What are you talking about? I haven't been in your bedroom for weeks." She looked to her mother, but the woman just shook her head, her expression sad. "Has something gone missing?"

"No, no," said her mother. "Nothing's gone."

"It's been touched. Damn it, I know when my things have been moved."

Moved? Touched? Papa didn't notice when Mama bought completely different furniture for the main parlor. It took him weeks to comment after Josephine laid off pastels in favor of brighter colors. And Mari believed he'd yet to realize the nursery had been remade into a sitting room eight years ago. But that wasn't his ledger. About certain things, her father was obsessive.

"I don't understand," she began. Worse, she was rather disconcerted to realize he cared more about his ledger than that she'd walked in at dawn, wearing a tavern woman's dress. Then she realized the thought had come too soon. Her father certainly did see what she wore and the hour. In fact, he made a point of sniffing her hair.

"Why do you smell like ale?"

How to answer that? "Well, I got into an accident while we were searching for Tie."

A man's voice came from behind. "She clapped two pints of ale across a villain's head. I assure you, sir, I had no desire for her to be there, but she appeared nonetheless, and I was grateful for her assistance."

She spun around to see Peter walking casually into the room, his expression rueful even as he nodded to her parents before looking intensely at the boy.

"Pet—um, Lord Whitly. What are you doing here?"

"I waited to make sure you got inside safely, then I heard the conversation." He flashed her a sad look. "Do you realize you are the worst liar I have ever heard? A masquerade party?"

"I was in disguise," she huffed. "It felt like a masquerade. Of sorts." In truth, it had felt like the most fun she'd ever had. Until, of course, she had gone to his rooms and learned about even better amusements.

Meanwhile, her father straightened to his full, lanky height. "Strange goings-on here. My things touched. A dirty boy appearing, asking after my daughter. And now you say she was in a fight with a villain. You will explain yourself this instant, or I will have you clapped in irons."

"Papa!"

"Quiet. I am waiting for Lord Whitly's explanation."

She reared up, furious about this, of all things, on this bizarre day. Her father demanding an explanation from Lord Whitly for *her* actions. "Well, you cannot have it," she snapped. "I am the one who jumped a hackney on the way to the docks. I am the one who found Tie. And I am the one responsible for clapping Silas on the head with two tankards of ale."

"Really, Mari," gasped her mother. "And here I thought Josephine was the wild one."

Mari threw up her hands. "She is, Mama. I am the wayward one."

Her father banged down his hand again, the clap echoing loudly in the kitchen. "And what has that to do with anything?"

Everything. It had to do with everything, but she couldn't begin to explain. Not with her father glaring daggers at Peter, and her fiancé accepting the blame for everything she had done. It was ridiculous, and she was tired of it.

"I am a grown woman, Papa, well into my majority."

Her father flashed her an irritated grimace, but it was Peter who spoke, his voice calm and deliberate. "The servants will be rousing soon." He glanced at the cook and butler. "The other servants. Perhaps there is a more private place we could speak?"

"Come to the library," her father answered, his voice gruff.

Mama didn't even bother getting to her feet, but Mari moved forward, only to be stopped by her father's glare.

"I will call when I am ready to speak to you."

She glared right back, but she knew better than to

press the point when he was in this mood. Her father was not generally mercurial, but when he became angry, everyone in the household stayed away. She was still trying to decide what to do, when Peter spoke to the boy.

"Tie, if you have finished eating, would you come with us? This concerns you."

The boy nodded, his eyes round as he hopped up from his seat.

"A ten-year-old boy gets to join you, but I—"

Peter touched her lips. His finger was large, but still gentle. Generally, she would have had no trouble speaking past his gesture, but the intimacy of what he did shocked her into silence. Certainly he had the right to touch her so openly, but it was still an announcement nonetheless. He'd effectively told everyone in the room that a proposal was imminent. And if there were any doubts, his next words made everything clear.

"I told you I would speak with your father today."

He had. She just hadn't expected it to be fifteen minutes after she'd snuck in the kitchen door.

"I should be there. This concerns me." Much more than it did the boy.

"Do you recall how you told me the dowagers would never dance the waltz?"

She nodded. "I won the wager."

"Because you know Society much better than I. Women's Society." He glanced at her father, who was watching them with a steady gaze. "In this, I am better equipped to handle the discussions of men."

"That was a ballroom game."

"And this is our future together. I will take care with it."

She wanted to say no! She wanted to stamp her foot like a child and then continue to stomp her feet right into the library. But she knew her father, and he would not tolerate such outright disobedience. The servants were watching, most especially Horrid Horace. She already appeared a scapegrace; she had no wish to compound that with a useless display of temper. Nevertheless, it grated on her to give way.

"Call me quickly," she finally said.

"Of course," he agreed. Then he gestured to Tie to precede him as the men trotted out of the kitchen to the library. Even Horace went, presumably to open the library door then stand with his ear pressed to it once the others were inside.

"Come along, Mari," her mother said with a sigh. "You can explain it all to me as Cook heats water for a bath. You cannot spend the day smelling like a tavern."

She knew she was beaten, so she nodded. It would be good to get out of this annoying corset. At least in her own clothing she'd be able to bellow with a full breath if her father became unreasonable later.

"I will tell you about the tavern fight," she said as they headed up the stairs, "if you will explain about Papa's ledger."

The deal was struck. She knew she could explain things to her mother's satisfaction. Mama understood better than most the need to do something wild and idiotic at times. And if Mari could gain insight into her father's worries, then it would be that much easier to handle him later.

# Twenty-three

PETER DIDN'T LIKE SPEAKING TO THE BOY IN FRONT OF Mari's father, but he'd faced thornier problems. The trick would be to watch both of them carefully without appearing threatening or even more than a genial buffoon. Fortunately, Mr. Powel was not an idiot and could be generally counted on to sit back and allow Peter to play out his hand, while keeping his own close to his heart. It was the way of a skilled negotiator.

So they stepped into the library, shut the door behind them, and found their seats. Mr. Powel even gestured for Tie to settle in the dark leather, despite his grubby clothing and generally filthy appearance.

Perfect.

Peter relaxed and began making friends with the boy.

"Your name is Tie, isn't it? Do you know who I am?"

"No, sir."

"He's the bloody heir to the Earl of Sommerfield," snapped Mr. Powel, "and I want to know what you were doing out at all hours with my daughter!"

Both Peter and Tie jolted at the man's explosive

tone. Apparently, his negotiating skills disappeared when confronted with a threat to his daughter.

"Sir," Peter began slowly, "there is no reason to discuss the marriage contract in front of young Tie here."

"And there will be no marriage if this is how you treat her! I've been asking about you. Learned an interesting tidbit about your time in the East India Company."

Well, he'd known his financial state wouldn't stay secret for long. Naturally, it was Mari's father who'd discovered that he wasn't the nabob everyone thought. But again, there was no need to discuss this before the boy.

"You've been woken in the middle of the night by some strange things, sir, but I have been awake all night trying to protect your daughter. She and I both went to a lot of trouble to bring this young man here, and I'm very interested in hearing what he has to say. Aren't you?"

And right here was the test of Mr. Powel. If the man chose temper instead of information, then he was a fool or worse. If he controlled himself to hear what was happening, then Peter would be inclined to trust the man. He waited, his expression as neutral as possible while the man visibly controlled himself.

"She's my daughter, man," he said with a huff. "The *sensible* one."

"She is still sensible, sir. Just too restricted." The man opened his mouth to argue, but Peter held up his hand. "We can discuss her choices later, sir."

"The boy," Mr. Powel said with a grudging acknowledgment. "Of course." He looked to the child. "Tie's your name? Do you have a last one?"

"Williams."

"Tie Williams. Good name."

Peter could see that the boy had never considered his name good or otherwise.

"I want to thank you, young man," Mr. Powel continued. "You came when my daughter asked you to. That was considerate of you. Decent thing to do, and all that."

Tie didn't know how to answer. Neither did Peter. Obviously Mr. Powel was skilled at talking kindly to people, servants and urchins included. He must save all his ire for suitors. Though clearly, his patience wasn't of long standing.

"So go ahead, Tie. Tell Lord Whitly whatever you need to."

The boy's eyes widened, and he shot Peter a panicked look. "I—I—"

He had no idea what to say, so Peter gave him a warm smile as he clapped his hand on his forehead. "I completely forgot." He reached into his pocket and pulled out the tarts his father's cook had given him. "Mrs. Evans had these for you. Said you like them."

He gave the boy the tarts. Dropped the packet into the child's lap, and watched him look at them with round, hungry eyes.

"Go ahead. I know how good they are. I used to sit at the table and eat until my belly burst. And then, when she wasn't looking, I'd stuff extras in my pockets."

Tie nodded. "Cricket likes 'em. He lets me sleep with the blanket if I get 'im one."

Cricket was older, then. Probably the bully in charge of the youngest ones.

"She'll make more tomorrow. You can sleep in the kitchen until they're done, then take some back to Cricket." It was a lie. Peter was never letting this child go back to the likes of Silas, but Tie wouldn't believe or trust that right now. These children lived on bartering—or what they could steal—and so that's what Peter would do. He just hadn't gotten to what he wanted in return.

The boy's eyes narrowed in suspicion, and he set the tarts away from him with obvious reluctance. "Why?" was all he said.

"Because I need to know something from you." He arched a brow. "Tell me about what you do with my father."

"I don't do nothing with 'im. He's a bleeding earl."

Peter didn't argue. An older child—or a harder one—wouldn't say anything. But Tie was still young enough to be manipulated. "You carry messages, right? Can you read them?"

"Course not!"

"And what's important is written down, right? That's why they send you. Because you can't read it." Peter shook his head. "They must think you're too stupid to understand."

"No," interrupted Mr. Powel. "That can't be right. Even I can see that this boy knows more than he says."

Peter nodded, pleased with the help from Mari's father. "I think so too. I think he knows the plan even if he can't read a single word."

"I ain't saying. Not for a couple of tarts."

Mr. Powel made a dismissive sound. "What do you want for it?"

Peter winced. That was the tactic of a wealthy man. Whatever nonsense came out of the boy's mouth, Mr. Powel could probably afford it. But Peter didn't bargain from a place of weakness.

"It's not worth more than a few pennies," Peter said with a grumble. "I'm just angry at my father for cutting me out." His eyes narrowed on the boy. "Unless you want to help me. I'll give you a piece of what I get."

The boy lifted his chin. He'd responded with a slight nod at the idea of a betraying father. And now he was clearly making calculations in his head. "What do you mean to do?"

"Nothing drastic," he lied. "Just watch. Say nothing now. Then I'll get my fair share from my father after it's done. And you can have a couple of quid just for telling me the when and where of it."

The boy sat there, chewing on his lip as he thought. A moment. Two. Damn it, the boy wasn't going to bite. And then Mr. Powel dropped his chin on his hand with a loud huff.

"He doesn't know anything. Best go get Cricket. He probably read the notes."

"He cain't read any more'n I can!" the boy cried. "And he don't know the plan, 'cause he didn't see the pictures. I did."

"Pictures, eh?" Mr. Powel said. Then he leaned back in his seat. "Well, that's interesting, but I have no more time for this." He pulled out a pound sterling and set it on the desk. "You'll get this now, boy, if you tell us everything. Pictures and all. And then you'll stay in my kitchen and take a bath until we've found out if what you say is true."

"And then wot?" the boy challenged.

And then the boy would be shipped off to Sommerfield to a new life, because the one he had here wouldn't last long. But Peter couldn't say that out loud. "Then I give you another quid as your share."

"My share oughta be bigger!"

Peter shook his head. He needed to stay firm to maintain the child's respect. So he kept his glare hard as he held out Mr. Powel's quid.

"Do you want this or not?"

Of course the child wanted it. It was more money than he'd touched in his entire life. He gave in with little grace and a great deal of grumbling, but Peter recognized the swagger for hidden glee. The child pocketed the coin, then set out with much gesturing and dramatic embellishes to tell the plan. Better yet, he was able to describe in great detail all the previous robberies orchestrated by the Earl of Sommerfield.

And wasn't that a grim realization? His own father was a thief. And not a common one, but a man who orchestrated the movements of children like Tie, all to his own benefit. What the hell was he going to do about that? And more worrisome, what was Mari's father going to do now that he knew?

⁂

Mari toweled off her hair and shoved a few pins in. There was no time for even a simple braid, but if she let it dry untamed, she'd spend the rest of the week fighting it. Or perhaps she was very focused on her hair as a way to avoid her mother's too-wise glare.

"You chose to leave the ball just like that? Mari, imagine what could have happened to you."

"I wished to be of help to Lord Whitly," she said primly. That was always her refrain with her parents when she did something untoward: she was trying to be useful. They accepted it because it was often true. They knew how much she fretted with endless days of doing nothing. It just happened that on this night, she'd been more concerned about finding Peter and doing other things than being useful.

"Lord Whitly is investigating something important," she continued. "And you know how men have no idea how to get information out of women or children. I had to help or watch him flounder."

"You mean you had to prove to him how valuable you can be." Her mother's hard stare met hers in the mirror, and she had the grace to flush.

"I…I like him, Mama. We're going to get married."

Her mother exhaled slowly, her expression narrowing as she studied Mari's face. "I can't quarrel with his pedigree, though your father said he found out something disturbing."

Mari paused as she settled a clean shift in place. "What do you mean, disturbing?"

"I don't know the details. He doesn't think the man is as rich as everyone believes. And your father doesn't like the earl at all."

"Oh. Well, Lord Whitly doesn't seem to care much for his father either. But not wealthy? Everyone says he's a nabob."

Mama waved that comment aside. "Everyone says you're wayward. What has that to do with the truth?"

A very great deal, given what she'd done this night. "Would you hand me my gown please?" she asked by way of distraction.

Her mother stood, picked up the rose gown, and pursed her lips. A moment later, she'd substituted it with a pale peach one so boring as to be virtually nonexistent. "This one is more demure."

Of course it was. "I'm tired of demure. I've learned that people will talk no matter what I do. So I might as well act as I please."

"Do that after you're married," her mother said tartly. "Until then, you will act as a proper lady and not wander through the docks in someone else's clothing."

Mari wanted to argue, but she could see that this was not the time. For all that her mother was acting calm and logical, there was still a heavy note of anger beneath. Mari had acted much beyond the pale, and she would do well to mitigate that damage.

"Of course, Mama," she said as she took the hated gown and began the tedious process of unbuttoning it before putting it on. They'd dismissed her maid in favor of frank talk, which meant that the silly parts of dressing would have to be accomplished by themselves. "Now tell me why Papa thinks his ledger has been touched. I thought the maids have been trained better."

"They have," her mother said with a wave of her fingers. "None of the staff would dare so much as dust the thing, if they even knew where it was. It's just one of your father's wild starts. You know how he can be."

She did, but this was not something her father

confused. On some things he was meticulous, and his ledger was at the top of that list. "But, Mama—"

"Do you love him?"

"What?" She'd just been about to step into her gown, but at her mother's words, she looked up in confusion. It wasn't that she didn't understand the question. She even knew that Mama was asking about her feelings toward Lord Whitly, not her father. But still, the question simply didn't make sense.

She looked to the list of suitors she kept on her dressing table. "Mama, you helped me write that list."

"I know."

"And Lord Whitly far outranks anyone on there."

"But you hated him. He's the one who named you wayward."

Mari shrugged, surprised that she could dismiss six years of fury so easily. "He meant it as a kindness."

"Don't be silly—"

"And perhaps it wasn't completely his fault."

"Oh?" her mother challenged.

Mari sighed. She was anxious to get downstairs and find out what the men were discussing, but she knew she'd end up cooling her heels in the hallway and appearing crass in front of Horace. So she might as well have this out with her mother now. The difficulty was that she'd only now come around to understanding it herself.

"He was discouraging that blighter Fitzhugh from pursuing me. That's why he said it in the first place. He had no idea the label would become so popular. He certainly didn't mean to make me completely boring for the last six years."

"No, that was your doing."

"And yours," she said with a tinge of reproach. After all, her mother had just handed her a bland peach gown that was demure.

"Very well, perhaps I can forgive him for his blunder. And I did encourage your efforts to become more refined."

More boring.

"But, darling, what about Lord Whitly the man?"

Mari frowned, then started ticking off attributes on her fingers. "He's titled, wealthy—"

"Maybe."

"Maybe wealthy," she amended. "He's handsome, and, Mama, he has this most glorious plan. It's quite idealistic, but I shall be able to help him bring it about. He values justice and responsible leadership. I think with my help, he could become eloquent when he enters the House of Lords."

"I don't think he needs your help to rule Sommerfield in a fair manner or take his place in the Lords."

"But I will be the perfect bride for that. Mama, I could help him be political. He doesn't understand Society the way I do. I would be an elegant hostess, and maybe I could assist with his speeches."

Her mother nodded, her expression troubled. "You would do well at all those things, but that's not love."

"I didn't love Mr. Camden either, but I was planning to marry him." And he certainly didn't kiss her the way Peter did. Or make her heart flutter and her body hunger.

"Mr. Camden was never my choice for you," her mother said, disapproval in every word.

"Well, that hardly matters, as I've decided on Lord Whitly." Mari punctuated her comment by presenting her back to her mother. Someone had to button up the gown without the maid there. Her mother obliged, her fingers swift and sure. But as the silence stretched, Mari ended up searching her mother's troubled expression in the mirror.

"I thought you'd like him," she finally said.

"It's not about him," her mother said. "Not exactly. I cannot understand all your lists and plans. I helped you with them, but I've never understood the necessity."

She knew this. It had always been so since her earliest days. It was her father who planned, jotted, and thought things through. She'd learned it from him.

Her mother finished buttoning the gown and then pressed a tender kiss to Mari's cheek. "I want you to fall in love."

"I am in love," she said. "With Peter." She spoke it firmly, because that was how she always stated things she wanted. It was a form of willing it into existence, and it sometimes worked. Either way, it was for her mother's benefit. Mama was the one who cared about love. Mari needed to be useful, and Peter was the perfect husband for that. Especially since he knew all sorts of fun ways to enjoy being wayward as well.

Their life together would be perfect.

Which was when she finally figured out who had bothered her father's ledger. She had no proof, of course. Nothing but the certain understanding that Peter had told her he was an accomplished thief. And he'd had notations from Papa's ledger in his bedroom. She'd seen it clearly and now knew what they meant.

Her breath froze in her chest.

The man was more clever than she'd even imagined. And he hadn't exactly been telling her the truth, had he? Add that to the realization that perhaps he wasn't as wealthy as everyone thought, and a number of difficult questions arose.

"Where are you going?" her mother demanded. "You haven't even put on shoes!"

Mari didn't stop. She had to ask Peter her questions. Why had he broken into the house to look at her father's ledger? What was he talking to Tie about? How did Silas fit in?

If she was going to help him, she needed to know the answers to those questions. And at the end of that she had one more question. Did he mean to marry her because he saw her value? Because she could help him with what he wanted in his life? Or because he needed her dowry?

And if it was the latter, if the only reason he'd courted and seduced her was because he needed her money, well, then…then…

She would hate him forever. Because she was done with proving herself to stupid, blind, idiotic men. And even after everything that had happened, the top of her husband requirements remained the same: Absolutely no fortune hunters.

# Twenty-four

MARI STORMED DOWN THE STAIRS WITH HER MOTHER scrambling after her. It was an unseemly thing for them both to do, but she had no interest in moderating her behavior. Or she didn't until she saw Horace with his ear pressed to the library door.

It was the last straw. Why had she spent the bulk of her life constantly controlling herself when even the butler felt it necessary to flout convention?

"Get away from that door!" she snapped.

Horace straightened with a startled gasp, and she glared at him.

"Mari, really!" cried her mother as she came up beside her. "There is no need to take out your temper on the staff."

"On the contrary, Mama, there is every reason. The man is a snoop and a snob. If you choose to tolerate such uncouth behavior, then that is your choice. But I shall unleash my temper on him every time I see him act in a way that does not fit with the character of this house."

Her mother sighed and dropped her hands on her

hips. "Darling, I thought you understood that your father prefers an obnoxious butler."

"He's supposed to be obnoxious to everyone else!"

"Well, who is Lord Whitly but someone *else*?"

How to answer that one? Mari certainly couldn't say he was the man she intended to marry. Not when she suspected she would try to claw his eyes out in the next few moments. So she chose to glare at Horace and speak in chilly tones.

"You will not listen to me," she said coldly. Then she realized exactly what she had said and huffed out a frustrated breath. "To my conversations," she amended.

"And how shall I stop myself, miss?" he intoned in the coldest, most pompous manner. "Shall I block my ears? Muzzle your suitors? Or perhaps you prefer I lock the back doors to all urchins speaking your name when they knock in the middle of the night?"

Well, he had a point, especially given what he'd seen this morning. She was hardly one to be throwing stones regarding proper behavior, but it didn't matter. She would be damned if she allowed their own servant to intimidate her. Also, she figured if she could vanquish this particular dragon, then facing Peter would be that much easier.

So she drew herself up to her full height, which left her still staring upward at the damned man. Papa also liked tall butlers, more's the pity. But when she spoke, she said each word in a clipped and imperious tone.

"I will tell you what you must do to avoid my ill temper, Horace. You must act in every way as someone who is kind. Kind to dirty street children, nervous suitors, and yes, even imperious lords who do not deserve such forgiveness. And then, sir, I will forgive you for failing to be kind to me."

It was a great deal more than she ever wanted to say to anyone, much less their obnoxious butler. But the words tumbled out, raw and clear. And while he gaped at her, she swept past him and pulled open the door to the library.

"Papa," she said loudly as she glared at Lord Whitly where he looked at a map of London. The boy, Tie, stood between him and her father and was pointing with a dirty finger at a single intersection. "I do hope you said nothing sensitive. There was at least one ear pressed to the door."

Her father looked up and frowned at the butler. "Damn it, Horace, I pay you to listen at *her* doorway, not mine."

"Papa!" Mari cried, but her father was still talking to Horace.

"Take young Tie here for his bath. He'll be staying with us for a few days. I'm making you personally responsible for his actions while he's here. He's to be clean and well fed throughout, is not to leave the house under any circumstances, and…" He glanced over at her mother. "What do you think, shall we teach him to read?"

"Of course we should teach him to read. If he's been of service to us, then we should help him in return."

Their butler had no chance to respond as her father kept talking. "An excellent suggestion. Horace, see to it personally, would you?"

Which was when poor Horace finally found his voice. "Teach him to read how, sir?"

"Kindly, Mr. Horace," Mari said somewhat gleefully. "There are books in the nursery that will help. And while you're at it, you might remember it was only an accident of birth that kept either one of us from this child's fate."

To which Horace drew up to his full height. "I was no *accident* of birth. My family has served in great houses for generations."

"Then be charitable to those who weren't so lucky by seeing to his bath and his education." And with that, she pressed the boy's hand into his and shut the door on them both.

There. One dragon slain, at least temporarily. But now it was time to face the larger, more difficult one: Lord Whitly. And with both her parents in attendance.

～∽～

The minute Mari burst through the door of her father's office, Peter knew she'd cause trouble. After all, she was a virgin who'd just had a grand adventure—her first bar fight, followed by her first sexual experience. Overwhelming for anyone, but she was a woman prone to grand schemes and elaborate rationalizations. Given the upset of this morning, she'd had just enough time to get it all wrong without enough time to realize she was making mountains out of molehills.

Which made it doubly bad that they were about to discuss things in front of her parents. He had to get her out of here now.

"Lord Whitly," she began.

Oh hell. She was in high dudgeon, making his name sound half summons, half curse.

Maybe he could derail her with a compliment. "Miss Powel, how lovely you look. I always appreciate it when your hair is left to curl more naturally." He counted himself especially clever, since that comment couldn't fail to remind her of the glorious way he'd worshiped her hair—and her body—not more than a few hours ago.

"My hair?" She blinked and ran a hand through the riotous locks. "Thank you."

Wonderful. The compliment worked. For about ten seconds. Then she frowned at him. "I have a question."

"Excellent," he said as he rolled up the map of London and passed it to her. "Perhaps we could go for a stroll in the park. I should be happy to discuss whatever you like there." Away from the too-intelligent gazes of her parents.

"No, my lord, it is something they should hear."

Damnation, she was being stubborn. "The marriage settlement has not been determined."

"Nor will it be until we—"

"Mari, we have both been awake through the night. Can this not wait until a more settled time?" After they'd both slept. After they'd had time to think things through. After she was past the overwrought emotions that were clearly upsetting her reason.

"Did you read my father's ledger?"

Oh. Blast and damnation. Far from getting things all wrong in her head, the brilliant woman had worked it all out right.

He glanced at her father, seeing the man's expression shocked to the core. Fortunately, his wife was of a more gullible sort. The woman threw up her hands in clear disgust.

"Mari, what a thing to say! Your father was just imagining it."

"I was not," the man growled. Then he took a step closer to his daughter. "Why would you ask this? Do you have any evidence?"

She pressed her mouth closed and shook her head. But her eyes were burning with unshed tears as she looked at him.

"Well," her mother exclaimed, "I can see you are one of those women who become irrational after staying awake all night. Young lady, I insist that you head straight for your bed."

Mari rolled her eyes. "I am not twelve years old."

"You can't just accuse people of—"

"He was a thief in India. He told me so. A very good one, adept at getting into places he was not supposed to go."

Her father huffed. "That means he *can* get in, not that he *did*."

"I told him, Papa. I told him where you kept your ledger."

"What?"

"I told him," she said in a low whisper. "And I am so very sorry about that."

Peter pinched the space between his brows. Damn it, this was not the way he meant to explain things to her. And certainly not with this audience.

"Even so," her mother continued, "that is not evidence, and you know it."

Mari nodded, her gaze still centered on him. "I

don't have to prove it," she said clearly. "I just have to ask him, and he'll tell me. Did you steal into the house and look at my father's ledger, recording things that you have no right to know?"

How to answer that except with the truth? "Yes." He wanted to say more. Hell, there were a thousand different explanations, but when it came time to voice them, the words crowded each other out. All he could see was the clear pain in her face. "Mari, I needed to know. I took nothing but the information, and I haven't shared that with anyone."

"Why?" she said, her voice a rasp.

"And how?" demanded her father.

That was the easiest thing of all. He'd been here as a guest enough times to know the lay of the land. Easy enough to wait until the staff was occupied below stairs while the family was out for the evening. But rather than explain that, he simply shrugged. "I learned to be an accomplished visitor in India, amusing when called upon and absent when out of mind."

"Because you were digging around where you didn't belong," her father said.

"Yes."

"In my ledgers." Her father leaned forward, his expression angry. "Did you think I was lying about her dowry?"

"No." He might as well tell it all. They'd figure it out soon enough, because he'd already told them the basics, but for her sake, he would explain it fully. "My father recorded money as coming from you. Large sums on specific dates."

"Not from me, he didn't. He hasn't made more than a few hundred pounds with me."

So Peter had surmised. "I had to be sure."

Now it was Mari's turn to be confused. "But why would the earl say that? Why would he give the credit to my father?"

He didn't answer at first. He saw her father look down at the rolled map of London and realize what young Tie had just told them. The Earl of Sommerfield was using a gang of boys to rob people. Most specifically, large chests of money coming from boats newly docked. At some point, those captains had to take the money from the ship to a London bank. The money was moved under guard, under cover of darkness, or some other scheme.

According to Tie, the earl learned the method and time of transfer, gave that information through Tie to Silas, and then waited for his cut of the robbery.

"My father robs people." Peter's voice was harsh, the words cutting. "But he can't record the income as a robbery, so it's written as profits from your father."

"Oh dear," her mother whispered as she half collapsed onto the settee. "Oh, you poor dear." Her gaze was hopping between Peter and Mari. Peter's eyes were on Mari's as she put the pieces together.

"You thought my father was the thief," she said slowly. "You thought it was his idea, his scheme."

Mr. Powel's head snapped up at that. Obviously, he hadn't even considered that aspect, but Mari had. Her mind was lightning fast.

"Yes," Peter said. "It's a hard thing to believe one's father is a thief. I was looking for a different explanation."

"So you looked to mine. You thought everything we have, all the money my father's made has been… that he stole it." It wasn't a question, but Peter answered it anyway.

"I needed to know the truth." After all, it made sense that Mr. Powel was a brilliant thief, disguising his income as profits from a myriad business ventures. The maharajas did it all the time, paying off debts before using bandits to steal the money back.

"One last question," she said, her voice soft but clear in the still room. "That day in the park when we met. You'd only been back in England a day or so, and yet you declared yourself to me immediately. I was so angry at you that I barely thought about it at the time, but you singled me out within days of landing."

"Yes. I knew I wanted you. I could barely believe my luck that you hadn't been snatched by someone else in the years that I was away."

She took a breath. "You wanted me."

"Yes."

"Because of my dowry."

He swallowed. He wasn't a man who spent time lingering in examination of his emotions. She had always burned bright in his mind, and meeting her in the park that day had shown him that she was everything he remembered and a thousand things more. "Because you are smart and prickly and beautiful. Because you speak your mind, and I like what you say." Because whenever he looked at her, he wanted her. And because he dreamed of the life they could have.

"It's because I'm an heiress, isn't it? How empty are your pockets, really?"

He could lie. God knew, he wanted to. He had come back from India with enough to keep him in a comfortable albeit simple life. Adding in his title and the family lands, he should have been a prince among men.

But one long, agonizing week with his father's ledgers, and he knew the truth. He didn't have enough to cover the expenses at Sommerfield, much less effect any improvements. His entire family fortune was gone, and worse, his father had turned to banditry to maintain the illusion of great wealth.

He sighed and looked at his hands. "You would be more secure financially with Ash, Lord Rimbury."

He heard her sigh as she dropped down to sit beside her mother. "So you are nothing more than a clever fortune hunter."

"I am a great deal more than that," he snapped. Except he wasn't. Every fortune hunter had dreams; every single one wanted the life they envisioned after the dowry was settled into their coffers. Just because she shone brighter in his mind than any coin, just because he ached for her with a desperation that went well beyond her money—well, that just said he was the best of a bad lot. "I want you, Mari." *And I have had you.*

Those words echoed in his mind. He could say them aloud and press the point. What decent man would have her then—heiress or not—if they knew she was no longer a virgin?

But he couldn't force her. As desperate as he was, he couldn't use what they'd shared last night to drag her into his arms. It would destroy what little affection she still had for him. So he stepped forward, and because she was sitting and staring at the floor, he dropped to his knees before her.

Never had he thought to humble himself this way before a woman, but he did it without more than a passing thought. He took her face in his hands and searched her gaze. He saw anger flashing in her eyes. Nothing so lackluster as pain from Mari Powel. It was only the exhaustion of a night spent awake that kept her from slapping his hands away.

"You love me," he said firmly, willing it to be so. She would not have gone to his bed if she did not. "The circumstances of how and why your heart found me are of no import. You love me, and we will be happy together."

He thought to see her heartbreak ease. Was that not what all women wanted? A sure knowledge that their future was safe? That they would have a man who cherished them and would see to their happiness? But her expression did not settle. It crumpled into dismay, while tears pooled and dropped, one by one, down her cheeks.

He drew back, confused. "Mari—" he began, but she shook her head, pulling away from his touch.

"I don't love you," she whispered. And lest he think she was lying, the pure torment in her expression told him it was the truth. "I love what you want to accomplish. I love that I could help you. But now I don't even know who you are. Oh God, another fortune hunter!" she cried.

"Mari—"

She broke away, shoving to her feet in a clumsy

display. Her sobs choked her, and she gasped even as she ran from him. He tried to catch her. He gripped her skirt as she stumbled away, but she tugged hard, and the fabric began to rip. He could not accost the woman. Not here on the floor of her father's library. He could not grab her and drag her to his rooms where he could hold her until she grew calm enough to converse.

So he let her go, though his left hand was already reaching for her even as the right released her gown.

"Mari, wait!" he repeated, but she was already fumbling with the latch. A moment later, she was gone, and two footmen were staring in at him, their eyes wide and their mouths agape.

"Well, that's a damned mess," Mr. Powel said behind him.

Yes, it was. Peter pushed to his feet and dusted off his clothing. What more could he do, with the footmen staring and her parents looking at him with enough sympathy to make his pride churn? He was the heir to an earldom, for God's sake. How dare two well-heeled cits look at him like he stood before them begging in rags?

Meanwhile, Mrs. Powel folded her hands together in her lap and shook her head. "Lord Whitly, I cannot understand what has occurred this night, nor do I approve."

And now he would have to make apologies, damn it. To the mother with her pursed lips and her tight fists. "Your daughter does not know her own mind," he said curtly.

"Don't be ridiculous," she snapped. "Mari has always

known her own *mind*. It's all the other things she muddles up."

His gaze jerked to her face, wondering if there was meaning in there, but he was too tired to understand it. And he kept thinking that he heard Mari. A footstep on the stairs. A thump in the room above them. Something that would tell him what she was doing. Was she calming enough to think? Was she cursing his name? Did she regret how he'd touched her last night? It distracted him and left his head thick, his chest tight.

"Lord Whitly!" Mrs. Powel's voice cut through his thoughts. He blinked and refocused, startled to realize that he'd been looking out the doorway.

"Lady Illston's ball is in two nights. No matter what else happens, Mari will not miss that night. She has spent weeks training that bird, and even in a temper, she will not cry off your wager. I suggest you resolve your difficulties." She gestured impatiently to the rolled map of London. "Whatever it is, see it done. And then think hard what you will say to her in two nights. I will be sure that she attends."

He looked at her, his mind churning slowly. Resolve a criminal parent. Put a thieving ring in gaol. And then find a way to woo the woman of his heart, when a month of steady courtship had yielded nothing but...

But one night when she might have conceived his child.

It was a measure of his desperation that he wanted that as a way to force her hand. "I never thought I would have to work so hard for the woman of my choosing," he mused absently.

Mr. Powel snorted. "Not for those timid English chits. But you picked a Welsh girl with fire in her. Of course she'll lead you a merry dance."

Peter gathered the pieces of his thoughts. "You'll still consider my hand for her? The marriage contract will be—"

"I'll set it out fairly for you. Had one drafted just yesterday." He walked around his desk and pulled a stack of papers out of his top drawer. "I already knew you hadn't much padding in your pocket, though I don't like what I've learned about your father."

Neither did Peter, but that was a problem left for later in the day. "I'd keep her safe from the earl."

Mrs. Powel sighed. "But not the scandal. You could never keep the scandal quiet."

No, he couldn't. But in this, Mr. Powel came to his rescue with a grumbled, "Tut tut. Wagging tongues only make a difference if you haven't the money. You've a good head. If you deal honestly with me, I'll see your coffers recover. But you have to handle your father first." His eyes narrowed. "Will you need men for tomorrow night?"

Peter shook his head. That at least he'd figured out while talking with Tie. "I'll see to my father's affairs."

"I'll keep Tie here and talking with no one." He passed over the draft of the marriage contract.

"Thank you, sir," Peter answered. Then he bowed to Mrs. Powel. "Madam."

"My lord," she returned, giving him her hand.

He finished the leave-taking, wondering how it was that he—the son of an earl—was grateful that two cits of heretofore questionable reputation could be so polite to him. They were treating him gently, when he had lied about his pocket and seduced their daughter after involving her in a tavern brawl.

But that was a thought for another time. First he had to find Ash and the constable, capture the thieves, and teach a damned parakeet something else to say. Something that wasn't going to get him kicked in the teeth in front of the entire *ton*. He caught a hackney and settled into it wearily. Then his gaze fell on Mr. Powel's document. He had no time to study the thing now. Mari's dowry was the smallest of his concerns, and in truth, he would take her without one, though how he would support her was another question.

And then he began to read.

Five minutes later, he was laughing hard enough to make his sides hurt. It wasn't funny. Nothing about this day was funny, but it was either that or sob like a tiny boy in leading strings. Because he finally understood just how deep he had fallen into disaster.

# Twenty-five

MARI ALWAYS CRIED IN PRIVATE. IT WAS A WEAKNESS of hers that she could never manage the tragic tears of so many stage heroines. A wilting facade or an elegant expression of dismay were beyond her.

No, when she cried, it was in a gasping, retching, oozing display. She had to muffle her voice in a pillow or alert the entire neighborhood. She had to cover that pillow with a rag to sop up the mess. And she had to wail so completely that when her body finally gave up the grief, she was head-sore and nauseated for at least a day afterward.

So she was upstairs, sobbing in a disgusting display, while the same litany of sentences whirled through her brain.

1. Lord Whitly was a fortune hunter, and she would marry no such man.

2. Peter was a liar and a fraud, and she would marry no such man.

3. He was a tender lover, who had shown her such wonderful things, and that was after her adventure by the docks. In a few short weeks, he had expanded her

world a thousandfold, and the idea that she would not marry him left her gasping and retching against her pillow.

4. She might marry a man—even a fortune hunter—if she loved him. But she did not love him.

Then she'd sob again before the litany restarted. She tried to distract herself. She tried to break the endless spin of statements with questions. Why didn't she love him? Why, after all they had done, didn't she worship the ground he walked upon? Why did her heart not pound the word "love" a thousand times whenever she thought of him?

If she knew in her soul that he was the only man for her, then she could forgive the lie about his money. She could convince herself not to care that he only wanted her dowry. She could do all those things if only she could think of him and feel that wave of adoration that women had for their true love.

But what she felt now was anger, wretchedness, and of course, that burning, hateful betrayal. He had lied to her. And he had crept into her house as a thief to steal things.

"I hate him," she said into her pillow. "I hate him. I hate him. I hate him."

Except that wasn't true. She didn't know how she felt about him. Which brought her back to the first statement again. Lord Whitly was a fortune hunter, and she would marry no such man.

So the cycle repeated until exhaustion claimed her and she slept.

She woke hours later. One glance outside told her it was late evening. Had she slept the day through?

What of her calls and the ball tonight? What of a visit to Lady Eleanor to scream out her frustration? But she'd slept the day through. One glance at the clock told her she could manage one event if she hurried, but she had no desire to be seen tonight, much less pursue another husband candidate. Not with her eyes still burning and her mouth like foul cotton. Best to stay home and handle her correspondence. Or rewrite her lists. Or read a book.

Or stare into the coals and cry some more. Fat tears that leaked silently down her cheeks. Which was how she occupied the next hour. Heavens, what a miserable bungler she was.

Sometime around eight, Mama came to visit. She brought Mari a plate of fruit and cheese. She talked about how boring tonight's soiree would be and that Mari was smart to miss it. They didn't speak of Lord Whitly, and for that Mari was grateful. Instead, her mother picked up her rewritten requirements for a husband and shook her head.

"No fortune hunter" was underlined this time and written in all capital letters. Mama pursed her lips, then set the page back down.

"Get some rest, darling," she said as she patted Mari's hand. "Perhaps you will think more clearly in the morning."

"I'm already thinking clearly," she said, though she winced at the peevish note in her voice. "That's why I wrote out the list again."

"Oh yes," her mother said dryly. "Isn't it lovely how everything in life can be boiled down to a number in a column or an ordered list of requirements?"

Mari didn't bother arguing. Her mother might be able to wander easily through life without the doubts and confusion that plagued Mari. Mama always knew that Papa was her true love. Her flexibility and his business brilliance made them a perfect pair and fully capable of managing the turmoil that came their way.

But Mari was of a weaker sort. Without the black-and-white letters on a page, a steady list of what was important and what was not, she found herself wandering off into the wilds of confusion. She might, for example, end up in a bar fight or making love in a liar's bed. These lists were her touchstone, and she would not abandon them now, when she felt most at sea.

Her mother watched her face closely, clearly waiting for something. But in the end, she shook her head. "You are so much like your father."

"You love my father," Mari returned, the words a smidge too defensive.

"I do indeed," Mama said as she pressed a kiss to Mari's forehead. "And I love you, my dear. I just wish that some part of you would look to your heart instead of your head."

"My heart has ever steered me wrong."

"That's because you're not experienced in listening to it. But practice makes perfect, you know."

Mari smoothed out the edge of the newest list. "I shall lead with my strengths, Mama. Now is not the time to bolster a weakness."

Her mother straightened with a sigh. "I shall never win an argument with you. You have too much logic." Then she kissed her child good-bye before setting out. And while Mari continued to stare at the dying coals, the rest of the house settled into night.

The doors were shut, the curtains drawn. The servants who lived elsewhere gathered their coats and departed. She even heard Horace bid the cook a good night. And as the minutes ticked by, Mari began to think. Instead of worrying over her conflicted feelings and the steady path of logic, she wandered through the other things that had happened. Most important, she focused on Tie. What exactly did he know? And what had he told Peter and her father?

Once the questions hit, the answers quickly became important to her. It didn't take long for her to realize that it would be easy to learn the truth. Ten minutes later, she was dressed and headed to the kitchen for a treat. Even if Tie had been well fed this day, little boys could always be tempted with a sweet.

An hour later, she had all the information she needed. And a new plan as well.

৺

"Are you sure you want to do this?" Ash's voice whispered through the shadows in the alleyway, mixing with the rustle of rats and the smell of piss.

Peter glared at the silhouette of his friend. Of course he was sure. No, he wasn't at all sure. Good God, was this the biggest mistake of his life? But it had to be done. So he put a finger to his mouth to demand silence, then he scanned the darkness wishing he could see something on this blighted foggy night.

Nothing.

He knew that somewhere the constable waited with

three of his most trusted men. Also in the darkness were two of Ash's favorite "footmen." Big men with scarred faces who were comfortable with weapons and had never, ever worn Ash's livery.

All of those men were well back from the narrow street they watched. Ash and he were the only two he'd allowed to slip close to this lonely stretch of London, if any part of the city could be called lonely.

He knew the attack would come soon. A boy had come through earlier, scampering up to extinguish the gas lamps. With the fog rolling in, the air felt like a thick pea soup that stank of fish.

That was when he heard it. A low grumble and a heavy thud like the blow of a big fist. A boy cried out, and there might have been sniffling. That told Peter that Silas was also waiting in the fog, probably farther down the street. Likely one of the boys had gotten restless and received a fist as discipline. Damnation, the waiting was interminable.

To his left, he heard Ash shuffle uncomfortably. A drip splattered across his brow, and he impatiently wiped it away.

And they waited.

Twenty minutes later came the sound of horses' hooves on cobblestones, the creak of wheels, and the groan of a harness. Turning toward the sound, Peter thought he saw the steady glow of lanterns.

"Idiot," murmured Ash, and Peter couldn't help but agree.

Lord Mooney had chosen the dark of a foggy night to transport his chest of gold from the docks to the London bank. A few well-placed questions had told Peter that the man had convinced the banker to receive the money in the dead of night, because he thought it was safer than in the light of a busy day.

Then, to make sure he was fully intimidating, the man had chosen his own carriage—complete with insignia emblazoned on the side—and outfitted it with two sharpshooters. That might have been smart if the men could see anything in this fog. They couldn't. And then—as if to fully prove his idiocy—he'd added lanterns to the vehicle, presumably to help the sharpshooters. Instead, the lights simply marked them as targets.

No wonder the earl felt no guilt about these thefts. He probably reasoned that a man this stupid didn't deserve to keep his gold.

Peter waited in silence, his fingers itching to do something, his toes curling and uncurling in his boots simply out of nerves. But he held himself still, and eventually the carriage made its way into the narrow gauntlet between a pair of dilapidated warehouses.

"Now," barked Silas, his voice crystal clear through the fog.

Rocks pelted the lanterns. Two were well aimed, and the things shattered instantly. The other two had to be pelted multiple times, and at least one of the sharpshooters cursed as he no doubt got hit hard by a rock. Within moments, the last two went dark, leaving the only light from the lantern inside the carriage.

The driver cried out; then there was a strangled gasp and a heavy thud. Shots exploded from the carriage. The sharpshooters fought back, but there was little chance anything was hit beyond the cobblestones. It was just too dark.

Next came the scream of a horse and the sound of a heavy mallet hitting wood. If only he could see. Beside him, Peter felt Ash stir uncomfortably. He understood the reason. It was bad enough to wait for an idiot to get robbed, but to sit still while a driver and his horses were damaged was beyond excruciating. Fortunately, it didn't take long.

A moment later, he heard the carriage door pull open, spilling light into the fog. The angle was wrong, tilted forward and down. That heavy mallet sound must have been against the wheel, breaking it enough that the carriage lurched awkwardly forward.

Meanwhile, two shots rang out, but they must not have found their mark, because Silas's voice came loud and clear. And only a few feet in front of Peter and Ash.

"'Ey now, no cause for that. I got lots o' men willing to pepper yer insides. I can get the gold from your dead body as easily as from yer live one."

"Shoot him! Shoot him!" squeaked a terrified man.

"I'm afraid they cain't, m'lord. I've got their guns."

Not to mention, everyone was still standing in the dark except for the gaunt and damned young face of Lord Mooney's eldest son. The boy was crouching inside the carriage. Jesus, he couldn't be more than nineteen.

"I'll never give it up!" the boy cried as he held out a pistol in a shaking hand.

Bloody idiot! He was going to die. Peter pushed forward—Ash a bare second behind him—but they needn't have worried. Before they could go more than a step, a weathered hand pulled the boy's pistol away. It came from a man inside the carriage. He'd been sitting twisted around so he wouldn't be visible from the open door. But his words were clear enough as he spoke.

"Don't be daft. They've got us surrounded, and we're sitting here like a bloody beacon."

Peter exhaled in relief. A voice of reason. Likely the ship's captain and a man experienced in violence. A moment later, his assessment proved correct as the man addressed Silas.

"I've got what you want right here."

"No!" squeaked the boy.

"But I need to be sure my men and his lordship are safe."

Silas released a dark chuckle. "Who knows? London's a dangerous city, especially at night." Peter moved silently forward.

"I still got my pistols, and I can shoot whoever comes near."

Silas didn't bother to answer. Instead, Peter saw the dark silhouette in front of him lift an arm. Then there was a bright flash as he fired, putting a hole straight through the side of the carriage.

That was it for Peter. Silas probably hadn't been aiming at anything in particular, but a shot from this distance could hit anyone. All he'd been waiting for was the proof of deadly intent.

And there it was.

So he sprang forward. Silas hadn't been expecting an attack, certainly not from behind. Peter tackled the villain quickly, knocking the pistol away then kicking the heavy mallet aside. But it was a *heavy* mallet, and it didn't go far. Silas wheeled around, but Peter had the upper hand. He didn't worry about other attackers.

He knew from experience that Ash would keep off anyone coming to Silas's aid.

The scuffle was quick. Within moments, Peter had the bastard subdued, though cursing enough to burn his ears. Then he called out in a strong voice.

"Constable? Have you caught the others?"

"Some," came the response as the man lit a lantern and set it on the ground. In the pool of light, Peter saw a couple of lanky adolescents struggling in the grip of larger men. "The little 'uns are quick little buggers."

Yes, the younger boys would have melted into the fog like water. Meanwhile, Lord Mooney's boy was peering owlishly out at the darkness.

"What's happening? What's going on?"

"Just a moment, sir," Peter said. "I'm with the constable, and we have been tracking this gang for a while now. Let us mop them up, and you'll be on your way."

"But the carriage—" the boy squeaked.

The captain's voice interrupted. "I'm grateful, sir. We'll be quiet in here, though I wouldn't mind a word from my men."

Peter understood that, and while the constable quickly produced some rope to tie up Silas and his boys, Peter looked to the carriage. "Speak up, men."

Not a word. Damnation.

While Ash lit another lamp, Peter went to the closest perch. The man there was messy with blood, but when he touched the man's throat, a pulse beat steady and strong.

"Alive but unconscious," he said. "Come on out, Captain, and tell me if you have any skill at physicking." He hadn't needed to speak. He'd felt the carriage lurch as the captain went to check on his other men.

A moment later, he heard the man's voice from the second perch. "Jones? Jones, man, wake up."

"Coachman's dead," said the constable from the other side. "Broken neck."

Peter cursed under his breath. He shouldn't have waited. He should have stopped the attack before it had begun. But then he wouldn't have known the exact intent of the robbery.

"What?" gasped the boy, who was still cowering inside the carriage. "Tom's dead? What?"

Peter grimaced and turned his attention to Silas. "So you were sent to rob the carriage. By whom?"

"I didn't do nothin'."

"You killed a man."

"That weren't me! I was just coming to 'elp." Then he got a glittering look in his eye. "Ain't no one can say different."

"I can say different. As can the men all around me." He leaned close. "You're going to hang, Silas. Unless you talk to me. Unless you tell me exactly who sent you and how you knew to come here."

The only answer was a string of profanities and spittle. Peter sighed, realizing he was in for a long night of interrogation. He needed to know the full extent of the ring. Was just his father involved? Or were there others? Then a female voice cut through the noise. A strong sound that nonetheless had him shooting to his feet in shocked horror.

"He won't talk," she said, "but the other one will. That one tied up near the constable."

Mari.

# Twenty-six

MARI KNEW SHE SHOULD HAVE STAYED QUIET. HELL, she knew she should have stayed at home. Even before that, she probably shouldn't have bribed Tie for the information on the robbery. But she had, and so why should she start doing what she ought now, when disobeying convention brought her so many answers? Albeit with a bit of a risk thrown in.

Fortunately, she'd been smart enough to bring Tie. He convinced her that she'd never get there unseen without him, and he'd been right. They'd slipped through shadows and scurried across roads like tiny mice. He was ten times faster than she—and much less averse to the city's filth—but he'd waited for her and even helped her when she'd needed it. And he'd guided her to a watch spot up the street from where everything had happened.

Then when she hadn't understood what was going on, he'd explained it in a low whisper, barely audible over the clatter of wheels and the shouts of the men. Which was how she'd known when it was over. So when the three largest children, plus Silas, were captured, they'd left their hiding place while Tie continued to explain.

He was the one who'd told her that Silas would never say anything, but Bobby would if they threatened him with his greatest fear. "Tell him you'll cover him in spiders if he doesn't explain," she said. It was a reasonable statement, and she considered it quite helpful.

Peter, of course, would focus on the fact that she was dressed as a barmaid again and out where she shouldn't be in the dark of a foggy London night. After he said her name—or more like strangled it—he made a quick gesture to Lord Rimbury who spoke gravely, but with an undercurrent of humor.

"Tend to her. I'll...er...cover the boy in spiders."

Bobby began howling at that, thrashing in his bonds like a demon possessed. But Mari had no more time to consider him as Peter rushed forward, grabbed her by the arm, and wheeled her into the shadows.

"What the bloody hell are you doing here?"

"I came to help," she lied. And what a bad lie it was, because he snorted.

"You know quite well that we didn't need your help."

True. "I knew about the spiders," she challenged.

"Tie knew about that. And he already told me."

Oh. That was disappointing. "Well—" she began, but he wasn't listening. While still keeping an incredibly firm grip on her arm, he squatted down to stare into Tie's face.

"I thought I said—"

"She were going to come anyway. I thought I'd keep her out of trouble."

Peter took a deep breath. "Apparently, that was beyond both of our abilities."

Mari smiled. "Glad you understand. I was well out of the way and very safe."

"There are more dangers in London than just these thieves," Peter ground out. "Do you have any idea what could have happened to you?"

"Yes," she said softly. In truth, the possibilities had been very present in her imagination, starting about one minute after she'd left the house with Tie. Pride had kept her feet pressing forward. "And none of them happened." Then she touched his face. "Peter, is it true? Was this…this attack orchestrated by your own father?"

"I don't know," he said with a growl. "That's why I had to capture them. So I could find—"

"Aye, it's planned by the earl," Tie piped up in an angry huff. "Silas ain't got the smarts for it."

Mari winced. His own father the head of a thieving ring. It was inconceivable.

Meanwhile, Peter dropped his voice. "You understand, don't you, Tie? If Silas knows you betrayed him—"

"I'm dead fer sure, but he ain't seen me." And he'd been keeping his voice low.

Peter exhaled in obvious relief. "Do you know how to get back to Miss Powel's home?"

"Want me to take 'er?"

"I'll escort her. You're the one in the most danger."

Tie nodded, his eyes wide. He might have ducked away, but Peter kept him still.

"I'll go with you if it would make you feel safer."

"Nah. I'm faster alone."

"Very well. If you stay at the Powels' residence, I'll come find you tomorrow and tell you what happened. I owe you for your help. Plus, I have other jobs that might work for you. I'll need a sharp pair of eyes seeing things I can't."

Tie's expression narrowed. Even in the darkness, she could see he was suspicious. Oh my. Did Peter fear he'd run away now? Disappear back onto the streets? She supposed that was a possibility, but she'd already thought of that.

"And don't forget that I'll pay you in the morning as well." At Peter's look, she explained. "I offered him a quid for seeing me safely here."

"Well, he's is becoming quite wealthy off of us, isn't he?" It was a joke.

Peter knew as well as she did that a few pounds weren't going to solve this boy's problems. But at the moment, there were other things to manage. Lord Mooney's chest of coin, for one thing. And the interrogation, spiders and all. Not to mention the questions she had for him. Ones she didn't relish trying to ask while surrounded by people at a ball.

"Go on home," she said to Tie with a reassuring smile. "I'll have Cook make us some more tarts tomorrow." If that didn't keep him safe at home, then she doubted anything would.

He flashed her a broad grin, then disappeared, melting into the fog faster than she could blink. She was still admiring the boy's skill when Peter tugged her closer. "You're hurt," she said as she reached out to stroke a smear of blood off his face.

"Not my blood."

Thank God.

"Mari, why did you come? Why risk yourself this way?" Then he rubbed a hand over his face. "Your father will have my head."

"My father will have *my* head, not yours. And…" She might as well explain as best she could. "I feared for you."

"And coming here put us both in danger."

"No," she said. "Just me. You were magnificent, by the way. I've never seen fisticuffs like that. So fast, so—"

"Brutal?"

"So decisive." She bit her lip. How had she ever thought him banal? The very idea was ludicrous to her now. "I've been so wrong about you for so long, I don't know what to think, except…"

"Except?"

"Except I want to know more. And I want to discover it without everyone watching us." Then she touched his mouth. She stroked her fingers across his lips, felt the heat of his breath, and knew that this man fascinated her. What she'd judged weak before was only the smallest fraction of him. Only now was she seeing the depths of the man. "Why did you lie to me?"

"Stupidity," he said softly as he pulled her gently against his body. "And habit. The appearance of power—or wealth—is often as good as the actual thing."

"But—"

He stopped her mouth with his thumb. "Not here. I need to get you home."

Behind them, the constable was issuing orders and directing his men in helping Lord Mooney's son with his coin. Lord Rimbury had already left with Silas and the other captives. Perhaps Peter wanted to be there.

"Did you need to join Lord Rimbury?"

"No. I think you had the right of it. We need to talk, you and I. Come this way."

He slid his hand down her arm, softening enough for her to entwine her fingers in his. Callused skin, big fingers, broad palm. Why didn't this man dwarf her into nothing? Given what she'd seen of his physical prowess, he should seem like a hulking brute to her. Instead, she felt protected and cherished.

She stepped closer to his side.

"Are you cold?"

"No, I'm fine. Where are we going?"

"To talk." He looked at her. "In my rooms."

She nodded. "Perfect."

He snorted. "Dangerous."

Perhaps. But she found she liked the danger.

They moved quickly through the dark streets. More than once they heard something that disturbed him. On those occasions, he pulled her into the darkest shadow and waited, while her heart pounded in her ears, and his breath slid hot against her cheek. Nothing ever happened. The sounds either faded away, or the people passed without seeing them. But the excitement made her grin in the darkness, and his body made her liquid with memories of the night before.

They made it to his rooms eventually. She ran as quietly as she could up his stairs, then slipped inside his room while he shut the door behind them. Then she leaned back against the wall, feeling her heart race and her breath—

Oh!

He was kissing her. Hot and hungry, his mouth covered hers, his tongue thrust inside, and his body pinned her to the wall.

She didn't mind in the least. She set her arms on his broad shoulders, twined her fingers through his hair, and kissed him with every part of her body and soul. It was wild abandon, and she loved it.

But then he pulled back. His right fist hit hard against the wall near her head while his left hand cupped her face. "I brought you here to talk. To explain."

She knew. She wanted that too, but those thoughts were so far away when he touched her. She stroked her fingers through his hair. "I don't know why I don't love you," she whispered. "You're everything I think about. I can't breathe without remembering some moment with you."

"You do love me," he said, his words harsh. "Good God, Mari, who else would you wander through the streets of London to be with?"

"Just you."

"Who drove you to six years of hiding?"

"You."

"And who makes you want this more than I?" He jerked the ties of her cloak apart before pressing his mouth to the mounds of her breasts above her bodice.

"Just you," she said as she let her head drop back. His mouth was hot, but it was nothing compared to the fire in her blood.

She felt his fingers on her bodice, unbuttoning her quickly. It wouldn't take long, since she hadn't been able to fasten it all the way. That's why she'd chosen her cloak that had been too heavy for sneaking about at night. But it was off her now. And within moments, her gown parted and slipped away.

"You love me," he said as if imprinting the words onto her skin.

She loved this. She knew that. She set her hands to his clothing, pushing off his rough coat then fumbling with the buttons on the shirt beneath. Then she pressed her hands to his chest. She felt the wiry hairs, the shift and flex of his muscles beneath, and then the exquisite heat of the man himself.

"I would never be cold around you," she said, knowing it was an odd comment.

He was kissing her, deep thrusts of his tongue as he pressed against her. She had no room to undress him more. All she could do was explore the feel of his chest as her hands were flattened between them. At least she could rub the edge of her nail against the hard rise of his nipple.

He growled as she did that, by which she guessed he liked it. Suddenly he was gone from her. She was left kissing nothing, her body falling from the sudden lack of support. Then she felt him scoop her up. Before she could do more than gasp, his arm was beneath her legs, and she toppled against him.

"You are mine, Mari. You have to know that."

Did she? She had promised him that she'd marry him. "You're a fortune hunter," she said without heat. He was carrying her so easily that she felt like she was floating. Then he set her down on his bed, seated upright with her legs dangling off the side. With quick movements, he untied her corset and stripped her out of her shift. Within seconds, she was naked before him. And far from being ashamed, she reached for his pants.

"You as well," she said.

"Light a candle," he said, his chin jerking toward the table as he pulled off his shirt.

She did, her fingers fumbling, but in the end she managed it. And when she looked back, he was naked, his cock thrust toward her, thick and ruddy red.

She loved the sight of him in his full prowess, but her hands seemed to have their own thoughts as she touched his organ, stroking across the velvety head, feeling its girth while slicking her thumb with his moisture. His breath hissed through his teeth, and his neck tightened, but he didn't move. If anything, she thought his entire body had gone rigid as she explored.

"Peter?" she asked, uncertain.

He tilted his head down to her. They weren't a far distance apart, but this motion seemed to come with deliberate tension. He moved slowly, his gaze dark as his fists settled onto the mattress on either side of her hips. She leaned back as he descended, keeping just far enough apart that she could watch the burning intensity in his eyes.

"You said you would marry me."

She swallowed. "I know."

"You could even now be carrying my child."

Her belly fluttered at that, and she bit her lip, both wishing and fearing it was true.

"We have gone too far for you to run from me now."

She touched his face, needing to soften the hard granite of his jaw. She stroked his cheek and brushed her fingertips into the curl along his temple. "I have never understood a single thing about you, even from the very beginning. I thought you cruel when you were doing a kindness. I thought you lazy when you were building a vision of your future. And I thought you wanted only me, when in fact you want my money." She swallowed down tears she didn't want to acknowledge. "Do you know how much that confuses me? Do you know how lost I feel?"

He nodded, a measured dip of his chin. And then he extended the motion, meeting her lips with a slow press that steadily grew to a full possession. He pressed her backward as he took her mouth. His fists had opened, and she felt his hands support her shoulders and head as he laid her out on the bed. And when she would have clutched his shoulders, he set her hands to the side and wrapped her fingers around the sheets.

"Hold here," he said as he began kissing down her neck.

"But—"

"Do you know what a French letter is?" he asked as he pressed his lips to her breast.

"No."

"It is a condom. A thing to prevent pregnancy."

His words were like a low vibration on her skin, the scratch of his chin an erotic counterpart to the soft press of his lips. She was so focused on those sensations that she barely heard his words.

"I cannot help yesterday, but I will not risk a child again until we are wed."

His chin brushed the side of her breast, and when he stopped speaking, his mouth found the point of her nipple. A tiny nip. A slow suck. And then another sharper nip.

"Mari, do you understand?"

"No," she said. "Did you not hear me? I understand nothing of what you do or why, and that frightens me."

His expression softened. "Or perhaps you do not understand the what and why of what *you* do, and that is terrifying."

She blinked. It was so hard to think with his breath wrapping around the wet of her nipple. "Maybe. Yes, that is true. When I am with you, I frighten me."

He smiled. "That I understand very well. You have pushed me in ways I never imagined."

He tongued her nipple, and she arched into his attention. Her hands slid to his shoulders, where she clutched at him, while her mind splintered into a thousand wonderful sensations.

He switched to the other breast, making her whimper as he suckled. And when she might have dragged him back to her mouth, he took her hand and gently reset it into the sheets.

"Hold there," he said as he kissed his way down her belly.

Her legs were splayed, her body quivering in hunger, and she had a fleeting question slip through her mind as he laved a circle around her navel. But she couldn't hold the thought for long, and so it slipped away as he…

He…

Oh!

He pushed her legs apart, settling between them so

his shoulders kept them wide. Part of her was alarmed by this, but then she felt his thumb slide between her folds. The rough pressure and the broad caress made her gasp even as she pressed up toward him.

She wanted to say something. She wanted to be eloquent and perfect, but there was no place for that with him between her thighs. And before she could even catch the idea of words, he spoke for her.

"You are everything I want," he said, his tone equal parts demand and reverence.

She didn't understand what was happening. The sensations were too wonderful for her to parse into meaning. Wet. Rough. Stroke. Suck. More and more while she thrust herself against him.

The tension was building. The sensations aggressive. She tightened her legs, but he held her knees down. And then it happened. Everything compressed together—a spring pressed tight—before releasing. Her body bucked. Her belly rippled. And everything was glorious experience as she flew.

Then she felt him, that thick presence at her entrance. Yes, that was what she'd been missing. Him filling her.

He was crouched above her, his body so wonderfully large. She arched, trying to take him inside. She was still contracting, her head thrown back into the bed, but she had the wherewithal to whisper.

"I would like to carry your child."

She didn't know where the words came from, and she couldn't hold onto them once they were spoken. They were simply part of the experience.

"When we are wed," he said.

"Yes."

He thrust.

Stretched. Full. Big.

He made her feel so expanded. As if she could take the whole of him and still have room for joy. Her thoughts made no sense, and yet they too were part of this lovemaking.

Open.

Embracing.

While he thrust.

Harder and faster.

Yes.

More.

She gripped him with her legs.

Every impact ratcheted her higher.

And then he seated himself and stopped.

"Mari," he said. "Mari!"

She opened her eyes.

"Say it."

"What?"

"You are mine. Say it!"

Of course she was. In this place, in this moment, she had no doubts at all.

"Yours," she said.

He grinned and became like a man driven to possess her. He thrust into her.

He: driven.

She: possessed.

*Yes!*

# Twenty-seven

PETER COLLAPSED SIDEWAYS, HIS HEART THUNDERING in his ears. His orgasm had been powerful enough to black out his vision and obliterate his mind for a few glorious moments. And while he was there, she had milked him like a woman taking every last drop. The squeeze and release had been like a fist pulling him into her, and he had wanted to go.

So hard. So fast. And so amazing that he had lost himself in her.

Until it was done.

He shuddered, barely having the wherewithal to keep from crushing her. And still she squeezed him. Tiny pulses that sent pleasure bursting through his system.

God, she was exquisite.

He didn't want to separate from her. So he pulled her on top, maneuvering her boneless body so she lay with her hips on his and her head on his shoulder.

She fit perfectly, and he pressed kisses to her hair in reverence. Then he exhaled in bliss and let himself doze.

Drowsy as he was, he allowed himself to be lulled

by a vision. The woman he'd wanted for six years finally beside him at the altar. She'd be dressed like an angel, and her words would ring strong and true.

"I do."

Yes. He wanted that enough to be tempted to sleep. Except Mari was not a woman to be held down, even by vows spoken in church. If forced, she would honor her word, of course. He did not worry that she would cuckold him. His fear was something else. That her attention would wander elsewhere. Her mind would take over, telling her to do some such nonsense here or there. And it would drive a wedge between them.

His parents were one such couple. His father's interests went to town, his mother's to her garden and her books. It made for a cold home of disinterested conversation, if not outright sneers and dismissals, until husband and wife could barely stand to be in the same room with one another. As for the children…he and his brother had fled the moment they were able.

He did not want that with Mari. He had to capture her heart as thoroughly as he'd ensnared her body. But how? How to woo a mind that would not settle? That saw him as a villain no matter what he did? Especially since he was not a man who was good with words.

"Mari," he murmured as he stroked a hand through her hair, "tell me why you hate fortune hunters."

"Hmmm?"

Her word was more a purr of contentment, but she was rousing. Her hand lifted to brush across his arm. Her breath stuttered once then pulled in deep.

"What happened?" he asked. "To make you put them at the top of your list?"

"What happened?" she murmured. "They happened."

"Who?"

She rattled off three names, most of them unfamiliar to him.

"What did they do?"

She snorted. "The usual. Dances. Parties. Flowers in the morning, sweet words in the afternoon, and then kisses in darkened alcoves at a ball."

His anger roused, a dark and growling thing at the idea that she would kiss anyone else.

"Nothing so bad, you understand. Twice under the mistletoe, once behind a statue of Cupid. And then there was the stroll in a garden." Her voice dropped on the last one, a clear note of fury.

"He forced you?"

"Into the garden? No. Against a tree? Yes. I hit him with my fan. Bloodied his nose."

"Good. I hope you broke it."

He felt her smile against his chest, and he stroked the hair from her forehead so he could plant a kiss to the skin there. Then he relaxed for a time, enjoying the simple sweetness of feeling her breath and relishing the vision of her bloodying the nose of an aggressive suitor. She was a firebrand, his Mari.

"I thought I loved them," she finally said. "All three. I would have said yes if they'd asked. I did say yes to the first one, but Papa refused to honor the dowry. Not for a blighter, he said. And without the money, they all ran away."

Given that he had firsthand experience with how her father negotiated marriage contracts, he understood how a young fortune hunter would disappear.

But it grieved him to see how strongly the bastards had wounded her heart.

"Your father would not be an easy father-in-law," he said. "I'm sure he did everything he could to frighten them away."

She swallowed. "Are you frightened?"

"Not of him," he said.

"Of me?"

"No."

"Then—"

"I fear what I will do to win you, Mari. Your father has offered me a new contract."

She lifted her head, her expression pinched. "Is it terrible?"

"No, it's quite generous." Then before she could ask, he explained. "It's an employment contract, Mari. He is offering me a job instead of your hand."

She gasped. "But you're the heir to the Earl of Sommerfield."

His lips quirked in a wry smile. "I don't think he cares."

"No, Papa wouldn't, but you do."

He thought he did. He certainly expected that he would. His parents would be horrified if they ever heard of the offer. They would name it an insult and set about damaging her father's name in any way they could. Future earls did not have jobs. It had been hard enough for his father to stomach him working for the East India Company, and that had been half a world away.

"I may still do it," he said, surprising himself as he spoke the words aloud. "If it meant earning your good graces." And because his family name would soon become the object of great scandal.

She pressed a kiss to his chest. "I do not know how much further into my graces you can get."

He smiled at that, but he knew her now. Knew her worries would get the better of her when she was no longer languid from pleasure and stretched bodily over him.

"What did these boys do to you, Mari? To make you write 'no fortune hunters' at the top of your list?"

She sighed. "They did not hurt me, Peter. They just showed me that I cannot trust my heart in these things."

"Because you were in love?"

"Because I believed myself desperately in love. And yet weeks after their defection, I felt nothing."

"Pain fades to numbness."

"You cannot imagine how stupid I was. I think of what they said, of what I believed." She huffed out a breath. "My heart is not a sure guide in these matters. If anything, it will steer me completely wrong."

"And so you trust your list and your mind, and ignore what your heart whispers."

"My heart has learned to be silent." She shifted then, lifting her head to set it on her fist. But the twist overbalanced her, and her hips slid away. He fell out of her and grimaced in regret.

"You put me in a quandary, then," he said as he resettled her against his side. "I will marry you, Mari." That was statement, not supposition. "But not until your heart wants me as fiercely as mine wants you."

Would she hear what he was saying? Did she

understand that he wanted her to feel? To know without reservation that he was the man for her? So he could marry her without constantly fearing that another one of her lists would put him out of favor? That at some point she wouldn't suddenly turn around and again name him the source of all her ills?

She sighed. "You make me rethink everything I thought I knew."

"You have sent me to India, where I changed everything I was. And now, because of you, I think to hire myself out to your father, humiliating myself before all of Society."

She looked at him, clearly stunned. "You would do that…for me?"

"I do that for money. So I will not need your dowry to wed you."

She touched his lips with her fingers. She searched his face for an answer. But in the end, she simply closed her eyes and set her head against his heart.

"I was wrong," she said. "You are not a fortune hunter."

"But I am," he said firmly. "I want your fortune, Mari. Without question. I just want you more."

She was silent a long time. Her breath shifted constantly though, one moment sharp and quick, the next a slow sigh of an exhale. He did not know what it meant, except that her mind was whirling again. Even without paper at hand, she was making a list in her mind. She was weighing his assets and her life as if they could be measured and balanced on a scale.

He didn't stop her. He knew he couldn't. All he could do was wait for her conclusion.

"I believe you," she finally said. "And I will marry you."

Not quite the passionate declaration he had hoped for.

"Tomorrow night at Lady Illston's ball," he said, "I will propose, and you will accept?"

"Yes."

He pressed a kiss to her forehead. Then he lifted her so he could find her lips. She returned his affection quickly enough. She opened herself to him, and he knew he could rouse her passion within moments. His was already heating his blood. But for all that, it was a lackluster acceptance to his proposal, and it left him feeling unenthusiastic.

"You still doubt this," he said, bitterness in his tone. "After everything, you still aren't sure."

She snorted and pulled herself off him. "I doubt everything." She pressed her hand to his chest. "Your faith. My heart." She gestured to the bed. "This choice. I doubt it all."

"Which is why you write lists, why you seek Lady Eleanor's advice, and why you allow your father to test and torture your suitors."

She shrugged, and her hair slipped down over her shoulder, covering her eyes and the glory of her right breast. "If you were looking for surety in a bride, you picked the wrong Welsh. My sister, Josephine, never doubts anything. I, on the other hand…" Her voice words trailed off, as if even in this sentence, she could not commit to what she wanted.

He took her hand and pressed it to his lips. "I fear you will change your mind before tomorrow night."

"Oh, I will," she said with a wry laugh. "At least a dozen times or more."

"That does not give me confidence, Miss Powel."

"Goodness, Lord Whitly, I had not realized you lacked for confidence in anything."

"It is a state I am becoming much too familiar with." He sat up and pulled her into his arms. She went easily, and he comforted himself that if he could only hold her whenever she doubted, in time all her fears would be erased.

He struggled to find the words to convince her, but he had given her his best arguments. She was so much better at words, so he resorted to the cheap and the easy. The only way he knew for certain that she was vulnerable to him.

He kissed her again. And as he kissed her, he palmed her breasts. And then he steadily, purposefully, stoked the fires of her passion. He spread her legs, rubbed her clit, and waited until she was crying out his name before he took her again.

And again.

All night long, if needed. Until she could think nothing—say nothing—but the word "yes."

# Twenty-eight

THE FIRST MARI REALIZED THAT SOMETHING MOMENTOUS had happened was when her maid pulled the curtains and flooded her room with morning sunlight. She knew not to do that. Which meant something important had happened.

But given that Mari hadn't snuck back into the house until a couple of hours before dawn, she had trouble caring. Let the world go hang for a bit. She was sleepy and happy from everything she and Peter had done, and in so many wonderful ways. She couldn't wait to get married and be able to do that in their own bed whenever they wanted.

But then her maid tsked, and Mari was forced to roll over.

"What?" she said, not even bothering to hide her irritation.

"Begging your pardon, miss, but you 'ave a caller. An *early* caller."

Mari frowned. "What time is it?"

"Nine twenty o' the clock, miss."

Nine twenty? She shoved the hair out of her eyes. "Who is it?"

"It's Lady Eleanor. And she's mighty anxious—oh, milady!" Ginny made a hasty curtsy while Mari was still realizing that someone had burst through her bedroom door. Someone dressed to perfection, with a smooth brow, elegantly coiffed hair, and as much of a frown of worry on her face as Eleanor would allow herself.

"Still abed, you poor dear," the lady said.

Sympathy from Eleanor? This couldn't be good. Cursing under her breath, Mari shoved herself into a semi-upright position as she looked at her maid. "Bring us tea, please. Strong."

"An excellent notion," Eleanor said with a serene smile. "And then together we'll make sure you're in your best looks for tonight."

Tonight was hours away, and Eleanor had never taken a personal hand in her grooming before. Mari closed her eyes and steeled her spine.

"What happened?" Had the government fallen? Had rioters taken to the streets? Was London riddled with disease? She could think of nothing else that would bring such a dramatic morning visit.

"Of course you haven't heard," Eleanor said as she settled herself pristinely on Mari's dresser chair. She started to speak, but then stopped herself, looking unusually awkward.

Mari began to feel real alarm. "Has someone died?" She couldn't even bring herself to say Peter's name aloud. It wasn't possible. God, no! Her hands were pressed to her mouth as she blinked tears away.

"Dead? No, not that. Though…" She shook her head. "I suppose some might prefer it. They definitely wish it so."

"What? Make sense."

Eleanor nodded then tilted her head at a precise angle so one curl draped enchantingly across her cheek. It was a practiced pose, one that conveyed consternation without wrinkling the face. "Please try to stay calm. It's about Lord Whitly. Rest assured that we will find you another husband. I have not lost faith yet."

Oh no. "I don't want another husband. Eleanor, I—"

Her bedroom door burst open again, this time with her mother in her best day gown as she rushed forward to press kisses to Mari's cheeks. "Never mind about anything today, Mari. We shall go shopping for some new gowns. Ones like you want, with dots or lines on them. Perhaps even some embroidery on a ruffle. Wouldn't that be nice?"

"No, Mama, that would not be nice!" Well, of course it would, but that was not the point. She gripped her mother's arms and forcibly sat her down on the bed. "What has happened to Lord Whitly?"

"Um, nothing, my dear," her mother said as she twitched her eyes to the maid who had followed her in with the tea tray. "Let's wait and discuss this after you've had something soothing."

She knew better than to argue. She waited with ill-disguised impatience as a small table was set out to hold tea for three. Eleanor presided over it from the dressing-table chair. Meanwhile, Mari straightened up to a fully seated position.

Except that motion pulled at a few of her sore

muscles, creating a sharp twinge followed by a dull ache. She knew how she'd gotten those pains. She wanted to be alone to fully savor the feelings, uncomfortable though they were. They were the result of a night spent in lovemaking, and she would not wish them away for anything. But she was not alone, and something had happened to Peter. So she waited, taking a moment to scrub her face with a cloth from the water basin.

"You should not be so vigorous in your ablutions," chided Eleanor. "It's detrimental to your skin."

So was getting slapped for choosing the wrong moment to pick at her, but Mari kept her tongue—and her hand—in check. Meanwhile, Mama began unplaiting Mari's hair to brush out the locks. The door finally closed behind the maid, Mari grabbed her mother's hand to still it, and spoke very clearly.

"Tell me immediately what has happened."

Mama and Eleanor exchanged glances, and by some unspoken agreement, Eleanor was the one to explain.

"The Earl of Sommerfield has been taken."

She blinked. "Taken? Where?"

"To gaol!" Mama said on a choked gasp. "An earl taken to gaol for thievery. Pulled right out of his bed and had the irons clapped on him like a common criminal."

Mari nodded. "Well, he is a common criminal. He should be arrested."

"Not an earl!" Mama cried.

"I know it's shocking," she began, but Eleanor interrupted her.

"That's not the horrible part."

Mari blinked. "It's not?"

"No. Lord Whitly was the one who had him arrested."

Of course it was. Peter would not leave such a thing to anyone else. "When did this happen?" She'd only just left him a few hours before.

"An hour ago," Mama said. "Lord Whitly sent a note to your papa, explaining matters."

Mari glanced to Eleanor, who shrugged. "I learned of it through a footman who was there at the time."

"At the earl's home?" How the devil was Eleanor connected to a servant at Sommerfield's establishment?

She nodded. "You showed marked interest in Lord Whitly. I felt it incumbent upon myself to gain insight into his particulars." Her arch look added the words she would never say aloud: *That is what you paid me for.*

Mari had no words in response, especially as her mind was wholly consumed by thoughts of Peter. How awful he must feel. How terrible to have to stand and see your father clapped in irons. Even worse to be the instrument of his father's destruction.

"Help me dress, Mama," she said as she scrambled out of bed. "I must go to him."

"What?" her mother gasped.

"You must absolutely not!"

Those were the sharpest words she'd ever heard from Eleanor, and she and her mother turned in shock.

"Let me explain this to you," Eleanor continued in a more moderated tone. "Lord Whitly has sent his own father to gaol. His father, an earl, has been incarcerated, and not by the hand of the King."

Mari slowly exhaled, beginning to fully understand everyone's reaction. She had spent so much time thinking about the crime the earl had tried to lay at her father's door that she hadn't really thought about the consequences of ending the thieving ring. It was one thing to incarcerate a wealthy cit like her father. It was quite another to lock up an earl. But either way, that did not change her mind. She would see Peter, if only to stand beside him. They were not married, but it was a wife's place to stand beside—

"You cannot see Lord Whitly, because he is right now speaking with Prinny, who is not pleased. Not pleased at all."

The Prince Regent was not a man to make angry. Still... "Naturally, I should think His Highness would be furious at the earl—"

"Not pleased that Lord Whitly would expose such a thing in so public a manner. Especially without informing him first."

Well, he probably couldn't have. Peter ran in good circles, but not quite so exalted as to call Prinny a friend. "Nevertheless, the earl was at fault—" Mari began.

"Listen, Mari!" Eleanor snapped, her words coming out crisp and cold. "If the lower orders lose faith in the peerage, then we will have chaos. People will riot, and Madame Guillotine will appear in Hyde Park. Do you want that?"

"Of course not," Mari returned with equal heat. "But if we allow the elite their corruptions—"

"No one said allow it. Simply end it, and do so quietly."

Mari compressed her lips. She understood Eleanor's fears. She might not agree with them, but she understood the worry. The peerage was expected to act in a superior manner. Show them to be as fallible as anyone else, and the entire government might collapse as it had in France.

But Peter wasn't worried about that. His fears were that the elite would become as venally corrupt as in India. And to prevent that, he would expose his own father as a thief. He would show the world—including England's most powerful—that they were not above the law.

She adored him for that, even as she now saw why Eleanor and her mother had rushed to her side. They knew the powerful did not like one of their own being exposed. And far from turning on his father, they would attack the son instead.

"How bad is it?" she asked.

Eleanor took a sip of her tea. "It is too early to tell. Much will depend on Prinny's reaction."

That made complete sense. Mari took a deep breath and thought about the gowns in her wardrobe. "What do I own that is appropriate for an early morning call on the prince?"

Eleanor's teacup clattered in the saucer. Another unexpected display from the usually serene woman. "You cannot be serious. Whyever would he see you?"

"He wouldn't, alone," Mari allowed. "But he would see you, wouldn't he? You're the exquisite Lady Eleanor, daughter of a duke who had once been friendly with His Majesty, are you not?"

"My father—my family—" The woman sputtered so much she had to fold her hands together and compress her lips. After a deep breath, she spoke. "I've only met the man a few dozen times. He *is* the Prince Regent."

"And you are Lady Eleanor, who opens closed doors. Who makes smooth that which has been ruffled." Mari made her gaze hard enough to transmit the words she wouldn't utter aloud. *And this is what we paid you for.*

# Twenty-nine

THEY DID NOT SEE THE PRINCE.

Mari laid the fault for that squarely at Eleanor's feet. First it had taken time to convince Eleanor that Mari intended to go with or without the woman. And that once at Carlton House, she would make liberal use of Eleanor's name.

It wasn't an idle threat, and Eleanor could see it. So she grudgingly agreed, but then had to leave to change into attire appropriate when visiting a prince. If it was a stall tactic, it worked, because that left Mari cooling her heels for another two hours. Fortunately, she put the time to good use and managed to persuade Eleanor's cousin, the sailor-turned-Duke of Bucklynde, to join their party.

Nevertheless, it was a wasted endeavor. By the time they made it to the prince's residence, the man wasn't there. Neither was Peter, nor would anyone tell them where they'd gone or what was the result of their discussion.

Maddening!

Fortunately, the duke had an excellent idea. He

promised to make a round of the gentlemen's clubs and find out what the general mood was. At that point, Mari was desperate for any sort of news, and she couldn't get the man moving fast enough.

Mari's next idea was to go directly to Peter's lodging, but Eleanor and her mother flatly refused and swore to lock her in chains if she attempted it. They were still set on her making a good marriage, and if the tide of favor had turned against Peter, they wanted her as far away from him as possible.

Mari ignored them and directed the carriage to her father's place of business. If anyone knew anything, it would be he. Except that when they got to his office, they discovered her father was doing exactly what the duke was doing: making the rounds to find out exactly which way the wind blew.

Damn and blast! Mari was nearly insane with worry. In the end, she had no thoughts other than to return home in hopes that someone had left a message. Which was when they received their first piece of real news, delivered, naturally, in condescending tones by Horrid Horace.

"Lady Illston awaits you in the parlor. She's had two pots of tea already."

Mari didn't bother to acknowledge the man but breezed into the parlor, intent on this potential source of news.

"Lady Illston," she said, taking the woman's hands in hers. "What brings you here this ill-favored afternoon?"

The woman rose and took her hands, her expression flustered. "Ill-favored?" she asked as she glanced out the window. The weather was bright and sunny. "Oh! I suppose you mean as regards Lord Whitly."

Mari kept hold of the lady's hands as she sank into the nearest settee. "We are most desperate for news. Have you heard anything?"

"My, yes! Lord Whitly has been summoned to Carlton House!"

Mari's teeth clenched. "Yes, we've just returned from there."

"You have? My goodness, what did Prinny say?"

"Nothing, I'm afraid. He'd already left."

"So you know then that Lord Whitly had his own father arrested for thievery. Can you imagine?"

"Yes, I can. His father is a thief and deserves it."

The woman paused a moment to gape, but then recovered quickly. "But I cannot credit it! He's an earl. My husband was most incensed. He stormed out of the house an hour after hearing the news. He knew Whitly, you see, in India."

"Then he must know—"

"Lady Illston, how pleased I am to see you," interrupted Lady Eleanor. She had just entered with Mama, and obviously meant to silence Mari's staunch support of Peter. They'd been counseling her all day to reserve her opinion of the matter until she saw which way the wind was blowing.

Mari had steadfastly ignored them.

Meanwhile, Lady Illston was straightening up off the settee again to greet the other women. Which was when Mari took the time to redirect her thoughts. She'd believed she needed to gather information, to find out what had happened between Peter and his father, Peter and the prince, Peter and God only knew who. But that information wasn't available to her now, and obviously Lady Illston would be of no help with it.

No, her job was to sway the tide of public opinion away from the earl and toward Peter. And that task began with taking control of the conversation. Which began with tea.

She ordered a new tea tray and made sure she was the one who served. It was a simple matter of grabbing the pot and interrupting anyone she wished to be silent with a simple question.

"Lady Eleanor, do you take cream?"

"Mama, I know you hate sugar, but do try one of these cakes."

"Lady Illston, let the footman take that old cup away. I'll make you a fresh one."

And when everyone was silenced with their drinks, Mari began the conversation as she wanted it to go.

"I'm so glad you came today, Lady Illston. I'm very excited about tonight's ball, you see, and wondered if you could give me a hint. Please tell me if you think Lord Whitly has managed to teach Greenie a new phrase. I am in such a state of anxiety to know if he has succeeded."

Lady Illston blinked at her, and no wonder. With the momentous news of the earl's arrest on everyone's tongues, she could not quite grasp the fact that Mari's greatest concern was their ridiculous wager and how it would play out tonight.

But that was the whole of Mari's plan. If she could reassert the trivial as the most important news of the day, then everything would settle back to normal.

Peter's part in his father's arrest would fade beneath the weight of the inconsequential question of whether he'd taught a phrase to a parakeet. And if that was the most pressing concern, then clearly England's peasants were not about to rebel, Madame Guillotine would not be established in Hyde Park, and everything would be exactly as it was yesterday. Except, of course, that a highborn thief would still be in gaol because—thank God—the English courts did not run on the tide of public opinion.

That was the plan. The question was: Would Lady Illston take the bait?

"Er…um, Miss Powel, you know I cannot disclose anything about what Greenie will or won't say."

Nonsense. She'd been trading on this wager for weeks now. According to her, her ball would be the event of the Season. Everyone needed to know the outcome of Miss Powel's scandalous wager with Lord Whitly.

"But you must give me a hint," she pleaded. "Surely you see that I must prepare myself…" She let her voice trail off suggestively. After all, the wager was that she would have to kiss him if he succeeded with Greenie.

"Well, as to that, I can say that he has not spent a great deal of time with Greenie. Not at all what I expected."

"Ah. Then I will be able to exact a punishment." She didn't relish winning this wager nearly as much as she'd once thought.

"Er, possibly not," Lady Illston hedged. "You see, I have lately come to learn that…er…well, my butler, it appears, has been working on Lord Whitly's behalf."

Mari wasn't nearly as startled as she should have been. Of course Peter would find a way to succeed in their wager even if he didn't have the time to see to it himself. Clever man. "Oh dear," she murmured with false dismay.

"Yes, well, you see, that's why I came to see you today. I could rule this as cheating, you see. He did bribe my butler." She shook her head in dismay. "I lay the blame completely at my father's feet. He's the one who promoted the man, and naturally, I couldn't fire him. He's been working for us for generations."

"Of course not," Mari muttered. "When I become mistress of my own home, I will dispense with butlers altogether. To a man, they are an unreliable, difficult lot!" She made her pronouncement especially dramatic in order to encourage the conversation in that direction. Problems with servants were a common complaint among the upper crust. And as easy as that, Lady Illston swallowed the bait hook, line, and sinker.

"Oh, you cannot know how I suffer at that man's hands!" On she went for at least another ten minutes, detailing her butler's perfidy.

Perfect.

But eventually, she wandered back to the point of her visit. "So, do you wish to cry off my ball tonight? To use Lord Whitly's cheating as the excuse, as it were?"

And there it was, just as she'd prayed back at the beginning of the Season. She now had the perfect opportunity for her to punish Lord Whitly in full view of the *ton*. All she had to do was take this pretend insult and use it to turn her back on him. To declare to all the world that he was beneath her, though he was the son of an earl and she a wealthy cit. Everyone would know it was a condemnation of his actions against his father. Or she could choose something completely different.

She grabbed Lady Illston's hands, squeezing them tightly to gain the lady's full attention. And when she was sure she had it—along with her mother's, and Lady Eleanor's—she spoke Peter's doom.

"You must tell everyone that I *will* be there tonight. Indeed, send round a note to Lord Whitly that he must attend or risk complete ruin. He must be there, for I will see the matter between us resolved once and for all. Will you do that, my lady? For me?"

"Oh my, yes! Of course! If you think that will help."

"It would indeed," she said. Just as it would cap Lady Illston's ball as the event of the Season. Everyone would come to see Peter's set down—or not—at the hands of the Wayward Welsh.

"Oh dear," Lady Illston said as she glanced at the mantel clock. "I have so much to do to prepare for tonight. I must be on my way."

Mari stood. "I completely understand," she said graciously. After all, she wanted the woman to spread the gossip as much as possible before tonight. Then, lest Mama and Lady Eleanor think she had forgotten them, Mari turned to them. Not surprisingly, Eleanor understood exactly what was happening.

"Please think about what you plan. Even in the best of circumstances, Lord Whitly will never regain the status he could have had. He will forever be tainted as the man who gaoled his own father."

"Just as I will forever be the Wayward Welsh."

Mari couldn't help but grin. "I think that makes us two of a kind, don't you?"

"No," Eleanor said repressively. "I think it makes you a fool. Your father hired me to find you an eligible husband appropriate to your rising status and massive dowry. A tainted future earl with no fortune does not qualify."

Mari paused. So that had come out as well. That Peter did not have the fortune everyone once believed. "How well known is that fact?"

Mama folded her hands and looked askance. "I told her, Mari. She's helping you, so she needed to know."

"I see," Mari said slowly. "Well, Eleanor, now you have a choice. As I intend to marry Lord Whitly, you can either exert your considerable influence to sway opinion in his favor, or you can admit to my father and the world that you failed in your endeavor. I am set to marry a bounder whom you initially encouraged."

She saw Eleanor's face pale. Her efforts on Mari's behalf were common knowledge. It was in her own interests to see Mari's situation resolved in the best manner possible. Which meant, of course, that she had to cede to Mari's wishes.

She did. And with typical Eleanor grace.

"Very well," she said slowly. "I will smooth the way." The woman departed, which left Mari to grab her mother's hand and head for the front door.

"Heavens, we've got no time and too much to do," Mari said.

"But, darling—"

"Please, Mama, don't argue. Just help me."

Her mother blinked in startled shock. "Of course!

What do you think I've been doing since the moment you were born?"

Mari's step hitched just a moment before she settled back into a brisk pace. "Exactly that, Mama. Thank you. And pray hurry."

"But where are we going?"

Mari grinned. "Shopping."

# Thirty

"ARE YOU HEARTSICK OR BORED? I CAN'T TELL."

Peter glared at his best friend, not wanting to be cajoled out of his foul mood. It took ten seconds before Ash got the hint and looked away.

They were disembarking from a hackney outside Lady Illston's ball. Tonight was the big moment when he would have Greenie say the words they'd been practicing for weeks now. Or rather Greenie and the butler had, but either way, the words were his. He just wasn't sure he should have the bird say them.

"It's not over, Peter," Ash said in a low voice. "It all depends on the women."

Not on *women*. It all depended on *Mari*, and despite everything they'd done together, he was not at all sure where her heart lay. Worse, he wasn't even sure if he should allow her to choose him. No, that wasn't true. He knew that the best thing for her to do would be to give him the cut direct. She should wash her hands of his whole benighted family, then find an honorable baron somewhere and put that bastard on the political path to glory. But the very idea made him want to retch.

Instead, he plastered on a bland expression that exactly resembled bored. He'd perfected it as a child when his father railed at him and he'd had no defense. He'd used it this morning when the man had been so shocked by his arrest—at his son's own hand—that he'd given Peter his back. Hard to do when being led out of his own home under guard, but he'd managed it.

And then Peter had used it over and over throughout the day. He'd worn it while the Prince Regent threatened to confiscate every inch of land his family owned. It had felt etched on his face when he'd gone for something to eat at his club, and the hatred aimed at him had been a palpable force in the room. And he'd put it on when he'd read Mari's note, pleading with him to meet her at tonight's ball if he couldn't manage earlier.

He hadn't managed it. He'd been too busy managing visits from his father's creditors. How the bloody hell had the man staved them off until now? No wonder he'd turned to thieving. It seemed the earl owed money to the whole of London.

Which was when he'd enlisted Ash's help. Together they'd figured out how to dance around his father's debts, but it would take every penny he had—or was likely to get—for years. In truth, his only option was Mr. Powel's offer of employment, but he couldn't even be sure that opportunity was still available. After all, Peter had grossly underestimated the reaction of the *ton*. He'd been so naive, thinking that they would understand what it cost a son to turn in his own father for thieving. Instead, they hailed him as a traitor to his own set and damned him to his face.

Bloody hell, was England truly this corrupt? Were the men in power that angry at having their faults exposed? Did no one see that the only way to have a strong nation was to make the bad ones pay, no matter who they were?

"Damn it, Peter, listen to me!" Ash said as he gripped Peter's arm. They were steps away from joining the line into the ballroom, but his friend halted him while still in the shadows. "It's the women who make the difference in this sort of thing. If they think you're a noble man fighting against evil, then their husbands will have no choice but to follow along."

"Don't be ridiculous. It's the men who control the purse strings. The men who will never do business with me again." Even so small a hope as breeding horses looked like a pipe dream now. His horse and his name were tainted with the same brush.

Ash shook his head. "The women control Society. They have a great deal more power than you imagine. And Miss Powel has more influence than you guess." Ash huffed out a breath. "Just marry the girl. Her dowry—"

"I won't marry her out of desperation." He said that firmly. Loud enough for others to hear him and turn in their direction. Loud enough, perhaps, for him to believe his own words. Because he very much feared that he would buckle under pressure. That he would let the woman rescue him, though she felt so little for him. And then his lands might be saved, but his bed would be a cold one. And the bright future he envisioned would feel dreary.

He turned away from Ash and stepped into line

like a man facing a court martial. And as he had done a thousand times already this day, he reviewed what might happen this evening. What exact thoughts might be twisting in Mari's head.

First off, she would approach this logically, as she did everything. She would think through the costs and benefits of an alliance with him. She would see that just about any honest husband was better than a disgraced future earl. That whatever ambition she wanted—and Mari had a great many ambitions—would be better served by one such as the lackluster Mr. Camden than by Peter.

And from that basis, she would make a public display of turning him down tonight. That was, after all, what she'd planned back when they'd first made this ridiculous wager on a parakeet's words.

Ash stepped in beside him. He greeted a few people, smiled at those who would respond. Mostly, he stood beside him in a show of staunch support, and Peter couldn't be more grateful. The man was the truest friend he could ever hope for.

The line inched forward.

At least his humiliation tonight would have a good audience.

Then a strange thing happened. Mrs. and Mr. Bailey greeted him, as did their three daughters. Cits, all of them, but they exchanged pleasantries with him as if he weren't a pariah.

Two feet farther up in line, and Lady Sylvia, daughter of the Earl of Crawford, flashed him a flirtatious look from behind her fan. Her father, naturally, was nowhere in sight. That man was an intimate of his own father and had already cursed the day Peter was born. But Lady Sylvia first, then her good friend Miss Koch did their best to encourage him from a distance. It was enough to make the young men in their environs give him a startled nod, especially as Lady Eleanor joined their party.

He glanced at Ash for explanation, but the man was doing the pretty with Lady Cowper. Peter knew better than to risk a harsh set-down from a patroness of Almack's, so he kept his face turned forward and stopped his hands from clenching nervously in his pockets. And so it continued until he at last made it into the ballroom.

Lady Illston greeted him with a dry kiss, a sympathetic pat to his wrist, and all the warmth that was lacking from her husband, his former associate at the East India Company. That man barely shook his hand before grumbling at him.

"Thought India taught men subtlety, but you seem to have learned the reverse."

"On the contrary, my lord," Peter answered with the same words he'd given Prinny. "India taught me that unchecked power is an evil thing. If men are not to pay for their crimes, then anarchy is a sure result."

"There's payment, boy, and then there's public spectacle." Then he turned his back on Peter to give his hand to Ash.

All in all, it wasn't a bad reproach. Given the kind of vehement condemnation he'd received throughout the day, it was barely a slap on the wrist. He would have to think longer on that, but the moment he turned away from his host, he saw her.

Mari.

Mari, with her hair barely restrained and in a gown of brilliant color. It even sported both embroidery *and* lace.

Now there was a gown fit for the Wayward Welsh. And by all appearances, she wore it proudly. Her chin was lifted, her eyes flashed in the candlelight, and there was a flush of color in her cheeks. She'd never looked more beautiful to him.

"You should talk to her before the big parakeet display," Ash murmured in his ear.

Peter took one step before he realized the futility of it. She was surrounded on all sides. "She's come into her own," he said, both pleased and dismayed. It was clear she'd finally found her purpose and was grasping it with both hands. He couldn't be prouder of her, even if it was in service of his set-down.

"I can clear the space," Ash said, "but you have to move quickly. Make your case. There's still time—"

"You do understand how marriage to me would only diminish her standing in the eyes of the *ton*."

"You do see that she'd never be the center of attention and wearing that stunning gown without you."

Very true. But that only meant she *had* needed him. Not that she still did. Or that she loved him.

"Too late," Ash grumbled. "The Greek chorus of old biddies has moved in."

It was true. The dowager ladies who had so put him in his place weeks ago had risen en masse as soon as they'd spotted him. He feared they were coming to give him the cut direct in a coordinated display. That or pelt him with their canes. But instead, they'd all abandoned their seats to circle Mari, as if she were in danger from him.

"Well, I'll be…" Ash said with a low whistle. "She's even got the dowagers stirred up."

"To do what?" Peter asked, keeping a wary eye on the placement of those canes.

"Damned if I know," Ash returned. "This is Mari's show."

And it was, he realized. Every bit of it was arrayed for her. The dowagers standing in support. Lady Illston's ball attended by the entire *ton*. Even the parakeet was there, he now saw, perched in its heavy cage right by Mari's shoulder.

"What say we go get something to drink?" Ash suggested. "Brandy?"

"Excellent notion," he agreed, though he couldn't manage to tear his eyes away from Mari. She hadn't seen him yet, being too absorbed by the dowagers as they clucked about her. If only she would look up. If only she would see him, he might have a clue from her reaction what her thoughts might be. But every time she started to turn in his direction, someone stepped in the way, and her view was blocked.

"Hmm," Ash muttered. "It might not be the best idea to venture toward the bar just yet."

"What?" Peter asked.

Then when Ash didn't answer, he forced himself to look.

As was typical, the men were gathered around the heavier spirits. Lots of men clutched into loose groupings of politicals, financials, and the sports mad. The first knot was the most overtly hostile to Peter, and unfortunately, the nearest to the drink. The sports mad Corinthians were distracted. Probably someone had bested someone else in a race, and so the affairs of the nation—or of an earl and his son—faded in importance. It was that middle group of the moneyed people that Peter watched, but they seemed not to notice him at all. No dark glowers or nods of encouragement. "I don't need to run that gauntlet just now," Peter said dully. He looked back to Mari, and then felt the gut punch.

She'd seen him.

Her gaze was trained on him, and when someone dared to step between them, she impatiently pushed the lady aside.

Peter felt himself drawn forward. He knew he couldn't get through the press of ladies, but he needed to speak to her. He needed to touch her skin one last time.

So he walked to her just as she maneuvered around the most planted of the dowagers. And they met in the middle—almost close enough to touch—and stood there looking.

"Peter, I was looking for you all day."

"You could not have found me. I have been at the banks." Three of them, to be exact.

"I hoped you would come here."

"I would not miss it. We had…" He glanced at Greenie, waiting like bored royalty as one girl after another tried to speak with him. "You deserve your moment of triumph."

"Triumph!" she said, clearly startled. "I've only managed to teach the creature 'sodding day,' and we both know that was not my intent."

His lips quirked at that. "Never fear. Lady Illston's butler has managed it. Just offer him some apple. He'll perform."

"I don't care about that." Her gaze searched his face. "How are you faring?"

He gestured about him without looking. "You see here only a tenth of the reaction. The news of my poverty is out. Prinny threatens to take Sommerfield by way of punishment." Unable to stop himself, he took hold of her gloved hands and held on. "I vastly misjudged Society's reaction."

"I doubt you misjudged it. You likely gave no thought to it at all."

Too true. That was where they were different. If he'd only thought to consult her, she could have predicted this to a T.

"But how are *you*?" she asked.

*Wretched without you.* "I shall be glad to get this done with, I suppose. I will have to return to Sommerfield if the prince allows me to keep it."

"Will he?"

"If I pay my father's debts, fines, and add in a gift of thanks to Prinny for his compassion."

She winced. "Do you have it?"

He shook his head. "Not even if I were the nabob everyone thought." Then he looked her in the eye and flat-out lied. "Not even with your dowry."

There. He'd said it. This was the statement she'd need to wash her hands of him. To realize that hitching herself to his boat was disaster for certain.

"Oh dear," she said, and he heard the death knell of his dreams in her tone.

But he couldn't end it like that. He couldn't let her think that any part of him still pursued her for her money. Some perverse part of his nature forced him to explain.

"That wasn't my plan, Mari. It was never my hope."

"I know. You wanted to build a utopia."

"Yes," he said. Then he shook his head. "But not like you think. I wanted a base. A solid place that would be our home."

"Sommerfield."

Damnation, why couldn't he ever find the right words? "Not just a place, Mari, but a financial base. A peaceful base. Someplace you could return home to whenever you needed rest."

She frowned at him. "Return to? But it would be my home."

"Yes, yes, of course, but don't you see? All those other men want you to be their support. They want you to dress their arms, hostess their tables, enhance their careers."

She nodded. "That's what a good wife does."

He pulled her hands together, and she moved a step closer to him. He hadn't intended to do that. Mostly he was gripping her hands in frustration as he fought for the idea that had been in his mind but never spoken aloud.

"No, Mari, *I* wanted to support *you*. So you could do whatever you want. So you could come home to Sommerfield, secure in your position there if the rest of your plans went awry."

She blinked at him. He could tell she'd never thought of the idea. She'd been reared to dress a man's arm, to read his ledgers, and set his table. "But what would I do without you?"

He felt his lips twist in a wry smile. "Whatever you wanted. You understand Society. You know money, too. You even thought to manage Mr. Camden's political career. You could have done all that from Sommerfield. Or the townhome in London." *With me*.

He could see the possibility hit her. He could see her mind work in its rapid-fire way. And he watched as her eyes widened and her words slipped out unbidden. "I had some ideas about what to do for Tie," she said. "But then I thought, what about the other boys? Where would they go?"

He smiled. She understood now. "What will you do?"

Her eyes began to dance. "I have no idea, but I did jot down some ideas. I know the men to speak with. The women too."

Of course she did. Hadn't she spent the last six years analyzing how the *ton* worked? "You'll need to make a list."

"It will take more than one, don't you think?"

He hadn't the foggiest clue.

She lifted their joined hands in what probably would have been a gesture if he'd released her. As it was, she simply swung their joined fists higher.

"Why didn't I see this before?"

"You were busy looking for a husband."

"But I could have been doing other things as well. I could have been *thinking*."

He smiled. He loved it when she grew animated like this. When she stopped obsessing about being wayward and stepped into her full self. Here was the woman he remembered from six years ago. And she was so very much more today than she'd been back then.

"I love you," he said. Glorious to finally say those words aloud. Heaven to finally see the woman he'd first fallen for six years ago at last come to beautiful life.

But at his words, she suddenly stilled. Her mouth grew slack in shock, and her eyes widened to an absurd degree. She stared at him. Worse, she gaped at him as if he hadn't been feeling these things from the very first day. When she'd showed him her intelligence, her perception, and that fire that burned so bright and in such a waywardly Welsh direction.

He loved her to the depths of his soul.

And now, he realized, was her perfect moment. Now when he'd at last bared his heart and soul to her, she could publicly destroy him.

# Thirty-one

He loved her.

She might have believed she'd imagined those words, except that he looked as startled as she was. And perhaps a little chagrined. But he didn't change his words. Instead, he looked about at the assembled peerage and gave her a rueful smile.

"Do it now, Mari," he said in an undertone. "You will never have a better audience."

"Do what?"

He sighed. "Declare yourself free of me. It is the only way to have any standing among them. You can't do anything you want with me as an anchor about your neck."

"Oh." Was that what he wanted? No, that was what he expected. And she could understand why. Perhaps a few weeks ago, she would have. Certainly when they'd made the wager, she'd intended to. But she'd changed this Season. And how odd a thing change was. She hadn't even recognized the shift within herself until it was already done. She hadn't noticed when she'd started speaking her mind.

She hadn't felt it when she'd begun to value her own thoughts.

She hadn't even believed it when she'd begun to feel wild and reckless. She'd only let it happen and never attached a word to it.

Love.

She'd fallen in love.

Not only with Peter, but with herself too. With the wayward woman she could be. In a gown with lace and embroidery, in a tavern maid's bartered dress, and in his arms. Most especially in his arms.

She looked about her, seeing the hundreds of eyes trained on her and Peter. He was right. There would never be a better time to declare herself than right here, right now. And so she gestured to Lady Illston, who came quickly to her side.

"Miss Powel, the dancing will begin—"

"Quite right," Mari interrupted. "You want to begin the ball, so we should dispense with this silly wager as soon as can be."

"Now?" That wasn't at all what the lady wanted. She knew that the longer people had to wait for the main spectacle, the more her fame would build. But Mari had no interest in prolonging the suspense.

"Lord Whitly and I are both ready, and besides, I begin to fear for Greenie's health."

"What? He seems fine." Indeed, if it were possible for a bird to thrive on attention, it would be this parakeet.

"But the stress is not good for a bird, you know. It's not at all what they're used to in India." That was true enough, so Lady Illston began waving people away.

The dowagers didn't move at first. They were standing in a kind of protective wall behind Mari, but at her nod, they reluctantly stomped aside. The crowd quieted immediately. Lady Illston had no need to clap her hands to get everyone's attention, but she did it anyway. This, after all, was her great moment.

"Everyone, everyone! Weeks ago, Lord Whitly and Miss Powel entered into a droll little wager with my Greenie. Which of them could teach the bird a new phrase first. I was honored to be selected as judge, along with the esteemed Ladies Jersey, Castlereigh, and Cowper."

The women in question stepped forward, patron-esses of Almack's and the most powerful purveyors of female opinion as was possible to get among the *ton*. Mari smiled at them. They nodded warmly at her and gave Peter the barest of glances.

"Naturally," continued Lady Illston, "Miss Powel was concerned about the propriety of such a thing, but we four here have declared this wager proper." She dimpled as she looked about the room. "All in good fun," she declared.

"Get to the forfeit," Lady Jersey said, clearly a bit tetchy about all the pomp being directed at Lady Illston.

"Er, yes. If Miss Powel manages to have Greenie say her phrase, then Lord Whitly shall drop to his knees before her and apologize for harming her. And he shall do it to her satisfaction."

A murmur of malicious glee seemed to roll through the crowd. Mari was dismayed. She hadn't thought the anger at him so entrenched. For his part, Peter appeared almost bored, though she read turbulent emotions beneath the flatness of his gaze. "And if Lord Whitly manages his phrase instead, then he shall be allowed to give her a *chaste* kiss."

Lady Jersey stepped forward. "And if they both manage the task," she said loudly, "then I declare this wager ill-conceived." She sniffed. "Truly, I cannot understand what made me think it was a good idea at the time." She glared at Peter. "Apparently India has badly damaged your understanding of what is proper and improper in civilized Society."

Well, Lady Jersey had certainly stated her opinion, and it fell firmly against Peter. Mari decided that lady would be her very first conquest in her new campaign to redeem Peter. But first, she had to handle Greenie.

At Lady Illston's command, a footman lifted the cage, his arm trembling from the weight, and then set it grandly between Mari and Peter. The place was quiet, everyone's breath held to hear better. Mari looked at Peter, wondering if she should just offer the apple and say, "sodding day." That was all she'd managed to teach him. But Peter held her gaze and silently mouthed, "happy day." And since she trusted him completely, she held up the bit of apple.

"Happy day, Greenie."

"Happy day!" the bird returned.

"He said it," she cried. "Happy day!"

"Happy day! Happy day!"

The applause was deafening. Loud enough, certainly, to drown out her whispered "Thank you" to Peter. Even so, he smiled and gave her a nod.

And then he went down on one knee before her.

Oh, such a pose, and him so handsome. Her heart

broke to see him do such a thing in service of a wager. Worse, with the whole *ton* watching and glorying in his humiliation.

"No, no," she said. "You must have Greenie say your phrase first."

To which Greenie said, "Winner, winner!"

But Peter remained down before her. And when she stepped toward him, he clasped her hand and bowed his head.

"You have won," he said loudly.

"No, not until—"

"I am awed by you, Miss Powel. You have a clarity of vision that I lack. An understanding and a determination that puts me to shame."

"Stop, Peter—" she began, but he didn't listen.

"If I have ever embarrassed you or caused you the least discomfort, I most humbly apologize. I have been so wrong in many things, but not in this. Not in the words I have wanted to say to you for so long."

Mari frowned. What the devil was he saying? And then he turned to the bird. He was tall enough, even on one knee, to offer the creature a nut.

"Your turn, Greenie," he said. "Say it for me, will you?"

"Marry me! Marry me!"

A collective gasp went up from all around them, but no more than from Mari herself. She couldn't credit it. Had he decided on that phrase on their first encounter at the beginning of the Season? Had he meant for this moment all along?

"And that," said Lady Illston loudly to Lady Jersey, "is why we allowed this wager."

He had planned it from the beginning! And now was her moment to choose. A lifetime of proper behavior, respected by Society, even in patterned gowns, if only she refused the heinous son who had his own father arrested. Or she could accept him, love him, and live outside of London in probable infamy, at least until their finances recovered.

"You call me clear-sighted," she said, "but I have been blind when it came to you. I thought you shallow and lazy. I did not understand how far your vision, how deep your honor."

"Mari—" he began, but she cut him off. Indeed, she dropped to her knees before him, pressing her fingers to his lips even as she spoke in ringing tones.

"Only a deeply honorable man would expose thievery at such personal cost. Only a patriotic man would consult with the prince and do as he was bid, despite the loss of money and power." Not quite the truth, but close enough that no one would gainsay her. "And only a man of hidden depth could show me the one thing I'd hidden from myself for so long."

He looked at her, his expression guarded.

"I love you," she said. "I have loved you for six years and was only angry before because I thought you'd spurned me. I thought you the cause of all my ills, but it was only because I did not trust my own heart. I love you, Peter. It would be my greatest delight to marry you."

He searched her face, not trusting her words. He lowered his voice and whispered to her. "Mari, think. I am disgraced."

"No, Peter, you are in love."

"Well, of course, but—"

"And Society adores nothing more than a great love story." She leaned forward. "I believe I owe you a kiss."

She kissed him. They kissed, in full view of all the *ton*. And when she thought to pull away, he pulled her close and lifted her up in his arms while everyone cheered.

With one kiss—and an obvious love story—the dowagers were touched. As one, they declared it an excellent match. Not to be outdone, the patronesses of Almack's agreed, adding that it was a well-done wager and all perfectly respectable. And besides, what else could be expected from the Wayward Welsh?

The men would take longer to come around, but they would not go so firmly against the ladies' opinion. And this, of course, was exactly what Prinny had been waiting for: a clear indication of which way England's powerful would sway on matters. Which meant Sommerfield was safe. Peter would have a scandal attached to his name for a bit, but it wouldn't last. And with the addition of Mari's dowry, his financials would recover. It was all perfect. In fact, they became so abruptly popular that Lady Illston asked them to open the ball with the first dance.

It wasn't until hours later when they were departing from the ball that he chanced to have a moment alone with her. They were strolling through Mayfair in the dark of night, their hands entwined and their heads pressed close together. Her mother was following a few feet behind in the carriage to maintain the proprieties.

"Did you mean what you said?" he asked. "Truly?"

"I did indeed."

"I cannot understand it. Mari, you said you didn't love me."

"I was wrong." It was so simple, and yet she could tell that he didn't quite believe her. "Very well, I see I shall have to prove it to you."

"I should accept a simple declaration every day for the rest of our lives."

"Oh, I could do that, I suppose, but I had something else in mind."

"Really?"

"Really." Then she reached into her reticule and pulled out the sheet of foolscap she had in there. "Here you go," she said as she handed it to him. "It's a list of all the logical, perfectly rational reasons why I am in love with you."

He held it up to the gaslight, squinting as he tried to make out the words. "I cry foul! I do not snore. And who would love a man for that anyway?"

"I do," she said as she turned into his arms and pressed her lips to his. "I love you."

"And I love you, my Wayward Welsh."

# Epilogue

MR. CAMDEN GLARED AT THE NEWSPRINT AND thought very unhappy thoughts. There in bold black and white was the announcement of the marriage between Lord Whitly and Miss Powel. According to the article, the couple were besotted with one another and were likely to have a glorious future, given that the Prince Regent himself had attended the festivities.

Some people were born lucky, he decided. Some people could defy custom and still succeed. She'd been labeled wayward, and had somehow become celebrated for it. He'd offended all decent thought by having his own father arrested for thievery, and emerged as a friend of the prince and a champion of justice. Even more lucky, Mr. Powel had tripled her dowry, thereby wiping out any financial concerns.

Of all the damned luck.

And to think it could have been his if only he'd been born lucky.

Mr. Camden reached for the gin bottle, only to remember that he no longer drank. He might be unlucky, but he'd learned from his mistakes, and a taste for gin was one of his biggest errors in judgment. Kissing her when he was three sheets to the wind ranked as his second stupidest mistake.

But without any gin to drink, he could only stare at the newspaper and hate his life. Which was when his door was unceremoniously opened by Ashley Tucker, Lord Rimbury.

"Capital day, isn't it?"

Mr. Camden blinked at the man. "It's raining."

"I know," Lord Rimbury said with a grin. "It's always dank in London, and I love it. Allow me to introduce myself. I'm—"

"I know who you are. How did you get in here?" Why the bloody hell did they pay the gents to mind the front door when they never bloody minded the front door?

"Don't blame them. I told them I was expected."

Mr. Camden pushed to his feet. The last thing he wanted was another bleeding nob in obviously new togs messing about in his office. He simply wasn't in the mood. "Well, you weren't expected. And you aren't—"

"I understand from the new Lady Whitly that you're an honest man of sterling reputation and learned political opinion. That with the right opportunity, you could have a very bright political future. And that, most important, your sentiments on a variety of issues exactly coincide with my own."

Mr. Camden frowned at the man, his hostility starting to fade beneath the glimmer of a possibly lucky star. "That all depends on what you want me to do in return for this opportunity."

"I wish you to be honest. If you think Lord Whitly

was extreme in gaoling his own father, I assure you that I would do nothing so public, but three times as deadly should I find you to be less than a sterling man of honor."

Camden swallowed, knowing from the pressures of the last few months that any man could crumble in his ideals. Truthfully, in his more honest moments with himself, he wondered exactly what he would have done at Rossgrove's behest. If things had gone differently with Miss Powel, would he right now be feeling caught between his patron and his morals?

"I find, my lord, that like any man, my feet are made of clay, but that I endeavor daily to ennoble them."

"Hmmm, now that was an honest answer. Rather refreshing, I might add." Lord Rimbury dislodged a stack of papers and settled into a seat. "Now, let us see if we do, in fact, align on salient matters. Shall we start with tariffs? What is your opinion on them?"

Mr. Camden leaned back in his chair and began to speak. He began with the most simplistic of statements, but soon discovered that Lord Rimbury had a sharp mind and was impatient with simple answers. What he loved most was learning something new, especially when statements were supported with fact, and seeing if Mr. Camden ever wavered in his thoughts.

Which meant that their discussion begun in the early afternoon soon became a lively debate that wound into a very exciting opportunity under the light of some very lucky stars.

Perhaps, he thought, he might not be born lucky, but between Miss Powel and Lord Rimbury, he might just have found his way there. Except for one very simple, very obvious fact.

"All this is very exciting," he said over the plain fish dinner they'd shared at the nearest tavern. "But it also requires blunt."

"And I don't have any?" Lord Rimbury challenged.

Mr. Camden shrugged. "Your new clothes are nice, but that won't hide what everybody knows: Your purse is near empty."

"Very true. It was."

Mr. Camden perked up. "Was?" he asked.

"I've recently accepted a job, you see. One that has already turned lucrative." His voice trailed away suggestively.

"You have the blunt for this?"

"Not me. Not exactly." He leaned forward. "But my employer does. And together we have some very exciting ideas that can include you."

"And who, exactly, is your employer?"

Lord Rimbury grinned. "You haven't guessed? It's Mr. Powel."

Of course it was. And right there was when Camden understood his largest and most obvious mistake. He'd been courting the girl, looking to advance the old way: through marriage and patronage. But with the way things were swinging in the world, there was a new order coming. And that was by way of new money, new jobs, and new lucky stars.

"I'm listening," Mr. Camden said. "What do you have in mind?"

An hour later, he knew the truth. It had been the luckiest day in his life when he'd set out to court Miss Mari Powel. He just hadn't expected that she would be the smallest part of his bright new future.

*Look for the first book in the Rakes and Rogues series*
*by USA Today bestselling author Jade Lee*

# 50 WAYS
## TO
# Ruin a Rake

*Make a plan, be sure of it, and do not deviate.*

THERE ARE CERTAIN THINGS A WOMAN KNOWS. SHE knows what the weather will be based on how easily her hair settles into the pins. She knows when the cook has quarreled with the butler by the taste of the morning eggs. And she knows when a man will completely upset her day.

And right now, that man was walking up her front drive as easy as if he expected to be welcomed.

Melinda Smithson bolted out of her bedroom where she'd been fighting with her curls—again—and rushed downstairs. "I'm just going for a quick walk!" she said much too brightly to their butler as she made it to the front door. Rowe hadn't even the time to reach for her gloves when she snatched her gardening bonnet off the table and headed outside. She had to get to the odious man before he rounded the rock and came into view from her father's laboratory. If her papa saw him, she would be done for. So she ran as fast as her legs could carry her.

She rounded the bend at the same moment he arrived at the rock. One step more, and she was doomed.

"Oh no, Mr. Anaedsley. Not today. You cannot come here today." She said the words breathlessly, but she punctuated with a severe tug on her bonnet. So hard, in fact, that three pins dug painfully into her scalp.

Mr. Anaedsley had been whistling, but now he drew up short. "You've punched your thumb through your bonnet." He spoke with a charming smile that made her grind her teeth in frustration. Everything about the man was charming, from his reddish-brown hair to the freckles that dotted his cheeks to the rich green of his eyes. An annoyance dressed as a prince of the realm, for all that he had no courtesy title. He was the son and heir of the Duke of Timby, and she hated him with a passion that bordered on insanity.

Unfortunately, he was right. She'd punched her thumb clean through the straw brim of her bonnet.

"Yes, I have," she said as she stepped directly in front of him. He would not pass around the rock. He simply wouldn't. "And that is one more crime I lay at your feet."

"A crime?" he replied. "To poke a hole in that ugly thing? Really, Miss Smithson, I call it more a mercy. The sun should not shine on something that hideous."

It was hideous, which was why it was her gardening bonnet. "The sun is not supposed to shine on my face either, so it is this ugly thing or stay inside."

"Come now, Miss Smithson," he said as he held

out his arm to escort her. "I am well aware that you have dozens of fetching bonnets—"

"But this was the one at hand." She ignored his arm and stared intimidatingly at him. Or at least she tried to. But he was a good six inches taller than her. Average for a man, but for her he was quite the perfect height. Not too tall as to dwarf her, but large enough to be handsome in his coat of bottle-green superfine. It brought out his eyes, which were made all the more stunning by the sunlight that shone full on his face.

"Shall we amble up your beautiful drive and fetch you a pretty bonnet?"

"No, Mr. Anaedsley, we shall not. Because you shall not come to the house today. Any other day, you will be very welcome. But not today."

His brows drew together in worry. "Is your father ill? Is there something amiss? Tell me, Miss Smithson. What can I do to help?"

It was the right thing to say. Of course it was because he *always* knew the right thing to say. Her father's health was precarious these days, a cough plaguing him despite all attempts to physic him. She might have ignored his words as simple politeness, but she saw genuine worry in his eyes. She couldn't help but soften toward him.

"Papa is the same as before. It's worst at night—"

"The gypsy tincture didn't help then." He took her arm and gently eased her hand into the crook of his elbow. Her fingers were placed there before she even realized it. "I'll ask a doctor friend I know as soon as I return to London. He may—"

She dug in her feet, tugging backward on his arm. He raised a perfect eyebrow in query, but she flashed him a warm smile. "An excellent idea. You should go there right now. In fact, pray fetch the doctor here."

His eyebrows rose in alarm. "I shall write down the man's direction and a message. You can send a footman—"

"No, sir. You must go yourself. Right now. It is most urgent."

He flashed her his dimple. Damn him for having such a very attractive dimple. "Now why do I get the feeling that you're trying to rush me away?"

"Because the first thing I said to you was go away!"

He cocked his head, and his expression grew even more delightful. She would swear she saw a twinkle in his eyes. "Miss Smithson, I thought you were a scientist. The first thing you said to me was, 'Oh no, Mr. Anaedsley, not today.'"

"Well, there you have it. Go away. We are not receiving callers."

And then, just to make a liar of her, her uncle's carriage trotted up the path. Four horses—matched chestnuts—stepping smartly as they pulled her uncle's polished, gilded monstrosity. And inside waving cheerily was her cousin Ronnie. Half cousin, actually, and she waved halfheartedly at the wan fop.

"It appears, Miss Smithson, that we have been spotted. I'm afraid politeness requires that I make my bow."

"No, we haven't!" She'd used the distraction to pull them back from the rock. They were, in fact, completely shielded from all windows of the Smithson residence including the laboratory. "Ronnie doesn't count. And he certainly doesn't care if you greet him or not. The most powerful snub only seems to inspire him to greater heights of poetry."

"A poet is he?"

"Yes," she groaned. "A good one too." Which made it all the worse.

"Ah. Your suitor, I assume?"

"Suitor" was too simple a word for her relationship with Ronnie, which involved a lot of private family history. "He's my cousin. Well, half cousin, as my father and uncle had different mothers. But he has convinced himself that we are fated to be wed."

"And as a practical woman of science, you do not believe in fate."

She didn't believe in a lot of things, but at the top of the list was Ronnie's fantasy. He thought fate had cast them as prince and princess in a make-believe future. She thought her cousin's obsession with her silly at best, but more likely a dark and dangerous thing. "I do not wish to wed the man," she said baldly.

"Well, the solution is obvious then, isn't it? I shall join you today as an afternoon caller, and Ronnie will not be able to press his suit upon you."

"That would be lovely," she said sourly, "if you actually did as you say. But we both know what will really happen."

"We do?" he countered, all innocence.

She tossed him her most irritated, ugly, and angry look, but it did absolutely nothing to diminish his smile. "Oh leave off, Mr. Anaedsley, I haven't the time for it today."

"But—" he began. She roughly jerked her hand from his arm and stepped away to glare at him.

"Five minutes after greeting everyone, my father will be excited to learn about your latest experiment."

"Actually, it is your father's experiment. I only execute the task he requests—"

"Two minutes after that," she continued as if he hadn't spoken, "the two of you will wander off to his laboratory. Uncle will follow, and I shall be left alone. With Ronnie." She spoke her cousin's name as she might refer to one of her father's experiments gone horribly wrong.

"Perhaps your uncle will remain—"

"Uncle desires the union above all things."

Clearly, she'd flummoxed him. He didn't even bother denying his plan to disappear with her father. And yet the more she glared at him, the more his expression shifted to one of charming apology. That was always the way with him. She'd even taken to calling him Lord Charming in her thoughts, and as she was not a woman prone to fairy tales, the name was not a positive one.

"I see your problem, Miss Smithson," he finally said. "Unfortunately, when I said we had been spotted, I wasn't referring to your half cousin."

She blinked. "What?"

His eyes lit up with genuine warmth as he gestured behind her. Then, before she could spin around, he opened his arms in true delight.

"Mr. Smithson, how absolutely wonderful to see you out and about. Why your daughter was just telling me that she feared for your existence. Was begging me to bring in a London physician—"

"What?" her father said as he strolled down the drive toward them. "Mellie, I've told you I'm right as rain."

"Papa? Where did you come from?"

"Down at Mr. Wilks's barn. Been looking at the sheep to see if the lice powder worked."

Damn it all! She should have known he'd be inspecting the neighbor's sheep. They were the subjects of his current experiment, after all. And naturally he'd be there instead of in his lab where he'd *promised* to look at what she'd done. "But you have been ill," she said, rather than snap at him for ignoring her latest chemical experiment. "You complain of the rain. It makes your joints ache."

"Well, that's what old men do, my dear." Then her papa turned to Lord Charming and embraced him as if the man were a lost son. It had always been this way between them, starting from when her father had been Mr. Anaedsley's tutor more than a decade ago. The two adored each other, and it was so pure a love that she couldn't even be jealous of it.

Well, she *shouldn't* be jealous, but she was. Especially as she knew that her plans for the day were doomed. The two would go off with her uncle and leave her with Ronnie. And worse, the main purpose of the day—the sole reason she had asked for her uncle and cousin to visit this afternoon—was completely destroyed.

And it was all Mr. Anaedsley's fault.

*And don't miss the second book in the*
*Rakes and Rogues series!*

# One ROGUE
## *at a* TIME

BRAMWELL WESLEY HALLOWSBY MISSED THE GREAT
love of his life because he was listening to the tale
of his first kill. She was right in front of the inn in a
blue dress and a bonnet with a matching ribbon. But
his attention was on the inside as Dicky spoke of his
Brave Deed. Not Bram's assassinations of vicious men
and once of a woman spy, but his very first kill at the
age of twelve.

It had been a rabid bear, according to Dicky,
escaped from the local fair and still wearing a bright
red and green ruffle around its neck. Horribly, this
only made it more terrifying to the onlookers as the
young Bram stepped forward to defend a child.

"A child?" gasped Dicky's wife, Clarissa. "Boy or girl?"

"Both!" cried Dicky, gesturing with his cheroot.
"Twins with kittens. One in each hand and completely defenseless!"

That part was new. Last time it had been piglets.
Bram looked out the inn window, idly scanning
the street. Though Dicky had easily a dozen men
who'd vowed to kill him, none of them would bestir

themselves this far north of London. They were in
Hull now, nearly to Scotland. If it hadn't been for
Clarissa's tetchy stomach, they would be there, and he
could get paid. That's all he wanted. To get them to
Scotland so he could get paid.

He narrowed his eyes. There was a thick brute of a
man coming toward them, but then the man stopped
to talk to the woman in blue. The man bowed only
slightly, then spent his time ogling the woman's
impressive bodice. Bram labeled him the local lecher
and let his attention wander back to Dicky.

"And there he stood, one tiny boy against a rabid
bear," continued Dicky as he patted the small treasure
chest on his lap. The heavy thing must have flattened
even Dicky's massive thighs, but the man would not
give up his gold even to sit in an inn with his sick wife.

"Terrifying!" gasped Clarissa. She always gasped
whenever she spoke. "Did it attack? Did it hurt you?
Are there scars?"

Bram barely stopped himself from rubbing his forearm. He knew the shape and the texture of the scars
there from memory. The origin of the bizarre tale that
had become his legend.

"Horribly disfigured, my dear," Dicky said, clearly
gleeful at the thought. "You shan't see it, of course.
He keeps it well covered."

"Oh my!" Clarissa's eyes grew sultry. Then she
pressed her sapphire necklace to her lips at such an
angle that her husband wouldn't see her lick it. But
Bram saw—as she had intended—and he idly wondered if he would take advantage of what was offered
tonight. It wouldn't be the first time he had used his

own mystique to open a woman's bedroom door. And Clarissa was stunningly beautiful, as was her husband. Of course, they were both rotten to the core.

As the bastard son of a duke, Bram had to make his own way through the world. Thanks to the connections of an elite education, he'd been able to hang on the outskirts of the moneyed *ton*, but it had cost him. Humiliation was the smallest price he'd had to pay as he played bodyguard and general strong arm for the peerage. He'd also had to split his mind into two pieces. One half hoped for goodness and beauty in the world. He couldn't shut it up no matter how he tried. The other half saw with clear, bitter eyes what went on and hated the world for the disappointment.

Meanwhile, Dicky continued the tale. "People were running about screaming, you understand. Everywhere was chaos as grown men dropped to their knees in terror. But not Bram. At the tender age of ten, he stood up for those poor children."

"Ten? I thought you said he was twelve."

Both husband and wife looked to Bram, and he knew they would stay like that until he answered. "Eleven," he said, choosing to split the difference.

"Eleven then. But you'd just had the birthday, right?" Dicky asked.

"Right." Wrong, but who was he to argue? Dicky was paying him to be mythic.

Something jerked in the window, and he glanced quickly back. It was the woman in blue as she'd twitched away from a grinning man. Oh. Likely she'd been pinched as she'd passed the thick-jowled man.

"The beast gave out a tremendous roar!" Dicky

bellowed as he leaped to his feet, one arm holding his gold, the other waving about while his wife squealed in mock terror.

"Uh, Dicky, you really shouldn't be so loud..." began Bram, but he needn't have bothered.

The door to their private room burst open as the innkeeper rushed in. "My lords! My lady! What is amiss?"

Dicky let his arm drop, not even embarrassed. "I was being a bear, sir."

The innkeeper was understandably flustered, and though Bram enjoyed a flustered innkeeper as much as the next man, he hardly thought it fair. But rather than point out Dicky's error—a sin for any paid servant—he redirected the man. "Have you got the posset yet? For my lady's stomach?"

"Oh, sir, not yet. But I've sent my son to find her—the woman I told you about—and not return until such time—"

"Oh, but I am so wretched!" gasped Clarissa as she pressed a limp hand to her brow, her sapphire earbobs waving wildly on their gold chains.

"A hot towel, milady? Perhaps a blanket?" Not much of the peerage traveled through here, and he was making the most of these two.

"I won't put you to the bother," she said, her voice fading.

"But milady, if it would ease your suffering—"

"Tut tut," Dicky interrupted, oblivious to his wife's need to be cosseted. "She said no. Get on with you. I was in the middle of my story." Bram sighed. "Bring her hot stew."

"I couldn't eat a thing," Clarissa protested.

"You will," he said, keeping his voice stern. She liked it when he was bold. Yes, her legs shifted restlessly, and she shot him another coy glance that made him vaguely nauseous.

The innkeeper's head bobbled yes as he rushed out the door in search of stew. Meanwhile, Dicky was annoyed that the attention had shifted off him. "Pay attention," he ordered. "I was about to get to the good part."

Pay attention to his own tale of derring-do? "Please, I adore this part," he lied as he looked back out the window.

He saw a mob of boys—four of them—barely into their first beards. They were calling raucous comments aimed at the woman in blue. Really, why was she walking alone—moving from one house to the next to the next—seemingly unprotected by a husband, father, or brother? Didn't she know better than to tempt the locals to harangue her?

"The bear attacked!" Dicky cried dramatically. He roared again, and Clarissa squealed. "Bram pulled out his father's dueling pistol and shot it right in the muzzle! Bang!"

"Bang," Clarissa echoed as she rubbed her thumb over and across the smallest sapphire in her necklace.

"And that, my dear, is the tale of how my dear Bram became the man he is today. And he will protect us, you see." Dicky returned to his seat and curled his arm around the treasure chest. "If he could protect tiny children—"

"And their kittens! Don't forget the kittens!"

"And their kittens from a rabid bear, then…"

"Then we are safe with him." Clarissa's gaze returned to him, her gaze growing more languid. "I feel so safe."

Dicky frowned, his face turning red. On any other man, it would be a hideously florid look, but it only seemed to enhance Dicky's easy charm. "That's why I hired him, Clary. To make you feel safe."

"You did a good job," his wife said, her eyes not leaving Bram.

Bram pushed to his feet, needing to stretch his long legs. "You do know that story has grown over the years."

"Tut tut," Dicky said. "We all know it's true. Or most of it."

Or none of it. When had his life become so absurd that he contemplated cuckolding a man—his employer— simply because he was bored? He despised himself, and by extension, he despised Dicky and Clarissa.

"There's no danger, Dicky. No one will chase you up here. They will ruin your reputation in town, destroy your financials simply because no one will do business with you, and certainly, you will never be invited to a *ton* party again. But there won't be a soul who offers you bodily harm."

"Course not!" cried Dicky as he patted his treasure again. "That's because you're here. That's because I had the foresight to befriend you as a child. I knew then that you would protect me. I knew then that you were a man who could save me from those blackguards…"

Bram stopped listening and headed for the door. Dicky noticed about the time he stepped into the hallway.

"Where are you going?"

"To have a look about. Just in case." It was a lie, but it was one that would satisfy Dicky, which would make sure he got paid when this was all done.

So he left the room, choosing to wander through the inn. He made it through the kitchen and out the back, to the garden behind with two lazy hounds dozing in the sun. And once outside, he took a deep breath of the summer air and a greedy look at the green land around him.

That was the life he wanted: stretched out in the sun like those hounds, with his eyes drooping shut, while a pup or three gamboled nearby. He saw no puppies, but he imagined them, and they made him smile.

Then he saw her. The woman in blue again, this time without anyone pinching or ogling her. The sight was striking enough, but then she paused under a tree, pulling off her bonnet to raise her face to what breeze could be had. Fine blond hair blew back from her cheeks, and her perfect bow of a mouth curved in delight. Beautiful. A country miss complete with a basket on her arm. Her lush, unspoiled beauty was the kind that could only grow in the wilds. In London, she would be painted and sullen, her body trussed into dresses that maximized assets and minimized flaws. But this woman had a simple gown, and while he watched, those puppies he'd imagined suddenly appeared. Four of them, barking and leaping from somewhere he couldn't see.

She smiled when she saw them, and then—to his shock—she laughed, so musical a sound that he was riveted. Bells could not have sounded so pure.

He was awed. It was his idealistic mind, he knew. The one that believed in unsullied beauty. She knelt down then, oblivious to the dirt that would coat her skirt, as she tickled the puppies, her laughter chiming in the air.

He found himself moving toward her without choosing to do so. He had no idea what to say to an innocent miss. He'd never known a woman who could be so sweet. And yet—

"Miss Bluebell! Miss Bluebell!"

A boy barely out of short pants came tearing around the corner. She looked up, her expression surprised as she held out her arms. He careened into them, so fast was he churning his short, stubby legs.

She said something too low for Bram to hear, especially as the boy kept talking right over her despite being short of breath. Rude brat.

"Da says…you come. Right away!"

At that moment, one of the puppies attacked the angel. It was nothing more than a growl and bite as it grabbed hold of her dress and shook. With a sharp word for the dog, she picked it up and took her time disentangling it from her skirt, but then the thing started licking her on the face.

He saw the wet tongue tasting her chin and neck. He heard her laugh, this time deeper—throatier—and he felt himself harden as he hadn't in years. Her cheeks were flushed, her hair now flying free as the dog laved her. His mouth was dry as he watched, and he abruptly thought of so many things, all dark and carnal.

"Miss Bluebell!" the child cried, and Bram wanted to spank the idiot child for drawing the woman's attention. *Don't look at him. Look at me!* The thought was bizarre in his mind, but it was no less loud.

The woman finally managed to pull the puppy away from her face. She must have said something because the boy nodded vigorously and pointed at the inn. At first Bram thought the child was directing her to look at him, but he soon realized the truth. Neither boy nor woman had seen him, and the disappointment of that was yet another shock. What was wrong with him?

# Author's Note

Longtime fans will notice that the heroine of this book originally appeared in *Winning a Bride* as Megan Powel. Research after that ebook was published indicated that the name Megan didn't come into popular use until the twentieth century. Oops! So rather than perpetuate an error, I have changed her name in this book to Mari. Hopefully you can forgive me for this mistake.

# About the Author

*USA Today* bestselling author Jade Lee has been scripting love stories since she first picked up a set of paper dolls. Ball gowns and rakish lords caught her attention early (thank you, Georgette Heyer), and her fascination with the Regency began. An author of more than fifty romance novels and winner of dozens of industry awards, Jade Lee delights readers with her vibrant, saucy Regency romances that deliver unusual stories with a lot of heart. Lee lives in Champaign, Illinois.

# If the Earl Only Knew

## The Daring Marriages

## by Amanda Forester

---

### A sizzling scandal just waiting to happen…

Orphaned at a young age, Lady Katherine Ashton and her brother have spent most of their lives on the high seas, seeking to restore their family fortune through somewhat dubious means. After that kind of adventure, Kate knows she won't ever be accepted as a proper society lady.

To the annoyingly clever, temptingly handsome, and altogether troublesome Earl of Wynbrook, society ladies are a dead bore. Kate, on the other hand, is scandalous, alluring, and altogether fascinating.

And Kate can't decide which she relishes more: the thrill of chasing fearsome pirates, or having Wynbrook chase after her…

---

### Praise for *Winter Wedding*:

"Pure ambrosia… Readers will delight."
—*Publishers Weekly* Starred Review

"A scintillating regency romance full of festive fun, intrigue, and subterfuge!" —*Fresh Fiction*

### For more Amanda Forester, visit:

www.sourcebooks.com

# The Rebel Heir

The Spare Heirs

## by Elizabeth Michels

— ❧ —

### The Spare Heirs Society Cordially Invites You to Meet Ash Claughbane: The Imposter

Lady Evangeline Green is living a lie. To please her family, she masquerades as the perfect debutante…until she meets the wickedly charming Lord Crosby. With him, there are no rules. She's finally free to do as she desires—but freedom comes with a price, and Lord Crosby is not what he seems…

Ash is not Lord Crosby. He's a con artist, a noble Spare Heir living off his silver tongue. When the Green family ruined his, he swore he'd make them pay, and he never doubted his devotion to revenge…until he met Evangeline. Now, caught in a web of lies, torn between duty and desire, what's a con to do but deceive all of London and steal the one lady who dared match wits with the devil himself?

— ❧ —

### Praise for *The Infamous Heir*:

"Readers are treated to Michels's strongest story yet. Savor this tale." —*RT Book Reviews* Top Pick

"Michels's latest is the complete package: a captivating romance with gripping suspense wrapped up in a novel to be savored." —*Publishers Weekly* Starred Review

### For more Elizabeth Michels, visit:

www.sourcebooks.com

# What the Duke Doesn't Know

## The Duke's Sons

## by Jane Ashford

---

### A proper English wife, or the freedom of the sea?

Lord James Gresham is the fifth son of the Duke of Langford, a captain in the Royal Navy, and at a loss for what to do next. He's made his fortune; perhaps now he should find a proper wife and set up his nursery. But the sea calls to him, while his search for a wife leaves him uninspired. And then, a dark beauty with a heart for revenge is swept into his life.

### He can't have both, but he won't give up either

Half-English, half-Polynesian Kawena Benson is out to avenge her father and reclaim a cache of stolen jewels. She informs James at gunpoint that he is her chief suspect. There's nothing for James to do but protest his innocence and help Kawena search for the jewels, even though it turns his world upside down

---

### Praise for *Heir to the Duke*:

### For more Jane Ashford, visit:

www.sourcebooks.com

# The Untouchable Earl

## Fallen Ladies

## by Amy Sandas

---

Lily Chadwick has spent her life playing by society's rules. But when an unscrupulous moneylender snatches her off the street and puts her up for auction at a pleasure house, she finds herself in the possession of a man who makes her breathless with terror and impossible yearning…

Though the reclusive Earl of Harte claimed Lily with the highest bid, he hides a painful secret—one that has kept him from ever knowing the pleasure of a lover's touch. Even the barest brush of skin brings him physical pain, and he's spent his life keeping the world at arms' length. But there's something about Lily that maddens him, bewitches him, compels him…and drives him toward the one woman brave and kind enough to heal his troubled heart.

---

### Praise for *Luck Is No Lady*:

"Smart and sexy." —*Booklist*

"Lively plot, engaging characters, and heated love scenes make this a page-turner." —*RT Book Reviews*, 4 Stars

### For more Amy Sandas, visit:

www.sourcebooks.com